Sergio Olguín was born in Buenos Aires in 1967. His first work of fiction, *Lanús*, was published in 2002. It was followed by a number of successful novels, including *Oscura monótona sangre* (*Dark Monotonous Blood*), which won the Tusquets Prize in 2009. His books have been translated into English, German, French and Italian. *There Are No Happy Loves*, following on from the success of *The Foreign Girls* and that of *The Fragility of Bodies*, is the third in a crime thriller series featuring journalist Verónica Rosenthal. Sergio Olguín is also a scriptwriter and has been the editor of a number of cultural publications.

THERE ARE NO HAPPY LOVES

Sergio Olguín

Translated by Miranda France

BITTER LEMON PRESS
LONDON

BITTER LEMON PRESS

First published in the United Kingdom in 2022 by
Bitter Lemon Press, 47 Wilmington Square, London WC1X OET

www.bitterlemonpress.com

First published in Spanish as *No Hay Amores Felices*
by Suma de Letras (Penguin Random House Grupo Editorial Argentina), 2016

Bitter Lemon Press gratefully acknowledges the financial
assistance of the Arts Council of England

Work published within the framework of "Sur" Translation Support Program
of the Ministry of Foreign Affairs and Worship of the Argentine Republic

Obra editada en el marco del Programa "Sur" de Apoyo a las Traducciones
del Ministerio de Relaciones Exteriores y Culto de la República Argentina

© Sergio Olguín, 2016

A CIP record for this book is available from the British Library

PB ISBN 978–1–913394–714
eBook USC ISBN 978-1-913394-721
eBook ROW ISBN 978-1-913394-738

Typeset by Tetragon, London
Printed and bound by the CPI Group (UK) Ltd, Croydon, CRO 4YY

*To Elena Oshiro, Carlos Arroyo
and Ignacio Palacios Videla*

Contents

Too often he relived in the present the lapsed moments of his own past, not out of remorse or nostalgia, but because the walls of time seemed to have burst.

MARGUERITE YOURCENAR, *The Abyss*

'It must have been murder. You don't kill a man to hide anything less.'

GRAHAM GREENE, *The Third Man*

'If it were sufficient to love, things would be too easy.'

ALBERT CAMUS, *The Myth of Sisyphus*

Prologue

THREE STORIES

I

He thought it was the end of the summer and didn't realize it was the end of everything. A few minutes from now, life as he had known it would fall apart once and for all. Nothing would ever be the same again.

White lines: double and continuous, avoid passing other vehicles; single and broken, accelerate and overtake the cars and trucks obstructing his steady progress towards the capital, Buenos Aires. That was all Darío saw: the white lines of Route 11, illuminated by the low beam of his car lights. Everything around him was black, dense and interminable. Like his mood.

The red lights in front of him gradually came into focus. Darío gently braked, shifted down a gear and fell in behind the car, which was travelling at less than sixty miles an hour. Double white lines on the asphalt indicated an approaching bend, so he couldn't overtake. As he took the bend, Darío checked the opposite carriageway and saw no white light to show a vehicle coming the other way. He accelerated and overtook the car. Once they were a safe distance ahead, he got back in his lane, and the other car soon dissolved into the nothingness behind them.

It was the end of the vacation. A fortnight during which Darío had confirmed what he already knew but couldn't yet bring himself to put into words: the relationship with Cecilia was over. They had to separate immediately. Those fourteen days had been a torment, barely mitigated by Jazmín's happiness on the beach, watching her run to meet the breaking waves, her contagious laughter at each new discovery. The photos they had taken on vacation would likely be the last in which Jazmín appeared with both parents. Would she remember anything from those days? What hazy memory might she retain in the future? Her father and mother drinking maté in the beach hut, perhaps, or her dozing in the shade of a parasol, playing in the arcade with her cousin in the evening, or getting ice cream on the main street of La Lucila del Mar.

The five women travelling with him were all asleep. Cecilia was next to him, her head resting against the window. Behind them were his mother-in-law, his sister-in-law, with her daughter on her lap, and Jazmín. He couldn't see her in the rearview mirror, but Darío could picture his daughter sleeping peacefully, her sun-kissed face, her rhythmic breathing. He had always liked to watch Jazmín when she slept, a habit that began when she was a baby and he used to fear that she might succumb to sudden infant death syndrome. He would sit beside the cot while she slept, or keep going to check that she was breathing. It's comforting, when you're a parent, to watch your children sleeping, safe from pain and danger.

Cecilia woke up. Wiping the saliva from around her mouth, she scanned the road for some reference point that would show their progress.

"Where are we?"

"We've just passed General Lavalle, still a long way to go."

Cecilia turned and looked at Jazmín. Seeing her asleep seemed to soothe some worry left over from her dreams.

"I think I had a nightmare," she said, but didn't elaborate.

Darío expressed no interest in his wife's dream. For several days now their conversations had been as brief as possible. That policy was at least an improvement on their previous tendency always to be saying hurtful things to each other. In fact, their last screaming match (unwitnessed, thankfully) still induced a physical response in Darío. He felt nauseous to think of it, especially when he remembered his wife's threat. He could still see her, her face burning as she said, "I'm going to take the girl and you'll never see us again, you bastard." She knew that Jazmín was his world, that nothing could hurt him like losing his daughter. What might Cecilia do to separate him from Jazmín? Make some false allegation? Anyone who knew him would testify that Darío was a good father, even his wife's mother and sister, who were travelling with them now, pained witnesses to the destruction of their marriage.

Nobody would ever separate him from his daughter.

Nobody.

He gripped the steering wheel harder, trying to discharge the sensations of frustration and hatred that had completely engulfed him. Cecilia settled into a more comfortable position for sleeping. Gradually Darío felt calmer. He would have liked to put on the radio, but he didn't want to disturb the girls' peaceful sleep.

Behind their car, he saw a light in the distance. It came from a vehicle travelling faster than theirs. In a few seconds it would pass them and he would fall behind, watching its tail lights get smaller and then disappear. In the rear-view mirror he saw the light become two low beams on a car like his own. Looking ahead, he saw more lights coming towards him.

It took one second, maybe two.

The car behind them pulled out to overtake, with no consideration for the light rapidly bearing down on them.

Darío dropped his speed, trying to facilitate the manoeuvre. But the other motorist's mistake was compounded by a bad decision on the part of the approaching fuel truck. Its driver must have thought that the overtaking car would mount the verge to avoid a collision and that he could steer a middle course, taking his vehicle between the two approaching cars. Instead, he crashed into both of them.

There was nothing Darío could have done. A giant cleaver seemed to slice him in two and he heard a metallic noise, like thunder inside his head, and a howl, one single howl made up of all their separate cries; he saw a white light, a gigantic flash. Had the car flipped over? Was it a wreck? Was it crushed beneath the truck? After a few seconds Darío lost all consciousness. He had no idea how much time passed before someone pulled him out of the vehicle and dragged him a few yards away from it. Nor did he know how long it was between that moment and the explosion of the fuel truck. He heard the blast, felt heat graze his skin. He tried to move his body towards the fireball, pushing forward with one sole aim: Jazmín. But he couldn't do it, he couldn't stand up. And everything after that was a blank.

I I

There's something worse than nightmares: dreams. Verónica Rosenthal was in a rowing boat. She was alone and enjoying a sunny day on the river. On both sides the banks were close and covered in trees. It could have been the Tigre delta, or somewhere similarly verdant. She could hear birdsong and the swish of water with each stroke of the oars. A gentle sound, water lapping against wood. It must have been spring, because there was a pleasant breeze on her face. She could spend hours like this without wanting anything more from life.

The nightmare began when she woke up, when the dream faded and gave way to memories. Then she saw herself in a similar boat, on a lake, in the company of someone she would rather not remember. Nightmares end where real life begins, but what happens when waking from a dream is painful? She closed her eyes tightly, trying to banish the memories and go back to sleep.

Just as she seemed about to achieve that aim, she felt someone trying to prise open her eyelid. At first it was gentle, but then the finger became more insistent, almost gouging her eye. Verónica resolutely kept her other eye closed: she refused to be woken up like this. Meanwhile, the open eye saw a face, close up, and a pair of eyes that were looking into hers much as an ophthalmologist would. The eyes looked curious.

"I'm hungry." Now a mouth was speaking into her open eye, perhaps confusing it with an ear.

"Yes," said Verónica but sleepily, so it came out more like *Yeeeh*.

"There's nothing to eat," the mouth continued, still talking into her eye.

"In the cupboard." She realized she should be more explicit, but it was hard to find the words when half asleep.

"I don't want a cup, I want breakfast."

Now Verónica felt someone kissing her neck, although *kissing* would be a generous way to describe the tongue licking and tickling her. She definitely wasn't going to be able to get back to sleep now.

She sat up in the bed, put Chicha down on the floor and lifted Santino, smoothing his ruffled hair. Her nephew looked seriously at her. The dog jumped back up on the bed.

"So what would you like for breakfast?"

"Chocolate milk and Oreos."

"That's a lot of chocolate."

Santino kept looking into her eyes, as if waiting for a more solid argument. He was a child of few words and a steady gaze.

"OK, OK. Aunty's going to get your milk. Go into the living room and put on some cartoons, and I'll be right there."

Santino went off and so did Chicha, who followed him everywhere, although it wasn't clear if that was because she had adopted him as her new alpha male, wanted a playmate or was simply keeping watch over him. Dogs are like their owners, thought Verónica as she went to the bathroom. She was used to waking up with a hangover, but waking up with a child in the house had a much more detrimental effect on the brain than mixing drinks.

Verónica had been delighted by the prospect of spending two days with her youngest nephew, although she didn't often look after her sisters' children. Daniela and Leticia had two children apiece. Verónica had never spent much time with them beyond taking them to the odd Pixar movie or to the zoo (two activities she enjoyed even without children), but since distancing herself from her father she had grown closer to her sisters. Plus Santino was particularly devoted to Chicha, the dachshund that Verónica had brought back from her trip to Tucumán, and that endeared him to her, as it did anyone who agreed that the little dog was the prettiest pooch in the universe. She liked seeing Santino and Chicha play together.

"Like cousins," she said and her sisters looked horrified, perhaps fearing that the youngest Rosenthal sister was turning into a dog lady.

But it wasn't easy to look after a three-year-old. Verónica was already exhausted, and the time when she could hand him back to Daniela seemed impossibly distant. Since the little boy's arrival the previous afternoon, Verónica hadn't been able to shake him off for one minute. He wouldn't even leave her time to shower. Santino had scattered the little toys he'd brought from home around the living room and bedroom, gone through her drawers, played with her CDs and even tried to insert sugar into a socket with a metal spoon (what goes on in the head of a child who does something like that?). Worst of all, he never stopped eating, drinking or going to the toilet and generally buzzed around like a cokehead unless he was watching children's TV. And she hated children's TV.

Verónica made breakfast, which Santino wolfed down before she got a chance to make herself coffee. She asked him to go and watch television again and even lent him a saucepan to put his toys in. It was still at least eight hours until her sister would come to pick him up. Those hours would last a century unless she found some activity they could do together.

They were out of cookies and juice, and that presented the opportunity for an outing. There was a Jumbo supermarket a few blocks away and she thought she might stock up on some other items while she was there: seafood sticks, hamburgers, wholegrain rice – not that she was planning to cook at lunchtime. She was going to take Santino to a McDonald's. With any luck he'd spend half an hour in the ball pit and another half hour eating and playing with the toy from his Happy Meal.

Two blocks from home, her nephew decided he was tired of walking and wanted to be carried. She tried reasoning that he was older now and that his aunt's arms were too weak to carry such a big boy. If he walked, she would buy him some chocolate in the supermarket. The promise of chocolate propelled the child two more blocks. She refused to let Santino play on the escalator or climb into the shopping cart, for fear he would hurt himself.

At that time of day, and that point in the month, the Jumbo was nearly empty of people, as supermarkets often are in American movies. Santino's shrill voice rang out loudly in that product-packed desert. Evidently her nephew had some experience of supermarkets, because he made straight for the dessert section and grabbed a packet of brownies. Verónica put it in the cart then failed to prevent Santino hanging off the cart's side like a refuse collector on a garbage truck. Before her nephew could fill the shopping cart with sweets, she took off towards the delicatessen section, trying not to let the child fall beneath the wheels of his own vehicle. She had remembered that she'd run out of ginger and was fed up with takeout sushi always skimping on it. Here she also found a new brand of wasabi and a man of about forty – tall, slim, good-looking – who was considering the marvellous offerings on the shelf with the eye of a connoisseur. Santino let go of the shopping cart and nearly went flying into the *Peppers, all varieties* section. The man gave first him and then her a meaningful look. Then he returned his gaze to the shelf, picked up an item and asked Verónica:

"Any idea what *maquereaux a l'ancienne* might be?"

"Mackerel, traditional style. I think they come with lemon and maybe mustard, but it should say on the box."

The man looked at her and smiled, like a teacher who has just awarded a good mark to a schoolgirl.

"*Maquereaux* sounds so much better than mackerel," he said, putting the box back on the shelf. "I prefer our own sardines."

"Actually, these tinned herrings are very good. I recommend them. Especially the ones in spicy sauce." Verónica pointed at the highest shelf.

The man took a couple of tins and dropped them into his basket. "Quite the gourmet mother," he said.

"No, he's not my son," she said quickly. "He's my nephew."

That would have been the right time for Verónica to stroke Santino's head, showing what a good aunt she was. She looked around for the boy, but he had gone off somewhere out of sight. Verónica turned around, worried, and still couldn't see him. She left the shopping cart and walked to the end of the shelving to look down the aisle. He wasn't there. She ran to the other aisle. Her head started to feel as though she were at the bottom of a swimming pool. No. She couldn't see him. Verónica turned abruptly, searching. She shouted "Santino", shouted again. She saw a woman looking at her, horrified. The woman must be reflecting the horror on Verónica's own face. Desperately, she ran towards the entrance. She couldn't see, or hear, or breathe, as she sank deeper and deeper, in that swimming pool the size of the supermarket.

III

They had been freezing cold for more than an hour now. Autumn, conceding defeat, was giving way to an early winter. Friday, 3 a.m.: not the best day or time to be in the port of Buenos Aires. An icy wind was blowing, slicing into his face, although a collective anticipation warmed the atmosphere. They were all gathered, print journalists and photographers, together with the TV station that had been given an exclusive. Everyone was crouching, as if at a surprise birthday party for someone who never arrives on time.

Federico hated this kind of thing. He hadn't organized it, but he was obliged to stay there and handle the press. Orders from above. And as a Justice Department attorney, he couldn't play dumb. Luckily, the job of answering questions would fall not to him but to the official responsible for special operations in the Argentine Naval Prefecture. And this prefect was more than happy to talk to the media about Operation White Ham. His unit was poised to seize a shipment of cocaine due to be loaded into a container that night. The drugs were hidden inside some fake cured hams – they looked innocent enough, but each one was stuffed with the purest blow.

There they were, huddled behind the containers lined up in the Wilson storage section of the port of Buenos Aires – journalists, men and women from the Naval Prefecture, members of the commando group Albatross and, representing Argentine justice, attorney Federico Córdova, a rising star in the judiciary, universally seen by all as a judge-in-waiting. The journalists were irritable, cold and unimpressed by the drug-busting operation. This kind of thing happened often, and readers weren't all that interested any more. So the newspapers had sent their second-string reporters, who viewed the assignment as a punishment. Some were leaning, smoking, against a Hamburg Süd container; over by a Maersk container, others were jumping up and down, trying to keep warm. One bored reporter asked Federico who he was. He answered her and returned the question, more out of courtesy than genuine interest.

"I'm María Vanini, from *Nuestro Tiempo.*"

"Right, I used to know someone who worked for that magazine," he said, pretending to search his memory for the name. "She was called Verónica Rosenthal."

"Ah, yes," was the journalist's terse response.

"Does she still work there?" Federico asked.

"Yes, she pops into the newsroom every now and then, when she's not off sick."

"Off sick? Is she ill?"

María Vanini whistled and made circular motions around her ear with her index finger. As if that gesture were not sufficiently clear, she added:

"Bit screwed up."

"Ah, I see."

"Hang on, you're not her boyfriend or anything, are you?"

"No, no, definitely not." His overreaction to the journalist's question made him feel like an idiot.

"Just as well. Although it wouldn't surprise me. She seems – or seemed – to have a man in every port. Like a sailor. Is it a while since you last saw her?"

"A long while, more than a year," he said, and mentally kicked himself again. Why was he even telling her all this?

His mobile vibrated. A text message. The reporter looked brazenly at his phone's screen and seemed surprised.

"It says *Vero*."

"Another Vero. My girlfriend, in fact."

María Vanini eyed him suspiciously.

"You're not Rosenthal's new man, are you?"

"No, my girlfriend happens to have the same name, but she's not a journalist. She works in PR."

María was going to ask another question when some of the police officers called for silence. The truck carrying the drugs was about to arrive. Everyone assumed their positions. The boredom induced by their long wait gave way to tension. Twenty officers and sub-officers from the Prefecture and eight members of the Albatross Group prepared for action.

The lights of a vehicle came closer. It was a white, medium-sized refrigerated truck, the kind that takes meat to retailers. It was travelling slowly, less than ten miles an hour. As it reached the middle of the operation, searchlights came on and there was shouting from the police. Like a white whale in a sea of containers, surrounded by fake sailors, the truck ground to a halt. A television camera was filming everything, and the photographers were taking the first pictures that would illustrate articles the following day. The driver was an overweight man of about sixty, with a moustache. His face, illuminated by the flashlights and captured in detail by the TV camera, was that of a man in shock – which was understandable, considering the big surprise they had just given him. But the shock redounded on those present when the driver took his right hand off the wheel and reached towards the passenger seat: he had picked up a gun. A commotion ensued as some journalists ducked behind the containers, the chief of the operation ordered the driver to drop his weapon immediately and the Albatross Group prepared to mobilize. However, the truck driver didn't point his gun at the law enforcement officers surrounding him, but at his own temple. Then he pulled the trigger. His body slumped over the wheel.

A few seconds of confusion followed as the officers and Federico went to the driver's cabin to check that the man was dead. The television camera followed them and the reporters clustered around the driver, sensing that there was something more for them here than a standard drugs bust. Other officers attempted to break the lock on the truck. Finally, the doors were opened, and the swearing and cries of alarm were enough to draw those who had been inspecting the dead man to the back of the vehicle.

The cameraman, who was used to being first on the scene, got there before the others. Federico saw how he focussed his lens on the truck's interior then immediately turned away and put down the camera. It was the first time he had seen someone in that line of work vomit.

The sub-officers who had opened the doors also turned away from the sight inside the refrigerated truck and only a few bystanders dared look at the scene inside, lit crudely by floodlights. Federico did the same, and saw not the expected cocaine-stuffed hams hanging there but human bodies. And not exactly bodies, either, but parts of them: legs, thoraxes, arms, all perfectly preserved. One of the Albatross Group commandos climbed into the truck, dodging the body parts, and levered open one of the two boxes in there. He studied the contents, then, without saying anything, quickly got out.

Federico climbed up to see what had shocked this last officer. Arranged in the boxes like plucked chickens, the naked bodies of several babies gave an illusion of resting in peace.

FIRST PART

1   *This Girl's Life*

I

Daniela was stroking her forehead, as though she were a small child. The pills she had been given a little while before were beginning to take effect; having a doctor as a sister brought certain advantages. Meanwhile, Leticia was crashing about in the kitchen: she would probably break the Nespresso, dent the Essen pan and blunt the knives, but Verónica decided to let her sisters get on with things. The three of them hadn't been together under one roof, with no children, husbands or parents, for a long time. It was a shame she was in bed, dosed up and nursing a guilt she couldn't shift.

Leticia appeared, holding a coffee. How typical of her sister to make herself a coffee without offering to make one for anyone else.

"I remember when we were at the zoo and Benjamín got it into his head to go off to the monkeys' enclosure while the rest of us were buying drinks. They had to call him over the PA system. There he was, happy as a clam, throwing trash at the poor chimpanzees."

"Come to think of it," said Daniela, "both Benja and Santino take after their Aunt Verónica. Don't you remember that time you ran away from home and gave Ramira a horrible shock? How old were you? Six, seven?"

"Five," said Verónica. "Where have you two left the kids?"

"With their fathers. Let them pull their weight for once."

I I

It was impossible now for Verónica to reconstruct the exact order of events. As soon as she had realized she couldn't see Santino in either of the two supermarket aisles, she had panicked and lost control. She had screamed, run about, frantically tried to enlist the help of other shoppers. People around her took up the search. Santino was eventually found playing on the escalator, Kinder egg in hand. He was eating the egg without having paid for it, but that was a small detail in the greater scheme of things.

Verónica remembered that the first thing she'd done when Santino appeared holding the hand of a security guard was to run towards him and violently shake him. It was all she could do not to slap him. Santino had burst into tears – and so had Verónica.

Then everything had gone blurry, not because of the tears but because her blood pressure was dropping and she was about to faint. People got her to sit on the floor. Seeing his aunt on the ground made Santino cry even harder. The supermarket staff offered to call a relation. Verónica found her sister's number and passed the phone to one of the people helping her, because she couldn't even speak. She certainly didn't feel able to take the boy back to her apartment on her own. Among the crowd gathered around Verónica and Santino had been the gentleman who preferred sardines to mackerel, and he offered to accompany them home, but she, still in a state of a shock, shouted at him:

"It's your fault I lost the child!" – words which a shopper stumbling upon this scene might have taken to mean that Verónica had just suffered a miscarriage. The gentleman decided not to argue the point and discreetly withdrew without having bought anything and perhaps making a mental note not to talk to strange women in supermarkets.

By the time Daniela had arrived fifteen minutes later, Verónica was already feeling better. Even so, her sister seemed more worried about her than Santino, who was still crying, but now because he was bored and wanted to leave, having consumed the Kinder egg, a cookie and a carton of juice someone had brought him. Daniela packed her sister and son into her car and, before getting in, made two phone calls. One to Leticia and the other to her husband, asking him to come and pick up Santino from Verónica's apartment. And now the three sisters were reunited there.

As the tranquillizers took effect, and Verónica felt a powerful weariness come over her, she noticed her sisters exchanging meaningful looks, as though they had been talking about something earlier and were now preparing to tell her about it.

"Verito" – her sister hadn't called her that for years, not since she was about ten years old – "Leticia and I are worried about you."

"Dani, I'm so incredibly sorry about what happened with Santino…" She didn't complete the sentence, sure that it would make her cry.

"Never mind that – kids are always getting lost. We ought to put him on a lead, like you do with Chicha. No. It's you we're worried about, because you haven't seemed right for a long time. You're not speaking to Dad, Fede wants nothing to do with you…"

"Is that what he told you, that he wants nothing to do with me?"

"It's obvious. He doesn't come to family parties any more, and we only see him if we ask him round to dinner on his own."

"You guys invite Federico round to dinner?"

"You need to change your attitude, Vero," Leticia chimed in. "You're in a depressive rut, you're alienated from everyone. You don't even care about your appearance, you look untidy."

"And you've always taken so much trouble over your clothes," Daniela added.

"Plus there are empty bottles of alcohol all over the apartment," said Leticia.

"So you're checking my apartment to see how much I'm drinking? What else? Do you want to know where I keep my weed and my cigarettes? The condoms are in my nightstand. In case you want to count them."

"What we want is for you to get better. You should go back to therapy, patch things up with Dad, get together with Fede, who's always been so good for you," said Leticia.

"Jesus, why don't you fuck off and leave me alone? Do I stick my nose into your shitty lives, with your stupid husbands and stuck-up friends? Do I give you advice? You'd better just go. I want to sleep."

Within five minutes Leticia and Daniela were gone. Verónica pretended to be asleep to hasten their departure, and in no time she had fallen asleep for real.

III

It was a deep, dreamless sleep. Verónica didn't know if she crashed out for the whole day or a couple of hours. Groping for her phone, she checked the time: three in the afternoon. It was the day she was due back at the magazine, and she was already running an hour late. Verónica sent a message to her editor, Patricia Beltrán, to let her know she would arrive at around four. Her boss wrote back curtly: *Hurry. We're about to close the section.* It was Tuesday. Society sent ten pages to press (plus sixteen on Wednesdays and another ten on Thursdays), and she was the deputy editor. She detested the role. Most of her colleagues saw it as a promotion, but Verónica and Patricia knew the truth. Verónica hadn't written anything worthwhile since her series on femicide in north-eastern Argentina. She never came up with any interesting pitches (and the definition of *interesting* was very broad at *Nuestro Tiempo*); the pieces Patricia asked her to write she banged out with no enthusiasm and, while it was true that some articles could be written that way, others deserved an energy that Verónica couldn't muster.

One afternoon, her editor took her for a coffee at the bar on the corner. Patricia asked what was wrong. Verónica answered, "I'm suffering from professional anorexia."

Patricia looked surprised and said, "Where did you get that nonsense from?"

"All this… I just don't find any of it interesting."

"'All this', as you put it, is your profession, one you chose quite a few years ago. Look, I know better than anyone that it's possible to get tired of your work, but bear in mind that this is the only world in which you'll ever be comfortable. If you really think you might prefer working in a boutique or as a lifeguard, you'd better hand in your notice and sail off in search of your destiny."

"You know that the only thing I can do well – OK, more or less well – is this."

"So make a decision to come back. I can't have a journalist who sits around like a houseplant. The intern's got more energy than you."

"He's young, he'll learn soon enough."

"If you don't want to write, then become an editor. I'm going to put you forward for deputy editor of the Society section."

"I wouldn't be any use as an editor."

"Right now you're even less use as a journalist. If one day you decide to go back to being what you were, I won't stand in your way."

Patricia requested the promotion. From now on, Verónica would have less time to write articles and would spend a large part of the day glued to a chair correcting basic journalistic mistakes made by her colleagues, something she could do in her sleep. It was a way to save her from the storm, although both women knew it was a punishment too. Verónica wasn't cut out to be an editor but a reporter, nose to the ground, mixing with people, sniffing out the shit, as she liked telling Patricia.

And yet a year later Verónica was still deputy editor of Society. Patricia hadn't tackled her on the subject again, and Verónica hadn't written anything more than the odd rehashed wire story or one of those articles that only require a couple of quotes and an opinion piece from some celebrity or an expert on the subject covered in the piece.

She didn't have time to shower or eat anything. She put on jeans, a T-shirt, a cardigan and the long coat she planned to wear throughout the coming winter. She washed her face, brushed her hair, which was getting too long and "untidy" – as Leticia would say – and tried not to look too closely at her face. She didn't have enough time or enthusiasm for make-up.

Verónica reached the newsroom at ten to four. Patricia passed her the articles for editing without a word, not even a reproach. Deep down, this tight-lipped restraint bothered Verónica, a lot. She would have preferred the kind of scene other editors visited on their underlings, or even a dressing-down from the editor-in-chief, a renowned bully. And if Patricia was going to be nice, then let her be genuinely nice, offering back rubs and saying everything was going to be all right, that one day she would go back to being the journalist she always had been and not some cut-price zombie from *The Walking Dead*.

IV

Tuesday nights were for "dinner with friends". In practice, that meant dinner with Paula. The weekly arrangement had originally been with Alma, Marian, Pili, Vale and a few others, but Verónica was increasingly intolerant of her friends, and several contretemps – nobody would describe these as actual fights – had led to them preferring to see each other sporadically at the odd birthday party rather than every week in her apartment. The only friend who had remained loyal, despite Verónica's mood swings, was Paula. On Tuesdays they would order in sushi, or ceviche, or Chinese, they'd polish off a bottle of wine, sometimes a tub of ice cream, and talk about their favourite subjects: their friends' character flaws, ex-boyfriends, the current and future men in their lives. Like some magic fountain, these subjects were never exhausted.

It was Paula who supplied the excitement and gossip, because Verónica had brought nothing to the table for a long time. Her relationships over the past year or so had been so fleeting that any commentary on them could be completed between the first and the third sip of coffee.

Paula generally talked about some current liaison, although she also liked to revisit previous relationships in search of comparisons or to draw parallels with potential lovers. Her capacity for analysis was like that of a professor who consults the collected wisdom of her library to explain a single book or event. Paula could have written a series of papers with enough citations on the masculine experience to make Harold Bloom wince with envy. And she didn't limit herself to analysis but also dabbled in practices of dubious morality: a while back she had managed to hack into the email account of a boyfriend – who soon discovered the breach and became an ex-boyfriend.

Verónica, on the other hand, had a one-track mind: any topic of conversation could be used to bad-mouth Federico. A cup got broken? She remembered that it was Federico's favourite. Her sister's birthday? Federico would doubtless get her a present, because that's how mixed up he was in Verónica's life, still in touch with her sisters, brothers-in-law, nephews and nieces. The food delivery was late? Federico must have something to do with it. It was raining? Verónica could go on about Federico for half an hour, eyes glassy from bourbon, without Paula grasping exactly what the connection between him and the rain was – not that it bothered her much. They were friends. They didn't have to be coherent.

On one occasion Verónica reminded Paula of her hacking skills. How, she wondered, had Paula got hold of her ex-boyfriend's password?

"Social engineering. It was his own name and his birthday. The self-centred prick."

After a second Jim Beam, Verónica confessed that she had attempted to get into Federico's email account, but that after trying several different guesses, the page had seemed to freeze or crash and she couldn't get in again.

Paula didn't take her to task. In fact, the next day she called her and said: "The IT guy in our office has some nifty program that lets you try out thousands of possible passwords without the security system detecting it. I'll email it to you. Good luck."

The nifty program had some drawbacks. The antivirus software had to be disabled before it would work. Presumably during that time, the program would be busily sending

Verónica's information off into cyberspace, but she didn't let that worry her; finding out the password to Federico's email account was a greater good. The world could be divided into two: people who needed an explanation as to why she wanted to get into his mailbox (and these people merited Verónica's absolute indifference and contempt), and those who understood without needing her to justify herself. That was the part of the universe to which Paula and she belonged.

After trying out dozens of variations, Verónica's initial optimism drifted towards a violent pessimism. With every batch of ten wrong passwords, she hit the table, thumped the keyboard, threw a book, swore as though she were on the terraces in the Atlanta soccer stadium. Finally, she conceded defeat. A few days went by before Verónica tried the program again, once more without luck. Soon she was trying out different variations each time she got bored, like someone playing Candy Crush. She had tried every combination of birthday, ID numbers, family names, friends, ex-girlfriends (the ones she knew about), Boca players and those in the Argentina team, leading tennis players and even all the NBA players she could think of. The bastard had better security than Obama.

V

That Tuesday Paula seemed odd, as though uncomfortable. They had opened a bottle of wine, trotted through the usual topics and the conversation was in full flow when Paula finally decided to tell her friend what she had known since that morning.

"Vero, there's something you should know. I found out that Federico has a girlfriend."

Like a bad actress in an Argentine movie, Verónica drank her wine, placed the empty glass down on the coffee table, crossed her legs and, in the tone of a television reporter, asked: "Who is she?"

"Someone who does public relations for companies. She's called Verónica Rinaldi."

The bad acting gave way to a much more natural burst of fury.

"Wow, what a piece of shit – he went out and found a girl with the same name."

"Just goes to show how he's still obsessed with you."

"Of course – he can't get me out of his head. The fact she's called Verónica is a provocation."

"I know her. She studied sociology with me."

"Is she your age?"

"Not exactly. I was in my final year when she started. I took my time graduating, remember?"

"So what does she do? Human resources?"

"No, public relations. She works – or used to – for Faena, and for IBM and I don't know who else."

"What an idiot. Dedicating her life to PR."

"It's like being a press officer, but you get paid more. She's not so stupid."

"Are there photos of her on the internet?"

"Bound to be. She must have Facebook."

"Let's look her up."

In a short time, they learned a lot about the other Verónica. Pictures of her on various websites attested to a life spent at private views and corporate events. She looked young (younger than Verónica), no prettier (Verónica and Paula agreed on that), well dressed (this they had to acknowledge) and was clearly screwing all those old perverts who ran the companies she worked for (a conclusion reached by Verónica but not particularly endorsed by Paula). On close inspection, you might say she looked like Verónica, save for one, devastating difference: Federico's new girlfriend had tits. Big ones.

"They're fake," was Paula's rapid assessment.

"I should get some too."

"Don't be ridiculous."

By the time they had finished their research, Verónica seemed in a better mood. She had never been the type to cry in a corner and wasn't going to start now. Later, on her own with Chicha, she looked through the images again and read everything she could find about the other Verónica. She took the little dog in her arms and showed her the screen.

"Look, Chicha, we have to get this bitch out of the way. What do you think?"

But the dog didn't answer. She didn't even deign to look at the screen.

VI

Verónica woke up listless and hung-over. She got dressed, ate a slice of cold, two-day-old pizza and went to work without even looking in the mirror. She had no idea that her life was about to recover a range of forgotten tones: emotion, memory, the feeling that life could still touch her somehow. Perhaps not in a good way, but providing a connection all the same – or, more than that, a shudder in the soul.

At *Nuestro Tiempo* she got stuck into some editing. Wednesdays were usually heavy-going. That was submission day for investigative pieces, interviews and op-eds. Thursdays were for late submissions, last-minute pieces and the occasional press release, hastily rewritten to plug a gap.

One of the articles she had to edit was by María Vanini, a reporter she didn't like. This woman had caused a scene with Patricia when Verónica had sent in her series of articles on femicide in north-eastern Argentina. María Vanini usually covered any stories concerning the struggles and injustices of womanhood. Patricia hadn't put her in charge of this area – nobody "owned" any aspect of Society – but whenever something related to the subject came up, Vanini promptly asked to be given the piece and Patricia let her have it. When Vanini had found out about the femicide articles, she'd hit the roof. Not content with making a complaint to Patricia, she marched to the magazine's editor to demand he send her to Tucumán to cover the murder of the foreign tourists. The editor replied that it wasn't his place to decide who wrote which article in each section of the magazine – Patricia Beltrán ran Society. Then he had taken Vanini by the shoulders, led her to the door of his office and shouted over to Patricia: "Beltrán, can you control your writers, for the sake of my blood pressure?"

Ever since then, Vanini had loathed Verónica, and Patricia had mistreated Vanini, sending her to cover crime stories at all hours of the day or at weekends. Her last assignment had been to report on the seizure of a shipment of cocaine in the port of Buenos Aires. Vanini had returned with some crazy story about a narco who had committed suicide during the operation and a truck that was carrying drugs hidden inside dead bodies. Verónica was editing the piece, grappling with its unintentional surrealism, when the first hammer blow of the day fell: in the middle of the article appeared the words "attorney Federico Córdoba". Lifting her gaze from the screen, she sought out Vanini, who was sitting almost opposite, on the other side of the Society desk.

"María, the attorney Federico Córdoba – shouldn't that be the attorney Federico Córdova, with a *v*?"

"I don't know. Crime's not my specialism."

Verónica considered giving this the response it deserved, but restrained herself and said simply: "You also haven't made clear what kind of attorney he is, in what field he works. Could you find that out and put it into your piece?"

Vanini responded with a snort and started making phone calls. Verónica was left thinking of Federico. She had a strong urge to call him, to ask if he was enjoying his job in the Justice Department, if he was happy with the stupid PR woman, if he missed her at all. The temptation to call him, to go and see him, had struck her often in the last year and a bit. But her friends could never have forgiven such a faux pas, not even Paula. Now seeing his name (misspelled) in the article she was editing gave Verónica the stupid sensation of being connected to him again. She wondered if he ever thought of her.

The second hammer blow was harder and caught her even more off guard. Verónica had finished editing Vanini's implausible article, the writer having checked her material, and was starting to edit another piece on La Salada, the biggest bootleg market in Latin America. She had gone to get a coffee from the vending machine and, while she was waiting for the cup to fill up with that dark liquid only distantly related to coffee, Adela, the receptionist, had appeared.

"Verónica, I've been calling on your line and getting no answer."

"That's because I have it on silent so nobody will bother me."

The receptionist let this comment pass and told her that somebody was waiting for her in the entrance hall.

Verónica took her plastic cup from the machine. It wasn't unusual for someone to turn up every now and then asking for one of the journalists. All kinds of people came. Crackpots who could communicate with extraterrestrials and wanted to tell the world their story; desperate people who needed medication or a wheelchair for their child and thought the magazine could help them; activists lobbying for (or against) a particular politician; press officers keen to promote an artist; out-of-work journalists who wanted to write for the magazine and didn't know who to approach. Verónica wondered which one of these assorted characters might be looking for her today.

"Did he say what he wanted?"

"No, just that he wanted to speak to you. He's called Darío Valrossa."

"Valrossa?"

"That's what he said."

"Are you sure?"

It was a long time since she'd last heard that surname. Valrossa. The name instantly transported her to the past: to her love affair, a few years previously, with Lucio Valrossa, the train driver who had died while helping her on an investigation. Was this merely a coincidence? How many people had that surname? She put her coffee down on the nearest desk and went to reception. There was the man waiting for her: tall, slim, short black hair. At first glance, this man bore no resemblance to Lucio. But when she stood next to him and looked into his eyes, she realized she was wrong: he had the same expression as Lucio. Verónica introduced herself. The man looked confused or lost.

"I'm sorry to bother you at work. My name's Darío Valrossa."

"It's no bother, Darío. How can I help you?"

"Everything I'm about to tell you is going to sound insane. But please listen until the end. I've come to ask for your help."

2 *Certainties*

I

Time was reduced to a single moment, animated by voices, by the sensation of someone touching or moving him. Every now and then he heard the *pip* of electronic equipment, instructions from nurses or doctors, a male voice giving orders. Nothing worried him, not even the fact that no one seemed to hear him. He was talking to himself. He didn't need anyone or anything. He was at the centre of a perfect whiteness.

When he opened his eyes, he saw the face of a nurse, watching him with a sombre expression. Darío closed his eyes. The next time it was another nurse: she was checking his drip and noticed him looking at her. It didn't occur to him to try to talk. He must have gone back to sleep, because when he opened his eyes again there were several doctors standing around his bed. The one checking his eyes with a small flashlight asked if Darío could see him. Darío made an effort to speak, and was unsurprised to find that he could. Why wouldn't he have been able to? And yet his voice sounded weak, like that of an old person, when he said *yes*.

After many sleeping and waking cycles – he wasn't sure exactly how many – Darío saw his parents. They were there beside the bed, watching him. Neither of them was crying, but they weren't smiling either. To reassure them he said, "I'm fine", then drifted off again.

He felt that he was back to life when he managed to tell a nurse that he wanted to defecate. All his movements were painful.

For a long time (but how long? He found it impossible to measure this period in hours or days), his body was something that hurt, that he could hardly move or touch, that other people manipulated with patience and understanding.

A doctor explained that he'd had two operations.

A nurse told him about the fortnight he had been in a coma.

He went to a physiotherapist who told him about the fractures to his ribs and his left arm.

Another nurse treated his wounds and burns, and that was how he found out he had injuries and cuts that still needed attention.

Darío never asked anyone anything, not even how he had arrived at the hospital. Nor did he have any recollection of what had happened, apart from a vague sensation of having been in an accident.

He opened his eyes and saw his mother, watchful, waiting.

"Jazmín. Where's Jazmín?"

His mother squeezed his hand. Hard enough to hurt it. She was crying and couldn't speak. He closed his eyes but couldn't sleep. Tears burned his tightened skin.

II

One by one, the tubes to which Darío had been connected all this time were removed. The wounds on his chest gradually became scars. A burn on his left wrist took on the shape of a watch that had calcified on his skin. Once he was able, despite the pain of swallowing, to take food by mouth, they put him in a private room. Now his parents could spend more time with him.

The answer his mother hadn't been able to give, when he asked about Jazmín, was finally provided by Doctor Anselman, the clinician in charge of his treatment. She told him that he had been the only person to survive the accident. His daughter, wife, mother-in-law, sister-in-law, niece, the two people travelling in the other car and the driver of the truck were all dead. Doctor Anselman spoke with a calm and resolve that combined to transmit serenity. Darío gave no reaction until a few minutes later, when they brought him lunch and he sent the tray spinning. His mother held him tightly to prevent him getting up; his father wept, not daring to come closer. And Darío howled. He was a wounded dog in a land of the dead.

Then the questions started. What had happened to Jazmín's body? Where had she been buried? How could he have survived and not the other occupants of the car? Had Jazmín died in the crash, the fire that followed it, on the way to the hospital, inside the hospital?

He asked everyone – the nurses, physiotherapists, doctors, Doctor Anselman, his parents, his maternal uncle, even his maternal uncle's wife when she came to visit him.

There were few answers, and none of them were satisfactory. Jazmín, like the rest of the family, had been burned to death. He had managed to get out of the car and drag himself away, avoiding the explosion that had carbonized the injured – or already dead – occupants and left him with first- and second-degree burns. How he had managed to get away from the site was something nobody could explain. Nor could they say why he hadn't tried to save his daughter. The answer most often given was that he had been suffering from trauma or shock.

Reconstructing the accident and identifying the bodies had proven very difficult. The investigators had to be guided by information given by the families and some forensic analysis at the scene, including the suitcases and bags that were stored in a roof box and had been thrown clear on impact. That was how police were able to establish who was travelling in the car.

Jazmín's remains had not been found. Nor had Cecilia's.

There was still a month to go before Darío could be discharged. He was now able to walk along the hospital corridors, but every so often he needed to go back to his bed and rest, or submit to more examinations. One of these required a general anaesthetic and, a few seconds before he came round from it, he saw Jazmín. She was alive. She was smiling at him and calling *papa-papa-papa*, like she had when she used to go running up to him for a hug. He knew that it was a dream. For Darío there was no confusion between waking and dreaming states; he didn't believe in premonitions or anything like that. And yet the evidence of those few seconds seemed clear and irrefutable. He woke up from the anaesthetic convinced that his daughter was alive. He had to get better as quickly as possible and go and find her.

III

Darío's parents tried to persuade him to go and live with them for a while, but he wanted to go back to his apartment in Caballito as soon as he was discharged. All the same, they went with him to his house and spent most of the day there. They bought food in the supermarket and his mother made a couple of pizzas along with some schnitzels and empanadas to put in the freezer. Darío quietly accepted everything. He knew it would be worse to put up a fight and that it was better to let his parents do as they wished.

By nightfall he was alone, and only then did he take possession of the house. He went to Jazmín's room. There were her toys, arranged as she had left them before they set off for

44

La Lucila del Mar. A few little figures were scattered across the floor – Jazmín must have left them there just before their departure. The princess-themed bedspread, the lampshade covered with little fishes, the multicoloured rug her aunt had brought back from Peru, the children's books he had bought her himself, the precariously balanced pile of soft toys, the little jackets hanging on a clothes rack, the family photos, the photos of her on the walls, on the bedside table. Darío touched her things, stroked them, seeing them as if for the first time.

The smallest toys were in a basket. It had always been a struggle getting her to put away all those unicorns, princesses and fairies, the little figures collected from McDonald's. Darío picked up the basket and emptied it over the carpet. Now the room looked as though Jazmín was in the house.

He sat on the floor and leaned against the bed. He stood up a prince and the characters from *Monsters, Inc.* From this vantage point he contemplated the photos stuck on the walls. Darío felt as though he could stay there for a long time. There was something living in the room, something that wasn't him, and that made him feel even more certain that Jazmín was alive. If he fixed his gaze on the photos for a few minutes, the images began to move slightly: Jazmín's hair fluttered in the breeze, her eyes narrowed, her lips murmured a word. And there she was, in front of him.

Darío fell asleep still propped against the bed, and it was dark when he woke. He got up and went to the living room, trying not to stand on any of the toys or to make any noise, as he used to when he left Jazmín sleeping every night.

IV

The following days were busy, with trips to La Plata and to General Lavalle. Darío was used to taking the bus, but it was

45

distressing to be back on the road. He spent much of the journey with his eyes closed, sweating, his legs restless. Although he couldn't remember everything about the accident, he knew there were things people weren't telling him. Cecilia and he had been experiencing a profound crisis; she had threatened to take away his daughter and not let him see her ever again. His wife had used this accident to disappear with Jazmín. It was she who had got him out of the car, dragged him away from it and left him beside the road, far from the accident. For that reason he needed the police, the courts or whatever agency was responsible to look for his wife, because she had kidnapped their daughter.

Darío visited the main police station in General Lavalle, the local cemetery, the courthouse in La Plata, the police department responsible for road safety. In every case he explained his situation, and nobody could do anything for him – some people barely gave him the time of day. They refused to open an investigation. His case perfectly fitted the profile of an accident. How could they open a missing persons file when everything pointed to his wife and daughter having died in the same way as the other occupants of the three vehicles? Even the people who heard him out made it clear that they understood his pain but couldn't do anything to help him.

"I've had five missing teenage girls in the last year," said the chief superintendent at General Lavalle. "Five families who come every week to ask what we've found out about them. And we've got nothing new. They've vanished into thin air. Imagine if I add to that the alleged disappearance of two people who are recorded as having died in an accident."

Darío also consulted two separate lawyers – prestigious, important, expensive ones. If he could get legal backing for his investigation request, that would make it easier to get the courts or the police to do their job. But neither of the lawyers wanted to take on his case. That he was in denial about the death of his daughter was the psychological assessment trotted out by the police, court officials, bureaucrats and lawyers as a way to get rid of him. Nobody even considered taking up the case.

But he wasn't deluded.

He wasn't in denial.

If Darío had survived the accident, it was because his wife had got him out of the car. She had wanted him to survive and to be tormented by the certainty that his daughter was dead. Cecilia had staged her own death along with her daughter's, to guarantee herself a new life with Jazmín and without him. Was that so hard to understand?

V

In between journeys and consultations – with a lawyer, with a retired police chief – Darío's life gradually returned to normal. Summer was behind him, and autumn was already leaning towards a hard winter.

One day, a package arrived at his door. It contained twenty copies of *The Witch's Broken Mirror*, sent by his publisher. Darío had handed in the completed manuscript just days before going on vacation and the plan had been that, on his return from La Lucila del Mar, he and his editor Emilse would choose an illustrator. It was a book for eight-year-olds, and he had suggested hiring a cartoonist. Emilse commissioned Rustikof, a brilliant Spanish illustrator, who had done some delightful drawings for the book. Along with the complimentary copies there was a note from Emilse: *I hope you like how our witch turned out. Whenever you want to get together, say the word. I'm with you at this terrible time. Very much love, Darío. Please feel you can turn to me – Emilse.*

He picked up one of the copies of *The Witch's Broken Mirror* and took it to the bookshelf in Jazmín's room. There were his seven previous books. They were all illustrated, and Jazmín had liked looking at them and pretending to read them. Her favourite was *The Dancing Monkey*. Darío had often read it to her before she went to sleep. He read it again now, aloud, then put it back on the shelf.

Every time he went into Jazmín's room he couldn't help looking at all the photos of his daughter. Now Darío remembered that there were many more of her on his computer. He spent the rest of that afternoon looking at pictures and videos. Then he searched Cecilia's album for the photos from nursery school. There she was with her teacher and the other two-year-olds in her group.

Next morning, he went to the nursery school Jazmín had been attending up until the summer vacation. It was a private one, quite exclusive, not so much on account of the fees but because its prestige fuelled a fierce competition for places. Cecilia had put a lot of work the previous year into getting a place for Jazmín.

Darío asked to speak to the headteacher. This woman – young, with the look of someone who took her job seriously – expressed her condolences. She knew what had happened and appeared saddened by the situation. It was clear that she wanted to be warm and attentive to Darío, and she was quick to say:

"I know at times like these this is the last thing on your mind, but I want you to know that the deposit you put down for next year's fees will be returned. Just let me have your bank details and I'll see to it."

"But that's what I wanted to talk to you about. My daughter isn't dead."

The headteacher looked at him, startled.

"It's a long story. But my relationship with her mother has been really bad recently. She took advantage of the accident to abduct my daughter."

"What you're telling me is terrible. Have you reported this to the police?"

"I'm doing everything I can to make them launch a search for Jazmín. And for her mother, of course."

The headteacher looked steadily at him. It seemed that she wasn't going to say anything more, so Darío added:

"I'm asking for only one thing: please keep Jazmín's place open next year. I know it's already June, but I wouldn't want her to have to make a new set of friends when she comes back. I promise you she'll be back at nursery very soon."

VI

Darío met Emilse at the corner cafe near the publishing house. She had clearly chosen that spot to spare him the pain of enduring the greetings and condolences of every single employee at the office. Emilse hugged him for a long time and seemed to be on the verge of tears. She asked how he was, what treatment he was still receiving after the long hospital stay. Darío didn't want to go into detail about his burns and injuries. He told her only about the pills he had to take daily and that they had advised him to keep up the physiotherapy even though he would prefer to have as little as possible to do with traditional medicine.

Emilse was a fan of yoga and tai chi. She had never come across as one of those people who want to convince everyone that their approach is best, but on this occasion she made a passionate pitch for both these regimes. She told him about her yoga teacher and the morning tai chi sessions in Parque Chacabuco. How through her understanding of these eastern disciplines she had achieved an equilibrium and an inner peace she hadn't found in eight years of psychoanalysis.

Darío listened politely, although he knew that he didn't need yoga, or psychoanalysis, or alternative therapies. He just needed to find Jazmín. So he let Emilse tell him in detail about all the things she did to feel good then, on the second round of coffees, he told her about his new writing project.

"I want to write a book of stories for Jazmín, all based around things she's said or done. It would be called simply *Jazmín's Stories.*"

"I think that's beautiful."

"And when I find her I'll read it to her at night, before she goes to sleep. She'll love it."

Darío noticed an involuntary change in Emilse, her body seeming to stiffen as she took a sip of coffee. He clarified:

"There's something I haven't told you, that you don't know. Jazmín and Cecilia are alive. Cecilia wanted to take my girl away from me. Various things happened while we were in La Lucila del Mar – complicated stuff. She told me that when we got back to Buenos Aires she was going to go off with Jazmín and that I wouldn't see them again. When the accident happened, I was conscious for a few seconds. Cecilia pulled me out of the car, I thought I heard Jazmín crying, but I couldn't move on my own. Cecilia took off with my daughter. While I was in hospital, they were declared dead and the case was closed. Now I'm trying to make the police launch a search. It's not fair, what Cecilia did to me. If she wants to leave, then let her go – but she can't separate me from my daughter."

Emilse listened to him intently. Now she raised a hand to her mouth and tears flowed down her face. Darío knew that the road ahead would be hard, but that he had the strength to carry on. He held Emilse's other hand on the table and told her not to cry, that everything would be all right. Now he was the one reassuring her. Emilse nodded and wiped away her tears.

VII

All children fear what may be lurking beneath the bed, especially at night, when the light goes off. Some imagine monsters, others picture wild animals, and the odd child believes there's a witch under the bed who sleeps all day and gets up at night. Everyone gets scared, but not Jazmín. She likes pretending to be asleep and, when her parents kiss her goodnight and leave the room, she quietly gets out of bed and dives into the secret world beneath it. That's where her only pet lives, a tarantula called Tula who she talks to her in her head: Jazmín thinks of things to say, and the spider responds in turn. They talk about all kinds of things: about school, about how difficult it is to spin a web, about how they would both like to be birds. Stuff like that, like any two friends who love each other.

When he got to this part, Darío paused. He wasn't sure whether to take the story towards horror or humour. He thought of filling the bedroom with horrible pets – cockroaches, bats, even a rat – but he didn't know whether to accentuate the funny side or the fear factor, so popular with some children.

Deciding it was time for a break, he got up from the computer and put on the kettle to make tea. That morning he had met a third lawyer, a celebrity type who took on the strangest cases so long as they guaranteed to raise his profile. Darío needed a sponsor because he wouldn't get anywhere on his own. But after listening closely to him, the lawyer had told him their chances of success were slim, that it might be better for him to hire a private detective – he had even recommended one.

Darío wasn't about to give up. While waiting for the kettle to boil, he realized what he had to do. His cousin Lucio. The train driver.

VIII

Darío had had a cousin a little older than him: Lucio. Many of his childhood summers had been spent with Lucio in Santa Teresita. Both cousins loved books. They read Jules Verne, Emilio Salgari, *Treasure Island, Ivanhoe, The Three Musketeers*. They liked talking about the books they read, telling each other the stories, imagining they were the characters.

Then they grew up. Lucio followed his father's wishes and became a train driver and probably lost all interest in books. Darío, meanwhile, kept reading and became a writer almost without ever planning to.

The last time they had seen each other had been at a family birthday party. They greeted one another with that affection that comes from having shared so much, although it was also tinged with the awkwardness of people who now have almost nothing in common. There was no doubt that they were fond of each other – they had watched each other grow up and each retained the clear memory of a time when they had been happy and carefree.

It may have been the effect of the alcohol, or boredom, or simply a desire to talk to someone he knew but who wasn't part of his daily life, that prompted Lucio to say that his life was hell, that he was sick of driving trains, that he lived with the constant fear some bastard would choose to end their life under his wheels. He told Darío that there was one thing keeping him going: his relationship with a woman. This woman was a journalist investigating a criminal organization, a gambling ring that bet on the lives of children from poor neighbourhoods.

As Lucio talked, Darío saw the boy who had imagined himself as Sandokan about to rescue Marianna from the clutches of the evil Baron Rosenthal. His eyes shone. Darío thought, somewhat enviously, that the light was a symptom of his love for the journalist.

Then Lucio's children had come running over, interrupting them, and they didn't reprise the conversation when they were alone again. At one point Lucio had seemed about to continue with his story, but instead he changed the subject.

"Do you remember Lucía?" he had asked.

Of course Darío remembered: both boys had been in love with her. They had been twelve or thirteen and she a few years older. She also used to spend the summers in Santa Teresita. Her parents rented an apartment in Pleamar IV, the same building in which Darío's family had three rooms. Despite the age difference she would talk to them and treat them like adults.

"I ran into her a few summers ago in Santa Teresita. She's gone to live there permanently. She's got a bar, and she sings and plays the guitar."

"She was always a bit strange."

"I've sometimes thought how much I'd like to go there with you. The three of us could get together."

"Wouldn't that be great? The two of us swimming right out to sea while she waits for us on the beach, just like when we were kids."

"I picture us both swimming to South Africa."

That's what they used to say as boys – *let's swim to South Africa!* But the reunion trip never got organized; in fact the cousins never saw each other again. Lucio was killed not long after that conversation. And a few days later Darío read the exposé on the train mafia in *Nuestro Tiempo*. The journalist credited Lucio in her piece. Thanks to him, she said, they had been able to thwart the criminals. He had noticed the journalist's surname: Rosenthal, like that character in Emilio Salgari's book.

And Darío realized that he didn't need to persist with judges, the police, bureaucrats, lawyers – not even with a private detective. What he needed was a journalist to investigate what had happened. A journalist. This woman, Rosenthal, would surely be able to help him.

3   *The Photograph Collector*

What had struck Verónica most about meeting Darío was less a physical resemblance to Lucio than the way her former lover appeared in certain gestures: a particular way of moving his eyes, or how he sat in the chair, or how he coughed. It was as though Lucio were hidden inside Darío and revealed himself only for a few seconds. She was unsettled by the similarities, and it was a while before she could concentrate on what he was saying.

She had taken him to the "goldfish bowl", the glass-walled meeting space that they used for interviews, in the newsroom. He told her about the accident, then explained the reasons why he believed his daughter to be alive, telling her about his wife's threat, the absence of a body, the lack of DNA evidence and his frustrated attempts to get the police to look for her.

"Have you never thought it might not have been your wife but someone else who pulled you out of the car?"

"It's crossed my mind. But the more I think back to the accident, the surer I am. For example, to start with I didn't realize that it was Jazmín I could hear crying. Now I have no doubt."

Verónica said nothing for a few seconds. She could see her colleagues outside the goldfish bowl. Álex Vilna had arrived in the office, with scarcely a word of greeting. A delivery boy was waiting for Matías Juárez to collect his order and pay for it, but Matías was over by the photocopier, looking for some back issues.

"I'm going to be frank, Darío. I'm not surprised the judges and police didn't pursue your case."

"I survived."

"Yes, of course. But the others – nearly ten people – died. It would be remarkable for only your wife and daughter to have come out alive."

"It's also remarkable that I survived." Darío tapped the table nervously. For the first time he seemed uncomfortable, perhaps even doubting himself. He stood up. "Clearly I won't be able to count on your help either."

Lucio would have reacted in the same way, Verónica thought, and the idea filled her with compassion for Darío. He was probably wrong, and his daughter and wife were dead, but she couldn't let him go like that. She couldn't. She owed it to Lucio. After Darío had gone, Verónica waited a few minutes and then left the newsroom. She didn't want to go to any of the bars nearby, for fear of running into a colleague. Instead she walked down Avenida Córdoba, crossed Avenida Dorrego then, once she felt far enough away, picked the first bar, one of those old ones that also function as a pizzeria. She ordered a whisky. They only had Argentine ones, so she asked for ice to curb the effect of kerosene hitting the stomach. And, although it tasted horrible, she needed more alcohol to calm her nerves and so she asked for another, this time without ice. The barman, seeing that she hadn't touched the complimentary selection of peanuts and pretzels, brought nothing with the second drink.

When she asked for a third, the barman looked doubtful, almost annoyed. As he poured out the drink, he seemed to be waiting for an explanation. It was at times like this that

Verónica wished she were a man: she'd punch him in the face. She paid, leaving no tip, and left the bar. She thought of going home, but it was early and she still had work to do back at the newsroom. Instead, she bought some chewing gum at a news stand to cover the smell of alcohol and went back to the office.

The cheap whisky was taking its toll on her stomach, but at least now she felt calmer. As she walked back to the magazine, she wondered if she was experiencing some strange dream, if Darío didn't exist, let alone his problems; at any moment she might open a door and find herself looking at the sea, or standing by a lake, or in a speeding car. Such images often cropped up in her nightmares. She felt nauseous and burped discreetly. There were some young women in the elevator – they must work in admin – and Verónica noticed them looking her up and down. She probably didn't smell good, or look tidy. Her clothes weren't clean and her hair was a bird's nest, but none of that justified these two bitches looking at her like they'd smelled a fart. Verónica returned the stare and the women glanced away, just as the elevator arrived at the floor where the *Nuestro Tiempo* offices were.

Verónica went straight to the toilets and locked herself in a cubicle. She vomited a yellow liquid that looked less like whisky than bile or some other strange bodily fluid. Her stomach was in revolt. She washed her face and tried to organize her hair. The mirror insisted on returning the image of a woman who looked like shit.

She went to Patricia Beltrán's desk and said she needed to talk to her. Patricia took one look at Verónica then stood up and, taking her arm, led her out of the newsroom and into the kitchen, which was empty.

"I want to talk to you about a piece," Verónica said.

"Have you been drinking?"

"A bit. Cheap whisky."

Patricia took her arm again, this time walking her right out of the office. She called the elevator and said: "Go home."

"But I've still got pieces to edit."

"You can't do anything in this state. How long since you last washed or changed this sweater?"

"It's called a pullover, I believe. I come to you with an idea for an article and you chuck me out. Isn't this what you wanted? For me to be a writer again?"

"Just go. Come back tomorrow and we'll talk articles. But for the moment go home, OK? If you turn up tomorrow like this I'll ask HR to suspend you. Is that clear?"

The elevator doors opened. Luckily there was nobody inside, especially not the two bitches from upstairs. She would have felt bad about having to hit them.

II

It was the first time since waking up in the intensive care unit that Darío had felt some measure of relief. Not calm exactly, or the absence of worry, but the sense that someone was by his side. He hadn't been wrong to call on Verónica Rosenthal. She would be able to access the right places, the ones beyond his reach.

He remembered how Lucio had spoken about her. And now he realized that his cousin had shown the same emotion as when he'd talked about Lucía.

Darío had also often thought back to their adolescent romance. Every time he and Cecilia argued, he fantasized about fleeing to that beach where Lucía was waiting. It wasn't only the bright afternoon when he and Lucio had seen her naked body that he remembered, but every other encounter and the long evening talks about life, death, fears and desires.

Now that he felt he could count on some help, Darío could start writing again. He began to work on a new collection of stories. He also spent much of the day opening files on his computer in search of some photo or recording of Jazmín that he hadn't yet seen. He looked on Cecilia's computer too and found several photos of Jazmín that he didn't have, taken by Cecilia on her mobile phone: one at some nursery event he hadn't been able to attend, one on a trip to the famous Recoleta cemetery, one playing in a ball pit. He copied all of the photos onto a USB stick and transferred them onto his computer.

The rest of the day he spent putting the photos of Jazmín into chronological order, until he arrived at the handful that had been on his phone at the time of the accident. There weren't many of those because they had taken a camera on vacation. All the same, there were about a dozen images of Jazmín playing on the beach at La Lucila del Mar.

There were also some photos on paper, with no digital copy: some from nursery, an official one taken at the entrance to the zoo, others that had been given to them by family or friends. He scanned all these images, as he planned to print off versions of the digital ones. He wanted two copies of everything.

Jazmín had started going to nursery the previous year, to the two-year-olds' class, which the nursery called the Strawberry Group (to differentiate it from the older Kiwi, Mandarin and Apple classes). Nursery had brought with it a bit of social life, and Jazmín often went to her little friends' birthday parties. There must have been photographs of Jazmín taken at those parties; they must have filmed her. Darío decided to call all the parents to ask a favour: that they let him copy those photos. He wanted all the photos of Jazmín that might exist in the world.

After the first phone call, which had turned awkward when he'd tried to explain to the mother that Jazmín was still alive, Darío decided to let the other parents believe the official line: that his daughter was dead. Thereafter the calls flowed more naturally. Condolences were expressed, to which he would make no reply, and that silence was proof enough for the other parents that he was grieving for his daughter. When he made his request, it no longer sounded so strange. One mother remembered that Jazmín had spent an afternoon at her house playing with her daughter and that she had taken photographs of them dressed up as princesses. He agreed to go and pick up the pictures of his daughter. While he was searching for Jazmín, trying to get her back, collecting all the available photos of her felt like the best plan for the days ahead.

III

She'd had a terrible night. Fits of vomiting had given way to an upset stomach and cramps that bent her double with pain. It couldn't be only the bad whisky that had made her feel like this. Chicha stayed beside her, in the cushioned dog basket to which she retreated when she was alone or could tell that Verónica wanted not to be bothered. And that night Verónica was in no fit state to look after her pet. In the middle of the night she made herself a tea, because she wanted something warm in her body, but that was worse because it brought the vomiting back. And so it continued until dawn: running to the bathroom, returning to bed, rubbing her stomach in an attempt to calm the pain. To make things worse, she didn't have any of that medicine that relieved cramps and nausea.

She took an ibuprofen, fearing that it might make her vomit again, or feel worse; against all predictions, though, it made her better. In the early hours she drifted off and didn't wake up again until morning. Verónica had managed to sleep for five hours straight and no longer felt any ill effects from the previous night, not even a hangover. She felt better, if weak, and stayed longer than usual in the shower, the water falling on her head and back helping her to order her thoughts so she could think more rationally about the previous day's encounter with Darío Valrossa.

Verónica washed her underwear and threw everything else in the dirty laundry basket. She needed to go to the launderette that day. While she made coffee and looked for a packet of crispbreads, planning to have them with a jam she didn't usually eat but which seemed ideal for a convalescent, she thought that it was still too early to go to the newsroom. There was more than enough time to go to the hairdresser and to get her legs waxed. She would get her hair cut the way she used to have it before this bird's nest appeared on her head.

Even though her appointment was with the same stylist who had cut her hair last, so much time had passed since then that this woman didn't recognize Verónica. She had to explain exactly what she wanted, not that it was complicated: she wanted her hair short enough to feel the autumn breeze on the nape of her neck.

The beautician, on the other hand, certainly knew her; she had been going to the same place for years. Roxi planted a noisy kiss on her cheek and then scolded her for not coming sooner. She was even more cross when she saw that Verónica had been shaving all this time.

There were two other women ahead of her. Verónica used the time to read old celebrity news in the magazines on a coffee table. On the radio, two presenters were swapping banter about their lives and every observation led to sex, to crass or crude jokes. A woman who was also waiting to be seen, and who looked about fifty, laughed at every gag. Verónica recognized the voice of a journalist she had worked with years ago.

Legs, armpits and bikini line. The classic trio, which she always requested without variation. Even so, Roxi invariably asked her: "Are you having a Brazilian? Shall I do the same as usual?"

Verónica liked to leave a landing strip. She didn't like a full wax, and that thin line made her feel more protected, as though a complete denuding of her pubic area would leave her more exposed to the world. Unfortunately, leaving that strip didn't spare her the intense pain of having such a sensitive area waxed. Although Roxi had a practised hand, Verónica always asked herself why she submitted to such torture. Lying on the treatment bed, with her legs a little bent, she could hardly see Roxi, but she felt her skilfully apply the wax then tear it off with brisk movements. Then the little taps against her skin as those red-nailed hands moved over her tender areas with the grace of a skilled pianist or a somewhat sadistic yet considerate lover. She liked the feel of Roxi's nails scraping away the stubborn residue from her skin.

After leaving the salon, Verónica had to hurry to the magazine. Her jeans felt uncomfortable next to her recently depilated skin. She wished there had been time to go home, shower and put on a skirt.

She arrived just in time for her section's weekly meeting. Patricia had called the other four journalists and the intern to the goldfish bowl, where everyone was pitching ideas for the following week. As deputy editor, Verónica usually noted down the different assignments while the others were talking about possible articles. On this occasion, though, she used the time to work out how she was going to talk to Patricia about the piece she wanted to write.

As Patricia was about to close the meeting, Verónica presented her idea: she told the others about the accident and the sole survivor's belief that his wife and daughter were alive and hiding somewhere.

"The guy sounds deluded," Patricia said.

"Yes, I know, but this man still has the right to an investigation establishing exactly what happened to his family. Up until now the only response he's had is negligence, red tape and a total lack of compassion for a terrible tragedy – the death of a child."

"OK, go ahead. Let's say two pages. Right, everyone back to work."

As the others all got up and left the room, Patricia asked Verónica: "So am I losing my deputy editor?"

"Maybe just for this week."

"Eighteen hundred words. Welcome back."

IV

After several days spent making calls and paying visits, Verónica had a few more details for her article. She had no doubt that there had been negligence in the case of the General Lavalle accident, and that nobody wanted to take responsibility for it. Everyone washed their hands of it. At the end of the day, it was an accident, not a crime, both police and lawyers told her in so many words.

At times like this she missed Federico. Professionally, at least – all other aspects would require further analysis. He would have known how to get to the bottom of this, how to find the Achilles heel of those nonentities who filled the judiciary.

But she couldn't call on Federico, or even on Rosenthal and Associates. Since Federico had left the law firm and she had argued with her father, who ran it, the Rosenthal practice no longer helped in any way with her journalistic work.

Verónica needed professional help. She remembered Doctor Renzi, the forensic expert who taught medical law at the Universidad de Buenos Aires and worked in the Ministry of Justice. The last time they met he had taken her to look at corpses in the morgue; this time he asked her to come to the Faculty of Medicine.

Renzi took her to an office, where he offered her an espresso and sat down to hear her out. He gave the impression of having all the time in the world – a nice gesture, Verónica thought. Renzi asked her which medical examiner had been charged with filling the accident report. Verónica looked through her papers and found the name: Doctor Augusto Pérez Riu.

Renzi raised his eyebrows, shaking his head. "I know him. He was a student of mine. A second-rater who barely looks at the bodies and likes to knock off early. I'm not surprised he's worked his way up. He's the kind of person who keeps within budget by refusing to do any complicated examinations."

Verónica handed him the few documents she had managed to secure on her visit to the courts. Renzi studied them carefully, then explained:

"When an accident involves fatalities, it's the medico-legal autopsy that determines the cause of death. It even establishes the likely position of the victim when the accident took place."

"But don't burned bodies disintegrate?"

"Well, not exactly – although, if the fire is very intense, the remains may disintegrate into ashes when you try to examine them. In those cases other aids to identification, like clothes, documentation and personal items, may be lost too."

"In this case, the suitcases were in a roof box and were thrown clear, which made it possible to retrieve the victims' documents. The documents and the family's statements were used to establish who was in the car."

"When flames make contact with the fibres in clothing, they can reach a temperature higher than a thousand degrees. It's very difficult to examine carbonized bodies – you have to try more specific methods."

"Such as?"

"It's more usual and effective to look for dental fragments. Often that's all you can find. Teeth can withstand temperatures up to 1,100 degrees before they disintegrate."

"So the teeth of the car's occupants should have survived, if nothing else?"

Renzi now seemed more interested in his own reasoning than in paying attention to Verónica's questions. After a few seconds he said: "How about this: I'll get hold of everything from the case. I think it could make a good case study for my students, to show them how not to work. I'll call you in a couple of days."

V

Darío knew Ivana's mother from picking up and dropping off at the nursery, and they had always got on well. Cecilia had gone for a coffee with her once or twice and Jazmín had been over to her house to play with Ivana a few times. Mariela was a single mother.

She had some photos that had been taken on a couple of afternoons Jazmín had spent with Ivana, her best friend, if such a thing can be said about girls of two or three years old. Darío dropped by their apartment in Almagro on Thursday morning. Mariela greeted him with a smile, skipped the condolences and behaved completely naturally. She told him that Ivana was at nursery, that the teacher wasn't nearly as good as the one last year. She led him to the living room, where there was a laptop on the coffee table.

"I've got loads of photos of them together and a few of Jazmín on her own. I think I already sent some to Ceci, in fact."

She left him looking at the pictures and went to make coffee, appearing a few minutes later with two cups. She passed one to Darío, who was absorbed by the photos.

"Ivana's mad on dressing up. So you're going to find a few princesses in there, plus a witch, even a Batman. That one she inherited from her cousin."

The apartment was dark, with low windows and weak artificial light. Everything seemed very old: the furniture, the little coverings on the sideboard and table, the reproduction of a Murillo painting on the wall. The room felt heavy.

"Did you see the video of them both bouncing on the bed? Those girls will be gymnasts when they grow up."

It was the first time since the accident that someone else had referred to Jazmín in the present tense. Hearing that was like a wave pushing him, throwing him onto the sand and crashing over him. For a few seconds he couldn't breathe and lost all sense of where he was.

"Cecilia's taken Jazmín. She's stolen her," he said quickly, before Mariela had a chance to correct herself.

But Mariela simply shook her head and, as though talking about a third party worthy of no more than passing comment, she said: "I never liked Cecilia." Then she went on without missing a beat: "Make copies of all the photos. There's something else, too." She went to the bedroom and returned holding a children's pop-up book, a version of Cinderella. "You should take this now. Jazmín lent it to us before the vacation and Ivana will throw a tantrum if she sees me give it back."

Darío hesitated for a few seconds. Mariela smiled at him. He took the book and clung onto it as a way to emerge from the wave and regain his balance.

There was no reason to spend any longer in the apartment now that he had made copies of the photos. Mariela said she would go with him downstairs to open the main door. In the elevator she asked him: "So, are you looking for them?"

Darío mumbled some response. He thought of telling her about all he had gone through in the last few weeks: the police, the court officials, the journalist, but instead he muttered some platitude. At the door she kissed him goodbye, stroking his face.

"You don't have to explain anything to me. But if you need anything, call me."

Darío walked quickly away, not fully understanding what had happened, doubting everything. Doubting himself, too, for the first time.

VI

There was something she wasn't getting right, or wasn't getting at all, though she couldn't work out what it was. Verónica needed to clear her mind, put some distance between herself and the investigation and consider the bigger picture. She thought of phoning Darío, then decided to leave that call for tomorrow. It was already too late for almost everything, apart from drinking. She texted Paula, but her friend already had plans for the evening. Then a call came through from Pili, her Spanish friend, recently separated. They arranged to meet an hour later at the Oak Bar in the Palacio Duhau hotel. It was a long round trip, but if her friend wanted to go to a fancy hotel, Verónica wasn't going to kick up a fuss.

By the time she arrived, Pili had already ordered a Bloody Mary and was boldly eyeing up the men at the bar. Verónica was thirsty, so – unusually for her – she ordered a cocktail, an Old Fashioned. There'd be time for a single bourbon later.

"You know what, Vero, I think what I like most about this city is the men. They're very basic."

Verónica had to admit there was some truth in this observation.

Pili was separated from her Argentine husband, with whom she had a five-year-old son. Motherhood had never held her back – she was always keen to try out a new bar, signing up for countless activities and finding all kinds of men to add to her collection. Verónica's other friends hated Pili, but they still wanted to hang out with her.

Verónica wasn't so extreme. She felt neither particularly close to Pili nor appalled by her – but she was curious to know what it would be like to live so freely. They were the same age and Pili had already lived abroad, been married, had a child. And she could act like a fiery teenager when she felt like it. You'd have to be very grudging to hate her. That's what she was going to say to Paula if her friend started criticizing her for going out drinking with Pili.

"I've made an Excel spreadsheet," Pili said as she ordered a second Bloody Mary, "with columns numbered between eighteen and fifty. In each column I put the number of men I've screwed, according to their age when we first fucked. For example, Agustín was twenty-eight our first time, and even though we carried on fucking for the next seven years – well, maybe not the last one – he just goes in the twenty-eight column."

"So much effort that could have gone on a worthier cause."

"Far from it, lovely Vero. I've come to some extremely interesting conclusions. For example: there are still five columns with no names in them. Do you grasp the significance of that?

Can you believe I've never done it with a nineteen-year-old, even when I was that age myself? On the other hand, I've got a surfeit of thirty-three-year-olds. No idea why. Could it have something to do with Jesus Christ?"

"You mean some kind of religious Oedipus complex, only with the Holy Father?"

"The thing is, I went to a school in Madrid run by Ursuline nuns. I don't suppose you have that problem?"

They left the bar at midnight, sharing a taxi as far as Córdoba and Medrano, from which point Verónica continued alone. The best thing about an outing with Pili was that there was no need to talk about personal or painful stuff. They kept the conversation light, sharing nothing more than, say, some strictly sexual indiscretion on the part of some guy or other. Pili didn't even ask why Verónica had recently been absent from their circle of friends, nor did she comment on the return to her old look.

The superficiality of their conversation allowed Verónica some respite from worrying about the Darío case. She had now been in touch with all the agencies implicated in the accident investigation; she had spoken to the top forensic expert. What was she missing?

When Verónica got home, she switched on her computer and poured herself a Jim Beam Black Label. She would spend tomorrow addressing the holes in her own investigation, but she wasn't yet ready to go to sleep. She walked over to the balcony and looked outside. Most of the lights were out now in the city that farcically claimed never to sleep. In her bedroom she took off her clothes and put on a nightshirt and some bedsocks, thick and soft, the kind she would never have thought of wearing in front of a lover – mind you, she wouldn't need bedsocks if she had a man to spend the night with.

The living room was lit only by the screen of her laptop. Verónica checked her mailbox and found no interesting messages. She tried repeatedly, and in vain, to hack into Federico's mail. That soon got boring. Then she half glanced at Sentimiento Bohemio, the fan site for the Atlanta soccer club, but didn't want to infuriate herself thinking about Atlanta's current woes.

That afternoon in the newsroom, the sports journalists had been talking about Belladonna, a porn star who had made a film while eight months pregnant. It wasn't hard to find the video. She was intrigued to see the body of a pregnant woman having sex, but in this film Belladonna appeared only with other girls. Verónica liked the way she fucked: strong, active, dominant. Would she also fuck that way if she were pregnant? Belladonna's belly was very attractive to her. Would hers be like that? She couldn't imagine herself pregnant. Loneliness was damaging her neurons. She could never take care of a child. Look at what had happened with Santino. She hadn't been up to the job: two hours after the little boy arrived she had been wishing she could hand him back to her sister. That's why she couldn't stop thinking that if Santino had been lost it would have been her fault, for wanting to get rid of him. No, she couldn't be a mother. She could fuck like Belladonna, though, with or without a pregnant belly, with girls like that or with guys like... like Federico? Like Darío? Was she attracted to Darío because he looked like Lucio? *Shut up, stupid woman,* she told herself, *you're horny, stop confusing things.* At this time of night, in these circumstances, she would have screwed any guy, but there was no guy. She could call Marcelo, the building's doorman, who would be happy to indulge her fantasies; if his wife found out, though, Verónica would have to move to another building. Another city, another country. Now Belladonna was going down on a bottle blonde. She was good at it. She liked Belladonna's underwear, pastel stripes. And the little cropped T-shirt was a nice touch. She wanted a T-shirt like that. And tits like that too. The tits more than the T-shirt. Some guys had broken into her apartment once, looking for information on her. Had they been turned on by her things? She should film herself fucking or masturbating. That would get them hot. She thought how surprised Federico would be to see her fucking someone else, maybe a girl like Belladonna. Or watching her masturbate, as she was now. She'd like to have a camera to film herself like this – lying back in the armchair, moaning softly, more softly than Belladonna and the bottle blonde on the screen. What if she called Federico and moaned like this to him? What if Marcelo was going down the stairs and heard her? She'd love him to see her right now, for him to discover her like this, with her fingers in her underwear. They would watch her, touching themselves, slowly, waiting for her to finish.

She squeezed her legs against her stronger hand and felt her breasts with the other. With the last spasms of her orgasm Federico disappeared, along with Marcelo, the men who had been in her apartment, Darío. Only Belladonna and the blonde girl were left. She bade them a polite farewell, as only two such generous girls deserved, then closed the laptop and drank what was left of the bourbon in her glass.

Why was she so determined to find out whether Darío's wife and daughter were still alive? The question rose clear in her mind. It was true that if she proved they were dead, the search was pointless. As long as there was no confirmation of that, though, these two women were dead and alive at the same time. So why not do two parallel investigations? If Verónica had faith in Darío, she should look for them. She had to find Cecilia. If she was alive then she couldn't have vanished, she couldn't even have left the country. If her escape had been spontaneous but somehow planned – even as a fantasy – there must be clues on her computer. First thing tomorrow, she would speak to Darío. If Cecilia was alive, Verónica was going to find her.

4   *The Search for a Daughter*

I

Verónica Rosenthal's call surprised him, even though there was a logic to what she proposed. If Cecilia had been planning to leave him, there might well be some trace of that on her computer. He felt no desire to comb through Cecilia's files. He had only looked for photos of Jazmín there, nothing else. Better to let the journalist open that can of worms. Photos aside, nothing she might find there would be good for him.

They agreed that she would come by at about three o'clock. Darío spent the hour beforehand trying to tidy the house a little and realized only then that there was nothing in the fridge he could offer his guest, apart from a bottle of water.

Verónica arrived punctually and brought him up to date with the latest developments. Before they sat down to look through Cecilia's computer, Darío took her to see Jazmín's bedroom. He seemed proud, as if he had recently finished decorating it. Verónica picked up a photo of Jazmín with her parents and studied it closely.

"That was taken in the square in Luján, in front of the cathedral," said Darío. He was pleased to see Verónica looking at photos of Jazmín, but he didn't tell her that he was collecting, copying and printing them, that he aimed to get hold of all the existing images of his daughter. Next he took her to the study, showed her Cecilia's computer and offered her a cup of tea.

For more than two hours Darío left Verónica alone, working. Every now and then he would look around the door and see her writing things down in a little notebook. What could she have found?

In truth, Darío didn't want to know anything about Cecilia. He was interested only in any information that could lead to finding Jazmín. If Verónica were to find evidence on the computer of an infidelity, or a diary in which Cecilia had written that she was sick of him, it wouldn't particularly hurt him. The circumstances of the accident had made everything that happened before it seem vulgar and devoid of any sentimental value.

Verónica appeared in the living room. She hadn't finished yet but said she'd prefer to carry on the next day. Darío was fine with that. He didn't want to ask anything about what she had found on the computer and, oddly, she didn't mention anything. While she drank the tea, she returned to the subject of the unfinished forensic investigations.

"They might need to take a DNA sample to compare with the remains they found. If there's no match, the likelihood is greater that Jazmín didn't die in the accident."

Darío said nothing. For the first time he realized the importance of something that until then had been buried deep in his memory.

"That won't be possible, because Jazmín is adopted."

Verónica nodded, without saying anything. When she had finished the tea she said goodbye until the following day.

Darío was left alone, remembering when Jazmín had come into their lives: she had been six months old. He thought too about all the paperwork they had done to register her as their own daughter, bypassing the usual adoption channels.

He remembered the judge in Santiago. Also Tonso, the man who had taken care of all the details. It occurred to him that there must be photos from the first months of Jazmín's life. He wondered what she was like when she was born. Or at one month old, two months. Would her biological mother have kept those photos or thrown them away? He decided to track down Tonso again, so he could get hold of those pictures.

II

The first thing Verónica did on leaving Darío's apartment was light a cigarette. That intake of smoke was like breathing again after more than two hours of feeling stifled. It had been a difficult afternoon, in an apartment she should never have entered, but there was no way round it: if she wanted to find out more about Cecilia, she had to look through her computer. Verónica hadn't expected Darío to take her into the little girl's room, showing her every photo and every toy as though he planned, despite his certainty that Jazmín was alive, to convert the place into some kind of museum. She had longed to make her excuses and leave.

Darío's presence had been troubling too, because of his similarity to Lucio. Verónica had tried not to look at him too much, to ignore the mannerisms, to concentrate on the conversation, but that got harder as time went on. While she was sniffing around Cecilia's computer, she was all too aware of Darío in the other room, and it was like sensing the ghost of Lucio.

It shouldn't have taken her more than an hour to look through Cecilia's files, but a lot of time had been lost to strange thoughts about Darío and Lucio and the fate of both cousins. She tried to remember if Lucio had ever spoken to her about him and vaguely recalled him telling her about a cousin who loved books. Veronica was no believer in fate or in any kind of god, or in the mysterious connections in people's lives. She was happy to put everything down to coincidence, with no deeper significance or meaning. All the same, the appearance of Darío in her life was making her doubt her faith in the lack of faith.

She didn't feel comfortable in that apartment, especially not looking through another person's computer. Even before beginning the search, Verónica had decided she wouldn't tell Darío about whatever she found. She needed to observe the professional confidentiality of a doctor or a priest in the confessional.

And, as she went through her computer files, Verónica began to feel she knew Cecilia. The thirty-five-year-old missing woman took shape in the photos and gradually Verónica got the measure of her personality: she was a sociologist and worked for a consultancy that specialized in political polling. She loved cooking, longed to have a garden and compensated for the lack of green space with assorted houseplants and by growing seedlings on the balcony. Cecilia was small, with a pretty face, blue eyes and long, straight black hair. She seemed like a forceful character; she listened to Alejandro Sanz and liked reading the books and blogs of political pundits. Verónica couldn't imagine her joining the gang for a night at Martataka, or sipping a gin and tonic at the bar in the Claridge – and that pleased her: there was no world in which they might have been friends.

Cecilia's inbox was open. There wasn't time to read all the emails, so she opened only the ones that looked personal. No sign of a lover, but Cecilia did write regularly to three friends, two of whom had got in touch after the accident. Those emails hadn't been opened and they were letters of farewell, heartfelt outpourings from grieving friends. Out of respect, Verónica marked them as unread. The third friend, who had not written, lived in Miami. None of the emails or files she looked at that afternoon contained any significant clues.

She seemed not to have any male friends, at least none she corresponded with. Cecilia's messages to men were generally to do with work. There were some with whom she seemed to enjoy a level of confidence bordering on camaraderie, but in no case were there intimate revelations or disparaging comments. In all instances, Cecilia came across as a faithful wife who ignored her husband (there were almost no references to him), and a devoted mother who took part in group mailings from the nursery, checked the prices of dressing-up costumes and bought tickets online for outings to the cinema or theatre with her little girl.

There was something Verónica wasn't seeing, without a doubt. And she needed to let the information she had found sink in. The most significant development had been provided by Darío: the revelation that Jazmín was adopted. Something was bothering Verónica: adoptive parents are usually proud of their status, yet Darío seemed uncomfortable; a shadow had seemed to pass over his face.

III

It felt strange going into a McDonald's, especially the one with the ball pit. He had been there so many times with Jazmín that walking in alone made his daughter's absence all the more palpable. He ordered a coffee and took his cup up to the first floor, which was where he had arranged to meet Mariela.

Ivana's mother had called him that morning to say she had found more photographs of Jazmín, taken on a phone she didn't use any more. She had suggested they meet at the McDonald's at Avenida La Plata and Rivadavia, where she was going to be marking some exams while Ivana entertained herself in the ball pit. Darío thought there couldn't be that many photos and she could have sent them by email; still, he liked the idea of seeing Mariela, the only person who had known Jazmín and could talk about her without feeling sorry for him.

Mariela looked up as he approached. She was sitting in the play area, where she could keep an eye on Ivana. Before he had settled into his seat, she asked: "Any news?"

"Nothing yet."

Mariela nodded, picked up her bag and rummaged in it for the phone. Smiling, she said: "These are from the afternoon I took the girls to Parque Centenario."

The photos were bad because the phone had a low-resolution camera. All the same, they brought Jazmín vividly before him: happy, radiant, having fun with her friend. Darío flicked through the same set of images several times, listening as Mariela described that afternoon at the park.

Ivana rushed out of the ball pit, perhaps after being pushed by another child. Running towards them, she misjudged her footing, crashed into the edge of a table and fell over. Mariela jumped out of her seat. The little girl was lying motionless on the floor, eyes closed, face covered in blood. Immediately there was a commotion all around them. Children cried, Mariela shouted, shaking Ivana and trying to wipe the blood off her face. Somebody called out for a doctor, pointlessly as there wasn't one on-site. Darío dialled 911 and requested an ambulance. Some McDonald's employees approached nervously, apparently reluctant to take charge of the situation. Then Ivana opened her eyes and, seeing the crowd around her and her mother's distress, burst into tears: a reassuring cry. Darío asked one of the employees to bring ice; the hapless boy brought it in a glass, but someone produced a handkerchief in which to wrap the ice before applying it to

78

Ivana's face. The cut, above her eyebrow, was soon bleeding less. Seeing her improve, Mariela decided not to wait for the ambulance and took her daughter to their local clinic instead. The McDonald's staff trailed after her as she left, like lost puppies, unsure what to do.

Mariela, Darío and the little girl, now hardly crying, got into a taxi, and five minutes later they were at the clinic. Despite Mariela's evident panic, they had to wait ten minutes before seeing a doctor. Ivana was given three stitches, prompting much screaming and crying, then all three of them went back to their apartment and Mariela asked Darío to please come up. He agreed.

They went to the kitchen to make coffee while Ivana settled to watching cartoons on TV. It was only when he sat down at the table that Darío felt all the tension of the last few hours come over him. When he went to pick up the cup, he could see his hand shaking. Then he felt pity for his shaking hand; looking at it, he wanted to cry. He wanted to speak to Mariela but couldn't: he felt as though something had finally broken that night. Covering his face, Darío began to cry. He felt a crushing sadness and no energy or desire to do anything. Although there were so many things he wanted to say to explain to Mariela why he was crying, all he could do was repeat "Poor Jazmín." Mariela put her arms around him and kissed his forehead, as though he were a child.

IV

Verónica had to go and see Doctor Renzi before heading to the magazine. These were difficult times in the newsroom. Too much upheaval: the resignation of the managing editor, a rumour of changes at the top, the possible layoff of editorial and administrative staff. At five o'clock there was going to be a conference, and on top of that they had to finalize sixteen pages. It would be a long day.

Renzi was waiting for her in his office. The doctor appeared to live between the Faculty of Medicine and the morgue; it was impossible to picture him in any other context. And he seemed to thrive on it – an older man who hadn't lost his passion for his work. Renzi greeted Verónica with a smile. He smelled of tobacco, as though he had been smoking until a few seconds before she arrived.

"All my suspicions have been confirmed," Renzi announced, allowing Verónica a few seconds to absorb this information before he went on. "No remains, pertaining either to mother or daughter, were found in Valrossa's car. Now, bearing in mind the carbonized state of the other victims travelling in the same vehicle, it's fair to assume that the dentition, at least, would have been found. It's unlikely that they too would have been reduced to ashes, especially given that other bodies less than two feet away retained a large part of their bone formation. The official line is that there was one survivor, three deaths confirmed by autopsy and another five deaths presumed through identification of elements external to the bodies. A travesty justified by budgetary constraints, although I'm sure it had more to do with laziness than anything else."

"So Cecilia Burgos and Jazmín Valrossa didn't die in the car?"

"I don't want to be so categorical. There would have to be another examination of the car wreck, taking DNA samples. Admittedly, the destruction caused by the fire was very extensive, but you can always find something. Do you know what happened to the car involved in the accident? Let's hope they've got it in some police or judicial storage facility. Analyses that should have been routine at the time will be harder to do now."

"In your opinion, Doctor, if we manage to reopen the case, will it be possible to do more forensic investigations?"

"Look, I'll tell you what I think may happen. You'll get administrative proceedings brought against the medical, police and legal officials responsible. Now, no judge is going to authorize a missing person search when the testimony of the only survivor is that those passengers were in the car at the time of the accident. He can protest that the wife was a child-stealing witch until he's blue in the face – no judge will give him the time of day. There are hundreds of missing person reports. They may look into ten or twenty, of which three or four will be fully investigated, with the most effort going into the higher-profile cases. I don't need to explain to you how that all works. In Argentina search protocols are ineffective, there's no digitized information, plus there's a lot of inertia. Don't expect them to go looking for a woman allegedly fleeing with her daughter when everything suggests they were burned to death, even if professional incompetence means there's no definitive proof."

Verónica asked a few more questions and got Renzi to write down the names of everyone he had spoken to, so that she could include these in the piece she was thinking of writing. With the evidence she had gathered, plus Renzi's own findings and the opinions of the pathologist, she could put together a solid article on the ineptitude of the Buenos Aires judicial and police apparatus in one specific case. As she was about to leave, Renzi broadened his habitual smile and said:

"Your friend came to see me the other day…" He searched his memory for the name. "The one who worked with your father in the law firm and who's an attorney now."

"Federico Córdova?"

"Attorney Córdova, exactly. Looks like you're missing some corpses and he's got too many. You should get together and do swapsies."

V

The article appeared in the next edition of *Nuestro Tiempo*. Darío had grudgingly posed for photographs when Verónica explained why they were necessary. He had also provided her with some photos of Cecilia and Jazmín, so their faces could be publicized, perhaps prompting readers to get in touch with any clues as to their whereabouts. He had already endured indifference, incompetence, the humiliating bureaucracy of police and lawyers. Now he must brace himself for the publication of this article, the images, his statements. Verónica Rosenthal had done a good job of putting into words all that he had suffered and was still suffering. But would the article help find Jazmín? Could Verónica find her? Would he ever have another chance to play with his daughter by the sea?

Back when he and Cecilia still loved one another, they had decided to have a child. They stopped using contraception and surrendered to this adventure with joy and the hope that a simple roll in the hay might ultimately bring a new life into their world. But the months went by and no pregnancy transpired. They embarked on a lengthy process of tests and analyses to establish what was wrong with their fertility and what other options were available to them.

It seemed that the quantity and quality of Cecilia's eggs were insufficient to result in pregnancy. The couple could have opted for *in vitro* fertilization, but there was no guarantee of success and they weren't prepared to endure years of frustration. Adopting a baby seemed to both of them like the most natural solution.

But if the fertility tests had felt drawn out, that was nothing compared to arranging a legal adoption. Every stage in the process was tedious and frustrating. The difficulty of adopting became an obsessive talking point between them. Then a political scientist friend offered to put them in touch with Carlos Tonso, a printer who could help them speed up the paperwork.

Using a printer as an intermediary sounded strange from the start. Moreover, all their communications were surreptitious and ultra-cautious. All the same, they decided to follow up on the contact. Cecilia went alone to the first appointment while Darío waited for her in Los Galgos, a bar a few blocks away. When she met him there afterwards, she seemed stricken with worry and doubts.

At first she had liked Tonso. He told her that he had been through a similar experience to theirs, and that was why he tried to help couples who wanted to be parents. He also explained that in the country's interior there were a great number of children at risk, many of whom died before their first birthdays from hunger, disease or maltreatment. There was a group that travelled around the provinces looking for these children, to find them families that could provide a good upbringing. Cecilia had wanted to know what kind of group this was, and Tonso answered her with another question: "Did you get married in church?"

They had done, and Tonso took it for granted that they were Catholic, but neither of them was particularly religious. Their decision to marry in church had been based on tradition rather than on faith.

"It's a group linked to certain parishes and a religious order that makes contact with the neediest. And a lot of the time what those people need most is someone to look after their children."

Tonso agreed that the process of legal adoption could be problematic and ineffective. For that reason, he and other church members had decided to use their position to help.

"Our work is very careful and painstaking. Every stage is overseen by judges, priests, respectable people. That's why I asked if you're married, because justices of the peace prefer to give children to marriages that have been sanctified by the Church."

Tonso also explained that there was no fee, in the strict sense, for this service, although they welcomed donations to support their mission. He asked about Cecilia's work and Darío's income, and suggested a figure that was three times their monthly revenue.

"Let's do it," said Darío.

There were two more meetings. The first took place in the parish of Flores. Darío and Cecilia met with Tonso and a priest who introduced himself as Father Eduardo. The conversation was somewhat overwhelming because they spent most of it talking about life and about God, His designs and the beauty of everything. Take out the Catholic bit, and it could have been a bunch of stoners chatting. Cecilia and Darío must have seemed to be on the same wavelength as the priest and the printer, though, because another appointment was organized there and then, this time at the couple's apartment. And not with Tonso or Father Eduardo, but with two diminutive nuns who were going to take care of all the necessary paperwork and to whom they must pay twenty per cent of the agreed fee. A kind of deposit, thought Cecilia and Darío.

Tonso had warned them it might be a long time before they heard anything – but two months later, there was news:

"We've got a baby girl. The only problem is, she's already six months old. She's healthy, beautiful and her mother is a teenager from Santiago who wants nothing to do with her. She didn't even register the birth. If you're interested, we can have her in Buenos Aires in three days. Have you already bought the crib, bottles and bibs?"

Six months old was still a baby. Of course they wanted her! Darío couldn't remember a happier time with Cecilia. And Tonso wasn't lying: she was bouncing and healthy. Soon after the little girl came into their lives, they had their papers in order. She was named as their daughter on their marriage document and on the birth certificate sent to them from Santiago del Estero.

Three years later, when Darío got back in touch with Tonso, the printer suggested they meet the following Monday, at four o'clock in Los Galgos, the same bar in which Darío had first dared to imagine he might become a father.

VI

Family photos aside, Darío was almost entirely absent from Cecilia's emails, diary or Facebook. It was as though he had died a long time before the accident. What if, in ignoring Darío, Cecilia was also hiding something else? Should Verónica be looking for a different email account to the one that was open on the computer? Perhaps Cecilia had led a double life so closely guarded that there was no trace of it anywhere else. She seemed intelligent, smart, incapable of putting a foot wrong. But even intelligent women made mistakes.

Verónica was useless at computer forensics. She had only one email account and got annoyed if anyone tried to talk to her through Google Chat (even though her status was permanently set to "invisible"). She had needed a lesson from Paula on how Facebook worked and only had WhatsApp because her eldest niece, Clara, had installed it on her phone to create a group called "Ros Sisters" comprising Leticia, Daniela and herself. After weeks of sending her sisters messages, Verónica had found out that Daniela didn't use WhatsApp and that Leticia had left the group. She had been messaging herself.

Notwithstanding, she had made a determined effort to gather information on Cecilia and discovered that sociology seemed to interest her only in a professional capacity. Verónica had looked through her internet searches and pages she bookmarked in the evenings, when people tend to put work aside to pursue personal interests. There was nothing connected to sociology or political science. On the other hand, there were lots of recipes and searches for rare ingredients, along with information about gardening and nature. Thanks to one website she visited regularly, Cecilia had managed to create a small herb garden on her balcony.

"Who picked La Lucila del Mar as a vacation destination?" she asked Darío when he brought her a cup of tea.

Darío considered this. He hadn't expected the question and struggled to give a clear answer. "I did – well no, not exactly. I think it was my sister-in-law. I wanted Jazmín to see the sea, and my sister-in-law had a friend who rented out a very nice apartment in La Lucila del Mar."

"And Cecilia? What did she want to do?"

He hesitated. "I don't know. I don't think she was against going to the beach."

In fact Cecilia had been making enquiries about the cost of renting a cabin in Entre Ríos, Córdoba or Mendoza. She had even bookmarked some pages offering vacation homes. In her emails, she asked what the rental price would be for two adults and a little girl. Apparently it had not been part of her original plan to go away with her mother, sister and niece, nor had she thought of going alone with the girl.

Cecilia's friends were still grieving for her and remembering her on Facebook, with the exception of one called Maru, who lived in Miami. Verónica was struck by this silence from a friend who had been in daily contact with Cecilia, sharing the tiniest details of her everyday life. She pulled up Maru's

Facebook page: since Cecilia's supposed death, Maru hadn't posted a single thing that mentioned her friend. She had merely "liked" some of the comments posted by other friends. Verónica always found it strange, not to say stupid, that people "liked" expressions of condolence. Maru was still in touch with the other friends, with lots of people in Buenos Aires and with Soledad, her sister who lived in the provinces.

Verónica searched for emails to Soledad in Cecilia's mailbox, but they seemed not to have written to one another. There were, however, many references to her in the exchanges with Maru, since all three shared an interest in plants. On Facebook Soledad had written to Maru saying that she now had lemon balm, sage and mint.

"Darío, did Cecilia grow lemon balm on the balcony?"

"No."

"Are you sure?"

"Yes, absolutely. Because we had an argument about that. She wanted to get permission from the residents' association to put a herb garden on the communal roof terrace. She wanted to plant lemon balm and mint and didn't have enough space to do it here. I said I thought it was a crazy idea. People would steal the plants."

Now you two can go into business exporting aromatic plants, wrote Maru. From what she could see on Facebook, Verónica deduced that the sister was single and had no children.

Soledad lived in San Javier, Córdoba. Now Verónica started a new search. Before the vacation, Cecilia had been looking at cottages in the Traslasierra Valley and even corresponded with someone who had mentioned San Javier more than once. In the emails that person appeared as Mieles Sol. And now Verónica realized that the email address belonged to Soledad. She, too, had not expressed any kind of sadness on Facebook or by email. It wasn't much to go on, but for now it was all she had.

5   *The Two Verónicas*

I

When Federico picked up the new edition of *Nuestro Tiempo*, he felt the same degree of tension he would have experienced buying a gay porn magazine. There wasn't anything wrong with it, nobody could have reproached him, yet on some level it was like sticking his nose into Verónica's life. He felt like a stalker.

At least this time he had the perfect excuse. This edition featured a piece on what had happened in the port during Operation White Ham. He wanted to see what the journalist who had asked so many questions about his private life had ended up writing. He feared some paragraph might start: *The prosecutor Federico Córdova, currently dating a Verónica, but not our Verónica, stated...* He was relieved to see María Vanini had written nothing like that, nor made any allusion to his private life. She had included his statements on what had happened; since Federico had no idea what had really happened, though, his comments were ambiguous and general. The journalist then went on to pursue a totally false lead: according to her, the bodies contained cocaine. Although she quoted an anonymous source, Federico knew that nobody in the judiciary or federal police was considering that hypothesis either a priori or in the light of subsequent investigations. María Vanini was clearly no Verónica Rosenthal. Verónica would have kept pushing until she reached the nub of the question; she wouldn't have leaped to outlandish theories but would have tried to establish the identity of the driver who had shot himself, for whom he was working, the real destination of those body parts and, above all, the origin of the babies' corpses. In other words, Verónica would have tried to find out all the things he now had to investigate.

After looking through the whole magazine and finding no article under the byline Verónica Rosenthal, he remembered what María Vanini had said: that she had been on sick leave more than once. Was something wrong with her? Surely Daniela or Leticia would have let him know. The sisters wouldn't have hidden something like that from him; they often encouraged him to get in touch with the youngest Rosenthal, although he always found an excuse not to attend any family gathering that included Verónica. Or her father Aarón, whom he hadn't seen since quitting the Rosenthal and Associates law firm. Federico had stopped attending large family events and preferred to visit Daniela or Leticia when they were alone or with their husbands and children. He was convinced that Aarón never wanted to see him again. And he was almost sure that Verónica had told her sisters nothing about the brief romance they'd had in north-eastern Argentina, two summers previously. But the two women suspected something, even if they didn't like to pry. How different these sisters were to Verónica. She wouldn't have rested until she'd found out exactly what had happened.

Federico realized he was idealizing Verónica again. He saw her as perfect. At least that's what Doctor Cohen had said to him. He had started having therapy, coincidentally or not, just after breaking off relations with the Rosenthal practice and with Verónica. *You idealize Verónica* was the verdict of the unorthodox psychologist Leticia had recommended to him. His analysis when Federico got together with the other Verónica was like a festival of clichés. Then again, they were the same opinions Leticia and Daniela had already expressed and which any taxi driver could have supplied on hearing Federico's story. Was it his fault if he happened to have met another Verónica who was charming, affectionate, loyal and predictable? The exact opposite of the first Verónica (except for the charming bit, but then he did have a broad concept of feminine charm)? He wasn't going out of his way to hunt down Verónicas. That's what he told everyone. And if he didn't leave the psychologist, it was because the guy had told him some interesting things about his life.

II

There was one thing nobody was saying and that seemed fundamental to him. *His* Verónica (to use patriarchal terminology; Rosenthal wasn't his any more, as the not-his Verónica would doubtless have pointed out) was from an Italian family, not a Jewish one. Rinaldi, not Rosenthal. Yes, the same initial, the same number of syllables, but that was it. The Russian Rosenthal and the Sicilian Rinaldi had nothing in common. Vero Rinaldi constantly exuded passion and was a bit clumsy in bed. Vero Rosenthal hated showing her feelings but, when it came to intimacy, knew all the tricks, or at least a lot more tricks than he did. His Verónica was proud of her sausage-manufacturing parents, from San Miguel. The other one was ashamed of her father, who was one of the most prestigious lawyers in Argentina. The young Rinaldi had left San Miguel as soon as she could and moved to Barrio Norte, one of the smarter areas in Buenos Aires, whereas the young Rosenthal had left her parents' home in uptown Recoleta and moved to Villa Crespo, the more modest neighbourhood where her grandparents lived. Verónica Rinaldi had confessed to him that in adolescence she'd had the fantasy – or desire, or mission – to be a virgin on her wedding day. Verónica Rosenthal planned never to get married. The Italian had Facebook, Twitter, Instagram and LinkedIn and liked to send him nude photos of herself. The Russian hardly knew how to send a text and hated having her picture taken, even with her clothes on. In her work as a public relations officer, Verónica sought out the company of like-minded people. As a journalist, Verónica sought the truth in things. Then there was the little matter of breast size, although Federico was too much of a gentleman to make the kind of observation, even to himself, that a friend of his from the Centeno Club had let slip one after one too many bottles of Norton Clásico.

III

He didn't need an alarm clock. Federico's body knew what time to wake up, depending on the day and his commitments. It never failed him. And besides, there was the morning WhatsApp Verónica always sent him as a greeting. Usually it would say *Good morning, mi amor,* and every so often there would be an accompanying photo. This ritual had begun soon after they first met at the Forum for Fast Justice, where she had been in charge of public relations. After a very professional chat, they swapped phone numbers, he called her, they met for drinks a couple of times and then she started sending him photos (with a few clothes on, to start with), before they had sex for the first time. There was no doubt that the photos were intended as an incentive for Federico to pursue the relationship.

It was six months now since they'd started going out, and Verónica had never dropped the snapshot habit. The image she had sent that morning – her facing the bathroom mirror, naked from the waist up – gave him the brio he needed for the day ahead and made him wish night-time would come sooner and Verónica with it.

When he arrived at the court, Federico applied himself to the "Mystery of the Mutilated Bodies", as the press were calling it. Anyone who wasn't familiar with judicial process might have thought the case was advancing rapidly, because it had already amassed more than three hundred pages, but there was still little to show for all the paper. So the press had been busy inventing all kinds of scenarios: from María Vanini's – bodies stuffed with cocaine – to the secret rites of an Umbanda sect in Brazil, using Argentine corpses. He wasn't ruling anything out because he was sure they were still a long way from exposing the truth of what had happened in the port.

For the time being, there were a few more details about the driver: he was Sandro Hernández, sixty-two years old, a widower, unemployed, resident of a boarding house in Bella Vista. He had three previous convictions for minor crimes. The first, in 1984, was for an attack on public property. Hernández belonged to an ultra-Catholic group that had attacked the Teatro Municipal San Martín during the run of a Dario Fo play. The second was for anti-Semitic graffiti in 1995. And the third was for drink-driving in 2004, which had resulted in him losing his last recorded job, as a truck driver. Unfortunately, the man had no family and was hardly known in the boarding house where he lived, according to statements collected by the police. The vehicle, meanwhile, had used a fake licence plate, and identifying numbers on the bodywork had been filed off, leaving no doubt that it was stolen. Federico imagined that it must be much harder to steal a truck than a car.

Once, when he was studying the 1994 bombing of AMIA,

the Jewish cultural centre, he had heard about a network that specialized in the theft and redeployment of trucks and vans for criminal purposes. He went to the central department of the federal police to visit a police chief who had acted as a witness in various cases represented by Rosenthal and Associates. Those contacts made during his time as a lawyer at the firm were still useful to him, although it was true that some of them now eyed him with suspicion because he was working for the Justice Department. Chief Superintendent Sosa had spent several years hunting the highway gangs who preyed on delivery trucks. Rumour had it that Sosa also stole some of the merchandise he intercepted, and only arrested felons who didn't belong to his group.

The chief superintendent welcomed Federico into his study like an old friend; doubtless he hoped to retire soon, to enjoy the money made during those years and treat himself to vacations in Las Vegas and expensive prostitutes.

"Sosa, I need to get in touch with people who sell stolen trucks."

"You're putting me on the spot here."

"It's so that I can make some enquiries about a truck that's turned up full of human body parts."

"Yes, I read about that in the papers. Is it true that they were destined for a cannibal restaurant in Montevideo?"

"Where did you read that?"

"I heard it on the radio."

"We still don't know what the hell they wanted those bodies for."

"There's only one dealer who'd be able to get a truck like that for you. Mosquito."

"Mosquito?"

"That's what they call him. His surname's Mosca and he's little and restless, like a little fucking mosquito." Sosa gave

Federico his contact details and added some advice: "Tread carefully. The guy is backed by some serious muscle."

"Whose muscle?"

The chief superintendent opened his arms wide, as though trying to encircle the universe. "You know how these things go, my friend. Sometimes the police need a van."

Mosquito had an auto parts business on Calle Warnes, a street known for its many car dealerships. Federico returned to his office thinking of ways he might get this character to talk. The man wasn't likely to blab out of a love of justice, especially not if he could rely on police protection. He mentioned the quandary to Doctor Laura Manukián, the court secretary, a lawyer with more than twenty years' experience who knew the judicial apparatus inside out.

"These types always end up falling the same way. Like Al Capone, taxes get them in the end. If he's got a business selling car parts, I bet he's working off the books and dealing in the black market. Try slapping him with a court order along those lines."

"But I don't have competency in commercial law."

"Call Judge Brunetti and say I told you to get in touch. Bear in mind you'll owe Brunetti a favour, though. Sooner or later he'll make you repay it."

Federico was familiar with that system of favours, oiled with money and the various forms of extortion that Aarón Rosenthal managed so well in his law practice, but he was surprised to find it flourishing within the Department of Justice. A prerequisite for working in the judiciary was to avoid annoying other judges or threatening their friends' interests. He called Brunetti, who demurred at first then let himself be persuaded, as though to show Federico that he was going out of his way to help.

Since Federico knew Mosquito had contacts in the police, Brunetti had to get the gendarmerie to act in this case.

Federico went along with Brunetti's court secretary and found Mosquito working from some impressive premises. The auto parts business was clearly going great guns. The guy was in his office which, although by no means large, still had an enormous LCD television and a PlayStation. He seemed relaxed, if a little irritated by the arrival of the law on his property. He asked to speak to his lawyer. Mosquito spoke in an annoying whine – perhaps the result of asthma – which fitted with his surname and nickname.

Federico dismissed the gendarmes who were present in the office and asked the court clerk to leave him alone with the car parts salesman.

"Look, Mosca, I don't care if you're up to date with your tax returns or if some Fed's asked you for a white van for tomorrow. You sold a refrigerator truck that was intercepted a few days ago in the port."

"The ham one. I saw it on TV. What makes you think I'm the one who sold them the truck?"

"Because they wouldn't have wanted an amateur for a job like that. Look, tell me what you know and I'll tell the court secretary we're going back to the office. Then you get to carry on as before, selling speakers for Fiat 600s."

Mosca got up, flitted nervously around the room and over to the window that overlooked the salesroom. From there he could see the people from the courthouse and the gendarmes.

"The old man who killed himself. He's the one who bought it from me."

"So any old geezer can turn up here looking for a refrigerated truck and you sort him out with one?"

"If they're paying upfront, why not?"

"Because it could be a trap. It could be a judge who wants to put you behind bars."

"The old man came recommended. By Barbosa."

"Who's Barbosa?"

Mosca flitted from one side of the room to the other. It would have felt good to slap him against the wall. He looked aggressively at Federico and whined:

"You don't know him? Álvaro Barbosa. He's in Dangerous Drugs."

IV

Federico went straight from Calle Warnes to the Hotel Faena. He would have liked to go home and change, put on something less formal, but there wasn't time if he was going to pick up Verónica. She was at a launch party at the Faena and they had arranged to meet in the hotel bar. He got there before Verónica had finished work, ordered a glass of red wine and settled down to watch the people around him. He always felt uncomfortable here, surrounded by people who gave the appearance of not having done any work that day (or perhaps ever).

Eventually Verónica appeared, accompanied by Agustín, her twenty-five-year-old assistant, a rugby player and student of marketing at a private, little-known business school. Agustín tended to look at his boss with a mix of lust and reverence. Verónica appeared not to notice this, or perhaps she simply enjoyed having a paid admirer to help her and celebrate her professional successes.

Vero was wearing a little suit that combined formality with a plunging neckline and invited the businessmen present to wonder if the professional veneer concealed a wild temptress. She gave Federico a long kiss. Then he offered his hand to Agustín, who crushed it as though it were the neck of a rugby halfback on an opposing team.

"Exhausting, but fruitful – right, Agustín?" said Verónica, putting an arm around Federico's shoulders.

"Everything was perfect."

Looking at her boyfriend, Verónica added: "We left them very drunk and very happy." Then, directing herself to Agustín: "You can get off home now. Mission accomplished."

The little prick ogled Verónica as though she were performing the Dance of the Seven Veils. "As you command, Ma'am." Agustín walked away, awkwardly manoeuvring his rugby player's body around the tables.

"Shall we get something to eat?" said Federico, who was beginning to feel hungry. It was only now that he realized he hadn't eaten since lunchtime.

"No, I'm shattered. Let's go to my place, open a bottle of wine and watch *Mad Men*. What d'you reckon?"

He would have added a pizza to the plan and subtracted *Mad Men*, a series Verónica watched in the same way he watched porn: to turn herself on. She must have some fantasy about living in 1960s New York, although she had never said so. He found *Mad Men* boring; he'd rather have watched an old episode of *Law and Order*.

They drove from the hotel to Las Heras and Junín almost in silence. His mind was still busy with everything Mosca had said. If there was a police chief involved and the guy was powerful, then he would need to proceed carefully. He couldn't start an investigation, at least not formally. Any request for information would ring alarm bells with the police chief and his cronies. The judicial machine was anything but discreet. The police chief could be a minnow with no influence at the courts, or the reverse, a heavyweight who could block the investigation with a couple of phone calls and put Federico's position in the Justice Department in jeopardy.

"Are you annoyed with me? What's wrong?" Verónica's voice brought him back to the car.

"No, sweetheart, not at all. It's just the usual stuff – judges, lawyers, police. All very tedious."

"I wondered if you were feeling jealous of Agustín."

"Should I be?"

"He's a kid. And a hard worker."

"I don't doubt it. The quality of his work is clearly exceptional."

"I knew you were annoyed!"

Fortunately, they had arrived at Verónica's apartment. She went to change and he went to the kitchen, without high hopes of finding anything appetizing in the fridge. At best there would be low-calorie drinks, water, perhaps a beer or a bottle of wine and a dried-up lemon. To Federico's surprise, there was a bowl and a plate. The bowl was brimming with sauce and on the plate was some kind of dessert.

"What's this?" he asked Verónica, who had returned barefoot, wearing white shorts and a black vest.

"I know, right," she said, sounding irritated. "My mother came over the other day and brought food. It's Sicilian aubergine and cannoli. I don't know how to make her understand that if I eat that I'll blow up like a balloon. It's been there four days. I was going to throw it out."

"Vero, I love your mother. I'd marry you just to have a mother-in-law who made me such delectable food."

Verónica slunk over to him, catlike, and put her arms around him. "Would you really marry me?"

Kissing her, Federico dodged the question. His hands went under her vest. Verónica didn't stop them.

"If I had a dollar for every guy who stares at my tits, I'd be a millionaire by now."

"There's something about that tally I don't like."

The T-shirt and bra had gone flying, and she was trying to unbutton his trousers. When he was down to his boxers, she suggested they go to the living room. Federico moved regretfully away from the aubergines, with the secret hope of returning fifteen minutes later to put them in the microwave.

V

Federico googled Chief Superintendent Barbosa and didn't turn up much: he had taken part in an operation that ended in the arrest of five Colombian drug traffickers. He had been at an event honouring the chief of police in Mar del Plata, and there were various other news items, nothing significant. The man kept a low profile. Whichever way he came at it, Federico couldn't see how to launch an investigation into Chief Superintendent Barbosa from the National Prosecutor's Office. Had Barbosa been merely a broker between the driver and Mosca, or was he a member of a gang that trafficked human tissue and body parts, even the bodies of babies? Was this what the gang was doing, or something else? Were they involved in other crimes as well?

A journalist might be able to access areas Federico couldn't reach. Verónica Rosenthal would have been so helpful here. She had the skill, courage and intelligence necessary for this kind of investigation. What if he called her? No – she'd think it was a pretext for something else. And worst of all, it probably was. He needed to stop thinking this way. He should write it in big letters on a sign: I'M NOT GOING TO CALL VERÓNICA ROSENTHAL.

There was one other journalist Federico knew could get his teeth into this: Rodolfo Corso. He had written articles about business mafias and had doggedly exposed the political and social morass surrounding the double murder of two female tourists in Tucumán. Federico called him, but Corso didn't pick up. Soon afterwards a text arrived: *Playing paddle. I'll call you when I've finished.* Corso's interests never ceased to surprise him.

They arranged to meet at Bar La Academia. Federico half expected to find Corso playing darts with the old-timers at the back of the bar, but he was sitting on his own by one of the windows, a glass of gin and a cup of tea in front of him. He explained to Federico that he had a chest infection, hence the tea with honey.

Federico knew that he could count on Corso's discretion. He explained that he was looking for someone to investigate Chief Superintendent Barbosa, laying out all the facts he had so far and the reasons why he needed more information on the police officer.

"If I can get a complete profile of the guy, I can make connections that may lead to whoever was behind the truck carrying body parts."

"Look, he may have just been in it for the money. A middleman with no firm ties to anyone involved. You could swim round in circles until you drown."

"It's the only lead I have."

Federico ordered a beer and Rodolfo followed suit, but added a gin. "Two gins and a beer," he said, "the best protection against suicide."

"Before I forget: let me know your fee. This is a private investigation, so I'll foot the bill."

"If old Rosenthal were mixed up in this, I'd take you to the cleaners. But what can I charge a public servant? Forget it. Let's do it this way: I'll write you up a report on this cop and you give me the exclusive when you're further into the investigation. Then I'll sell it as a piece somewhere."

A waitress brought their drinks and they toasted with beer.

"Tell you who I haven't seen for a while," said Corso. "Your little friend and partner in crime, Verónica Rosenthal."

Corso took a swig of beer, savouring this as much as he did teasing Federico.

"Me neither."

"You could have asked her to do this investigation. Girl knows her stuff. Maybe she's a bit ditsy sometimes, but she has a way about her."

"I think a man might be better for this job."

"True. Although I can picture her swinging that pretty ass from one police station to the next, swearing at the old cops who won't cooperate."

Corso laughed dramatically and Federico knocked back half his beer in one go, to avoid having to reply.

VI

One advantage of working in the judiciary was having the best coroner in Argentina at your disposal. Doctor Osvaldo Renzi was an eminence whose seminar on thanatology – the study of death and dying – Federico had once attended. Rosenthal and Associates had brought him in as an expert witness on several cases and Federico had stayed in touch. He had no hesitation in sending him all the information about the impounded truck and, that afternoon, Renzi had some answers for him. They met in the Judicial Morgue, not somewhere Federico much enjoyed visiting but practically a second home for Renzi. He would have been offended had a different meeting place been proposed.

Federico entered his office to find Renzi blowing smoke out of the window. Renzi finished the cigarette and put it out in an ashtray he kept in his top drawer. Despite these precautions, there was a strong smell of tobacco in the room.

They sat opposite one another, the desk between them. Renzi had his work in front of him in a folder but, before coming to that, he said, "Talk about a strange coincidence: your journalist friend gets in touch with me because she's lost two bodies, and you bring me a whole heap of bodies like an early Christmas present."

"My journalist friend?"

"That young woman… Verónica Rosenthal. Aarón Rosenthal's daughter, no? She's writing an article about a clear case of irregular practice following a car accident. Nothing out of the usual in Buenos Aires province."

"Ah, I don't know anything about that."

"Just a strange coincidence. Right, let's get to your bodies."

Renzi adjusted his glasses, opened his folder and scanned the uppermost pages. "First of all, let me be clear that this isn't a case of organ trafficking. There are no hearts or kidneys. It would be difficult to keep them in a usable state given the conditions inside the vehicle. A heart or liver stored like that wouldn't be good for anything, apart from a cannibals' barbecue, as I read somewhere."

"But some kind of trafficking is going on," Federico put in.

The pathologist took out a cigarette but didn't light it. "Yes, of course. It's a strange cargo. I mean, there were a lot of elements you could traffic there, but in small quantities. To be clear, though, we're definitely looking at a case of traffic in cadavers."

"Parts of cadavers."

"Cadaverous parts – except in the case of the babies – and, obviously, only parts that could be used. Why would they take a cranium if they weren't going to sell it to someone?"

"Sorry, Doctor, but all this sounds a bit nineteenth-century to me."

"The nineteenth century gave bodysnatching an air of romance, but people have been secretly using cadavers since the Middle Ages. I'll tell you something: if there's one kind of trafficking that's particularly of our time, it's not drugs – very twentieth-century – or human trafficking, which is a version of slavery. Or stolen artworks. The hallmark of our time is the traffic in body parts to be used in industries linked to health or beauty."

"You mean they're selling body parts?"

"Do you remember when you were at school and you had to write an essay on the cow? Everything had a use: the hide, the meat, the milk. The same is true of our bodies. Human tissue is in high demand for skin implants or to lengthen penises. It can also be used in products to plump up lips or smooth away wrinkles. It looks like these people didn't have the wherewithal to remove and preserve the skin. It's a fairly simple procedure but requires a certain amount of care. They seem to be sending the bodies abroad and having them flayed there."

"It would be easier to set up a good laboratory here and just send the skin, since it doesn't take up much space."

"That's true. They aren't only using human tissue, though, but ligaments and tendons which can be used to make knees as good as new in the case of athletes, or even in people who can't walk. The bones are very useful for making screws and bolts for orthopaedic and dental implants. They can also be ground down and mixed with chemicals to make prosthetic glues that are far superior to the artificial ones. There are gentlemen in funeral homes and morgues who'll remove all the bones from a corpse then fill the body with PVC tubes before it's returned to the family."

"This sounds like a really bad horror movie."

"Except that it's true. There are documented cases in countries like Ukraine."

"Who buys human remains?"

"Like I said, medical labs, multinational corporations involved in the health industry."

"Those are legal companies, I imagine, not shady, back-street operations led by some kind of Doctor Frankenstein. How can they bring themselves to use skin and organs bought on the black market?"

"First of all, because there aren't as many controls as there are with transplants, for example. Nobody asks where the skin used to remove a burn mark came from or what the dental implant is made of. There's a great demand for human tissue: bones, cartilage, tendons – but there are never enough donors. High demand equals high prices. It's almost inevitable that would create a black market that crosses borders. The multinational health companies have an advantage in that, once these illegally obtained remains are turned into products, they can easily be sold to other countries. They get cadavers from Argentina or Slovakia, then take them, let's say, to the United States, where they are manufactured and sold as products – which may even be approved by the FDA – or to Germany or South Korea. In countries where violent death is part of life, bodies are never left lying around – they're sold. Bear in mind that a corpse can be worth a thousand dollars at the point of death, and that a good reseller can make between twenty and thirty thousand dollars cutting it up and selling it on."

"And we're the providers, like cows and sheep."

"There's such a lack of supervision in morgues that it's not surprising deals are done in some of them. You see, a lot of dead bodies are never identified. After a certain time has elapsed with nobody claiming them, and given the choice of continuing to store them or portioning them up and selling them, some people are going to choose the second option.

You wouldn't believe how many bodies there are in morgues with no known next of kin."

They fell silent, Federico trying to assimilate everything Renzi had said to him. There were still some parts he didn't understand.

"And the babies' bodies?"

"Same thing: the beauty industry. It's strange there were no foetuses – they tend to be highly sought after."

"There's something I find even more worrying than all of this. I'm wondering if this black market could be useful as a way of making the victims of criminals or mafiosos disappear. And whether there might be such a thing as corpses on demand. Like, I need some good tendons, so I'll kill a young athlete to take his legs."

"Both cases are possible, the first more than the second. And it wouldn't surprise me if they were happening."

VII

On the second Tuesday of every month, Federico met up for dinner with the rest of his Centeno Club friends. The name may have had the ring of a political posse, a masonic society, a closed shop, even of a sect devoted to the worship of rye – *centeno* – above all other cereals; in fact it comprised ex-schoolmates of the bombastically named Doctor Dámaso Centeno Military Social Institute, the private high school at which Federico had been a student. He still had four friends from that far-off time. For years they had only seen each other occasionally. But as they'd reached their thirties, they all agreed that the time had come to tend to their friendship, and a decision was made to get together once a month. They would meet for dinner in the Boedo area, at places like Cantina Pantaleón, Spiagge di Napoli or Lo de Beto – or San

Antonio, if they were in the mood for pizza. The dinner was a pretext to chat, to give teenage anecdotes yet another airing, to argue about soccer or politics and to philosophize about women in general. Sometimes their conversation touched on more personal or private matters, like the death of Sebastián's father, who had been a teacher at Centeno and so known to all of them, or Diego's divorce, the scandalous firing of Ignacio from a public body, Ramiro's lung cancer (now in remission) or Federico's dealings with the Rosenthal family, especially its younger daughter.

"I reckon you should fuck all three sisters," had been Ramiro's advice, and there was general agreement.

"Jewish girls are strange," observed Diego and the conversation turned to the sexual variations between women depending on their religious beliefs or the degree of their atheism ("Because an atheist isn't the same as an agnostic – they blow you differently," Sebastián asserted, and he was, after all, a philosophy teacher.)

That late October night, they were in Pantaleón, Ignacio's favourite place because it was a shrine to San Lorenzo, his soccer club. Once they had even taken down a Colombia shirt that had belonged to Chicho Serna, with the silly excuse that it had fallen off the wall. Federico was enjoying some *fusilli al fierrito all vongole* when his phone rang. It was Chief Superintendent Sosa, who wanted to see him urgently. Right now. Federico told him where he was, and the police chief said he would come and find him there in twenty minutes.

It was odd that Sosa was so agitated. A man of his experience should be able to keep calm in any situation, even if the world were falling apart around him. What could have happened? Federico left his meal half finished, unable to eat while he waited for Sosa to arrive. As soon as he saw his car pull up at the door, Federico went out to meet him.

"What did Mosca say to you?" the chief superintendent asked, visibly irritated.

"He confirmed that he had sold a truck to the guy who committed suicide."

"What else?"

Whose side would Sosa take if he found out that another police chief was involved in the trafficking of body parts? Since he couldn't be sure, Federico decided to be evasive.

"Nothing else. Either the driver was his only contact, which is possible, or Mosca knew when to keep his mouth shut. Why are you asking this now?"

Sosa nodded, seeming to endorse all that Federico had said. He seemed agitated, as though finding it difficult to breathe normally.

"Mosca was found dead an hour ago at his dealership. It was made to look like a burglary, but there's no doubt someone was sent to kill him. And if the murder is linked to your case, you're also in danger."

Mosca dead? Could Chief Superintendent Barbosa have acted so quickly? Was he really in danger? Corso too? Federico felt dazed. Looking back into the cantina, he saw his friends chatting animatedly and felt a strong desire to be with them, sitting at the table, waiting for dessert, ordering more wine and coffee.

"Listen, Sosa, Mosca told me only that he had sold the truck. If he knew anything else, he took it with him to the grave. Don't worry – I don't think this is linked to my case."

The chief superintendent seemed to relax. Federico's phone rang and he saw that the call was from his girlfriend, but he didn't answer, so he could finish the conversation with Sosa. When the phone rang a second, then a third time, he asked Sosa to wait while he took the call. At the other end of the line came not Verónica's voice but the well-fed voice of Agustín.

"Federico, I need you to come to the Museo de Arte Decorativo. Verónica's been attacked."

"What do you mean, *attacked*?"

"You're coming, right?"

"Yes, yes, what happened though?"

But Agustín had already hung up and Federico was left with the phone pressed against his ear, powerless to react.

"Are you all right?" Sosa asked.

Federico, in a daze, answered robotically.

Sosa offered to drive him to the museum, and minutes later they were speeding towards Palermo Chico. While he had been out with his friends, Verónica had been at a literary prize-giving at the Museo de Arte Decorativo. She often went to similarly glamorous events on the lookout for new clients who might need a publicist. Could she have been attacked because of what had happened with Mosca? What had they done to her? Please, God, let her be OK, he thought, let them not have hurt her. He shouldn't involve his loved ones in complex cases he was investigating. He called Verónica's number; nobody answered. He imagined Agustín must already have dialled 911, but called it anyway. When he was asked for details of what had happened he had to invent them. An ambulance would be there in a few minutes.

They arrived at the museum, and Federico practically threw himself out of the car. There was no sign of an ambulance, unless one had already come and was now on its way to hospital with Verónica in it. That clearly wasn't the case, though, because there she was, sitting on the staircase, Agustín crouching beside her. Verónica had reddish stains on her white dress. They looked like blood. But to see her alive and in one piece calmed him. If she was hurt, at least it wasn't serious. When she saw him, Verónica got to her feet and hugged him, sobbing. Federico gently moved her away, to get a better look at her injuries.

"She attacked me, Fede, she attacked me."

"What happened to you, Vero?"

The stains on her dress weren't blood.

"I was sitting talking to Agustín in the patio at the back when two women came up to me. One used to be at university with me. I didn't know the other one."

"Both drunk," Agustín added.

"They started saying weird things I didn't understand. The one I didn't know was really aggressive. She said I should leave you alone. I couldn't help laughing, more out of nerves than anything else, because I was so shocked that she knew who my boyfriend was."

"Then the crazy bitch threw a glass of wine over her," said Agustín.

"And I started screaming and everyone looked round. And this nutcase was saying, 'Shut up, you slut, I know you, I know where you live.' And the other one, whose name is Paula Locatti, took her by the arm and led her away. That bitch threatened me." And Verónica started crying.

"You should have seen her eyes," said Agustín, still shaken. "She looked wild, as if she might go for Verónica at any minute."

As Verónica told him what had happened, Federico willed the conversation to veer towards some accomplice of Mosquito, hoping Verónica Rinaldi had been threatened by a mafioso, someone who operated according to a predictable code. But no, he thought. Verónica Rosenthal is back with a vengeance. The situation was worse than he could have imagined.

I

Darío tried to be as clear as possible: he told Tonso about the accident, the presumption of death, his search, the journalist who had helped, the article she had published. He also explained that during this time he had been collecting photos of his daughter. All the photos of her in existence. He reminded Tonso that, when they had adopted her, Jazmín was already six months old. Darío supposed the biological family might have photos from her birth or from the first six months of her life. The use of mobile phones was so widespread now and everyone took photos on all kinds of occasions. That was why he wanted Tonso to put him in touch with the birth parents. He understood that it was an unusual request but, bearing in mind his current circumstances (including his wife's disappearance with their daughter), they might make an exception and allow him to contact the other family.

Tonso eyed him with some apprehension, as though confronting a psychotic and wondering whether or not to call in the nurses from a mental hospital.

"What you're asking is impossible. Once the baby is handed over to a new family, all connection with the biological mother is severed. So I have nothing for you."

"Our adoption wasn't that long ago. I don't need you to give me a full address. If you could tell me the name of the village, what the mother was called – even if it's only a first name."

"For a start, you didn't adopt her. The girl was registered as yours and that's the line we have to stick to – you, your wife, all of us. Secondly, I don't think you realize the grave implications of what you're proposing."

"How could it be grave for me to meet the biological mother?"

Tonso seemed about to lose his patience. As he spoke he repeatedly banged his right hand on the table. One of his legs was shaking. "Leave it there, Valrossa. You're walking on quicksand. You could sink."

"Perhaps I'm not being clear enough."

"You're being very clear. You want to bring about a disaster that will ruin all of us who helped you."

"If you can't give me an answer, I'll speak to Father Eduardo."

"He died a year ago."

"I'm going to look for Jazmín's biological mother by whatever means necessary. Even if I have to search the whole of Santiago del Estero."

If Darío seemed irritated, Tonso looked furious, managing to contain himself only because the bar was a public space. Darío was like a puppy barking at a Rottweiler. Tonso stood up, making no move to pay for the coffees. Again, he slammed the table with his hand.

"You've already got enough trouble looking for your family. Don't go looking for any more. Put your energy into finding Jazmín. A lot of people were involved in helping you have a daughter. None of those good people would thank you for going around telling the world how you came to be a father."

Tonso left the bar and Darío stayed behind, puzzled. His first reaction was that Tonso didn't grasp what he was asking

111

for, didn't understand why he needed to find the biological mother. But he also saw that it had been wrong for him and Cecilia to register Jazmín as their own daughter. For the first time he felt some compassion and concern for Jazmín's biological family. Why shouldn't they be put in touch with each other? For the first time since beginning the adoption process, Darío asked himself if everything had been as straightforward and consensual in the transfer of parenthood as he and Cecilia had been led to believe.

II

It had been a long time since Verónica last attended a social event. But Paula, Pili and Valeria had kept badgering her until she agreed to go to this one. The party was being given by a publisher, to honour the winner of an obscure literary prize. Not the most promising environment for meeting someone – lots of gay men, lots of sad marrieds, lots of guys with pathetically inflated egos, lots of drunks who thought they were funny – though she had to admit that the food and drink were good, and, if she was with her friends, she was going to have fun.

Verónica went home straight from the office to shower and get changed. She put on the short, strapless black H&M dress Leticia had brought her back from Chile, some transparent underwear and leather knee boots. On top of that went a leather jacket that didn't offer much in the way of warmth but gave her a vintage rocker look she liked.

Pili came by in the car to pick her up. On the way to the Museo de Arte Decorativo, she asked her to light a joint that was in the glove compartment. Verónica would have preferred a normal cigarette, but she wasn't going to argue with a friend who had bothered to drive out of her way to give her a lift.

They were at the start of a night out in Buenos Aires: anything could happen. This was the best time of the day for Verónica. Leaving her apartment in the evening, stepping out onto the street with a plan, she felt like someone stepping into life. She didn't mind staying late to work in the newsroom, or working late at home, but nothing compared with the feeling of going out at the start of a night. It was like the first minutes of a movie in the cinema, when the lights go down, the people fall silent and you enter a different world. Going out at night was like entering your own movie.

She used to go to this kind of event with the fantasy of meeting a man who swept her off her feet, who energized her. Nothing that starts at a party can end badly, she used to think, with the optimism of a teenager. Now her fantasy took a different form. She liked to imagine that she was going to run into Federico, that he would say something funny to her and she would look at him with feigned scorn and make some witty riposte. She put together conversations in her head, as though this were an Oscar Wilde play; she could almost picture herself dressed as Lady Windermere and him in a tailcoat. The joint was beginning to make her sleepy.

They parked where they could, then walked two blocks to the museum. As they headed through Palermo Chico, the sound of their clicking heels resonated in the quiet streets. The entrance to the museum was empty and it looked as though nobody was there but, after crossing the front courtyard, they heard a growing murmur from the throng heaving inside. Some smiling girls asked to see their invitation, then let them through anyway, because Paula had appeared from the back of the room with an expression that conveyed both stress and a determination to have fun. She greeted them both with a quick kiss, pointed them towards the place where she had last seen Valeria and Rita, and went off to talk to the catering team.

The women intercepted a passing waiter to get drinks: red wine for Pili and champagne for Verónica. Fortunately, they didn't know many people from the world of books, so there were only four or five familiar faces to greet, and then only briefly, because the constant ebb and flow of bodies made a sustained conversation almost impossible. It was better to let yourself be swept along in the tide of guests, clutching at waiters as they passed with glasses and canapés.

The women found Valeria and Rita in the second room, chatting to two guys, both badly dressed and easily identifiable as cultural commentators. They said hello and joined the group. One of the journalists seemed to be weighing up which of the two, Rita or Valeria, might be more interested in him and the other wouldn't let a single tray go by without taking something from it. Verónica did the same, because she was hungry.

Years ago she had gone out with a publisher, but luckily the guy had gone off to live in Spain, so there was no danger of running into him here. She was embarking on her second glass of wine when she saw a woman coming towards her, a former press officer Verónica knew from the days when she was starting out as a journalist and used to review books for a legal magazine. They embraced each other with surprise and happiness. Although Alicia was retired now, she still came to these parties.

"After loathing them for so many years, I now quite enjoy observing these atrocious types in their natural habitat," said Alicia.

The human tide pushed them towards the back courtyard, where they chatted for a while and ate some little sandwiches, warm and filled with roast pork. They talked to a couple of cheerful and entertaining writers, both of whom recommended their own books to Verónica, who promised to read them soon. She spotted Pili heading for the roast pork queue in the company of a man she didn't recognize: from the animated way in which she was talking and gesticulating, Verónica guessed Pili was talking about her ex.

"Better not come to the magazine in that get-up."

Álex Vilna, *Nuestro Tiempo*'s assistant editor and head of Politics, had sidled up without her noticing him. The last time they had spoken outside the newsroom, she had punched him in the face. She hoped she wouldn't have to deliver another cross to the jaw.

"Vilna, what a surprise. I had you down as someone uninterested in culture. Although interested in sandwiches, come to think of it."

She introduced him to Alicia, and Vilna nodded indifferently. Ignoring Verónica's barb, he told her: "I've actually got a book coming out with this publisher. It's already commissioned."

"Congratulations," said Alicia, sizing up the man before her.

"Some unauthorized biography?" Verónica asked.

"This publisher doesn't do that kind of book. No, it's a portrait of a day in Argentina's political life. A congresswoman goes shopping, a minister goes to a parents' evening at school, a senator dances tango on Friday evenings."

"Fascinating."

"It has a certain something," said Vilna, smiling with barely contained pride.

Verónica saw Paula in the distance, beckoning her over to the other side of the courtyard. She didn't want to leave poor Alicia alone; then again, the veteran publicist would know how to get rid of Vilna when she tired of him.

"I've got a bombshell for you," said Paula, grabbing her friend's arm once she came close enough. "Verónica's here."

"Which Verónica? What bombshell?"

115

"Verónica's here. The other Verónica, Verónica Rinaldi, your boyfriend's girlfriend."

"He isn't my boyfriend – he never was."

"OK, Federico's squeeze."

She felt a cold wave course through her body. Was Federico here too, then?

"Is she on her own?"

"She's talking to people, but I haven't seen Federico."

Verónica asked Paula to go with her to the bathroom. She needed to piss, to splash water on her face, to touch up her make-up. She could see that Paula looked worried.

"Don't be an idiot. I'm fine."

"I know you better than you think."

She washed and dried her face. Luckily she'd brought foundation, and she applied some more. She had forgotten her lipstick, though.

"Fuck's sake."

They returned to the throng, which seemed to be talking and laughing louder and louder, as though all the guests were actors in a bad horror movie.

"Is there any whisky? I need a whisky."

"You were on champagne, no? Don't go mixing," said Paula and intercepted a waiter, taking another glass.

Verónica knocked it back in one gulp. "You know her, don't you? Introduce me."

"Are you sure?"

"Just casually, like it's no big deal."

Paula looked into her eyes, like a trainer studying her boxer in the corner of the ring. She knew that smile well. It was Jack Nicholson's smile in *The Shining*. But it wasn't the worst smile in Verónica's armoury, nor the most dangerous, so Paula decided that it was safe to introduce her friend to the other Verónica. Before braving the sea of bodies they had another drink, then began a stealthy approach, like friends admiring pictures in an exhibition. When they were a few feet away from their target, Paula wheeled round. Verónica Rinaldi was talking to a very young, good-looking man.

"Hey, Vero!"

"Paulita, how are you? Did you organize all this?"

"Well, I do the press, but at a publisher's you have to do a bit of everything, from sorting out the catering to getting the writer's tie straight. Let me introduce you to Verónica Rosenthal, who's a journalist. Vero, meet Vero," she laughed nervously. "Namesakes."

The women exchanged kisses. Verónica brushed against the cheek that Federico must touch every day. She tried to identify the other woman's perfume but couldn't place it. She noticed how the other woman's white dress showcased her breasts. Easy to be seductive, dressed like that.

"This is Agustín, one of the young guns in our agency."

"Very young," said Paula, in the tone of a woman long past thirty.

"We met at university," Verónica Rinaldi explained to Agustín.

"So you're a teacher?" he asked Paula.

"No, we were both students."

Verónica Rinaldi slightly narrowed her eyes, as if that might give her a clearer view into the human soul or help her locate some memory others might prefer forgotten, and she asked Verónica Rosenthal: "Don't you write for *Tiempo Nuevo*?"

"For *Nuestro Tiempo*."

"Ah, I know who you are then. Do you know who I am?"

A strumpet, she would have liked to fire back, using the language of a bad translation, but she was from Buenos Aires, so the words came out in Argentinian: "The one who's banging Federico."

117

Verónica Rinaldi laughed like an actress in a play. The hand in which she held a glass of red wine shook slightly. "Exactly," she confirmed and, with the temerity of someone who doesn't know exactly who she's talking to, added: "I imagined you as prettier, with a better body."

"Whereas I imagined you exactly like this: as a badly waxed cross-dresser."

"Look! Here comes the prize-winning author!" shouted Paula, firmly taking Verónica Rosenthal by the arm. "Come on, I'll introduce you, he's lovely."

Verónica shook herself free, then uttered perhaps the most pathetic phrase she had ever spoken in the thirty years since she first acquired the power of speech: "I'm the one Federico loves. You're simply a sex doll."

Pathetic phrases can sometimes hit home, though, because just then Verónica Rinaldi threw her red wine in the face of Verónica Rosenthal, who stepped back, dramatically flailing her arms, catching the tray of a waiter who was collecting empty glasses. Tray and glasses went flying and the uproar was such that the whole room fell silent, while the rest of the museum carried on partying regardless. Paula grabbed Verónica from behind, anticipating a catfight that would have delighted all the other guests. She manoeuvred her friend away while motioning to the other Verónica to stay back.

"Did you see what the stupid cow did? She threw wine all over me. Let me kill the bitch."

"You're not going to kill anyone."

"I'm going to call Federico and tell him."

Paula got Verónica out to the front courtyard, which was empty now, and called Pili. A minute later their Spanish friend arrived.

"What happened, girls? Isn't it a bit early to be throwing up?"

Paula asked her to take Verónica home and in God's name not to let her use her phone. "I have to stay until the end of the party, but in two hours I'll head over there."

"The bitch ruined my clothes," muttered Verónica.

"What do I do if she doesn't cooperate?" Pili asked anxiously.

"Give her a good smack. Maybe that'll teach her."

III

Verónica didn't have a hangover in the morning, just an annoying feeling of things not having gone as well as they might. The absence of a hangover confirmed what she knew anyway: that she hadn't been drunk and therefore had been completely aware of everything she had done – or rather said, because she hadn't done much. Perhaps she would have acted more intelligently the previous night if she had been drunk.

Thankfully, Pili and Paula had now both left. They had looked after her like someone who was sick, or a recovering addict, or maddened by love. She knew they loved her, but they also underestimated her. She was perfectly able to handle what was happening in her emotional life. Put simply, she had been curious to meet Federico's current girlfriend – to see her up close, smell her. Given the opportunity, anyone in her position would have done the same. If anyone had come across as deranged, it was that stupid, fat, big tits who had ruined her brand-new dress. If she had been drunk she would have done the right thing: grabbed the bitch's face and scraped it against the wall like sandpaper.

Her phone had been ringing for a while. Verónica hadn't answered it and the calls were coming every few minutes. When she finally got up and checked her missed calls, she saw that they were all from Darío. She called him back immediately. They arranged to meet in the Café del Sol on Avenida Primera Junta.

As soon as she arrived, Darío cut to the chase. At first what he was saying made no sense, but gradually Verónica began to grasp what he was telling her: Darío was explaining the story of Jazmín's adoption. Now she understood why a shadow had crossed his face when he first told her the girl was adopted. She tried to understand the details, not to assume anything. Various parts of the story weren't entirely clear.

"How many people did you have contact with during the whole adoption process?"

"Four. Tonso the printer, Father Eduardo, and two nuns whose names I don't recall."

"Tonso mentioned a Justice of the Peace – is that right?"

"Yes, but we never had any direct contact with him."

"And he didn't say anything about the people at the civil registry office?"

"No, he didn't mention that. He just brought us the birth certificate, as though she were our biological daughter."

Verónica looked over the notes she had made while Darío was talking. She could certainly get an article out of all this. She had the sudden sensation of opening a Pandora's box.

"Darío, you do realize that if I publish this the consequences could also be negative for you?"

"Yes, I think so."

"You've been an accomplice to identity theft. We don't know in what context the biological parents handed over their baby."

"At the time we preferred not to think about it."

"They may have been coerced, or tricked into giving her up."

"All the more reason to get this out in the open. Perhaps the accident was no more than a warning that this could come to light. Perhaps what I'm going through now is what happened to them, when Jazmín became our daughter."

"I don't have to write about this. I believe what you're telling me should be published, because what happened with Jazmín is bound not to be an isolated case. But I don't want to expose you to the press, to the law. Once the article comes out you'll have to give evidence – you could even face a trial."

"I want to do it. For Jazmín."

IV

She arrived at the newsroom to find an atmosphere of lingering tension caused by the changes that had recently been announced. A conference was called for six o'clock that evening, and the editor-in-chief had also called a meeting of section heads, together with an extraordinary meeting of the editorial team, at three o'clock in the fishbowl. This was Verónica's first formal meeting as deputy editor of Society and she was delighted to be finding out before her colleagues what changes were planned to the magazine's direction. But when, twenty minutes after the meeting had started, the editors and deputies were still engaged in small talk, she began to regret having to be there. Forty minutes in, the editor-in-chief made a brief announcement: he wasn't leaving, these rumours came from a media company competitor of the magazine and should be ignored. They should calm the troops and try to have fewer meetings, because that was why they kept falling behind with everything.

As they left the fishbowl, Verónica asked Patricia if she had five minutes to hear about Darío's revelation.

Patricia, getting a coffee from the machine, said: "The same person we published in the last edition alleging his family have gone missing is now reporting an illegal adoption in which he is also implicated. Could he be a serial fantasist?"

"Everything last week checked out, exactly as it was published. I haven't looked into this new angle much yet, but I'm sure he wasn't lying to me."

"Illegal adoptions. There's definitely a cover in it, if you can get some good stuff. Do you want more time to get to the bottom of this and we'll run it in a few weeks?"

"I'd rather do something on this case first, then, if we find more material, write a longer piece for a future edition."

Patricia studied her. "Normally you'd hold this back to do a bigger exposé later on. The fact you aren't doing that makes me suspect you're more interested in helping this Darío character than in working on an in-depth article."

"It's partly that, admittedly."

"Listen, Verónica, I don't mind publishing what you give me so long as it's journalistically sound, but I'm worried that your investment in all this is too personal."

Verónica had neither the time nor the inclination to submit to her boss's psychoanalysis. She asked permission not to stay at the office for the rest of the afternoon; she wanted to visit the printer and find out about Father Eduardo. First she would go to the church, hoping to arm herself with more information if that was possible, before confronting Tonso.

It was windy and pouring with rain when she came out of the newsroom, and the temperature seemed to have dropped ten degrees. Verónica shivered beneath her overcoat. She would have liked to have had a coffee and waited for the rain to subside, but the taxi ordered for her by the magazine's receptionist was already waiting to take her to the church.

When they arrived there, she asked the driver to give her a few minutes. Verónica found Catholic churches troubling.

They had always seemed to her like dark places where people gathered to carry out magic rituals.

The main entrance to the church was closed. There was a side door, but it had no bell and she didn't know if anyone could walk in or if she should knock and wait for an answer. She banged on the door twice and no one came. The rain, falling diagonally, struck her full in the face. She felt as though she were sitting in the prow of a boat in the middle of a storm. Tired of waiting, she tried the latch and the door opened into a narrow passage. Verónica then passed through another door, which took her to the church's nave. It was almost dark, barely illuminated by a few candles. A saint with a bloody leg watched her from a few yards away. Rain pelted the roof as though God were rapping on it with his knuckles to enter his own house. A woman was lighting candles in the portico.

"They're votives," explained the old woman when Verónica approached her and apologized for interrupting her candle-lighting.

"Votives. Of course. I'm looking for the priest in charge of this church."

"Father Anselmo."

"Exactly. I'd like to speak to him."

The woman took her to a side door and asked her to wait in an office that abounded with images of Jesus and the Virgin Mary. Before the woman left, Verónica asked her: "Have you been coming to this church for long?"

"More than twenty years."

"So you knew Father Eduardo."

"Yes, a saintly man. God rest his soul. I used to clean his house."

"He really liked travelling round the country, right?"

The woman eyed her suspiciously. "Did you know him?" she asked.

"I never had that pleasure."

The woman left the room, cutting their conversation short. Two minutes later, Father Anselmo appeared. He was a man of about seventy, balding and somewhat obese. Verónica remembered Father Pedro, a priest who worked in the shanty town, whom she had got to know while investigating the train mafia and who had helped her greatly. She had a feeling she wouldn't be so lucky with this priest.

The priest was wearing everyday clothes and was in shirt-sleeves despite the cold in the office. He sat down at the other side of the desk and smiled beatifically. Verónica introduced herself, explaining that she was a journalist from *Nuestro Tiempo*. The priest nodded, as though he agreed with what she was telling him.

"I'm looking for information about Father Eduardo. Did you know him?"

"Father Eduardo had already died by the time I came to this parish, but lots of people have told me about him. A great man and a great priest, concerned for the poor and determined to spread comfort and the word of God to all."

"Did he work on anything to do with adoptions?"

"I don't understand the question."

"I'm asking if he helped Catholic couples to adopt children from low-income families."

"We have a vigorous programme of pastoral work to help the very poor. Father Eduardo is sure to have been involved with it, like the rest of us."

The priest was playing the innocent to a tee. At times like this, Verónica struggled to contain her fury. Putting aside any thought of coaxing information from her subject, she decided to go for the jugular instead.

"What I'm asking, specifically, is if you and the others were taking children from poor families in the interior and giving them to wealthy families in Buenos Aires."

"That would be unlawful, if I'm not mistaken."

"Three years ago, Father Eduardo was an active partici-
pant in such a case, and everything leads me to believe that
it wasn't a one-off."

"Listen, señorita, I think you're wrong. Sadly, Father
Eduardo isn't here to defend himself, but I assure you that
someone like him would never have contravened the laws of
God, nor the laws of man."

Verónica took her leave with the feeling that Father
Anselmo knew more than he was letting on, but she had no
means of pressuring him more than she had already. She left
the church to find that the taxi driver had moved his car a
few yards further on. As she walked towards it, she realized
that the church was contained within a bigger building, something like a convent.

On these late autumn days it got dark early and the skies
above the taxi were thundery, making them darker still. By
the time Verónica reached the printworks, it was fully night,
but the business was still open. She glanced at her watch:
quarter to seven.

The printworks smelled strongly of ink. There were piles
of publications everywhere, and machines could be heard
working away in the distance. Tonso's office was no more
welcoming than the priest's but, while the latter's had been
papered with portraits of virgins and saints, here magazine
and book covers were stuck up alongside print adverts from
earlier times. Also, it was very hot, thanks to an electric heater
on full blast. Verónica, already wet from the rain, found the
change of temperature uncomfortable. Tonso looked about
fifty-five and could have passed for Father Anselmo's younger
brother: he was also obese, with a receding hairline that
would soon progress to baldness, and wore a shirt with three
buttons left undone. In contrast to the priest, Tonso didn't

125

smile beatifically at her and instead fixed her with a violent glare, as though close to boiling point before she had even said anything. He did offer her a coffee, though, and that wasn't the only thing that caught her attention. Nobody had asked her why she wanted to see Tonso. Granted, she might have been mistaken for a client, so she decided to dispel any confusion straight away.

"I'm from the magazine *Nuestro Tiempo*. We're doing an investigation into adoption practices and received information saying you had helped arrange some special adoptions."

"I don't know what you're talking about."

"Specifically, that you acted as a mediator for Cecilia Burgos and Darío Valrossa in the adoption of their little girl, with the approval of certain priests and judges."

"I don't know these people you mention."

"You never met with Father Eduardo and this couple to discuss the details of their adoption?"

Tonso shifted in his seat. He took his time answering. Perhaps he was wondering whether to throw her out immediately or keep listening, to see what direction her questions would take.

"I don't recall having met anyone with those names, nor did I make any such arrangement with other couples."

"You don't recall… Excuse me while I check my notes, because my memory also fails me sometimes… You and the deceased Father Eduardo were part of an organization that might be described as criminal, which took children away from poor mothers and brought them to Buenos Aires. It's very likely that you're still doing this, with the support of other members of the Church. Is that correct – or don't you recall?"

"You said Rosenthal, right? Are you Jewish?"

"That's not relevant, but yes, I am Jewish."

"Now I understand."

126

"It's great that you understand. I hope that you also remember."

"Listen, señorita, I'm not going to enter into some Zionist game aimed at attacking our Church. I'd like you to leave."

Verónica put on an expression of resignation and returned her notebook to her bag. She stood up and gestured goodbye. As she reached the door, she turned back.

"One more question, Tonso. How many adoptions did you facilitate? Ten, a hundred, a thousand? Know that from now on, each one of those adoptions is going to be a problem for you."

V

It took Verónica longer than expected to write the article. Although the words came out easily enough, what she had written didn't entirely convince her. She was uneasy about exposing Darío. Her article gave the impression that Tonso and the dead priest had been involved only in this one case. A reader might conclude that they were not regularly making such deals – and she didn't believe that to be true. She still didn't know whether the little girl had been stolen, abandoned or freely handed over by her birth family. Verónica was hopeful that the article would get some traction and bring other cases to light that might allow her to get to the bottom of what was currently no more than a hunch.

It had been raining with no let-up for two days now. And, as luck would have it, there was no bus that could take her straight from the newsroom to Darío's apartment. She took the 39 first, then picked up the 160 on Avenida Medrano. That meant nearly an hour on public transport, observing how rain complicated everything. And this was an oily, cold, hectoring kind of rain. She hated rain in winter.

Verónica arrived at Darío's apartment a little before eight. There wasn't much more to do on Cecilia's computer. She was thinking of following the San Javier line of enquiry and going to Córdoba that weekend, but she didn't want to say anything about that to Darío. Better to spend another day raking through Cecilia's files, so that he didn't suspect she already had a possible lead.

Around nine o'clock, Darío told her that he'd ordered a pizza and a big soda. She finished her search when the delivery arrived and they both sat at the coffee table in the living room, although Verónica would have preferred to eat in the kitchen. The living room was a dark space, made gloomier by the noise of rain. She imagined Jazmín running around in here, some children's show on the television and Cecilia bringing in dinner, and had a sense of the agonizing loneliness that surrounded Darío in that apartment now.

"Lucio talked to me about you once."

They had finished eating. Verónica had been about to leave, but when Darío mentioned Lucio she felt an urge to cry. She didn't know if that was because of her memories, or seeing Darío so alone, or because Darío seemed to share many of Lucio's gestures and perhaps for that reason was also marked for tragedy.

"He told me he had a cousin who was very into reading, but he wasn't called Darío."

"Claudio. He called me by my second name."

"You used to read books together – Verne, Salgari..."

"Lucio and I hardly ever saw each other, and yet every time we met at some family party it was like a reunion between two guys who know each other incredibly well. When he talked about you, I realized the two of you had something special."

"We were lovers."

128

"When he and I were kids, almost teenagers, we met a girl on a beach and we both fell in love with her. She was older than us. Obviously we were both enthralled by our first real encounter with female beauty. But that wasn't what drew us to her. It was something deeper, harder to describe. And I think that's what he felt for you."

"I'd like to believe that. Sometimes I think that if he hadn't died, we might not have seen each other again anyway."

"A few years ago Lucio met up with Lucía, the girl from the beach we fell in love with as teenagers. He told me this in the same conversation he told me about you. I hadn't thought about her for years. Then I realized that Lucía was the connection between us. The secret love we had shared. What was he trying to say when he spoke to me about you?"

"Maybe nothing. Just finding a way to put his new love story into words. If he were alive now he'd tell you that we split up, that we didn't carry on together. But he's not here to say that to you."

"We're both dead."

"Don't say that. You still have a hope of finding Jazmín. You still have books to write."

"I've got nothing, Verónica. One day I'll realize that everything has been a desperate attempt not to die, that there's no sense any more in writing, in carrying on as though nothing has happened. I'm open wounds, scars, a wrecked body, a spirit stuck onto burned skin, like a synthetic material."

"You're a man, and you'll see the light again, you'll be happy again."

Darío stood up. With some difficulty he took off his sweatshirt and T-shirt, baring his chest. She saw his burned body, the welts raised by the fire and the scars that criss-crossed his torso, as though he had been the victim of some crazed assassin. His skin oscillated between the brown of his burn marks and the red of his unhealed wounds. Verónica saw Lucio's body again, bleeding on the tracks of the Sarmiento railway line. She saw, through his eyes, the mutilated corpses on the tracks. She pictured Darío dragging himself through fire and blood to search for his daughter in the middle of the night. She moved closer to Darío and touched his chest, running her hand over the lacerated, burned and hardened skin. Every mark was like a needle stuck in the body. And what was beneath those wounds but more and more wounds that would never heal? She put her arms around him, feeling the irregular form of those marks against her arms. She held the ravaged body and it was like holding Lucio again, and when she had caressed Lucio's body she didn't know that those caresses were also for Darío. Because time had lost meaning, the stories were getting mixed up and she didn't feel like thinking any more. She wanted only to hold that body, not let it die.

VI

Verónica had decided to travel by night, arriving in the morning at San Javier. Marcelo and his family were looking after Chicha until she got back. She didn't like leaving her little dog alone, even though Paula had offered to drop in and water the plants while she was there. A dog isn't a plant, something Paula found hard to understand.

Before leaving, she grabbed a novel she hadn't yet read from the bookshelf: Evelyn Waugh's *Brideshead Revisited*. She had read other books by Waugh and they were always good company. She also took the latest edition of *Nuestro Tiempo*. Her article about Jazmín's illegal adoption was in the magazine and she saw now that Patricia was right: she should have waited to investigate more cases before going public with the one she already had. But, if it was the wrong decision, why hadn't Patricia stopped her? It wouldn't be the first time she had held a piece back. Perhaps Patricia wasn't on top form either, and she hadn't thought about this because she was too taken up with her own worries. When Verónica got back to Buenos Aires she would try to talk to her editor.

She slept fairly well on the coach in the end, after being served a meal that, though bad, was not as awful as she had expected. The seat was comfortable and designed for sleeping. Her only regret was not being able to smoke a cigarette while she looked out at the dark, unfurling road.

The coach arrived at the Villa Dolores terminal at eight o'clock in the morning. San Javier was a few miles away; she could get a taxi there. Verónica's phone rang: it was María, her friend who worked as a television reporter.

"Where are you?"

" In Córdoba, on my way to San Javier."

"Always on vacation."

"Ha ha."

"I read your piece about the illegal adoption of that baby. Do you have Darío Valrossa's phone number? We'd like to interview him."

"I'll text it to you."

If they interviewed him on TV, Darío's case was sure to get more publicity.

Verónica found a taxi and asked the driver to take her to the main square in San Javier. She hadn't reserved a hotel room because she didn't know how long she was going to stay. She didn't even know if the trip would prove worthwhile. She was clutching at slim straws: a shared interest in plants, a friend who had said nothing after Cecilia's death, the ambiguous use of a personal pronoun in the plural. She'd have more faith in a lottery ticket than she had now of being on the right trail.

She liked this deserted road heading towards the sierra. In the distance she could see what must be Mount Champaquí. If she really had been going on vacation, as María had joked, she'd have loved to trek up the mountain. Perhaps she could come back one day.

The taxi left her in the square which, because of its similarity to many other rural towns, reminded her of the one in Yacanto del Valle, where she had stayed two summers ago: the church in pole position, a couple of supermarkets, a restaurant, a newsagent, a real estate place, various stores selling antiques or regional products.

There was almost nobody around at that time in the morning and Verónica could hear birdsong, something she always noticed. A diaphanous sky took the edge off the morning chill. She spotted a small grocery store she would have liked to go into, but it didn't seem the right place to start the day. Across the square, there was a bar open, and she sat down at one of the outside tables. Although the view wasn't particularly good, at least she could smoke while she had her croissant and double cortado.

Now people were beginning to arrive in the square. They seemed to be installing an artisanal market. She loved that sort of thing and usually ended up buying a little pair of earrings and some balsamic vinegar, or napkins and farmhouse cheese. If she could get her hands on an authentic Cordoban salami, the journey wouldn't have been in vain.

Verónica paid for breakfast, lit another cigarette and saw that it was her last one. As she passed the news stand she bought another packet and headed for the square. There were already a few people browsing the crafts and natural products. One of the stands was selling honey. Mieles Sol, the same name that had appeared on that email to Cecilia.

Verónica had enough willpower not to look up as she passed the honey stall. She walked casually past then continued until she was a short distance from the market and could look back without being noticed. Soledad was at the Mieles Sol stand. Verónica recognized her from the photos she had seen on Facebook.

She found a bench in the square from which she could observe Soledad without raising suspicion, looked in her bag for some dark glasses and substituted these, which hid her gaze, for the prescription ones. Now she looked like a young woman enjoying the morning and the winter sun. Nobody paid her any attention, least of all Soledad, who was smiling and talking to potential customers.

The best plan now, Verónica thought, was to wait. She'd had some beginner's luck and hoped to have more: an appearance from Cecilia. But as the time passed it seemed increasingly unlikely that Cecilia would come to the fair.

At midday she decided that the time for action had arrived. She walked over to the Mieles Sol stand, looked at the different jars and enquired about the prices. There were liquid and set honeys, along with royal jelly and honey sweets. Verónica said she would like a jar of set honey.

"Do you make it yourself, here?"

"Yes, we've been doing this for ten years now," said Soledad.

"That must be a lot of work. Do you do it alone?"

"No, I have a team of people working with me."

As they talked, Verónica noticed that the honey had a label with nutritional information and also the address of the Mieles Sol business: *Camino al Cerro Champaquí 1.3 miles.*

She went back to the news stand where she had bought the cigarettes and asked the woman in charge: "Which way is the Camino al Champaquí?"

The woman pointed towards a road beyond the bar where Verónica had had breakfast.

"I have to go down it for 1.3 miles, but I don't have any way of measuring that," said Verónica.

"The road begins at that corner. After a mile or so it'll take you past a couple of sharp bends, then the road splits in two: one way leads to a bar called El Mirador. Don't go that way. On the other road you'll find a house which is also called El Mirador, and further on there's a bar called Las Violetas, where they do snacks. The place you're looking for is between the house and Las Violetas."

"Do you know Mieles Sol?"

"Yes, of course, it's Soledad's business. She's here in the square now."

"I'm looking for a friend who came to San Javier to work with her."

"Ask Sole – she's right there."

Verónica began to walk down the Camino al Champaquí. Luckily it was cold, because it was tiring, tramping that road under the sun. You couldn't tell at first, but the road was clearly climbing. Ballet flats weren't the best footwear for this sort of walking.

She passed a watering hole, and beyond it the asphalt road gave way to a dirt track. Weekend and vacation homes followed, one after the other. The bends the woman had mentioned turned out to be ravines, which she gently descended. She reached the house called El Mirador and saw the road splitting in two. Slowly she walked on, looking at the signs for houses to rent. In the distance she saw the snack bar. A partly concealed sign said SOL APIARY – PURE HONEY FROM BEES.

Verónica was about to knock at the door, but held back briefly. The midday sun was blinding and it was hard to make anything out. She had to put her prescription glasses back on because she could barely see anything with the other ones and wanted to be sure that she was in the right place and not experiencing some hallucination, a mirage created by this blinding white sun.

A woman was coming down from the top of the road and she sensed that it was Cecilia. Someone who looked like Cecilia, anyway. Was it her, though? In the last few days Verónica had seen dozens of photos of the woman, she had read her emails, her files, her notes. She felt as though she had known her for a long time. And Verónica recognized this thirty-something woman who was walking down the hill with a serious expression, who walked past apparently without noticing her and headed towards the entrance of the Mieles Sol apiary.

"Cecilia."

The woman turned and looked at her. Verónica walked towards her. Every step confirmed what she had intuited since first seeing the woman come down the road.

"Cecilia Burgos?"

Cecilia briskly turned away, as though to enter the house. Verónica feared that she was going to hide, or that she might make an escape through the back of the property. But instead Cecilia turned back and asked: "Who are you? What do you want?"

7   *Thirty-three*

I

Agustín had started working for Verónica six months ago. Strictly speaking, he worked for D'Alessandro and Associates, the public relations company where Verónica was content manager. After passing a stringent selection process (which included tests on English and general knowledge and an hour-and-a-half-long interview with the heads of Human Resources), he had spent a month as secretary to everyone until Verónica asked if he could work with her as a replacement for her assistant, who was taking maternity leave. Agustín was delighted because Verónica worked in the area he liked most. In fact, he dreamed of having her job one day.

Being an assistant meant supporting the manager in all areas (work, professional, personal, emotional) and absolute deference to her every decision. To be an assistant was to be a soldier and Agustín was determined to be the best, just as he had been in rowing, as a teenager, and was now, on the marketing course at the small private university he attended, even though he missed a lot of classes through work.

Some days Verónica and Agustín would be together from nine o'clock in the morning until the early hours of the next day (only to start again a few hours later). He discovered that Verónica could be brilliant, but that she could also make silly mistakes (like trying to organize a concert sponsored by Pepsi in the Coca-Cola Stadium), and that was when he stepped up for her. They made a good team.

When Verónica was on a roll she was a joy to behold. Agustín loved watching her make an entrance in the meeting room and then dazzle the clients with her presentation. There was no signature she couldn't secure, and that made her the most valuable employee in the company. The directors let her do her own thing while they pursued other kinds of business, the exact nature of which wasn't always clear to him.

What Agustín felt for Verónica was an admiration close to desire. Or the other way round. Sometimes he felt like Anne Baxter in *All About Eve*. Plus Verónica was less Bette Davis and more Silvana Mangano in *Bitter Rice*. He had once told her she looked like Mangano and Verónica asked which movies she had been in, though she didn't know any of the ones he mentioned. He suspected Verónica hadn't seen any movie made before the 1980s. That made him admire her less, but only a little.

So many hours spent together, so much alcohol flowing between them (there's a lot of drinking in the world of public relations), meant it wasn't long before they were sharing confidences, too. Hers, mostly, because he was careful not to reveal to her his most secret feelings. That was how Agustín found out that Federico, her attorney boyfriend, had had another girlfriend also called Verónica, for whom she (Rinaldi) suspected he still carried a torch. In the odd spare moment (not that there were many of those) they used to try to find out more about her. That wasn't easy, since she didn't have Facebook, or LinkedIn, or Pinterest, or Instagram, or Twitter, or a website. She was a journalist, but not particularly well known. She had never worked in television and the magazine where her articles appeared wasn't one of the biggest titles.

Agustín didn't like the way Verónica was so hung up on her boyfriend and his ex. The guy was certainly attractive and, whenever he imagined an erotic encounter with Verónica Rinaldi, Agustín liked to fantasize about a threesome involving himself, Federico and her. And he was sure Verónica would be delighted by such a scenario. They would just need to convince the boyfriend.

When he decided to accompany her to the publishing party – an event of minor importance in their world but which Verónica had insisted on attending – it never crossed his mind that the evening would be a turning point in the war between Verónica and the attorney's ex-girlfriend.

The party itself was really boring, full of people wearing glasses and with no sign of bankable clients, which he had thought was the main reason for being there, drinking second-rate wine. The only positive was that the lack of interesting people to talk to meant they had more time to speak to each other, to gaze into each other's eyes as he breathed in the scent of her Escada perfume. But Verónica had stiffened, the blood draining from her face.

"I've just seen Federico's ex walk past."

"The other Verónica?"

"Who else? The flirty receptionist?" she asked, violently.

They watched the other woman approach, accompanied by an old classmate from university, and Agustín realized how nervous Verónica was when she shakily raised a wine glass to her lips. The women exchanged a few words, in an increasingly aggressive tone. He was about to come out in defence of his Verónica when she, his elegant boss, the most *public relations* of public relations officers, threw her glass of wine into her rival's face.

The gambit worked, because the other Verónica and her friend left, but then his Verónica started to panic. She was convinced that the ex would call Federico, play the victim and make her look like a lunatic. And that was when he had a brainwave. She should get in first.

After calming Verónica down, he accompanied her to the door of the ladies' room and waited for her there. Then he told her his plan.

Agustín took a glass of red wine and sprinkled it over Verónica's lovely dress. Then he used his boss's phone to call Federico. He should come right away, Agustín said, and see what a terrible state his girlfriend was in. Then they sat at the entrance to the museum and waited for him to appear. Verónica, who was still in a state of shock, didn't find it hard to play the part of victim. Her anger and surprise were genuine; only the circumstances and the attribution of names were invented.

II

Federico asked himself whether Verónica Rosenthal was capable of attacking and injuring his girlfriend and came up with two possible answers: yes, and yes, of course. If she had thrown a glass of red wine at someone in front of hundreds of witnesses, he shuddered to think what she might do if the two Verónicas ever met each other alone. He ought to do something, though he had no idea what. Every course of action was problematic. The most logical thing would be to call Verónica Rosenthal and confront her, establish boundaries (which Aarón Rosenthal had so clearly failed to do, patriarchy notwithstanding). But she'd laugh in his face (he knew her crazy woman laugh – he could hardly forget it) and say that this was a just a pretext to get in touch with her. And he wasn't ready to be hurt again.

There were two options. He could get professional protection for his Verónica, a security guard to watch over her.

But that would look like spying on his girlfriend; if she found out, she'd think he was monitoring her and no explanation would seem credible. The other option would be to get someone to spy on Verónica Rosenthal. Vero would certainly find out, though. She was brilliant at that kind of thing. And if that happened it would be better to lie, to say that he put an investigator on to her because he missed her and wanted to know what she was doing. At the end of the day, that idea had crossed his mind before.

He was going mad. Or he was being a total fuckwit, as another member of the Centeno Club would doubtless say.

Thinking of his friends always brought clarity. Inspiration struck, and he knew what he had to do. He called La Sombra, "The Shadow", a hacker who had worked for him when Federico was still on the team at Rosenthal and Associates. La Sombra was capable of solving the most complex problems in total silence.

"It's a simple job," Federico explained to him. "I'm going to give you two telephone numbers. When you see the second one coming within a one-mile radius of the first, let me know."

"Yeah, that's simple enough. If the telephones have a GPS tracker."

"Check that and get back to me."

"OK. Round the clock?"

Federico thought of Verónica Rosenthal's routine. "No. From 5 a.m. until 11 a.m. you can take your eyes off her."

"Man, one of these numbers belongs to Aarón Rosenthal's daughter."

"I don't work for him any more."

"So who's this for?"

"For me."

"Women problems?"

"Something like that."

"I'll charge you half, then. I always overcharged Rosenthal."

With this worry about protecting his girlfriend allayed, Federico resolved not to think about the other Verónica any more. But she had such a knack for getting into his head. It was as if she'd hijacked one of his neurons. And that neuron was always working away. Now he needed to focus his mind fully on the body parts investigation, on Mosquito's murder and on the police involvement in this plot, which he still couldn't untangle. He had to concentrate on work and forget about Verónica Rosenthal for a while.

III

Rodolfo Corso was a great journalist, no doubting that. An honest guy who had the run of all the newsrooms, as well as good sources, a winning prose style, erratic social behaviour and an ability not to worry too much every time he landed in trouble or got fired from a job.

Federico didn't understand the world of journalism well – Verónica had never spoken much about her work – but he suspected that the media companies who employed him made Corso pay for his free-spiritedness by not publishing him much, only turning to him when he had a scoop or could beat a rival publication to an exclusive. He could easily imagine an editor saying of Rodolfo: *Great journalist, shame he drinks too much* (or *He does too much coke,* or *Screws too many colleagues,* or *Arrives late* – or whatever excuse served to keep employing mediocre journalists while sidelining the talented but difficult Corso).

And it was true that Corso could be eccentric. He had asked Federico to meet him at midday at a paddle court a few blocks away from the old Caseros prison. Federico didn't object (perhaps Corso had his reasons) and set off for this location like someone preparing to visit a Roman ruin.

It turned out to be a kind of neighbourhood club, with paddle courts, a gym and a bar. Federico was still settling into his seat at one of the tables in the bar room when Corso appeared in shorts, sweating and holding a paddle racquet.

"We won: 6–4, 6–7, 6–2."

Corso greeted him with a sweaty kiss. Federico felt it wouldn't be right to wipe the moisture from his cheek.

"Congratulations."

"I'm going to go and get the notes I have in my bag." He stood up and shouted to a man behind the bar: "Medina, get the boy a drink – whatever he wants."

Five minutes later, Corso returned carrying a folder. He was still wearing his sports kit, but seemed to have freshened up and combed his hair. He took a grapefruit Gatorade out of a cooler on one side of the room and sat down opposite Federico, who already had the coffee in a glass that Medina had brought him.

"Very tough."

"The game?"

"No, no, the job you gave me."

Corso opened the folder. The chaotic arrangement of the papers inside suggested that they had been dropped on the floor and hastily retrieved. After brief consideration, he selected a couple of small sheets covered in unintelligible handwriting. He squinted at them as though even he didn't understand his writing. Then he put them to one side, apparently dismissing them, and started speaking:

"Let's start with the patsy, the poor driver, Sandro Hernández. He was sixty-two but looked seventy. Alcohol ravages the face, you see. There's something that does even more damage than booze, though, and that's religion. The opium of the people, as that unfairly discredited Karl Marx wrote so truly. Our friend Sandro was one of those Catholics. An ultra-Catholic or an ultramontane, although I would reserve that particular definition for people who are ideological about their religion, people who, at the very least, have read Saint Augustine. Hernández was a fervent Catholic without much knowledge or interest in the principles of ecclesiastical doctrine. He was happy enough with nice moral tales about Jesus, the Cross and the miracles. You don't need much more to be a Catholic.

"The guy wasn't always like that, mind you. He got married young, had two children, a boy and a girl, who grew up estranged from their father. By the age of thirty he was already an alcoholic. Some acquaintance in the José C. Paz neighbourhood took him to an Alcoholics Anonymous meeting that was held in a church. The guy came out cured, but all that exposure to holiness turned him into the kind of Christian who prays every day and does church on Sundays. He didn't go back to his wife and children, but he embarked on a solitary life marked only by his activities in a Catholic group called The Triumph of Christ, a name that reminds me of that sadly famous chant, 'Christ Conquers', used by the Catholics who deposed General Perón."

"Which year are we talking about."

"Perón's defeat was in 1955."

"Seriously."

"We're at the beginning of the 1980s, the end of the military dictatorship. The Triumph of Christ disbands in 1983 and Hernández starts attending a church in Liniers, where the priest was one Ignacio Salvi, known as Father Nacho, an ultramontane priest, pre-Vatican II and almost certainly a paedophile, but I can't be sure of that and it's of no interest to us as regards this investigation. That was the meeting place for a little group, unnamed but sharing a conviction that Catholicism offered the only possible salvation for humanity. Sandro, and some fellow members of this congregation, get invited to take part in a demonstration against a Dario Fo play at the Teatro San Martín. I once saw a Dario Fo play, and I can assure you I'd also have protested against it if I'd had the chance. Anyway, you know the story: they smashed the theatre windows, threw stones around, handed out leaflets and even recited the rosary. The police arrested some of them, Hernández among them. And here's the good bit."

"Go on."

"Who do you think got him out of the police station and paid the lawyer who defended him?"

"*Touché.*"

"Father Ignacio. What a bastard that priest must be, over ninety years old and still alive. God clearly doesn't want him for an angel."

Corso finished his Gatorade, looked over at the cooler as though wondering about getting himself another one, then said to the man behind the bar: "Medina, bring me a cortado like my friend's." Then, to Federico: "Would you like another one? OK, I'll go on. During those years, Sandro Hernández had various, low-skilled jobs. He didn't last long in any of them. As far as we know, there were no other relationships and he didn't go back to his wife and children, except on the odd occasion. His loyalty was to the parish of Father Ignacio."

"Incredible."

"I'll be coming back to this priest. At the start of the 1990s, Hernández starts drinking again. He doesn't show up in police records because they don't record many drunk and disorderlies, but he gets admitted to public hospitals on various occasions with alcohol-related complications. He even spends two months in the Muñiz with a chest infection. Have you ever spent time in a public hospital?"

"No."

"One day I'll tell you my life story and you'll be moved to tears. In the Muñiz, he gets to know a nurse – hang on while I find the name – that's it, Romualdo Profano. A strange name if ever there was one. Romualdo was a militant in the Partido Nacionalista, an ultra-right group that mixes Naziism, cut-price nationalism and Catholicism. Profano introduces Hernández to the group, in which he now becomes an activist. In 1995, as you know, he receives a prison sentence for anti-Semitic graffiti. Well, once again, Father Ignacio saves him from prison. At the beginning of 2000, Romualdo Profano, his sponsor within the Partido Nacionalista, dies in strange circumstances. Supposedly they were celebrating a birthday at a house in Ciudadela when some men came in, stabbed Romualdo then ran off. At the party were twenty far-right militants. Not one of those criminals had the *cojones* to stab them. What's clear is that, with the death of the nurse, Hernández distances himself from the Partido Nacionalista and is increasingly confined to the parish. He spends more time there than even the priest himself. A year later, he gets a job as driver for a candy manufacturer. He lasts a few years there until 2004, when he's fired for driving while under the influence and gets arrested for the third time."

"Whereupon the priest saves him again."

"No."

"No?"

"That's the strange part. The guy walks free. There's only one explanation: somebody important put pressure on for him to be freed without their intervention being recorded. Someone more important than a priest. So Hernández goes back to the parish, but this time to work as a driver for Father

Ignacio, who gets a car because he sits on certain commissions within the metropolitan curia, which brings him into contact with the Archbishop of Buenos Aires. One of the commissions he's worked on, since the start of 2000, is on the prevention of drug abuse, a mixed group comprising priests and various establishment movers and shakers: well-to-do ladies, church-loving journalists, politicians on their way down and police officers who defy categorization. Guess who else sat on that commission."

"You tell me."

"Chief Superintendent Barbosa, head of Dangerous Drugs in the Argentine federal police."

IV

Rodolfo Corso sipped his cortado, enjoying the look of shock on Federico's face. The attorney had been noting down names and dates in a little notebook, which had once been a gift from Verónica Rosenthal, something he hadn't remembered either now or when he'd distractedly picked it up at home.

"Up until now it's all been quite picturesque. An alcoholic who discovers Jesus and then Nazism, who's protected by a priest and ends up shooting himself in the head because you lot spoiled his plan. It could be an Argentine movie with five-minute shots of the guy driving his truck along a deserted road. But Chief Superintendent Barbosa takes this somewhere else. You know why? Because he has a spotless record. Look at him. He's not your typical neighbourhood police chief, whoring, getting free pizza and doing the odd line of coke. Barbosa is an intellectual. Given that he chose to work in the police force, I would say he's an intellectual of violence. He speaks perfect English, he's done various specialist courses in the US and one in Germany. I wouldn't be surprised if he's worked for the DEA or the CIA, although I don't have any proof of that. His parents were middle-class yet he married an heiress from a rich family: Margarita Loaiza. His wife is a Catholic who takes daily Communion. She attends the church of Santísimo Sacramento, near to Plaza San Martín, just as her parents did. Margarita and the chief superintendent have five children: none joined the police, but there is an agronomist who looks after the family estate, a psychologist who works with her father in the field of drug prevention, a classical violinist who lives in Brussels and two younger children still in high school. As I said, it was his wife Margarita who introduced him into the most rancid circles of the Catholic Church. He's been the head of the Dangerous Drugs section for ten years. A not insignificant detail: five years ago there was one of those periodic panics about security. The government wanted to be seen taking a tough line and to choose someone from the police corps as Secretary of Security. They picked Barbosa, but he turned down the job. Apparently he was more interested in keeping an eye on dangerous drugs than in being a public servant."

"It's like that old Spanish proverb, 'under the master's gaze, the livestock fattens'."

"It's legitimate to ask if the guy's involved in drug trafficking. But there are other questions without answers here. Why would a man who's trafficking drugs get into trafficking organs and bodies? Why did he facilitate the contact between Hernández and Mosquito? Was Hernández working for Father Ignacio, for Barbosa, or for someone else we don't know about yet? Why would a guy who knows he can count on the support of priests and police officers, who surely would have walked free, shoot himself?"

"Because there's something very dark behind all this."

"Or not – perhaps he was really screwed up, or tired of living a shitty life and in the last ten seconds of his life decided to go out with a bang. I'm going to try to find out more about Barbosa and I imagine you are too. Be careful, though. If this guy has a clean sheet, he most likely paid for it by taking out anyone who tried to stain it."

They both got up. Federico went to the bar to pay for their drinks. As they said goodbye, Corso added: "Come along next Friday."

"Why – will you have more information for me then?"

"No idea, but we're a man short for paddle. And don't worry about a racquet – they can lend you one here."

V

The cases were piling up on Federico's desk. Without looking, he could pick up any one of several folders on crimes completely unrelated to the suicide driver. Sometimes he wondered why he got so obsessed by a particular case. And his obsessions nearly always led to him working semi-secretly. Back when he was employed by the Rosenthal practice that had been because Aarón alone decided what was a priority and, if another case looked more interesting to Federico, he had to pursue it in his own time – which had been almost non-existent because working at Rosenthal and Associates meant being busy seven days a week. Not that Aarón demanded this; the dynamic of a successful law firm simply made it inevitable.

Nowadays he had the pressure of court timetables, of judges, of public attorneys, of prosecutions, of the media (in the unhappy event of a case hitting the headlines) and even the court secretaries, who believed themselves to be more important than the entire justice system.

There was something very strange about this case, but he could have dispatched it quickly enough if he wanted: the guy had committed suicide; his vehicle was carrying an illegal load. Federico ought to pass everything on to the judge and leave the police and judicial system to spend the next few years investigating what those body parts were doing in the truck.

That was how the judiciary worked, and he wasn't going to change it. He couldn't count on the budget he would have had at Rosenthal and Associates, nor on qualified assistants, not even on a supportive judge motivating him to keep going. Federico had reached a point where it would be feasible to draw a line. This shit was too much for him.

He thought back to the case of the trains, investigated by Verónica Rosenthal. That had also begun with a suicide.

"Do you think there's a connection between that and my obsession with this case?" Federico asked Doctor Cohen, his psychoanalyst.

"It seems quite clear, doesn't it?"

"What does?"

"There's a marked thanatic component in the relationship between you. Curious, this: there's currently no relationship between you. You could say that the relationship is dead. And you feel that the only way to revive it is through a dead person."

"So why did I ask Corso to do the investigation and not her?"

"There are two possible answers, one of which is pretty basic. You're scared: of rejection, of your girlfriend finding out – which in your case would be like your mother finding out – and of asking for help. An answer more worthy of the fee you're paying me would be that desire doesn't follow a straight line between the desirer and the object of desire. Desire is always baroque. Sometimes it follows a curve. And the relationship with this Rosenthal girl is like a spiral for

149

you. It twists and turns as it comes closer, as you see it getting nearer. But it's not like one of those spiral repellents you use against mosquitoes which has an end point – you marry the girl, and bingo. It's a spiral with a vanishing point. As you get closer, it shoots off in a straight line, into the distance. I don't know if you understand me."

"I don't."

"Never mind. If I wanted you to understand I'd give you a course, not sessions. And tell me, have you had any more erotic dreams about your mother?"

"No, Doctor! That was only once, and I wish I hadn't told you. It wasn't even her, it was my girlfriend, Verónica."

"In the dream they were the same person, Federico. Doesn't it get tiring having to add 'my girlfriend' every time you mention your girlfriend's name?"

"I don't understand."

"Yes you do. Let's leave it there. We'll continue next week."

"I think I'm going to discharge myself."

"Only a professional can do that. You can stop coming, but that would be something different. Same time next Wednesday?"

"OK then."

VI

La Sombra hadn't called him. That was a good sign. If Verónica Rosenthal was capable of attacking his girlfriend, that must mean that deep down she was still interested in him, or at least interested in ruining his life, a gesture that, in women, could be taken as a sign of love. No, he shouldn't even go there... He knew Verónica Rosenthal was no longer remotely interested in him. He had always been like her brother (older or younger, depending on the situation), the guy who helped her tap the power of Rosenthal and Associates. Although circumstances may have led to her lowering her guard enough for the brief romance they had enjoyed in Tucumán, that had been a moment of weakness. He was just another lay for her. Perhaps more affectionate, more familiar than some, but still a lay at the end of the day. True, he had taken the decision to leave her, but then she had never tried to get him back. For a time he nursed the illusion that the Rosenthal sisters might convey messages from her, or that on some occasion when he was meeting Leticia and Daniela, their younger sister might show up, but that had never happened. It was easy to conclude that these things hadn't happened because Verónica had a boyfriend. Who was the bastard, though? A journalist, maybe, someone prominent. Or a millionaire economist. Or a construction worker. Anyone – it could literally be anyone. There was less logic to the woman's choices than to the spinning of a roulette wheel. Or maybe there was a logic he didn't know about, something related to the body or its capacity for love. Had he not lived up to her expectations? Could that be the reason she had never spoken to him again? It must be. Now it was crystal clear: that was why, when they'd had a fling in their early twenties, she had abandoned him and now, in their early thirties, he had left her and she hadn't made an effort to get him back. He knew her to be capable of fighting like a lioness for the things she wanted. Evidently he wasn't one of them. Anyway, if he ever ran into her somewhere with her boyfriend, he'd punch the guy's lights out, to get her back for what she did to his girlfriend.

Thirty-three – not his lucky lottery number but the age he would be in three days' time. Perhaps because it was Christ's age when they crucified him, or because it felt like the beginning of old age, or because Verónica kept going on about it, Federico had decided to celebrate his birthday this year. His parents were away in Mexico, so he could have the party at their place. Although it wouldn't be a massive event, his girlfriend insisted on doing it there and on taking care of all the details herself. She loved organizing parties. She also liked play-acting that they were married and living there together. She wanted to have sex in his parents' room, but Federico refused point-blank to do that. They could sleep in the master bedroom; for sex, though, they would have to resort to his childhood bedroom or, at a push, the armchairs or the carpet in the living room.

Federico handled the invitations. First off, his friends from the Centeno Club with their partners; three colleagues from the prosecutor's office; a couple of lawyers, old friends from university; another female lawyer from Rosenthal and Associates with whom he kept up a fraternal camaraderie; the Rosenthal sisters, Daniela and Leticia, with their husbands; and Rodolfo Corso. Verónica asked if she could invite Agustín, her assistant, who could also act as DJ since he loved playing music.

Verónica had done a fantastic job. There would be more than enough food and drink. She had also been able to draw on the invaluable support of Agustín, who turned up three hours before the time stipulated on the invitation.

Federico decided to leave them to organize everything and went to his parents' bedroom, which had an en suite bathroom, to shower and get changed. He answered various birthday greetings on WhatsApp and tried not to think about Verónica Rosenthal, from whom there hadn't been a peep. Which showed a basic lack of courtesy, he thought. Because, even if she hadn't remembered his birthday (and, for as long as they had known each other, he had never known her to forget it), she must at least know that her sisters were coming to his party. He wasn't expecting her to turn up without an invitation, gift in hand, but at least a little text message, a WhatsApp (he had, despite himself, established that she now also had WhatsApp), a measly email. There was nothing, though.

He took off his clothes and got into the shower, applying some of his father's anti-hair-loss shampoo. A noise came from the bedroom, like a shoe falling onto the floor, and Federico rinsed out the shampoo, his eyes burning. He was about to turn thirty-three, but he still made the same mistakes with shampoo as when he was eight years old. Then Verónica appeared, completely naked.

"May I?" she asked, slipping into the shower.

"Seriously? In my parents' shower?" Federico asked, in a tone contradicted by the erection he was getting.

"Don't be a prude. I have to wash too."

Verónica picked up the soap, but instead of using it on herself, she started lathering up Federico's chest. Strictly speaking, he supposed the bathroom didn't count as his parents' bedroom. Federico kissed her, enjoying the sensation of her smooth body sliding against his.

There was another noise in the bedroom, the noise of a slamming door. Federico moved away a little from his girlfriend and listened, expectantly. From the door of the bedroom (from outside or inside?), Agustín asked loudly: "Vero, shall I take the cheeses out of the fridge so that they'll be at room temperature when the guests arrive?"

"Do you prefer cheese cold or warm?" Verónica asked Federico.

"Christ, I don't know how I like it. Do whatever you want."

"Do whatever you think, Agustín," shouted Verónica.

"Would you like me to check with Federico, then?" Agustín called back.

"Federico's right here."

For a few seconds there was silence. Then Agustín added: "Right. I'll take the cheeses out and put them on the counter."

"That Agustín never stops, he's a machine," she said, as she took hold of his cock. Then she crouched down and began to suck him off as the water fell over them both like a benediction.

VII

The party was dominated by lawyers merrily comparing cases, something that quickly became tedious for the other guests, who congregated on the other side of the living room. In that group were Daniela, Leticia, their husbands, the friends from Centeno and their partners. At some point in the night, Federico overheard this group discussing Verónica. Doubtless his bastard friends were on the hunt for gossip they could drop into the conversation next time they all had dinner.

All evening Rodolfo Corso had stalked the partygoers like a lone predator, glass of whisky in hand, until he identified his prey: the court secretary, thirty-eight years old, unmarried and willing to believe everything Corso told her that night.

Verónica had organized things so people could serve themselves, and the Centeno friends were taking full advantage, perhaps because they had known this apartment for nearly twenty years. They were the ones investigating the fridge and freezer, replenishing plates and throwing cans of beer to anyone who asked for one. Agustín was in charge of music (obviously he thought himself quite the DJ, because he kept putting on those techno tracks that nobody there liked) and followed Verónica everywhere, like a little lapdog. One of the few times they separated was when Verónica went to the kitchen and he to change the music to another track that sounded the same as the last. Federico was chatting to the group of lawyers and Rodolfo Corso took the opportunity to pass on some new findings from his investigation, keeping his voice low and his tone conspiratorial.

"Barbosa, he's so by the book, isn't he? Somehow he manages to combine a public image more immaculate than the Virgin Mary's with assets greater than King Midas's. Evidently a chief superintendent's salary can get you a lot: a Mercedes-Benz, a Renault for the wife, a Honda for his eldest son, a mansion in Villa Devoto, a pretty country house in Pilar and land in Santa Fe province."

"The millionaire lifestyle."

"And then I don't know how much cash he's got stashed away here and abroad. Think about it: if everything I've just mentioned is in his own name, he must have ten times more under fake names or shell companies, as per that quaint Argentine custom."

"Obviously he's never been investigated for illicit earnings."

"No judge would dare to pin the tail on the donkey. Well, maybe the veteran would."

"What do you mean?"

"The woman you work with."

"Ah, she's hardly a veteran. She's only thirty-eight."

"That counts. I don't trust single women of her age. How come they haven't found a guy to marry and have children with? And single men over forty make me suspicious too, by the way, unless they're gay."

"You're over forty, not gay and still single."

"But I lost five years to alcohol and cocaine. That counts the same as a marriage."

Federico spotted Daniela going to the kitchen, which was empty apart from Verónica. When a few minutes went by and neither of them had returned to the party, Federico found he had stopped paying attention to Rodolfo Corso and was worrying about Verónica. At least Daniela wasn't violent, like her younger sister. Or was she? Better check. He got up and went to join the two women.

Daniela was leaning against the counter, a glass of white wine in her hand, while his girlfriend was holding a tray of sushi, ready to take into the living room. They were smiling and chatting. Federico caught the end of an exchange.

"That happened to me once and I nearly cried. Plus it was a horrible party full of doctors from the hospital where I'd been doing my residency," said Daniela.

"I can't stand them. I swear I'll never use them again."

"Here comes the birthday boy."

Both of them looked at him tenderly, and Federico felt ashamed to have feared the worst. Daniela rubbed his arm and Verónica took her chance to carry the tray through to the living room.

"What were you two talking about?"

"Women's things. Your girlfriend's a delight, by the way."

"You think?"

"Attractive, intelligent, sociable."

"Yes, you're right. She's all that and then some."

"You deserve someone like that."

"That's what I tell myself every morning."

"I'm just sorry you're not officially a member of the Rosenthal family."

"Officially."

"Of course, in that you're not marrying Vero, our Vero. But unofficially, my children will always call you Uncle."

"That's part of the Rosenthal family charm: once they get hold of you, they never let you go."

"You should go back to work in the firm. I've no idea what happened between my father and you, I don't even know much about what happened between Vero and you, but both Rosenthals need you."

"I thought you just said that Vero, my Vero, was the ideal woman."

"Obviously she's the ideal woman for you – but who wants to spend their life with an ideal woman?"

"I should have suspected as much: you're a Rosenthal too, after all."

The conversation might have continued in this slightly dangerous direction had it not been for the arrival of Sebastián, his Centeno Club friend, looking upset.

"I'm off, we're off, I've come to say goodbye." Sebastián gave him a quick kiss, then abruptly walked out of the kitchen.

"Wait – what's happened?" Federico asked, following behind him.

"Same thing as always. Luciana."

Luciana was his partner. Federico looked round and saw her crying in a corner of the living room. The people closest to her were pretending not to notice, apart from Diego's girlfriend, who was trying to comfort her.

"See what she's like?" Sebastián said to him. "The stupid cow has to cause a scene wherever she goes."

He didn't know what she was like, though. Federico had no idea. Sebastián had never mentioned any problems with his relationship. He didn't know if Luciana was weird, if he was an emotional bully, or if both of them enjoyed causing a scene at their friends' parties. He watched them leave without understanding what had happened.

Verónica came up to Federico and whispered in his ear: "Your friends are fucking in your parents' bedroom."

Federico wanted to reply *I don't have any friends.* Then he realized that all the guests were friends of his, apart from Agustín and the partners of some of those present, which meant that Verónica's observation was not only calamitous but unhelpfully vague. Scanning the room, he quickly concluded that she must be talking about Rodolfo Corso and the court secretary. Verónica confirmed his hunch and seemed annoyed, or disdainful, about it. Perhaps because they had never had sex in the parental bedroom. But how did she know, anyway?

"Agustín told me."

What was Agustín doing checking all the rooms in the house? How did he know it was those two and not another couple? Had he spied on them? Federico felt as though all the alcohol he had drunk that night was starting to take a toll. He watched Agustín walk towards them.

"Listen up, what are you doing looking in the bedrooms?"

"What about what your friends are doing?" Verónica quickly intervened. Agustín seemed to be trying to say something and unable to get the words out. His pale face emulated the contortions of a trainee mime artist. Only this routine ended in the worst kind of gag as he bent his head and vomited, right in front of them. A few people screamed, or perhaps it was Federico who screamed, drowning out the *ker-chunk, ker-chunk* of the techno music.

"Poor thing, he's not well," said Verónica, putting a hand on her assistant's forehead, then his shoulders, and leading him to the bathroom. Agustín faltered, as though he might faint.

"Where do you keep cloths and a bucket?" asked the girlfriend of one of the Centeno gang, the same woman who had earlier consoled Sebastián's partner and now seemed prepared to clean up vomit. Evidently a true Samaritan.

Federico walked robotically towards the stereo and tore out the cables connecting it to the speakers. There followed a strange, profound silence, like when you dive into a swimming pool. Some people looked at him, others stood up – to give him a hand, or to leave, or perhaps to do something else he neither knew nor cared about. Federico picked up a half-glass of wine from the table and drank it in one go. As though in a dream, he watched his friend's girlfriend wiping the floor. Some people came smiling towards him to say that they were leaving. The goodbyes went on for a while, and he wasn't sure if he had managed to speak to everyone because at some point he fell asleep, sitting in an armchair. Verónica woke him, stroking his face. There was nobody left in the living room.

It was half past three in the morning. Federico made an effort to wake up. He looked towards the place where Agustín had vomited, and it was clean.

"Let's go to the bedroom," Verónica said, and Federico stood up. He needed a piss.

He noticed that the bed in his parents' room was unmade, and walked past it to the bathroom.

"Lucky your friends didn't leave any used condoms or stain the quilt," said Verónica, pulling back the covers and starting to take off her clothes. Federico washed his face with cold water and looked at himself in the mirror: he definitely looked thirty-three.

"Come on, my love, I need some attention," said Verónica, kneeling on the mattress in her underwear.

"More? What about this morning in the shower?"

"I sucked you off. It's not the same."

"It was perfect for me."

"Stop being silly and come here."

"Let's go to my room then."

"I forgot to tell you that I told Agustín to sleep in your old room, since he didn't feel well. He's already asleep."

"Your assistant is sleeping in my bed?"

"Don't be a dick. Come and give me a kiss."

First he went to close the bedroom door. The last thing he wanted was for Agustín to show up in the middle of sex. Then he took off his trousers and shirt, trying not to look at the family photos positioned around the room. He would have to keep his eyes closed to have any hope of an erection in the next few minutes. As Federico's trousers dropped, his phone fell onto the floor. He picked it up and looked at it: there was a WhatsApp message from 23.59. It was from Verónica Rosenthal and read: *Happy birthday! I hope you have a great day and enjoy yourself.* Federico noticed that her last activity on WhatsApp had been only two minutes ago. He thought of writing something back, some witty, hilarious comment that would make her want to send a clever response, and then he would also answer that and they would continue in the same vein for hours. But his Verónica had stood up, taken off her bra and was walking over to kiss him.

VIII

Federico's stomach was a bit unsettled, but otherwise he didn't feel too bad. He arrived at the prosecutor's office at around midday and saw his desk piled high with jobs pending. For the next three hours he worked on a case that concerned the falsification of government bonds, allocated various tasks and requested some procedures to be carried out. Then he settled down to study Chief Superintendent Barbosa's service record. There he found something that struck him as odd. The man had begun his career in the Bonaerense, the Buenos Aires force, then some years into his career had moved to the federal police. That was in 1987. He called Rodolfo Corso.

"That was a very good year to leave the Bonaerense."

"Why so?"

"There were purges, clear-outs. The Bonaerense was still the same force it had been under the dictatorship. In the first years of the democracy there was a minister, Luis Brizuela, who tried to rid the force of corrupt officers, criminals and murderers. Some joined the ranks of the unemployed, others clung on to their positions, and a few moved to other forces. Brizuela was torn to shreds within a year – don't you remember?"

"I was barely out of kindergarten, Corso."

"Nice party, by the way. Your lawyer friend was a bit wild. Listen, go and see Brizuela. He's a man of integrity who was thrown out because he wanted to do things honestly."

"He won't remember a young officer who jumped ship, not considering all the other stuff he had to deal with."

"Brizuela's a wily old fox. He knows a lot and he lives far away from everyone, on an island in the Tigre delta. You'll feel like Martin Sheen going to visit Colonel Kurtz in *Apocalypse Now*."

"Can't I just call him?"

"Or tweet him, while we're at it? The man's going to want to talk face to face. He's a politician from the old school."

Once he had Brizuela's details, Federico called him, introduced himself and explained about the case he was investigating and how the security forces might be implicated. As Corso had anticipated, Brizuela invited him to come to Tigre.

At ten o'clock the next morning, Federico was at the port in Tigre, waiting for the ferry that would take him to the island where Brizuela lived. It was a sunny day, but cold. Even so, Federico was in the mood for an excursion. He ought to get out of Buenos Aires more often.

He got off the ferry at the dock indicated by the old minister. A few large but friendly-looking dogs approached. Then Brizuela appeared. He looked like an islander, like someone who had lived his whole life in this place and never been in high office debating with congressmen and national senators. Wild hair, beard, simple clothes.

"I take it you drink maté?"

They sat in the sun, sheltered from the breeze coming off the river by the house in front of them. The dogs lay at their feet. Brizuela passed him the maté gourd and Federico spoke frankly about his suspicions concerning Barbosa.

"I'm guessing you don't remember him."

"The name definitely rings a bell. I don't particularly remember him, but I do remember various officers transferring to the federal police. It's quite common for Bonaerense police officers to move to other forces that pay better. Not so much in the higher ranks, though. And anyway, they were being investigated. They might have faced suspension. I say 'might' because the pressure on my ministry was so great that we never knew how far we could go."

"You were forced out after less than a year."

"That's right. Tell me the name again."

"Chief Superintendent Álvaro Barbosa."

Brizuela got up and walked towards the house, leaving Federico alone with the maté in hand and the two dogs lying at his feet for company. He could hear the cheeping of birds and the humming of a boat's engine in the distance. It wouldn't be bad to live somewhere like this, thought Federico, far from everything and everyone.

The other man reappeared, holding some papers. "You're in luck. I haven't kept many papers, at least I haven't kept them all, but I did hang on to some that could be useful for future investigations. And good thing too. Here's your Chief Superintendent Barbosa."

"Drug trafficking?"

"No. Cast your mind back to Buenos Aires in the eighties. There were drugs being sold, but it was a limited market compared to other crimes. Barbosa worked with Chief Superintendent Lauro, who ran the illegal lottery in the Tercer Distrito in Buenos Aires province. He dabbled in stolen cars too, but gambling was his main thing. We suspended Lauro and, when his people saw the way things were going, they asked to be discharged and went over to the federal force. I've got papers on this Barbosa up until the mid-nineties, when he arrives with a glowing record at the Bureau of Complex Crimes. Then there's an allegation of a cover-up in a human trafficking case. It seems that Chief Superintendent Barbosa suppressed a series of cases that took place in several northern provinces. Once again, before the scandal could break, the man moved to Dangerous Drugs, at which point the trail went cold."

"Could I photograph those papers?"

"No need. I'll scan them and email them to you. That'll be easier."

By the time Federico arrived back at his apartment, Brizuela's email was already in his inbox. He sent it on to Corso, who said he would do some quick checks.

Federico didn't see Verónica or any of his friends that day. Instead he decided to make himself a couple of hamburgers with fried egg and bacon, and have a few beers while watching the repeat of the Barcelona game he had missed that afternoon. Around midnight, fatigue got the better of him and he went off to bed, but not long afterwards the phone rang. It was Rodolfo Corso who, realizing that he'd been asleep, urged him to wake up.

"What I have to say will give you insomnia for a week."

"What's up?"

"After reading the papers you sent me, I got in touch with a few sources. Turns out that when Barbosa went from Complex Crimes to Dangerous Drugs, it was to save his neck after covering up a trafficking network. Young girls brought from the interior and prostituted in Buenos Aires or roadside clubs in Patagonia. The usual story."

"All that info was in Brizuela's material."

"Yes, but what it doesn't say is who saved his ass, who did the paperwork, pressured the politicians and even met with the president to make sure Barbosa wouldn't be touched. It was Monseñor Quarracino, the archbishop of Buenos Aires."

"Wow. That's intense – but I can assure you it won't stop me sleeping."

"Don't you see the similarities with the truck driver? Hernández gets protection from Father Ignacio, Barbosa gets it from Archbishop Quarracino."

"True enough. There's something there, no?"

"Well… if that was all I had to tell you I'd have let it wait until tomorrow. This is the part that's going to make you lose sleep. Do you know who Barbosa protected, for whom he put his career at risk?"

"No idea."

"A mobster, capable of murder, who's tried his hand at every crime known to humanity and doubtless a few we don't yet know. A guy who can never be pinned down. A big fish who didn't think twice about trying to murder a journalist we both know, you better than me, admittedly."

"Juan García?"

"The very one. The wickedest villain of them all is back."

"You were right. I won't sleep tonight."

8   *Cecilia, Jazmín, Lucía*

I

First she had felt herself entering a shaft of light, only it wasn't so much entering as falling, or flying. That's how confused everything was. Then there was also a dry, metallic noise and a sudden human scream. It was her screaming, blocking out all the other noises. Then the white light went out and gave way to an absolute blackness.

Cecilia felt that her face was wet. With blood, not water, although it didn't hurt. She immediately thought of Jazmín. Tried to turn round. Couldn't. She undid her seat belt and tried to open the car door. Then she pushed as hard as she could, but it was useless because part of the chassis had buckled and the door had been forced inwards. She managed to climb through the window, which had shattered, then fell onto the ground. Leaning against the car, she pulled herself upright. All she could see around her was metal, twisted into monstrous shapes. She heard moans and a noise that sounded like tyres deflating.

When Cecilia opened the back door there was Jazmín, who had freed herself from her grandmother's arms. She seemed to be asleep. Next to Jazmín, her grandmother, face shattered, covered in blood. Her sister and niece must be further in, but Cecilia couldn't see anything else, just Jazmín. Leaving her mother, she pulled her daughter from the car, hugged and kissed her, searching for vital signs. She shook Jazmín to wake her, spoke to her, shouted at her. There was no reply. Her voice rang out in the night.

Then she saw Darío emerge from the car, like a ghost. He had opened the door on his side and half his body had fallen outside it. Like a snake, he dragged himself out of the car and seemed to be trying, in vain, to get further away. Cecilia felt an enormous hatred bursting out of her, with the same force as the crash. Gently she laid the girl down on the grass and went towards him as he kept struggling, fruitlessly, to move away from the car. She considered kicking him, stamping on his head, but she limited herself to crouching beside him and insulting him. Telling him he had killed his daughter. Their daughter. That it was his fault Jazmín was dead. Darío didn't see her, he seemed to be locked inside his own nightmare. However, when he heard Jazmín's name he let out a scream, like a howl, and summoned the energy to advance a few yards more. Cecilia was like the voice of a devil, condemning him to Hell for all eternity.

"Look at me, you bastard, you've killed our daughter," she said to him a hundred times and he raised his eyes, staring at her as though he really were seeing a terrifying vision. He wanted to speak and his voice came out as a howl, again, a bubbling of hiccups, a cry he couldn't release. Cecilia left him there and went back to Jazmín. She picked the girl up and there was a miracle: Jazmín coughed, or went into spasm. She didn't open her eyes or make any other gesture. She breathed. Very weakly, her lungs filled up and expelled the air.

With the girl in her arms, Cecilia started walking back along the deserted road. Five minutes later there was an explosion that lit up the sky. Behind Cecilia the bodies burned and she thought neither of her mother, her sister, nor even of her niece. She just wanted to carry her daughter as far as a hospital.

166

Cecilia had walked for nearly half an hour, perhaps more, when a truck pulled up alongside her. She climbed up into the cab. The driver offered to take her to the hospital in General Lavalle. He drove there as fast as he could. They met only two other cars on the road.

In the cab, Cecilia kept talking to Jazmín, to keep her alive. She gazed at her, hoping she would open her eyes. She stroked her hair and felt her daughter's warm skin. When they arrived at the hospital, the truck driver offered half-heartedly to accompany them inside, but Cecilia thanked him and went in alone. At the entrance to the hospital, she shouted for help. She cried as the medical staff hurried towards her. They took the little girl and carried her away. She followed them and waited outside the room where they tried to resuscitate Jazmín.

The miracle never arrived: Jazmín died an hour after she arrived at the hospital.

A doctor was talking to Cecilia, someone asked for the girl's details; someone else said she would need to reclaim the body from the morgue. She wasn't aware of them talking to her, she paid them no heed, gave them no answers. She thought of Jazmín, of the tantrum she had thrown before they got in the car because her favourite doll had been packed away in a suitcase. Cecilia wondered where that doll might be now.

No. She didn't want to see her dead daughter.

Without telling anyone, without speaking to any of the doctors and nurses looking after her, Cecilia went to the door of the hospital, walked out and kept on walking until she reached the main road.

She hitched her way back to La Lucila del Mar. There she got someone to lend her a phone and called her friend in Córdoba. She told her two things: that Jazmín had died, and that she needed to be picked up.

For the rest of the night and part of the morning she sat on the sand, scarcely moving. She had turned into a granite statue, sunk in the sand. Twelve hours after receiving the phone call, her friend Soledad found her there, looking at the sea.

During that time Cecilia had resolved to die with her daughter, that Darío would know nothing of her, nor of Jazmín. Let him writhe in Hell, never knowing what had happened to them both.

Jazmín's body was still in that provincial hospital. Jazmín was alive, in her. Since arriving in Córdoba, she had spent two or three hours every day meditating and watching her daughter playing, eating, crying, walking, laughing. If Cecilia wanted, she could see Jazmín alive, as she had been before the accident.

II

In his dream, Darío was on a crowded beach. Jazmín was playing in the sand with her friend Ivana, both of them laughing. But he didn't like having so many people around him and felt increasingly hemmed in, because he was seeing everything from the girls' viewpoint, as if he were crouching or lying down. Among the multitude of legs, Darío recognized Mariela, who was bending down to kiss him. He liked kissing her, but he didn't want to lose sight of his daughter. When he broke away from Mariela, though, only her daughter was there. He asked Ivana where Jazmín was and the girl laughed, as though this were a joke. He woke up, panicking, in the bedroom of the apartment they had rented in La Lucila del Mar. Cecilia was beside him and he asked her about Jazmín. With that hatred in her eyes that had become habitual, she replied: *Jazmín is dead.*

He woke up again. Now he was in his apartment in Caballito. In the loneliness and pain of aftermath.

Jazmín was dead.

Sitting on his bed, still sleep-dazed, Darío knew for the first time with absolute certainty that his daughter was no longer alive. Now everything was clear and luminous, because that was what death was like: it shone like the sun.

He lay down again, staring at the ceiling, fists clenched. He wanted to die, drowned by his own tears and snot. He cried aloud, and hearing himself cry made him as sad as the realization that his daughter was dead. Dead, dead, dead. Every time he repeated it, the memory of Jazmín as she was in the first dream grew more distant, confined now to her image in those photos he had kept. He got out of bed and looked for them: she was dead in the pictures, too. Jazmín was no longer alive anywhere.

How many hours did he stay sitting on the floor, surrounded by photos, without looking at anything, without thinking? He had to make a decision, but lacked the strength to draw any conclusions about his life. The book of Jazmín's stories was half complete. He could finish writing it, though he knew he wouldn't find her there, either. Writing didn't bring back things that were lost, nor even mitigate the pain. Writing was merely a passing distraction.

Sometime after dusk, his phone rang. It was Mariela, wondering if he would like to have dinner with them. She was making pizza. Darío didn't feel like talking, so he said yes without thinking much about it. He said he would drop round in an hour.

Then he wondered if he'd done the right thing. What did the invitation mean? Was it a continuation of his dream? He pictured himself kissing Mariela, then watching her daughter playing with her toys. And Jazmín? Jazmín was dead.

His mobile rang again. It was Verónica Rosenthal.

"Hello, Darío, I was wondering if you're going to be home tomorrow morning? I'm in Córdoba, but I'd like to drop by around eleven o'clock, if possible."

"Jazmín is dead."

"Hello – Darío?"

"Jazmín is dead, Verónica. I know it."

"How... how did you find out?"

"I don't know, but I'm sure."

There was silence at the other end of the line. Had Verónica reached the same conclusion as him?

"Is that why you wanted to see me? To tell me that?"

"Yes."

"How did you find out?"

"I'm in Córdoba, in San Javier. I've found Cecilia living here. Darío, these are things I should tell you in person."

"It doesn't make any difference."

"There is something important. Cecilia told me that she was able to get Jazmín out of the car. That she was still alive at that point, that she managed to get to the hospital in General Lavalle and that Jazmín died while the doctors were treating her."

Now he was the one to fall silent. The idea of Jazmín's death had blocked out the possibility of knowing more about what had happened. Verónica was supplying the details that made that death more painful.

"Darío – can you hear me?"

"Yes."

"Cecilia reacted strangely when she found out that Jazmín had died – she ran away from the hospital. She didn't give them her name, nor your daughter's, nor any information."

"What are you saying?"

"That she never claimed Jazmín's body."

"I don't understand."

"I've recently spoken to a doctor who works in forensics. He said that she's probably still in the morgue as an unidentified body."

"You're saying her body is in the morgue?"

"Yes, it must be in the hospital morgue."

"I'm going there."

"Listen, Darío, wait for me to come and we can go together."

"Thanks, Verónica, but I'll go on my own."

"I really don't think that's a good idea."

"I'll never be able to repay you for all you've done for me. For me and for Jazmín."

"Darío, let me go with you."

"Lucio was right about you."

"About me?"

"I understand why he fell in love with you. Thank you."

"Don't do this."

"Goodbye, Verónica."

Darío ended the call and switched off his phone. He put all the photos of Jazmín into a bag, along with the USB stick containing the digital images, documents he might need, some clothes for himself and some matching clothes for his daughter: her Disney princesses sweatshirt, her turquoise trousers and flowery sneakers. Some of her dolls, too. Unfortunately her favourite ones had been lost in the accident.

He left the house and headed for Retiro bus station, planning to take the first coach leaving for General Lavalle. It was a while before he realized he hadn't let Mariela know he wouldn't be going to her house. They'd never kiss. They wouldn't see each other again. None of that mattered to him.

In the coach, Darío thought that he should also go back to the law courts and to the police to see the people who had refused to investigate his daughter's disappearance. By rights he should insult them, hit them, do something to them. Her body had been lying minutes away from where they had parked their lazy backsides. What would the court secretary, who'd been so busy on his phone he didn't even pay attention to what Darío was telling him, say now? And that police chief who had looked at him as if he were mad? His daughter had not been burned to death, as everyone had claimed – her body was in a hospital morgue. If only he had the energy to revisit all those police and court officials. But he was exhausted and all meaning had gone out of things.

"I've come to claim a body that has been registered as unidentified," he told various people at the hospital who gradually, some with indifference and others with compassion, directed him to the right person in the hospital morgue.

An administrator asked him for the date Jazmín had been brought to the hospital. Could there really be so many children's corpses that they didn't remember one belonging to a three-year-old girl? He hoped to meet a doctor, someone who could tell him about Jazmín's last moments, but none of the people there had anything to do with clinical work. The doctor who had signed the death certificate was in charge of the emergency room. He might sign around a hundred death certificates a month. He probably didn't remember this case.

That was how the person who finally took Darío into a room to identify Jazmín explained it. The room was cold and smelled strange, disagreeable, as though bleach had not been enough to mask the smell of death.

The morgue assistant asked him to wait a few minutes and went to an adjoining room. Darío heard him manoeuvring different metallic compartments. Finally, he motioned Darío through. There was a gurney on which a small, covered shape lay. The employee lifted the shroud to allow identification to take place.

He could have said that it wasn't Jazmín. That waxen figure, with its deformed and lacerated face, the scorched hair, couldn't be and never could have been his daughter. She resembled her in the same way a bad portrait resembles its subject. He put out his hand and stroked her cold face. His fingers, more sensitive than his eyes, told a different story: this body had once been Jazmín's; he had held it, hugged it, kissed it. This body, which had grown so astonishingly in three years, had been the vessel for the daughter he loved and wept for, the little girl who had run through parks, who sometimes had fits of giggles, who sang lullabies to her dolls.

"Yes, that's my daughter."

The morgue assistant said he would have to do some paperwork, sign documents, get authorization, especially if Darío planned to remove the body to a different district. Darío said he would rather bury her in General Lavalle. The man recommended that he go to an undertaker who would take care of the formalities. There was one a few blocks from the hospital.

At Parisi Hermanos, the funeral home, Darío was served by a lady of about sixty called Rosa de Parisi, who listened attentively and told him not to worry, that they would handle everything and that the funeral could take place the next day in the cemetery. The woman suggested they retrieve the body then, before leaving for the cemetery. But Darío didn't want to leave Jazmín in that place any longer. He asked if they would let him stay with the coffin in a room at the funeral home; he would pay, of course.

The woman introduced him to her husband, Señor Parisi, who owned the business. Together they went to collect Jazmín's body in a private ambulance and brought it to the funeral home. Darío asked Señora Rosa to dress Jazmín in the clothes he had brought and to put her dolls in the coffin with her.

When everything was ready, they took him to the place where the coffin would remain until the following day. It was a large room, with scores of coffins lined up on both sides. This was where clients came to choose a casket in which to bury or cremate a deceased relation. Darío had been spared that moment in which the macabre and the commercial collide, Señora Rosa herself having made the decision to lay Jazmín in a little white coffin. Now that whiteness shone at the end of a room dominated by so many dark boxes.

Darío looked at his daughter, dressed in the clothes he had brought. Her hair had been oddly arranged, in a style quite different to the one Cecilia favoured. It was the first time he had thought of his ex-wife since Verónica had called him. Nothing she might be doing now interested him.

Señora Rosa told him that it would be better to close the coffin, and Darío consented. They had put a chair for him beside it and, a few hours later, Señora Rosa returned with a cup of tea and some cookies. She did the same at night. That was all Darío ate in twenty-four hours.

Apart from trips to the bathroom, he didn't move from Jazmín's side. It was a long day, a time to consider his life before and after the accident. There was no hope for him now of a tranquil and ordinary existence. The loss of Jazmín destroyed everything he had achieved, the family he had nurtured, the professional successes, the social bonds that protected him. What was there left to live for?

At some point his phone lit up. There were hundreds of missed calls from Verónica Rosenthal and from Mariela. Text messages, too. He skimmed through them, without paying attention to the details. He wrote back to Verónica, who sounded very concerned.

When they came to collect the coffin to take it to the cemetery, Darío had fallen asleep. There was no funeral procession, just the hearse that carried the coffin, himself, Parisi and an employee who also acted as driver.

Although it wasn't raining, it was cloudy and a cold, sharp wind was blowing. The cemetery was smaller than Chacarita in Buenos Aires, yet the rows of family mausoleums and funerary monuments seemed interminable. When they arrived at what was to be Jazmín's grave, the diggers were finishing preparing the plot and waiting for the small cortège. The coffin was light – three of them could have carried it – but one of the cemetery workers hurried over to help balance the two sides of the casket. The diggers arranged it in the pit, the undertakers withdrew a few steps and Darío was left alone to face the abyss of opened earth. He wanted to pray, but he couldn't remember a single one of the prayers he had learned in childhood. He wanted to speak to Jazmín, to give some last message to the body down there, but he couldn't do that either. He noticed that the white casket was already dirty from soil that had come loose and fallen onto it, and this observation made him cry.

A few yards away, a woman in her seventies was arranging flowers on a grave. She had watched the scene and now came to stand by Darío's side. The woman did remember how to pray and recited the Lord's prayer, which Darío, in the midst of his tears, tried to repeat. When she had finished, the woman bent down and threw a handful of earth into the grave. She told Darío to do the same, but he shook his head and walked away. The gravediggers began to cover the coffin with earth.

175

Whether the woman stayed beside the grave or went away immediately, Darío never knew, because he didn't turn back to look. Parisi helped him into the car and, when they had left the cemetery, asked where he would like to be dropped off. Darío asked them to take him to the bus station. He had decided to go to Santa Teresita.

IV

He knew the name – Lucía – remembered the surname – Marchesini – and knew that nearly three years ago she'd had a bar in Santa Teresita, near to the coast. It took him an hour's stroll through the empty streets of the seaside town to find the place. Rockamor, on Calle 35, just off Avenida Costanera, a few yards from the beach. An employee was mopping the sidewalk. The bar was closed but opening at seven o'clock. Darío asked if the owner was called Lucía Marchesini and the man said simply: "Sí."

He gave the man his name, although he wasn't sure Lucía would remember his surname. And she may have known so many Daríos in the intervening years that she wouldn't know which one was looking for her now.

The man asked him to wait – she'd be down soon. Apparently Lucía was there, on the first floor. Darío wondered what he would say to her. He hadn't given any thought to what, or how, he would tell her about recent events. He wasn't even sure what he was doing in that place, how she might react; perhaps they would simply have a coffee and then he'd feel obliged to leave. Darío had fallen into a chasm and hoped to catch a branch that could break, or stop, his fall. Lucía was the branch. His chance of not crashing into the bottom of the chasm was that fragile.

A woman appeared. Lucía. Old, loose jeans, a red pullover

wide enough to hide the shape of her body; her long curly hair was all that remained of the teenager who had taken off her clothes for Lucio and for him.

Lucía approached him with a sad smile and embraced him. "It feels good to know that you thought of me at such a difficult time," she said, to his surprise.

"You know about what happened to me?"

"Yes, yes. To you and to Lucio before you, poor thing. Murdered by gangsters."

"But how do you know about everything?"

"I read the article in *Nuestro Tiempo* that mentioned Lucio's death. There was something about the tone that made me think it wasn't simply a news report, that there was a message hidden in it. So I started buying *Nuestro Tiempo* every week. I know there's no such thing as coincidence. I knew that sooner or later that journalist was going to tell me something more. And it happened with you. I wanted so much to see you, for you to come to me."

"Why?"

"I don't know. Do we need to know?"

SECOND PART

9 *The Others*

I

Patricia Beltrán liked to recall that more than twenty years ago her friend Carlos Arroyo, foreign editor for the morning edition of *La Razón*, had turned down the chance to be editor or assistant editor of said newspaper with an excuse she found delightful: "I don't want to have to have lunch with Timerman."

The by then ancient Jacobo Timerman had been editor-in-chief of *La Razón*, which had abandoned its successful evening edition in favour of a disastrous morning one. Arroyo didn't want anyone making his life harder. The higher you go in a journalistic career, the further you get from journalism. Patricia had learned that lesson from Maestro Arroyo. She had always known that being an editor was a way to distance herself from the job she had loved for decades but which now left her cold.

But she wasn't ready to move even further from it. For that reason she had turned down an invitation to become *Nuestro Tiempo*'s new assistant editor. She, too, would waste no time lunching with Goicochea. Or with whoever replaced him, because rumours of change at the top were getting louder. The company – the owner of a small but profitable stable of publications – was frustrated because sales of *Nuestro Tiempo* were stagnant, if not actively falling, and they were contemplating major surgery. Meanwhile the editor-in-chief, desperately clutching at straws, experimented with changes and redundancies. Any journalist who left was replaced by one who was already there and who then took on double the workload, or by an intern.

Her decision to turn down the promotion obviously hadn't gone down well. Goicochea took it as a sign of conspiracy (was she biding her time in case there was a new editor-in-chief? Did she know something he didn't?) and the managing editor, Atilio Forte, and the other assistant editor, Álex Vilna, saw it as priggishness. The writers suspected that Patricia was thinking of going to a national newspaper. In any case, the post was filled immediately, since it was offered to the Entertainment editor, Elena Cardozo, a not very bright woman who regularly confused gossip with information, celebrity with entertainment and trends with culture.

Patricia Beltrán's section remained under suspicion, and her articles were gone over with a fine-tooth comb. Given these developments, it wasn't surprising that she was called to a meeting to discuss Verónica Rosenthal's article about a case of illegal adoption. Verónica stood accused of alarmism, lack of sources, sensationalism, of making absurd claims. The article was also criticized because it featured the same person who, the previous week, had demanded an investigation into the disappearance of his wife and daughter.

Vilna, the little shit, pointed out that these were the first articles Rosenthal had written for a long time and that she seemed to be out of practice. "We can't let our writers use the magazine for creative writing," he asserted.

"At least we can't accuse her of having a stake in some radio programme and using the magazine to flatter its sponsors."

Patricia's jibe was aimed squarely at Vilna, who had a couple of radio shows that were financed by insurance companies, foundations and several businesses whose owners were actively involved in the country's political life.

"If an article like that landed on my desk, I wouldn't publish it," said Elena Cardozo.

"Perhaps it was too long for you to read – although that's your obligation as editor," replied Patricia.

"I read it," put in Forte, "and I didn't think it was terrible. That's why it came out."

"Well, if you all wanted me to know you didn't like the piece, job done." Patricia got up to leave, but Vilna made her sit down again.

"There's something you should know: if your star reporter submits another article like this or continues with her lazy student lifestyle, we're going to have to let her go."

Patricia walked out of the newsroom, furious. More than anything, she was annoyed with herself. Putting animosity to one side, Vilna and Cardozo were partly right about Verónica's article. Patricia ought to have asked her to rewrite it, using more evidence. If she hadn't done that, it was because she had feared Verónica might revert to her journalistic mutism. The deputy editor role was no longer enough of a cover to keep the people upstairs off her back.

It wouldn't surprise her if they did fire Verónica. She was too much of a journalist for those people, who preferred articles written by the agents of vested interests. Most of the journalists working at *Nuestro Tiempo* – underpaid and often badly treated by the editor or his deputies – had jobs on the side: some sold advertising for their radio programmes or their spots on cable TV, others offered media coaching to business people and politicians, some were invited on trips abroad paid for by multinationals or foundations of dubious renown, and more than one directly received bribes from trade unionists, businesses and even the intelligence services. And the priority, for all these people, was that whoever was giving them money got special treatment in the magazine, that they were looked after, that nothing negative was ever published about them.

Verónica wasn't like them. Her job was her life, a quest for truth, a way to fight injustice. She didn't dream of being on TV or on the radio. She wasn't interested in writing copy for a public relations pamphlet. She did journalism. They weren't going to fire Verónica without firing Patricia first. She wouldn't permit it. At the end of the day, one of the best things about being an editor was having the power to protect your writers. If they wanted Verónica's head, they would have to cut hers off first. And nobody in this newsroom had the balls for that.

II

Her name was María Magdalena and, with a name like that, she was destined to be a nun. María Magdalena Cortez. Sister María in the Order of the Daughters of St Paul. Magui once she had abandoned the habit and gone to work in the plastics factory that belonged to her younger brother, Pablo Cortez. She liked to be called by both names: María Magdalena. At school, people used to mock her and say that she was always crying, like Mary Magdalene, yet she had learned to cry only on rare occasions. *Proceed as God, who never weeps / or Lucifer, who never prays.* She knew Almafuerte's poem by heart and often found herself reciting it. It was like praying.

Nobody had mocked her name at the convent, but many sisters envied her and others straight out detested her. They said, under their breath, behind her back, that such a name was a sign of pride. The Marcelas, the Susanas, the Lilianas couldn't bear to share their religious destiny with someone whose name was the same as the first woman to follow Christ. They all wanted to be like Mary Magdalene. Only she had the name, though.

Would she even have entered the Pauline order if her parents hadn't thought to name her after the young woman from Magdala? Yes, she was sure she would have taken the veil, because she had heard the call of Christ as a teenager.

But María Magdalena had another vocation too: journalism. It was Father Arnoldo who told her that there was a religious order dedicated to working with the press and broadcasters, dubbed the Media Nuns. She didn't want to be a cloistered nun, nor to work in a church-run soup kitchen. María Magdalena wanted to spread Christ's message through journalism, and to tackle the problems that led to people using soup kitchens in the first place. Her confessor told her about the Paulines, and María Magdalena couldn't imagine a more perfect match for her than this Order.

After consecrating herself to Christ she moved to the Pauline house in Calle Nazca. Her duties included cleaning, cooking and general upkeep in the Daughters' home. Even though she had never confessed this (not even to Father Arnoldo), it bothered her that members of the female branch of the Order of Saint Paul were called Daughters and the men were Brothers. It was as if the women were destined always to be children, while the men could have a fraternal relationship with Jesus.

Anyway, off she went to clean toilets and peel potatoes. It was a while before she could persuade the Provincial Superior to let her contribute to the magazine *Vida Cristiana*, the publication produced by the Order. The sister in charge of proofreading had fallen ill and the magazine planned to pay for an external editor on the following edition. María Magdalena convinced them of her superior knowledge of grammar and spelling. Besides, her services – unlike the external editor's – came for free. Proofreading an edition of *Vida Cristiana* was her first job in journalism.

After that came Church-related articles, covering activities organized by the parishes or Catholic associations, and reporting on the social life of the Christian Church in Buenos Aires, in the correct house style. Yet she wasn't satisfied: she didn't want to write a parish newsletter but a serious magazine. In a few years she progressed from contributor to lead writer, then managing editor and finally, thanks to the support of a new Provincial Superior and a retirement at the top, editor-in-chief of *Vida Cristiana*. It was the 1990s. Nobody was too worried about what a nun might get up to on a magazine, so she made the most of her freedom and a decent budget to put together a professional publication. First she got rid of all the parishioners who wanted to try their hand at journalism, then she started commissioning pieces from real journalists, initially ones who were known to be Catholic and then ones who were good at their job. She retained the social pages, with their surveys of Catholic institutions, as well as articles about worship, opinion pieces by priests and sermons. But alongside all that, articles started to appear about medical breakthroughs, community work (whether Christian or otherwise) in deprived neighbourhoods, and interviews with artists (including atheist artists) and with politicians and philosophers who weren't necessarily graduates of the Universidad Católica Autónoma.

María Magdalena was proud of her work. Her first days in the Order seemed as distant now as her devout adolescence. She was still profoundly a believer, but she no longer felt that faith was enough, as she had at the age of fifteen.

The Order didn't place many restrictions on her, so long as the magazine preserved the most confessional articles. And she wasn't on her own. She had managed to put together a team with the few nuns who could do more than clean or cook (and they were few) plus a couple of journalists who understood the ethos of the magazine: anything could be published if it respected the Church's ethical principles.

At the start of the new millennium, the Provincial Superior responsible for the Order, who had placed her trust in María Magdalena, died. A couple of Provincials came and went, and eventually a Chilean nun arrived who made her life impossible. If theirs had been a commercial proposition, rather than a magazine produced within a religious order, María Magdalena could have accused the new Provincial of harassment. Including sexual harassment. But she didn't do that; she simply told her confessor, who advised her to pray hard that the new head of the Order would change her behaviour.

Not only did this woman not alter in the slightest her disagreeable bearing, she began actively to involve herself in the running of the magazine. She was a bad person, but clever, too. First she marshalled the support of a few bishops, some important priests, the recalcitrant Catholic journalists María Magdalena had kept at arm's length. From all sides, her authority was undermined. Then María Magdalena made a risky move: she took the opportunity of a trip to Rome to speak to the Superior General leading the Order worldwide. She spoke honestly about what was happening in Buenos Aires, how she had put together a Christian magazine that reached large sectors of the population, with a particular interest in social issues, and how the Provincial had been harassing her (she didn't clarify what kind of harassment) and trying to turn the magazine into a publication that was purely confessional, with no concern for real people and much less for the needy. The sister listened to her attentively and said she would take matters into her own hands. María Magdalena left the meeting with a sense that things hadn't gone exactly as she had hoped. What if this Italian nun and the Chilean one were friends, accomplices or something else?

Her fears were confirmed when she arrived back in Buenos Aires to find that she had been removed from her position as editor. The Provincial Superior had brought in another Chilean nun to take the job. As she was now too old to be cleaning toilets, and in recognition of her intellectual work, María Magdalena was named convent librarian. The following week she left the convent. In silence.

She was nearly fifty years old and, even though she had contacts in the world of journalism (after all, lots of journalists had published their first articles in *Vida Cristiana* and now occupied important positions on other newspapers), she realized nobody would give her work. She would never stop being a nun in their eyes and would never be a journalist either.

With an inheritance from her parents she bought an apartment, and her brother Pablo gave her work in his small firm. María Magdalena had abandoned her vow of obedience, but not of chastity – if she had ever felt anything for anyone, she had hidden it so well that it was impossible for her not to be chaste at this stage in her life – nor of poverty. Her apartment evoked the simplicity of a Franciscan convent: she had only a few family photographs, a crucifix, a rosary blessed by Pope John Paul II and an image of Our Lady of Sorrows that had always moved her. She had no television, though she owned a battery-operated radio. María Magdalena's only vice was buying newspapers and general interest magazines. She liked to keep informed. One of the publications she bought regularly was *Nuestro Tiempo*, where one of the journalists was a woman whose first published articles had appeared in *Vida Cristiana*.

She read Rosenthal's article on illegal adoptions very carefully. One particular detail caught her eye: the implicated priest was called Eduardo.

Too much of a coincidence.

Shortly before that fateful trip to Rome, Ignacio Gómez Brest, a journalist on *Vida Cristiana*, had investigated a series of cases from the 1970s to the present day, in which children were adopted or given up through a Catholic institution called the Christian Home Movement. Gómez Brest was also a Catholic, from a traditional background, who had first-hand knowledge of similar cases. Intellectual integrity had motivated him to investigate a case involving people close to him. It had been a tough assignment, hard to substantiate, involving cast-iron pacts of silence and direct and circumstantial evidence. It would doubtless have yielded journalistic fruit, though, had it not been for two things: María Magdalena being dismissed from her position as editor, and the journalist – who was far advanced in his work – dying in a senseless traffic accident, knocked down by a car a block from his home.

Somewhere she must still have the article outline that Gómez Brest had sent her. She hadn't kept much material from *Vida Cristiana* and yet she had hung on to those pages for some reason, perhaps as a small homage to that Catholic journalist who had helped make *Vida Cristiana* a respected publication. Her papers were well ordered and, searching through them, she found what she was looking for. Father Eduardo, from the Order of the Most Holy Charity, advisor to the Christian Home Movement, was mentioned several times.

Should she get in touch with Verónica Rosenthal? Would she still be interested in the case? For the first time in ages,

María Magdalena felt that tingle that journalists experience when they know they're on to something.

III

He took off the violet skullcap and arranged it in its case. Next to that he laid the immaculately white archbishop's mantle. He kissed it, as he did all the different elements of his priestly attire after celebrating Mass. Archbishop Arturo Nogués locked the vestments and sacred ornaments away in the sacristy, then he went to the bathroom, looked at himself in the mirror and applied some aftershave. He repeated this action several times a day, enjoying the fresh feeling on his skin.

Leaving the cathedral by a side door, he walked towards the provincial government house, on the other side of the square. He had a meeting there with the governor to arrange the details of the More for Less campaign that would be launched in a few weeks. The governor was a crafty, irritable and cunning politician, licking your boots one day and sidelining you the next, negotiating on his own with other archbishops. Nogués had to get him to commit a significant chunk of money to promote the charitable campaign, with a sizeable donation for his own diocese thrown in. He wouldn't settle for less if the governor wanted to be in the front pew at the next Midnight Mass.

He walked unhurriedly through the square. The archbishop had lived here for more than forty years, and this space always felt like an extension of his own garden. He knew every person he passed. They all respected him, feared him, perhaps. There were even some who venerated him with an exaggerated zeal for the Christian faith, something that didn't entirely displease him. On one side of the square, in the shade of a hundred-year-old palo borracho tree, he found Luisito, the shoeshiner. Nogués walked over to Luis, who kissed his ring as the archbishop himself had taught him to do. He made the boy polish his shoes even though they were already shiny and without a speck of dust. Luis made them even shinier. The archbishop liked looking down on the teenager working diligently on his shoes. When Luisito had finished, he gave him a bigger note than usual and continued to the government house.

The politician was waiting for him there with two of his ministers, well-known Catholics and regular intermediaries in the dialogue between Church and provincial government. Nogués was pleased to see them. These two were more loyal to his ecclesiastical investiture than to the whims of that demagogic charlatan: they knew that politicians come and go but the Church remains.

This meeting was short and amicable. The governor seemed resigned to shelling out money, but he dressed up his resignation as fervent religiosity. Nogués despised men who confused faith and personal interest.

He returned to the bishop's palace with time to spare for lunch and then a siesta. He didn't anticipate his secretary upsetting his plans and his digestion.

The archbishop always had green soup for lunch in winter. He had the maid bring him a deep bowl, not too full, while he waited for the main course. It was after the soup and before the grilled pork fillet with pureed potato that Fernando Converti, his private secretary, appeared. They never lunched together – the archbishop liked to eat alone – and it was rare for Converti to interrupt him. It must be something important if he was prepared to brave the cleric's reproving glare.

Converti was holding a magazine: a copy of *Nuestro Tiempo*. He looked shaken. Opening the magazine, he placed it in front of the archbishop. Nogués helped himself to a bread roll, broke it in two and chewed a piece while casting an unworried eye over the item his secretary was showing him: an article on illegal adoption. He looked at the photos and read the headings and intro without finding anything that merited his attention.

"The article names Tonso as an intermediary in the adoption of children," said Converti, to clarify his concern.

"Tonso? No idea who he is."

"It names Father Eduardo."

"God bless him and keep him."

Luisa, the maid, watched the scene unfolding between the archbishop and his assistant, trying to decide whether she could bring in the main course. Judging that nothing too serious was going on, she brought out the pork to serve the archbishop.

"Something must be done," said Converti in a peremptory tone that irritated Nogués.

"Do you know how many bishops there have been in the history of this diocese? Eleven, in more than a hundred years. I'm as far from whatever this article says as I am from the first bishop of this province. There's a century between me and any calumny."

Nogués tried the meat: a bit overdone for his liking. He chewed slowly. He was counting on Converti having left before he swallowed this piece. But his secretary was still there.

"I spoke to Doctor Rossi, and he's worried too."

"Who else have you spoken to?"

"To Doctor Rossi, Herminia de García and Sister Ofelia."

"And they're all worried."

"Press is never a good thing. It wouldn't be the first time an article that seemed innocuous later snowballed out of control."

"What did Rossi say?"

"He's been able to stop various articles, but he didn't see this one coming. He says Tonso's to blame for not telling him."

"So Tonso knew about the article?"

"In the magazine there's a quote from him, denying everything."

Nogués would have eaten more meat, but he'd lost enthusiasm. He threw down his cutlery in annoyance. "Rossi thinks there could be consequences?"

"He's been looking into it, and his findings aren't very encouraging. For one thing, there's the girl's father, who seems to want to talk. And then the journalist who wrote this has a history of writing sensationalist articles with accusations and that kind of thing."

"And she's a Jew."

"That too."

The archbishop called Luisa and asked her to take his coffee up to his bedroom. At least his secretary wouldn't follow him there.

"Converti, do you remember the motto of the Crusades?"

His secretary considered this for a few seconds.

"*God wills it?*"

"Exactly, *Deus vult*. God wanted the liberation of the Holy Sepulchre, but he also wanted the faithful to take action. However much God wanted it, without the action of the crusaders, the Holy Sepulchre would have continued in the hands of the infidel." He left a short silence so that his secretary could absorb the lesson. "It's simple, Converti. God wills it. God has willed everything we've done and wants us to keep doing it. But we have to act too, as though we were on a crusade."

"So…?"

"Act. Do everything necessary for the will of God to be accomplished. Speak to Rossi again. He'll know what to do."

The archbishop stood. He flicked through the magazine. It struck him as vulgar, mundane, so far from his life, that the article on adoptions looked unworthy of his attention. He left the magazine on the table and went to his room.

IV

She walked into the kitchen and smelled meat grilling. Although Fabiana didn't like this way of preparing food, it was still a familiar aroma, typical of the food her mother used to cook when she was a little girl. There was some potato puree left in the saucepan. She took a spoon out of the cutlery drawer and ate it straight from the pot, even though it was cold. Her mother came in from the dining room and walked straight up to her, not to kiss her hello but to snatch away the saucepan.

"If you want to eat, use a plate. And warm it up."

Fabiana couldn't resist finishing off the puree. She always had and always would, so long as her mother kept serving pureed or mashed potatoes as a side dish.

Her mother put a steak on the grill. She always had her lunch after the archbishop had finished his.

Fabiana wasn't hungry, but she wanted a piece of fruit. There were apples on the counter, so she took one, rubbed it against her pullover and bit deeply into it. The apple's acidity was strangely satisfying; she had a sense of being in a safe place in that kitchen. Although perhaps that was an illusion. The bishop's palace had never been safe for her.

"What news?" she asked, as her mother made an espresso to take to Nogués.

"Converti's here. I think there's some problem."

Fabiana shrugged, indifferent. She no longer willed problems on the archbishop. It was three decades since her mother had started working with Nogués. Fabiana had been ten at the time and the memory of her father's death was still fresh. In all those years she had never seen the archbishop suffer a setback. At most, he got irritated when things didn't go exactly as he wanted.

Although Fabiana didn't live there any more, she often came back. She couldn't help it. People get habituated, even to the most atrocious things. Fabiana found she could operate comfortably in a kind of double life. She could move from the one in which she was a political activist, denouncing exploitative businessmen, pursuing human traffickers, fighting for the needy, to the one here: at the back end of the cathedral, the back end of faith, the back end of an existence she had always denied but which still carried on, in the same place, just like her mother's grilled steaks.

Her mother watched her fearfully. She was frightened of Fabiana getting into trouble, ending up dead in a gorge, which had been the fate of other girls. She would have liked her to marry, to have children. When her mother said this to her, in that pitiful tone Fabiana detested, she would reply: "I've already had a daughter." Then her mother would look away, take a cloth and wipe down the already spotless tablecloth and say nothing. She was always saying nothing.

As for relationships, for the last two years Fabiana had been with Pablo, an activist like her. He supported her in her activism, he listened to her; he was more affectionate than any other boyfriend she'd ever had. Men didn't last long with Fabiana. They dissolved into thin air. The idea of losing Pablo, though, was inconceivable. It would be like losing a leg or an eye.

The espresso was ready. Her mother quickly prepared a tray with a cup, sweetener and a glass of cold, still water.

"Leave it, I'll take it up."

"Are you sure?"

Fabiana hated her mother's expression of fear, innocence, complicity. Without answering, she took the tray and, as so often before, carried it through the dining room, library and private chapel to the room of Archbishop Nogués. She knocked on the door and he called her in. He was in a T-shirt and the high-waisted trousers he always wore.

"You?" said Nogués in a tone more quizzical than surprised.

"Is that a problem?"

"On the contrary."

The bishop sat down on the bed. She left the tray on an oak table on one side of it.

"Shall I go?" she asked in the same fearful, innocent, complicit tone she hated to hear herself use.

"Take off your clothes," said the archbishop.

The room was tidy and smelled of wood, of old and elegant furniture. Nobody cleaned a house better than her mother.

Fabiana took off her clothes.

V

Marcelo hadn't had a pet since childhood. As a boy he had owned dogs, birds, the odd cat. So his feelings were mixed when Verónica asked him to look after her dog for the first time. It wasn't that he was out of practice when it came to handling animals, but that he would have to persuade his wife. She had always been wary of doing favours for the girl on the second floor. Even so, Marcelo didn't hesitate.

"Don't you worry, you go off and I'll look after Chicha."

The little dog wasn't badly behaved, but she wasn't particularly good, either. Although she urinated on chair legs and on the cables of a power strip they had in the living room, she also liked playing with Manuel, their five-year-old son, and was never aggressive towards Luciana, the five-month-old. He just had to be quick to clean up the accidents before his wife spotted them, and to take the dog out for a walk with Manuel twice a day. It was the promise of getting their son out of the house that had secured his wife's grudging agreement.

Marcelo had known Verónica for more than seven years. They had both arrived at the building on the same day (he as the new doorman and she as a resident), and ever since then they had had a special relationship. He fantasized about her. How could it be otherwise with a woman who was tall, slim, sensual, funny and – the fatal clincher for him – fragile? Because he realized that behind the woman who got through boyfriends, lovers and affairs at a pace the neighbours found scandalous, there was, first and foremost, a girl who went looking for trouble and sometimes risked her life in the process. For years he had been there to watch out for her. He would never allow anyone to hurt her. It wasn't desire or romantic love that motivated him (he was a bit too close to forty to believe in anything like that) but a more complex sentiment, hard for him to define. His mission in life? He did still lust after her, at any rate, though he wasn't going to make any moves in that direction.

Verónica had told him that she needed to travel to Córdoba for a journalistic investigation and asked him if he could look after Chicha for a couple of days. Of course he could.

"You're my hero," she said, and he believed her. She sounded convincing.

Verónica handed over the dog, with lead, balanced food, bowls for food and water, a bed, a toy and a promise to bring Marcelo back a box of Cordoban cookies. He stood at the door to the building with all this kit, watching as the journalist, carrying a small backpack and wearing tight jeans and a leather jacket, climbed into a taxi.

That night he argued with his wife. Chicha had urinated against the leg of the marital bed and his wife had stepped in the puddle, barefoot. To make things worse, Marcelo had had a long day at work, fixing the plumbing in the kitchen of 4C. He hadn't been able to take the dog (or his son) out for a walk. His wife had threatened to abandon the crazy woman's bitch – her exact words – in the middle of Avenida Córdoba.

Marcelo was in no mood to argue. He might as well take the dog out. She could relieve herself on all the trees while he relieved himself of his wife's bad temper. He put on a heavy jacket and went out with Chicha.

There was almost no one in the street save for the odd hurried passer-by and a few cars. Marcelo walked two blocks away, then turned back towards the building after Chicha had smelled all the trees. Half a block away from home, she decided to crap. Marcelo took out a couple of paper towels and a bag. He squatted down, picked up the dog shit and put it in the bag. When he stood up, his knees hurt and he waited briefly, looking towards the building, gathering strength in his legs.

A car pulled up a few yards in front of him. Two men got out and went towards the entrance. They didn't call the intercom but let themselves in with a key. Nothing unusual in that, except that he didn't know them. They didn't live there.

Marcelo walked past the car and out of the corner of his eye saw that a driver was waiting in it. The dog strained at her lead towards the car, perhaps hoping to piss on its wheels, but he didn't let her, dragging her back to the building.

As they approached the door he decided to keep going, to walk inconspicuously to the next block and stay there for a few minutes. He squatted down again, as though to pick up more dog shit, and from this vantage point looked up towards Verónica's apartment. Someone had put on the living room light. The men were in there.

He thought of calling the police, but what if the men in the apartment *were* police? Should he confront them? And what would he do with the dog in the meantime – leave her out here tied to a tree? Absurd idea. He walked slowly along the sidewalk, crouched down to sort out Chicha's lead (damn joints hurting) and combed her fur with his fingers, to the surprise of the dog, who looked up at him with concern. The living room light went out then, and on came the bedroom light. Someone opened the door to the balcony and stepped outside, protected by the darkness. Marcelo couldn't see his face clearly. What had brought this person out onto the balcony? Was he searching the plant pots? The man stood back from the railing and looked upwards, then shook his head. Was that a sign to someone or an empty gesture? The man went back inside the apartment, closing the balcony door.

Marcelo walked to the corner of the block. From there he couldn't see much, but the intruders also couldn't see him watching. Three minutes later, the two men came out of the building and got back into the car, which immediately pulled away. Marcelo went into the building and up to his apartment on the top floor, legs shaking. Everyone at home was asleep. As he had done once before, he went to get his .22 pistol, a flashlight and the keys to Verónica's apartment. He was breathing heavily and tried to calm down, reminding himself that the men had gone, there was nothing to fear. Then he went quietly down the stairs, alert to the slightest noise. The life of the building was following its usual rhythm, marked out by the television sets in almost every living room. He reached the second floor and waited. No sound came from inside Verónica's apartment. Silently, he opened the door and switched on his flashlight. A tornado had passed through there: papers and books had been thrown about; the computer's central processing unit had been dismantled;

pictures had been taken off the walls and flung onto the floor. He went to the bedroom: the entire contents of the closet were scattered over the bed.

He reached for his phone and, with no thought for the late hour, called Verónica. It looked like the girl from 2A was in trouble again.

VI

The typical image of a hacker as lazy, dirty, fat, ill-shaven, a serial eater of pizza, accumulator of cans (soda, beer, energy drinks), onanist, anarchist, desperately enamoured of an international porn star, corresponded only in part to La Sombra. True, he was a little overweight, but he would prefer a schnitzel sandwich with the works to a pizza, and red wine to any other drink. He washed every day, was in a relationship (with a local porn star! Or rather, an ex-porn star) and there was nothing lazy about him. La Sombra worked longer hours than anyone (his two assistants included), and whatever time he didn't spend in front of the computer went on negotiating deals that sometimes sailed close to the wind. He tried to stay on the right side of the law, though, because he had no intention of ending up back in court. If he wasn't in prison it was thanks to Rosenthal and Associates, or rather, to their lawyer Federico Córdova, who had saved him *in extremis* from a sentence for computer fraud. Since then he had worked for the Rosenthal practice (which also sailed close to the wind with the advantage that they knew which way the wind was blowing), for Federico, and had even done the odd job for Doctor Rosenthal's youngest daughter.

He liked Federico and Doctor Rosenthal's daughter, above all because they always asked him to stick it to powerful types, usually complete bastards. And that was where his anarchist streak came out: he enjoyed working against those people. That was why he hesitated when Federico asked him to track Verónica Rosenthal. He didn't like to think Federico might be monitoring Verónica's phone. Federico had asked to be informed if Rosenthal's phone came into proximity with another one, which was in the name of a marketing firm.

Right now, for example, the Rosenthal girl was in Córdoba and had boarded a bus in Villa Dolores which, presumably, was bringing her to Buenos Aires. La Sombra could sleep easy, because that telephone was at least eight hours away from the other telephone he had to monitor.

He was thinking of heading to bed, perhaps of watching a box set, when his phone rang. It couldn't be. He looked at the number several times and couldn't believe it. For the first time in years, La Sombra felt disconcerted – he even considered not answering. No. He had to take this call. But how could she have found out that he was tracking her? What technology was she using? The phone was still ringing. Verónica Rosenthal wanted answers. He pressed *Accept* and said hello, trying to maintain a normal, unruffled tone.

"Sombra, tell me something: how can I stop someone monitoring my phone?"

10   *Meetings*

I

San Javier was behind her now. It seemed like a long time since she had sat watching the square, waiting with no guarantee of finding anything. Now, by contrast, everything was clear, and she felt the disquiet that comes when a story has a sad or unsettling ending. When she met Cecilia on the road to Champaquí and was invited to dinner, Verónica had fully expected to find Jazmín in that house, playing with a doll. If Cecilia was alive, it followed that the little girl would be, too.

The woman had led her to the back of the property, which opened onto an enormous garden crossed by a fast-flowing stream. Both women treated each other with suspicion. Verónica wondered if they were staying outside the house because Jazmín was having a siesta or watching cartoons on TV. They sat in wicker armchairs, facing one another. Verónica got straight to the point: she was there on behalf of Darío; he had asked her to find out where his daughter was.

"How is he?" Cecilia interrupted.

"Darío?"

"Yes."

In anguish, thanks to your fucked-up stunt, she thought of saying, but she contained herself and attempted a summary of everything she knew: the convalescence in hospital, the futile run of police stations and hospitals, the certainty that mother and daughter were both alive.

"He's wrong."

"In what respect?"

"Jazmín's dead."

The bitch is lying, Verónica thought. She should force her way into the house and look for Jazmín. She'd find her in front of a TV set, the girl would turn around to see her, Verónica would discover that Jazmín had the same expression as her adoptive father.

"So you survived and Darío did too, but Jazmín died?"

Cecilia smiled. It was the saddest smile in the world. "Unimaginable, right?"

During the hour that followed, Cecilia spoke without stopping. How many times had she gone over what happened that night on Route 11? Would she forever keep remembering the moment they told her Jazmín had died? Verónica pictured Cecilia carrying Jazmín's wounded body along the road, she saw her sitting in the truck on the way to the hospital, stroking her face. She could imagine Jazmín in her mother's exhausted arms. The woman must still feel the weight of her daughter's dead body in her lap.

By the end of the story, Verónica was crying. Cecilia's expression was sombre, but she remained poised. The mistrust was gone.

Verónica tried to compose herself. She found a tissue and blew her nose. She took off her glasses and rubbed her knuckles into her eyes.

"I'll tell Darío everything you've just told me."

"Do whatever you want."

Verónica thought of asking her why she had made these decisions – to cut herself off from the world, to conceal the truth from Darío, to hide away in this distant town – but before she could ask anything, Cecilia said: "You've got what you came for. Please leave now."

Seconds later, Verónica was back on the road to Champaquí. She needed to get away from there like someone needs to get rid of a bad memory. She walked down the road that led to Plaza San Javier and only stopped to catch her breath when she reached the giant, overflowing water tank. Verónica lit a cigarette. She had to speak to Darío, to tell him about her encounter with Cecilia, no details spared. But she should do this in person and not by telephone. The earliest opportunity would be tomorrow morning, as soon as she got back to Buenos Aires. She could go straight from Retiro station to his apartment.

She looked around her and saw no one: no cars, no bicycles, nobody walking. The place seemed desolate. Perhaps that was for the best: she could think without distractions, mull over everything Cecilia had told her.

There was one thing that bothered her: Cecilia's flight from the hospital, leaving Jazmín's body behind. What had happened to it? She called Renzi, and the pathologist answered with his usual professional calm. Verónica told him what had happened.

"What would have happened to Jazmín's body?"

"It must still be in the hospital morgue."

Renzi explained the procedure in cases where it hasn't been possible to establish a body's identity and next-of-kin. All around the country, morgues were full of unidentified bodies waiting for someone to claim them, he said.

She decided to ask Darío to wait for her the following morning at his apartment. Telling him the truth was going to be very hard. She also wanted to go with him to General Lavalle, so he didn't have to witness the sight of his daughter's corpse alone.

Their phone conversation had been freighted with anguish, and anguish builds a wall around those who suffer. Verónica and Darío were separated by a sense of insurmountable fear and helplessness. She hadn't expected him to say that he already knew Jazmín was dead. After the call she felt even worse.

Once more she gathered herself; she had to get back to the square, take a taxi to Villa Dolores then wait for her bus. Walk, concentrate on each step. She came to a couple of teahouses and was tempted to leave the main road and follow a track that led down towards a wood. She took this path and arrived at a river crossed by a small, rudimentary bridge. It must be the same river that ran through Cecilia's land. Verónica looked in her bag for a joint. She lit it and sat on the steps to the bridge. She needed a moment of calm, to understand what had happened.

Right from the start, Darío had been honest: he wanted her to help him find his daughter. Now they knew for sure that Jazmín was dead and where her body could be found, she no longer needed to be involved in Darío's life.

She remembered Lucio's naked body and Darío's scars. Weren't those marks like the pain that Lucio carried inside? Why had Darío mentioned Lucio before ending their call? Why had he said that he understood why Lucio had fallen in love with her? Lucio had never spoken of love to her. His silence on that matter had been a constant in their relationship. So, had Lucio told Darío he was in love with her? Did he frame it as a confession, a betrayal of his marriage vows? Another answer occurred to her, but she must be wrong: Lucio's declaration of love to Darío had been intended as a message that his cousin would one day be able to convey to Verónica. Closing her eyes, she saw Darío's wounds on Lucio's body. She put out her hands and caressed them while he (Lucio? Darío?) told her he loved her.

I I

This time Rodolfo Corso didn't ask him to come to a paddle court but to the Havanna bar on Córdoba and Rodríguez Peña. Corso was already there by the time Federico arrived a little before seven in the evening. The revelation that Juan García could be behind the trafficking of bodies obliged them to consider their next steps carefully. Corso had a large plastic glass in front of him, topped off with a transparent straw.

"Sorry for making you come to such a den of decadent modernity. We should have gone to the Peña grill, but it's still a bit early for sweetbreads."

"It's all good. What are you drinking?"

"Better not to ask."

Federico ordered a coffee and opened the folder he was carrying. "I've got part of Juan García's criminal record here. He's still got a case pending for money laundering," he said, and passed the folder to Corso.

"Thanks to an article I wrote and, *noblesse oblige*, thanks to the material the delectable Verónica Rosenthal passed to me at the time."

"And, just to close the circle, that information Verónica gave you was pulled together at Rosenthal and Associates. Back in the day."

"The investigation into money laundering is stuck in the court of Doctor Basavilbaso, and she's a judge who seems to look fondly on powerful people. There's nothing useful for us in this document. The guy doesn't live or have offices in the place where he was a few years ago."

Corso returned the folder to Federico, who was stirring sugar into his coffee. "So he's an invisible man again."

"I've been thinking," said Corso. "What if our friend Juan García has nothing to do with this? Perhaps Barbosa helped him because of other business interests they have in common. So far, all we know for sure is that the chief superintendent arranged for a truck to be bought by a fervent Catholic, an alcoholic who had the backing of Father Ignacio. Both Father Ignacio and the chief superintendent, good Christian souls that they are, belong to the same Action on Drug Addiction commission in the archdiocese of Buenos Aires. At some point or other, the archbishop of Buenos Aires saved Barbosa's skin, who had himself saved García's skin."

"Supposing Barbosa is involved in drug trafficking? Wouldn't that be a big enough market to warrant his full attention? Why also get involved in selling human skin, bones and babies' bodies?"

"There are two answers to that. First: if García is involved, such a diversification of businesses wouldn't surprise me. The guy's always liked to put his eggs in different baskets. Remember that in El Chaco he was involved in human trafficking. He's also dabbled in the train mafias and money laundering. It's a crime empire."

"And the second?"

"Barbosa's getting rid of inconvenient bodies by exporting them."

"Wouldn't it be easier to bury them or burn them?"

"Not necessarily. Plus this way he makes money."

"There's something I'm still not getting."

"There's something you haven't taken into account and which has been bothering me since you brought me in on this laborious but fascinating investigation. Why did the Prefecture go off and organize the detention of a truck carrying drugs, without alerting the federal police; in other words, Barbosa?"

"Perhaps the Prefecture knows about Barbosa's links with drug trafficking and was trying to trap him."

"I love how childlike your reasoning can be. Why didn't they find a truck full of drugs? I think the Prefecture knew there would be body parts, not drugs, in the truck. This was a message to Barbosa. We're putting the squeeze on your side hustle – your main business is next."

Corso asked for the bill and Federico quickly offered to pay. From the receipt he saw that Corso had had a dulce de leche frappé and a chocolate *alfajor*.

"I didn't pick this place by chance," Corso said, reading his mind. "Let's go, it's nearly time."

They left the cafe and walked down Avenida Rodríguez Peña towards the Palacio Pizzurno. Corso suggested they sit on a bench in the little square that offered a good view of the church opposite.

"The Iglesia del Carmen," said Corso, nodding towards the church. "That's where the diocesan Commission for Action on Drug Addiction meets. They're meeting there right now, and they'll be out soon."

"And what are you planning?"

"Don't panic. I'm no Verónica Rosenthal, I'm not going to jump on them shouting and swearing or anything like that. I just wanted to see them in the flesh. It's always something that intrigues me. What a criminal looks like, how they walk, how they breathe."

An imported car pulled up in front of the church.

"Here's the driver. They must be about to come out." Corso stood up. "Come on, let's get a bit closer."

They crossed the square as the members of the commission reached the main door. The Catholic activists advanced slowly, chatting, not paying attention to their surroundings. There were a few older women and some cautious-looking men. Behind them came a woman of about sixty, on the arm of Father Ignacio, and then Chief Superintendent Barbosa. The priest was a wizened-looking character who moved slowly. He still looked younger than his ninety years. Beside him, the chief superintendent had a martial bearing, even in civilian clothes. He kept pace with his elderly companion, but he looked like someone taking part in a slow-motion military parade.

Corso and Federico pretended to be reading the bulletin board at the entrance. None of the three Catholics seemed to notice them. They walked towards the car, where the woman kissed the men goodbye. Barbosa helped Father Ignacio into the car then turned to get in himself. The car pulled away and the remaining members of the party went off in different directions.

"We should have come by car so that we could follow them," said Corso.

"So what shall we do?"

"What shall we do? Head to the Peña grill – I'm paying."

III

It was dark by the time Verónica arrived at Villa Dolores. She couldn't face the station bar, but bought herself a snack and a bottle of water in the kiosk. Then she went to sit on one of the benches facing the departure bays, waiting patiently for the Chevallier coach that would take her to Buenos Aires. At some point she nodded off, hugging her backpack.

The sound of her ringtone woke her with a start. Seeing it was Marcelo, Verónica immediately thought something bad must have happened to Chicha. When Marcelo told her that two men had entered her home while he was walking the dog, she felt heart and body reuniting.

"They've turned the place upside down, Vero."

"Are you there now?"

"No, no."

"Please, don't go back into the apartment."

"Something else happened: the guy who was inside came out onto the balcony and I got the impression he was making a sign to another person, who must have been in one of the buildings opposite."

Verónica thought the same as Marcelo: they were watching her, perhaps waiting for her return. Clearly her article about illegal adoptions had touched a nerve. Had Tonso sent them, then? Or the priest from the church? One thing was clear: she couldn't go back to her apartment.

"Marcelo, three things. One: don't even think about going into my apartment, don't take that risk – even if you see that someone has gone in and is still there. Two: please will you keep Chicha a few more days? Three: thank you, Marce, thank you."

Verónica ended the call and stood up, glancing towards the far side of the terminal. It was in complete darkness. A couple in their twenties with backpacks sat down next to her. To her right was the bar, weakly lit. An elderly man arrived, on his own, then two middle-aged women. They all seemed to be waiting for the same coach. Verónica was wondering whether to go into the bar or wait where she was when the Chevallier coach arrived in the terminal, its sign reading RETIRO. She stood on Platform 4, waiting for it, and was the first to get on board.

They had gone into her apartment, ransacked her belongings, broken things. They were either looking for information or looking for her. Did they want to frighten her, kill her? Was this a warning or a lesson? Was someone still watching from the building opposite? After a year of writing no journalism worthy of the name, Verónica was certain this attack had been prompted by her piece on illegal adoptions. If she had learned anything, it was that those men wanted to do her harm.

Darío was in danger too. Verónica called to warn him, but his phone kept ringing with no answer. She tried several times more as the coach left Villa Dolores and joined the highway. No reply. Finally she sent him a text message: *Leave your apartment. Your life's in danger. Tonso or someone else is looking for us.* Minutes later Darío replied: *I left a couple of hours ago. En route to General Lavalle. Not going back to my place.*

Verónica thought of trying to call him again, but it was pointless. This exchange of messages felt like the death rattle of something already broken for ever. At least she knew he wouldn't be at home if the criminals went there.

When she was thirteen, her sister Leticia had taught Verónica to play poker, Truco and Tute, over one summer. They were spending the vacation in Punta del Este and Leticia, as a punishment for getting poor exam results in six subjects, wasn't allowed to go out in the evenings with her friends. To keep boredom at bay, she organized a nightly poker session with her sisters and two friends who came to the apartment. The five of them would play until dawn. It was during these late nights that Verónica first tried alcohol: Tía María, drunk straight from the bottle, which Verónica thought disgusting, but it was the only thing they could drink without their father – who kept a close eye on the whiskies, vodkas and gins in his bar – noticing. In the afternoons they would play Truco with Daniela and one of the friends. On rainy days they played Tute with their father. In every case they played for money – small change. Even though Verónica was a risk-taker, she knew that in some games it's better to pass and save your chips for

211

the next hand. That summer she went home with a haul of Uruguayan fifty centavo coins. Ever since then, whenever she had to make strategic decisions, she thought of them in terms of poker games. In writing about illegal adoptions she had played with her cards face up. She had made her opponents nervous and they were starting to show their hands. That was her small triumph in that round. They had attacked her and were waiting for her to double her stake, to expose herself, so her next move had to be smart. Not showing her hand until she had all the winning cards. Making herself invisible.

If there was another thing she had learned, it was that bringing others into the game put their lives at risk. She must distance herself not only from places but from people. Verónica couldn't take refuge with her sisters, or at Paula's apartment, or go into the newsroom. She was no longer prepared to let a loved one become the victim of people who were hunting her.

Verónica reclined the seat and tried to relax. A thought occurred to her: the mobile phone. If they were looking for her, it wouldn't be difficult to find her location from the tracker. It could be that the people trailing her already knew that she was in the province of Córdoba, on a coach, on her way to Buenos Aires. She needed help from someone who understood these things, so she called La Sombra, the hacker who sometimes worked for the Rosenthal practice. He was slow to pick up and, when he did speak, he sounded tense, annoyed even, so she got to the point.

"Sombra, tell me something: how can I stop someone monitoring my phone?"

La Sombra took a while to formulate a clear response, as though debating whether to help her or not. She probably should have offered him money, to pay for his time, but this hadn't occurred to her before and it would sound strange if she said it now. It turned out not to be necessary: La Sombra launched into a long, technical explanation about how mobile phones worked.

"Change your phone, both the handset and the number."

"And what do I do with this one?"

"You can turn it off, throw it through the bus window, or take out the battery and chip."

"OK."

Verónica was about to say thank you and end the call when La Sombra said something disconcerting:

"I shouldn't really get involved in these things. Do whatever you want, but I think you and Federico should talk."

"Me and Federico?"

"It would avoid the need to go around spying on each other."

"Who told you I tried to get into his computer? Have you been in mine? Did he ask you to?"

"You're both grown-ups. Stop playing silly computer games."

Verónica cut off, bewildered: she couldn't believe that La Sombra knew all about her problems with Federico. Clearly her ex had told him. He must be bad-mouthing her to everyone, even the hacker. If he was capable of making up stories about her spying on him, when all she had done was try to look at his email, he must still be hung up on her. On top of that, he had rudely left her birthday WhatsApp unanswered. He wanted to humiliate her; he wouldn't succeed. Anyway, she had more important problems to worry about now. She switched off the phone, put the chip in her backpack and left the disabled device, together with its battery, in the pocket of the seat in front of her.

She slept little and badly. The few times she did fall asleep she had tortuous dreams which, luckily, she forgot on arrival at Retiro bus station. There, Verónica hesitated between leaving the phone on the coach or throwing it away in the station, finally deciding on the second option. But would her trackers know that she was in Retiro? If she wanted them off her back, she would have to proceed carefully. As Verónica walked, she scanned the people around her, pretending to look in windows, stopping at the exit to light a cigarette, to see if anyone else stopped at the same time. She skirted the train terminals until spotting some stairs to the metro which she went down, ever alert to the people coming down behind her. A train arrived and she boarded the last compartment, then remained standing by the door until the last minute, when the signal announced the departure and she jumped back off again. Nobody followed her out, and the train departed. She felt pleased with herself and her cinematic education: the advantages of having watched *The French Connection*.

Back at street level, Verónica took the first passing bus. It was a 150 that crossed Retiro, Barrio Norte, the Congress area, then continued to the southern side of the city. She got off the bus in Calle Solís, just before Avenida Independencia. Talk about nowheresville, she thought, as someone more used to navigating the north of the capital. If she walked towards the east, she could get to San Telmo, a neighbourhood she knew better. There was something she liked about this area, though. Instead she went west, looking for a bar. When she found one with Wi-Fi, she went in, ordered a *café doble* and set to planning her life for the next few days. Verónica took her laptop out of the backpack and started searching for places to stay. She had in mind a hotel, or a guest house, but ended up searching hostels in San Cristóbal. To her surprise – she hadn't thought that tourists favoured the area – there were several to choose from. She picked one that looked pleasant and was only three blocks from the bar. So many old houses in Buenos Aires had been recycled and converted into hostels for young tourists. Verónica didn't know if she still belonged in that category (not the tourist one but the age group), but she liked turning up there with her backpack: it was like revisiting her twenties.

And she liked the house. It had five bedrooms, two with en suites, one of which was available. It was very expensive, but she took it all the same. How much would a good hotel cost, then? The bathroom had a beautiful old tub, although she couldn't see herself filling it up and throwing in bath salts. The last time she had been in a hostel like this was on her first trip to Europe.

If this sojourn was going to last a few days, Verónica would need to buy some things: underwear, a long-sleeved T-shirt, perhaps another top and some trousers. She went out for a walk and got as far as Avenida Entre Ríos without finding a single clothes store. There were several on the avenue itself, though, and, even if they weren't the kind of places she usually shopped, they would do for now. She didn't spend a long time browsing – just went for the basics and comfort. She also visited a pharmacy and bought tampons, shampoo and conditioner.

It was already about two in the afternoon. While Verónica was walking along Avenida Carlos Calvo on her way back to the hostel, she spotted a small tavern with an unusual feature: a public telephone just inside the door. She went into the Nuevo Lisboa and a Spanish lady offered her the dish of the day: roast chicken with potatoes. Verónica requested leg and thigh, left her things on the chair and went to use the telephone. First she called Leticia to say that her mobile phone had broken and she was going to be away for work for a few days. That in a few days she would call her, and that if Leticia needed to be in touch in the meantime she should email her. Then she called the newsroom and asked to speak to Patricia. She explained what had happened in her apartment while she was in Córdoba. That this was connected with her last article. Patricia asked if her trip to Córdoba had anything to do with her investigation into the missing little girl and her mother. Verónica said that it did, but followed up with a lie: she had found nothing interesting, it was a dead end.

"So what are you going to do? You can't go on hiding all the time."

"I have to find out more about how Tonso is connected to all this. And the last priest I interviewed."

"If you find something, we've got ourselves a nice cover feature. If not, we may be writing your obituary."

"Fine by me, so long as you don't let that idiot Vilna write it."

"You've got to be really careful."

"I'm no kamikaze."

"And I can't give you lots of days off with the excuse that you're working on a piece. They'll crucify me."

"Just give me a few days and I'll keep you posted."

Patricia broke off to speak to someone in the newsroom. A few seconds later her voice came back on the line: "Joaquín says that someone came here today who wanted to see you about your piece on the illegal adoptions."

"Could it have been someone from the gang that's hunting me?"

"Did they look like gangsters?" Patricia asked Joaquín. "He says no. The person left a name and phone number. It was a woman."

"I've got a pen and paper. Tell me."

"She's called María Magdalena Cortez. What a name. Do you know her?"

"It rings a bell. Wait, yes, I do know her. The nun!"

"The nun?"

"My first female editor."

"So I wasn't the first? You're full of surprises, Verónica."

IV

Small acts of vengeance. Once she had taken a sandal, another time a scarf; it could be a Bible, a missal, a rosary; it could also be an anti-ageing cream (because Nogués liked his beauty products) or toothpaste, his floss, anything he would miss, if only for a moment. Fabiana wasn't particularly interested in any of the things she took. She usually abandoned them somewhere. Nogués never mentioned them the next time they met. It was his way of depriving her of the pleasure of seeing him annoyed. She could never make him angry. "Eagles don't hunt flies," she heard him say once, in that complacent tone that gave her a deep desire to kill him.

She had never taken money from him. Not once. Even though he left his bulging wallet on the chest of drawers. She didn't take the money because she wasn't a whore. Even when she had needed cash, she didn't take it.

That day, Fabiana had stolen the copy of *Nuestro Tiempo* lying on the dining room table. She wasn't particularly interested in it, but she hadn't spotted anything else that caught her eye and didn't want to waste time looking. She needed to get away quickly.

The same thing always happened: Fabiana would arrive at the bishop's palace without thinking about it, without planning it. She wanted to be with her mother and chat to her. And yet she didn't stick to the kitchen, her mother's hideaway, but always ended up going to see Nogués. There were times when he simply looked at her, as if he didn't know her, and asked for nothing. Other times he groped her, as though she were a cow or a mare, then told her to leave. Every so often he asked her to take her clothes off, to suck him off, or to masturbate while he did the same. And there were times he fucked her, insulting her through gritted teeth, in that low murmur that contained a violence she had known so well for twenty-five years. Afterwards she would get away from there, disgusted, furious, yet with the reassuring feeling that at least he hadn't rejected her.

Nobody in the Party had any inkling of what she was doing with the archbishop. A few of them knew that her mother worked in the bishop's palace. That was all. Her fellow activists let it go. At the end of the day her mother was a worker, another woman exploited by a system of which the Catholic Church was a part and an accomplice. Fabiana didn't even want to imagine how much her *compañeros* in the Party would hate and despise her if they found out she was having sex with a priest. Even her worst nightmares didn't conjure up such a prospect.

Fabiana arrived at the committee meeting at which they were going to plan a demonstration over the next few days against human trafficking. A girl from Barrio Río Dulce had disappeared, and all the signs were that she had been kidnapped and prostituted in some other part of the country, perhaps even taken abroad illegally.

The meeting was attended by women from Las Muchas Otras (The Many Others), a feminist collective based in Córdoba that travelled the country denouncing trafficking and pimping in all its forms. And representing the Party, among others, were Rolando Belinsky, a historian who had led the occupation of the Alplex factory in 1975; Amanda González, a gynaecologist, president of the Centre for Medical Students at the Universidad Nacional de Santiago del Estero in the 1990s; and Pablo Belinsky, a carpenter and cabinetmaker, Rolando's son and Fabiana's partner. She had met Pablo shortly after becoming an activist more than a decade ago now, but they had only been together for two years.

Amanda was Fabiana's gynaecologist first, then her friend, and later her sister in arms. Rolando, an honest and uncompromising fighter, was the model to follow. Pablo represented the peace she needed every day. She never thought of her secret activity in the bishop's palace as having anything at all to do with this, her real life.

Of these three, Amanda was the only one who knew Fabiana had had a child. What she "knew" was a toned-down version of the truth: a teenage boyfriend had got Fabiana pregnant, her mother didn't want her to have an abortion, and she wasn't ready to look after a baby, as her own mother had done. The child was adopted by a couple, and Fabiana never knew anything more about her. Fabiana relayed this story to Amanda with the tone of someone who has already overcome any pain caused by the event. She had repeated this story to herself thousands of times to convince herself these were indeed the facts, but Fabiana never managed to forget the real details, even the smallest ones: the colour of the underwear she was wearing when the bishop touched her for the first time, the slap her mother gave her the day she dared to reveal what Nogués was doing when he was supposed to be giving her maths tuition, the fifteenth birthday she spent locked up in a country house so nobody would discover she was pregnant, giving birth in that same place, with a rough, rude midwife, the sweet smell of meconium the only time she ever changed her daughter's nappy, the baby crying when they took her away, her mother forbidding her to give the baby a name. The name she had given her daughter and which she never dared say aloud: Betina.

The women from Las Muchas Otras were proposing a sit-in in front of the city hall that Tuesday morning and calling on activists and people from the city to support their protest. They planned to denounce the mayor publicly, provincial police and the local judges, as well as the complicity of the governor, and to call in the press, including the Buenos Aires newspapers and TV channels.

Everybody agreed to this, and the meeting came to an end. The Cordobans left first, Amanda returned to her clinical work, Pablo went off to speak to his father. Fabiana waited for him, sitting on one of the uncomfortable white plastic chairs. To fill the time, she flicked through *Nuestro Tiempo*. She read the article on illegal adoptions. There weren't a lot of details, but a couple of priests from Buenos Aires were mentioned and there was an allusion to Misiones, a province Nogués visited more regularly than the others. Was that how her daughter's adoption had been organized? The article suggested there might be a network that supplied children to Catholic families and that priests were involved in it. What if Nogués were one of them? She saw a way to get at the archbishop, even at the risk of destroying her real life, the life she loved.

V

Now Verónica Rosenthal had a change of clothes and a new phone with a prepaid SIM card and she was back in her hostel room, listening to the voices of other guests. She heard a woman speaking Italian and couldn't help thinking of Petra, and then of Frida, the two girls she had met a few summers ago and who had been murdered. She still had Frida's MP3 player and took it everywhere with her. Verónica put the player on "Random Play" and the voice of Ornella Vanoni came on, singing "L'appuntamento". A song in Italian. It had to be a message. Verónica closed her eyes and thought of them both.

She fell asleep and woke up to the sound of a boy speaking English. It was time to get on with some work.

Verónica decided to go for a walk and call María Magdalena while she was out. She wondered what the nun from *Vida Cristiana* wanted. Verónica had written a few pieces, years ago, for that strange magazine, a publication that combined papal homilies with articles on macramé, investigations into police shootings or political corruption, and which even challenged the ecclesiastical leadership with articles about paedophilia in the Church.

"Hello, María Magdalena? It's Verónica Rosenthal. You left me a message at the *Nuestro Tiempo* office."

"Hello Verónica, how nice to hear from you."

It was strange to be talking to the woman who had been her boss when she was barely twenty years old. And a nun, to boot.

They arranged to meet in a bar in Boedo. Verónica felt safer knowing their meeting place was in the south of the city, as if the hitmen looking for her wouldn't dream of crossing Avenida Rivadavia.

When she arrived María Magdalena was already there waiting, looking very different from how Verónica remembered her, and not only because she had aged more than a decade. There was something else, perhaps her clothes, although those weren't so different from the light blue shirt and navy, below-the-knee skirt she used to wear and which had surprised Verónica, who thought all nuns wore habits. Now she had on a pink blouse under a neat violet jacket. Perhaps what was most striking was to find her not surrounded by papers and newspapers but nursing a glass of whisky.

They greeted each other with a kiss and Verónica guessed that María Magdalena was also evaluating the passage of time in her own appearance.

"What are you drinking?"

"A Vat 69. Don't bet on getting anything better."

Verónica ordered the same. She asked if María Magdalena had left the magazine.

"Actually, I was thrown out. I've thrown off my habit, too."

"So you're no longer…?"

"I'm no longer a Daughter of Saint Paul."

"And now you can get married if you want?"

María Magdalena burst out laughing. "Yes. If I wanted, I could get married, or just have a partner. What about you – are you married, do you have children?"

"No."

"So you haven't thrown off the singleton's habit."

María Magdalena took a copy of *Nuestro Tiempo* out of her bag and opened it at the page with Verónica's article. Then she brought out a folder containing printed sheets.

"Ignacio Gómez Brest. Have you heard of him? A great journalist and an excellent person. Four years ago, not long before they kicked me off the magazine, he was investigating a series of illegal adoptions in which the Christian Home Movement was involved. It's an association devoted to family matters. The nuns tend to work on maternity wards, they take part in the life of Catholic colleges, give support to married couples."

"Are they the people responsible for that work within the Catholic Church?"

"Not the only ones. All kinds of movements and religious orders support the Catholic family in religious and social matters. But the Christian Home Movement has always been an elitist group, connected to the Order of the Most Holy Charity, one of the oldest orders in Christendom. It was started in the twelfth century, during the Crusades. Its original mission was to rescue Christians held in Muslim captivity."

"And how did they rescue them?"

"Generally they paid a ransom, as with a kidnapping nowadays. According to chronicles written at the time, the Order became particularly powerful when its redemptive mission enabled the rescue of about a thousand minors who had set off on a Children's Crusade."

"A thousand children?"

"Even back then reports were more than likely prone to exaggeration. What is true is that the Order evolved from an organization rescuing captives to one specifically concerned with the plight of children at the hands of infidels, atheists and bad Christians. Their aim was to get those children into the care of good people. But that power to take children away from one set of people and reallocate them to another was ended by a bull issued by Pope Paul III in the sixteenth century. Obviously they kept doing it, though now more discreetly and with the rest of Catholicism looking the other way. The Order of the Most Holy Charity arrived in Argentina at the beginning of the 1900s and the Christian Home Movement was formed in the 1920s, although it wasn't until the 1930s that it became powerful. Both institutions expanded throughout the country. Homes were opened for abandoned children, religious houses and so on. Everyone knows that the Movement helps arrange the adoption of children at risk, but nobody condemns it."

"And that's where Gómez Brest comes in."

"Not yet. There are well-intentioned people in the Church who strongly believe that using religious intermediaries to facilitate the adoption of children is a very good thing. According to them, this is a positive solution to the problems of unwanted pregnancy, infant mortality and a childhood marked by deprivation. Ignacio Gómez Brest shared that view. But he suspected that the Movement was overstepping the mark. He investigated and found there was more to it than met the eye. It was something he was obsessed with for years, but then, a few months before his death, he dug up some new information.

"The majority of families who received babies via this method of adoption were Catholic. Gómez Brest was familiar with lots of couples who belonged to lay groups connected to the Church. Among them, he had identified at least three cases in which the Movement had facilitated the adoption. The children came from Misiones and Santiago del Estero, two provinces in which the Order of the Most Holy Charity has a base. One case concerned a woman of about forty whose father, on his deathbed, revealed that her adoption had been 'irregular'. Another involved a couple who, at the suggestion of their marriage guidance counsellor, decided to speak out about how they had come to adopt their two children. The third case was also initiated by the parents. Their son needed a bone marrow transplant, and it's always better to do that with a direct relative. The parents set about looking for the boy's biological family and came up against the Movement's refusal to provide any information. They hired private investigators, who managed to find the birth parents. It turned out that the mother had been pressured into giving up her newborn son for adoption. She was young, illiterate and unmarried. Sister Ofelia had threatened that she could go to prison for having a child outside wedlock – she convinced the girl that this was a crime and that she was going to Hell."

"Who is Sister Ofelia?"

"Ofelia Dorín, the current Provincial Superior of the Sisters of the Most Holy Charity, the female line of the Order."

"Do you know her? What kind of woman is she?"

"Yes, I know her. You could say she's one nun who hasn't been blessed with the milk of human kindness."

"In other words…"

"She's a vile piece of scum, may God forgive me. There are two other cases mentioned in the material Gómez Brest passed to me: one concerned a man looking for his brother. From what the mother, now deceased, said, she'd had a son in 1969. She was single and had an affair with a married man, who left her when he found out about the pregnancy. A young, well-intentioned nun, called Ofelia, persuaded her to give up the baby, using arguments similar to the ones she gave the illiterate girl: that she would go to Hell if she didn't give her son an orderly, Christian home. The woman persuaded herself this was the right course, then later regretted her decision. She never saw Sister Ofelia again, though the woman's younger son continued the search and tracked down the nun, Ofelia Dorín, who didn't deny organizing the adoption of his brother but didn't give any clue to his whereabouts either."

"The nun still remembered a case from 1969?"

"Sister Ofelia keeps a register of all these cases. She's proud of it. She even showed it to the man who was looking for his brother."

"What a twisted woman."

"Look. Most of us nuns talk to God. But there are some who believe God talks back. They're the dangerous ones.

"The last case we have is that of a girl from Santiago, also a single mother, who was pressured throughout her pregnancy by a nun – perhaps Sister Ofelia – to give up the baby for adoption. She refused, and was still refusing even in the delivery room. She was given a Caesarean under general anaesthetic, and when she came round they told her that the baby had died. I have the name of the obstetrician who delivered her, one Salvador Rossi, a member of the Association of Catholic

Doctors and an advisor to the Christian Home Movement. And another thing: the president of the Movement is Herminia Dorín, sister of Ofelia, a layperson married to a missionary businessman.

"Gómez Brest managed to show me an early draft of his article, and I've brought a copy for you. I went on a trip to Rome. When I came back, I'd been fired from the magazine and he'd been knocked down by a car."

"You think it could have been a murder, organized by Sister Ofelia?"

"This isn't the work of one crazed nun. There's a whole criminal network here. Look at the dates of the cases we have: 1969, 1973, 1979, 1984, 1992 and then the little girl you've investigated, Jazmín, which was about three years ago. We're looking at a group that has been active for more than forty years at least, regardless of what kind of government or Church doctrine prevailed."

"María Magdalena, I don't know how to thank you for all this."

"It's not only what's in Gómez Brest's drafts. I have more. I think I could get the people involved to restate their testimony, so that we could include it in a new article. And one last thing. The doctor I mentioned to you, Salvador Rossi, was married for years to a gynaecologist. They separated against his will. She was a Catholic doctor who ended up turning her life around and she hates her husband now. I think she'd be prepared to talk about him. And in one of those strange paradoxes of life, Doctor Laura Rivarola carried out an abortion on a sister from my order."

"Nuns get abortions?"

"Nuns don't get abortions. Architects don't get abortions. Housewives don't get abortions. Women get abortions. Any woman can find herself in that desperate and terrible situation."

Verónica was visibly shaken. María Magdalena smiled at her.

"That said, I think we need a couple of whiskies and something to eat."

They ordered another round of drinks and a board of cheese and salami. Verónica detected an excess of passion in María Magdalena. This didn't concern her, but it made her curious. Was the ex-nun helping her because she had unfinished business with the Church? Because she wanted justice?

"How can I help you?" Verónica asked.

"I want to be a journalist again. I want to write this article with you."

"I love that idea."

They raised their glasses and toasted with whisky.

11   *Crossed Lives*

I

After her meeting with María Magdalena, Verónica decided to walk back to the hostel. She needed to process the information the ex-editor of *Vida Cristiana* had supplied. They now had enough cases for an exposé revealing the workings of this group of powerful Catholics. She just needed to find the threads that linked the cases and establish who else had been involved, apart from Sister Ofelia, Father Eduardo and Tonso. Verónica enjoyed picturing the printer's face when he saw all the material they had gathered. Perhaps she should pay him a second visit.

Several times in their conversation, María Magdalena had thrown Verónica off her guard; she wasn't sure she liked that. And yet she was fascinated by the path the ex-nun had taken. Their conversation about adoptions hadn't left room to talk about anything else, and there was so much she wanted to ask – and also to tell. After all, in a long, long, distant past she had thought of becoming a rabbi. Not so different from becoming a nun.

A few blocks from the hostel she stopped at a bar. The place was nearly empty. She sat down next to a window and took out the papers María Magdalena had given her. Ignacio Gómez Brest had done a meticulous job. How much further might he have got if he hadn't been killed in that accident? There had already been obvious reasons for writing a thorough article, and now there was another: to be worthy of the groundwork laid by Gómez Brest. But what if María Magdalena had been in love with Gómez Brest? Perhaps the nun was enacting a variation of her own story with Lucio. Her mind was wandering. The result of two whiskies, no doubt, although Verónica didn't feel at all drunk – in fact, she decided to have a third. She asked the waiter for a JB Red Label, and made a mental note to buy a bottle of Jim Beam to keep in her room.

"I'm sorry, but I can't sell you alcohol."

Had the waiter actually said that? Was she drunk without realizing it? In a tone that sounded more aggressive than intended, she asked him why.

"Because we don't sell to under-eighteens."

Verónica looked at the waiter, who must have been a few years younger than her. He had short, black, dishevelled hair, tanned skin and was studiedly unshaven. He was a sexy bastard and he knew it, hence the impudent smile.

"Bring it without ice, please," she said, gravely.

When he came back with her order, Verónica moved the papers aside to make room on the table. The waiter, serving her, asked: "Are you studying for an exam?"

"I can't work out if you're bored because there are no customers, if you're a schmo who talks to everyone, or if you're trying to pick me up."

The waiter considered this. "All three."

"How old are you?"

"How old do you think?"

"Well, the last time I heard someone say that, it was a boy of fourteen."

"I'm twenty-two."

"OK, come back when you're of age," said Verónica and turned her attention back to the papers. The boy walked away, but she couldn't help feeling that he was still watching her. It didn't bother her. Why should she care if some guy found her attractive?

When she had finished the whisky, she called over the guy her friends would surely have dubbed "bar boy", to ask for the bill.

"At least tell me your name, if you're from round here, and if you have a boyfriend or a husband," said the waiter as he handed her the bill.

Verónica replied wearily: "I'm called Verónica and no, I'm not from the barrio. Or rather I am, but not for long."

"Snap. I'm not from here, either. I'm from Quilmes, but my destiny is Hollywood."

"Hollywood?"

"I study acting. As soon as I can I'm going there to try my luck. So you're married, right?"

"How did you know?"

"Because you didn't reply when I asked you and because you didn't want to tell me where you lived."

"Very sharp." Verónica stood up to leave.

"At least give me your phone number. I promise only to use WhatsApp, so your husband doesn't find out."

"My husband is terribly jealous, so I'd better not give you anything. I can always come and find you at the bar. And if you're not here, it'll be because you went to Hollywood, right?"

"My name is Harrison."

"What?"

"I'm called Harrison."

"Nobody can be called Harrison."

"My mother's crazy about Harrison Ford."

"OK, that makes sense. Goodbye then, Harrison."

And Verónica went happily off to her room. She felt as though, instead of whisky, she had drunk champagne.

II

Mala fariña was what Federico's Galician grandmother used to say whenever she mistrusted something, disliked someone or had a bad premonition. And all the way from his apartment to the courthouse on Avenida Comodoro Py, Federico found himself repeating his grandmother's "bad flour" mantra. Judge Tagliaferro, who was leading the trafficking case, had asked him to come to his office first thing. Federico planned to act the innocent. He had to get this right; put a foot wrong and he might soon find himself joining the beggars, round the corner at Retiro station.

As soon as he arrived, Tagliaferro called him in. The man was dressed and smelled like an Italian banker. He was even wearing an Armani suit.

"When are you going to close the pretrial proceedings?" he asked, straight out, as Federico's buttocks were about to make contact with the chair.

"I still have a few enquiries to make, Doctor Tagliaferro, but in a week I should —"

"Stop fucking about and pass me the case. We've got the driver who committed suicide. Go and find out where he stole the cadavers from. Doubtless from some cemetery. A nutjob."

"Possibly," said Federico, rather than explain that there were no signs of the body parts ever having been buried.

"What's all this about going with Judge Brunetti to meet the man who's supposed to have sold him the truck?"

"Doctor Brunetti was investigating financial irregularities in connection with that man, who coincidentally appears to have been responsible for providing the stolen vehicle."

"The alleged vendor was murdered by thieves last week. So leave him out of the case and let's not complicate the investigation."

Federico suppressed an urge to say that a prosecutor is not the judge's employee, much less his assistant. He left the courtroom with assurances that he would hand in his report a few days later, and with a promise to focus on other pending cases. It was surprising that Tagliaferro knew about the visit to Mosquito. Did he also know that Barbosa was in Federico's sights? Who was pressuring Tagliaferro to close the case? Clearly, if Federico wanted to carry on investigating he would have to keep it on the low. Apparently he couldn't count on the support of the judiciary. And without the safety net of Rosenthal and Associates it looked as though he was completely alone in this quagmire. Well, there was always Rodolfo Corso. He gave him a ring.

"Father Ignacio – is he still priest at the church in Liniers?"

"He's a Pastor Emeritus. He lives in a religious house owned by his Order. It's in Floresta."

"Give me the address. I'm going to pay him a visit as an officer of the law."

"Watch your back."

"Yeah, I know."

"Father Ignacio belongs to the Order of the Most Holy Charity. Did you know it's incredibly ancient – older than the Franciscans, the Templars and anyone else you might care to think of?"

"I bet it doesn't predate Benedict of Nursia."

"Who's that? Bah – never mind. What I'm trying to tell you is that these guys have survived everything. They're like *Highlander*, but in cassocks. Make a note of this address."

Federico decided to go straight to the religious house. Travelling there on a number 5 bus, it occurred to him that it might be a bad idea to introduce himself as an attorney. It was possible that the priest would tell Chief Superintendent Barbosa about their meeting, then the cop would move his pieces in such a way as to outmanoeuvre him. Suddenly he had an idea: he could pretend to be a lawyer acting for the widow of Hernández, the poor driver who had shot himself.

The Order of the Most Holy Charity comprised a school, a church and a convent, and occupied most of one block. Federico entered by an open side door and was greeted by an older man he judged to be about seventy. Federico introduced himself as Doctor Marcos Mendoza. He explained that he was representing the family of Sandro Hernández and that he was looking for Father Ignacio Salvi.

Five minutes later he was ushered down a series of silent corridors, finally arriving at a magnificent courtyard with palm trees and a variety of plants that seemed well adapted to the winter conditions. Sitting in the sun, in a rocking chair, was Father Ignacio. Opposite him, a wooden bench. Federico extended his hand. The priest's was soft and warm. Close up and sitting down, he didn't seem as old as he had when Federico saw him coming out of the Iglesia del Carmen.

"Forgive me for receiving you in the middle of the court-yard, but this is the time of day when I like to take the winter sun. Please sit down."

Federico explained the reason for his visit: "The widow of Hernández is convinced that her husband committed suicide because he was the victim of brainwashing. She holds the parish of San Félix responsible and you in particular, because you were his mentor."

"How ridiculous."

"Before taking the corresponding legal steps, I wanted to come and chat with you and gauge the degree to which my client's suspicions are accurate."

"Hernández was a great Catholic: devout, hospitable, generous to everyone."

"Yet he abandoned his family."

"That was always a difficult subject which we talked about under the protection of confession. As you will know, it's something I cannot speak about under any circumstances. Are you a Catholic, Doctor Mendoza?"

"Yes, of course. I wish I could be one who took Communion daily, but I only go to Mass on Sundays."

"It's important to make time. The Lord needs all of us."

"That's what Father Rodolfo, my confessor, always says. I'm sorry to press the point – you knew Hernández for many years, is that correct?"

"About thirty years, if memory serves."

"From when he started attending Alcoholics Anonymous meetings."

"Not exactly. Our group is similar to the AA, but its work is based on the wisdom and compassion of Christ. Hernández came to our help centre for victims of alcohol and left it reborn."

"And once he was cured of his addiction, he stopped attending the group."

"No, far from it. We believe that the true cure implies staying on at the recovery centre to help new arrivals."

"And what do you believe happened? Why did he commit suicide? And how did he come to be driving a truck containing parts of cadavers?"

Father Ignacio considered this, gently rocking his chair. He looked at him with dry, cold eyes. Federico shivered slightly.

"Ours is not to reason why, Doctor. The haughty pursuit of knowledge is a sin. Father Rodolfo can explain this to you in detail."

The priest was like granite – no way in, no way to crack him. He remained firm and courteous in his responses. At no point did he seem ruffled by the interrogation, but neither did he gave away any valuable information.

"Thank you, Father. I may be back to bother you. I hope it won't be necessary to take this all the way to court."

"In any case, the judgement awaiting us is God's."

As he walked away from the priest in his rocking chair, Federico breathed deeply, taking in the perfume of the waxed floors and polished mahogany. Before he reached the exit, a bulletin board caught his eye. There was the invitation to take part in help groups at different branches of the Most Holy Charity. He made a note of the group for alcoholics at the church of Liniers. They were holding a meeting that same evening at 7 p.m. He would go along as a hardened drinker. He hoped not to overplay the part.

III

Their protest had exceeded expectations. People in Santiago del Estero were becoming more aware of the urgent need to end the trafficking of women and hold those responsible to account. The sit-in organized by the Las Muchas Otras collective and by the Party had grown into a full-blown demonstration, with more than a thousand people and a strong showing from local and national media.

Fabiana took particular interest in the journalists from Buenos Aires. She noticed a woman of about thirty interviewing members of Las Muchas Otras, and heard her introduce herself as a journalist from the weekly magazine *Nuestro Tiempo*. Fabiana waited patiently for her to finish the interview. Once the journalist was on her own, she walked over to her.

"Are you from *Nuestro Tiempo* magazine?"

"Yes."

"You did the article on illegal adoption?"

The woman responded brusquely: "No, no. A colleague wrote that."

Fabiana was disappointed. Perhaps this journalist wouldn't be able to help her, after all.

"Ah, because I wanted to tell her something about the babies who were stolen."

"You can tell me. I'm María Vanini. I know the story. Obviously I've read my colleague's piece, and I also write about this sort of thing."

Fabiana felt that her own story was going to take a lot of explaining. She wasn't sure where to start to be sure of holding this journalist's attention. She decided to tell it straight, without showing any emotion, as though she were talking about someone else.

"When I was a teenager, my daughter was taken away and adopted without my consent."

The journalist suggested they go to a bar, so they went to the pizzeria that looked onto the square. From there you could see the cathedral and the bishop's palace. Every so often Fabiana glanced towards them. Not because she was frightened. On the contrary, she felt as though all this time she had been waiting to tell her story. The article she had read in *Nuestro Tiempo* was like a doorway she was ready to go through. Nothing was going to stop her. Not even herself.

They talked for nearly an hour. The journalist asked questions and watched her with a certain wariness. Or perhaps Fabiana was the one worrying that her evidence wouldn't stack up against a powerful priest like Nogués. Exhausted from so much talking, she paused. It crossed her mind to tell the woman how she had used the pain of her humiliation at the hands of Nogués to sustain herself all these years. She could tell her what it was like to live each day terrified that your secret will be discovered by your partner (the current one and previous ones), your friends, your fellow activists. As she was thinking of saying all this, the journalist confirmed what she had already suspected.

"I'm going to be honest: I think your story could make an article, but we've only got your testimony to go on. The archbishop could claim that you're lying, that you're not in your right mind, all kinds of things."

"Abusers always have alibis."

"Exactly."

"There's something else I have no evidence of: the archbishop often travels to Posadas, and sometimes I've heard him talk about children given up for adoption. I don't have any way to prove this, and I can't give you any specific details, but I promise you it's true. There may be other women who'll see your article then feel encouraged to speak out. Just as I was by the article in your magazine."

María Vanini agreed. She asked if she could take some photos from behind to accompany the article. Fabiana consented to that, so long as she couldn't be recognized. She couldn't help worrying that all of Santiago was going to find out it was her.

Fabiana said goodbye to the journalist and they agreed to touch base if more information were needed. She crossed the square and walked towards the bishop's palace. Her mother was there, ironing while she watched a gossip show. It was still a little while until teatime, which was when the archbishop finished his siesta.

Without saying anything to her mother – she never did, nor did her mother want to hear about or know the details – she went to the cleric's bedroom. She entered silently. Nogués was asleep, snoring gently. She stood and watched him. Seeing him asleep was like seeing him dead. His corpse would look like this, she thought. Like a defenceless old man, incapable of harming anyone. Fabiana took off her clothes and got into the bed. She began to caress him. The priest woke up. First he looked at her somewhat aggressively, which was not an unusual response in him, then he turned towards her, pinching her breasts until it hurt. She accepted the pain. As she climbed on top of him, she told herself this was the last time. She waited for the archbishop's final spasms before climbing off. Then she quickly got dressed.

"Why are you in such a hurry?"

"I need to go and see a friend."

"One of those Vietnamese who want a socialist country."

As she did up her jeans, Fabiana said: "I want you to know that today I spoke to a journalist from Buenos Aires and I told her everything: how you fucked me when I was a child, how you stole my daughter, how you steal the children of other women."

The archbishop got out of bed. He looked ridiculous wearing only his pyjama top, naked from the waist down.

"What are you saying?"

"Literally what I just said."

"You're crazy. No, you didn't say anything – you're just trying to annoy me. If you keep this up I won't have you back in the house."

"Think whatever you like."

"Even if you did say anything, who's going to believe a little slut like you?"

She smiled to herself and left the room. This time she took nothing, no magazine, rosary, crucifix or any other material thing, because she was taking something better: Nogués's peace of mind.

Fabiana left the bishop's palace knowing what she had to do. She would go and see her friend Amanda and get her to take her to a trusted hospital, quickly, while the archbishop's semen was still in her body. Then she would have to tell Pablo the truth. She didn't feel happy, but she was relieved.

After trying for ages, Verónica finally got Doctor Laura Rivarola on the phone. An overzealous secretary had been blocking her way, clearly suspicious of Verónica's intentions, but after much back and forth, a lot of questions and objections, Verónica managed to get an appointment with the doctor in two days' time, at her practice in Barrio Norte.

By now she had read the material gathered by Gómez Brest several times. She was sure the key to this case lay in the north-eastern provinces and at the Order of the Most Holy Charity. If María Magdalena and she could gather more evidence, they could put together an article denouncing the Order and perhaps also naming Tonso. María Magdalena had asked her for the printer's details because she wanted to go and visit him. Perhaps Tonso would prove more talkative with a Catholic than he had been with a Jew.

She had some time on her hands. She did something she shouldn't.

There are times, when harassing an ex, that you wonder how low you can go, without realizing you've already hit rock bottom: you're at the very gates of Hell. So it was with Verónica that afternoon.

For no particular reason, she had switched on her computer. She wasn't in the mood to read online newspapers, or peruse bizarre websites, or look up offers from hotels in places she had no intention of visiting in the years to come. Bored, she did something shameful: she entered the address of Federico's building into Google Street View. Verónica was past looking for scraps of his life on court-related websites, or on his fucking girlfriend's Facebook page. Now she let herself sink into the mire with no trace of dignity. What did she hope to find? An image of Federico waving at the Google camera? Obviously she didn't find that; nevertheless, she stayed on Street View, navigating around the blocks near his building. She identified the bar where Federico went nearly every morning for breakfast. On a whim, she opened the program that tested email passwords and typed in the bar's name. As suspected, the program returned an error. She tried the name of the street where the bar was: that didn't work either. One more go. She put in the street name and the number, all together. And to her amazement, the Gmail page opened up, like the door to Ali Baba's cave at the command of "Open sesame."

To start with Verónica didn't see anything, couldn't even read a line. She almost couldn't understand what was happening. It was as if she were looking at an advert imitating an open mailbox. Or as if she could only see the email headers. Then she clicked on one message at random and the whole thing appeared. It was from a colleague in the prosecutor's office asking for time off to make up for work he had done during a public holiday. She read it several times. Then she checked the sender, confirming that he had sent it to Federico Córdova. She was inside Federico's mailbox!

Verónica poured herself a glass of Jim Beam White Label she'd bought in the supermarket on Avenida San Juan. She told herself to calm down, but couldn't. She was terrified that a sign might pop up saying *Verónica, stop reading my emails.* Could he know that she was reading them? She needed to master the basics of internet snooping. It was tempting to call La Sombra and ask him. Too late for that, though. She had managed to get into Federico's emails. Now to read them.

First she put the other Verónica's name in the search box and up came her address (she hated that writing *Verón* brought up the other Verónica first, followed by a Sebastián Verón, with her in third place). She was curious to know if Verón

240

was the soccer star and what he might be writing to Federico about, but she wasn't here to mess around. She went straight to the girlfriend's emails.

There weren't as many as she might have expected; reading one of them, she realized that the couple communicated more via WhatsApp. Could she get into his WhatsApps too? She would need to find that out. All the same, the emails were telling. The little tart was sending him nude photos of herself. Verónica would never do anything like that. She urgently needed to talk to Paula about this. She saved the photos on her computer; she'd decide what to do with them later, whether to throw them away, upload them to an ex-girlfriend's porn site or whatever else came to mind when she had a cool head and could think rationally.

Verónica read every single one of the emails written by this semi-literate girl. How could such a moron end up working in public relations? Now she understood better all the cleavage-flaunting and the selfies she sent to Federico. And his drooling replies, the jerk-off.

The more she read, the less she understood how an intelligent, sensitive man like him could be with a woman like that. Were men really so obvious? You send them a photo of yourself squeezing your tits together and they rush you up the aisle? Admittedly, these two hadn't actually got married, but she wouldn't be surprised if they did.

And that wasn't all. She was amazed to see that Federico was still writing to Fernanda, his ex-girlfriend, who had been the receptionist at Rosenthal and Associates. And the bitch was leading him on. She wasn't sending him photos, but her emails were full of insinuations, like that she was alone in bed, missing him. And he replied *Same here!* (meaning that he missed her too, or that he was alone in bed?). There were various exchanges in this masturbatory tone. And all written while he was going out with the other Verónica. An idea flashed into her mind: should she write anonymously to the girlfriend to tell her that the shithead was still in touch with his ex?

Verónica went to the bathroom, splashed her face with cold water and looked in the mirror. Had her eyes always bulged so much, or had they just gone like that now?

Back to Federico's inbox. She found the welcome page to a porn website. That was intense, but there was worse to come.

Denial is a human instinct. You see something terrible right in front of you and deny it with all your being. Verónica had spotted her sister's name flash past while reading other emails and not paid it any attention. But now she was beginning to realize that there were too many emails from her sister Daniela to Federico. She read them and her heart crumpled like something plastic thrown in a fire. The fire of betrayal.

Daniela had written him long letters full of drivel (why would Federico be interested in the plot of *Toy Story 3*, which she had been to see with the children?), which had gradually become more intimate, revealing that her marriage to husband Sebastián was on the rocks. Daniela had never spoken to Verónica about any problem with her dimwit brother-in-law. And here was the little hypocrite telling Federico that she felt alone, that nobody listened to her (and she clarified *apart from you* before pathetically adding *hahahaha*), and that she ought to leave Sebastián but couldn't bring herself to hurt the children. And Federico, who wrote only two or three lines per email to his girlfriend, was lavishing long screeds on Verónica's sister. Like a Catholic priest, or a TV psychologist, he gave her advice, he assured her that we're all alone. He was getting poetic on her, son of a bitch!

Those two were going to end up screwing. No doubt about it.

Exhausted, devastated, she closed his inbox. But it was too late: Pandora's fucking box was open now, and all her secrets had escaped.

She called Paula (it could have been worse: she was sorely tempted to call Daniela and scream at her, or demand explanations, or do both at the same time). Paula was asleep.

"What are you doing asleep at this time of day?"

"I was up at six o'clock this morning and tomorrow I'll be up then too. My son is with his father. Give me one good reason why I shouldn't be asleep."

"I need to talk to you."

"Oh, Vero. Where are you calling from? Your number didn't come up."

"It's a long story. I'm not at home and I'm using a different phone. I've hacked into Federico's email account."

"From the sound of your voice I should be regretting giving you that nifty program."

"Far from it – it was the best thing that could have happened. Now I really know Federico. I've seen his true face."

"Vero, darling. Calm down."

"For one thing, he's a cheating bastard who's going out with a slut who takes nude pictures of herself while he carries on with my father's receptionist. As if that weren't enough for him, he's visiting a porn site, and I haven't even told you the worst."

"So far everything you've told me could apply to your life or mine, with some small variations."

"Daniela wants to get in his pants, and evidently the feeling's mutual."

"Oh my God, your sister's such a bitch!" shouted Paula, and seemed to wake up.

For the next twenty minutes they analysed the likelihood of a sexual encounter taking place between Daniela and

Federico. And, if Paula thought this unlikely to happen, whatever fantasies the two correspondents might have, she agreed that Verónica ought to talk to Daniela about it, although without admitting that she had read the emails.

"Listen, Vero, there are two things you must never, ever do: don't ever, ever go back into his mailbox, and don't ever, ever tell him what you did. Under any condition. Understood?"

V

Federico arrived at the church of San Félix a few minutes before the meeting of the alcoholics' group. First he had to register at an office next door to the church, where an elderly gentleman was greeting new members. Federico found himself fielding questions and explained that he handled admin for a small factory in Ciudadela, that he had taken part in other Alcoholics Anonymous groups and that he felt the need of God's support on his journey towards sobriety. The man wrote down his details (name, address, telephone number) on a notepad. Then he wrote his name in another book. The man asked if he could donate anything for the church and Federico gave him a twenty-peso note. This figure went down beside his name in the second notebook. Federico saw that the names of people attending each meeting were listed there, along with the sums they had donated.

The man showed him into a room at the back of the church, where a few people were already waiting. Presently, a man and woman of about fifty appeared. They were the group leaders and had the appearance of Old Testament catechists whose teaching on alcoholism might cite the drunkenness of Noah as its only professional source. The other participants arrived punctually and took their places in the bucket chairs that had been arranged in an irregular semicircle. Federico had to introduce himself and tell his story. He recited the dull backstory he had invented that afternoon: the alcoholic past, the recovery, the need for a connection with God through the Church so as not to fall into the temptation of drunkenness again.

While he talked, the others listened to him patiently but without much interest. They must have heard so many stories like this. Federico was hoping to stand out as little as possible, and he seemed to have achieved that. The others updated their own stories; there were a few triumphs, a lot of fears and doubts.

As one story followed another, Federico began to wonder if joining the group was really such a good strategy. It would be difficult to win the others' confidence in a short time, and he didn't know if he could keep up the lies in the longer term.

After the meeting everyone dispersed, but Federico lingered as long as possible so that he could observe the others. He noticed a group of four men gather on one side of the room and then go through a door leading into the church. Were they going to meet the priest? He thought of following them then decided it would be too risky, especially as one of the coordinators was watching him now and coming towards him. He had the appearance of a humanized monkey: overgrown and hairy, with a serious voice and a warmth that didn't seem put on.

"I hope you felt comfortable in the group."

The coordinator spoke earnestly to him about God's infinite love and Jesus's sacrifice, about Mary's example of courage and piety. Federico calculated that if he kept going to these meetings, in about a month the coordinator would move him to the group that went into the church. It was too much time, though, too risky.

He needed to walk and tire himself out. That would help him find clarity on what to do next. Close to Liniers train station, he felt the draw of an old-fashioned bar but resolved not to stop, to keep walking towards the city's south side. Federico crossed a bridge over the tracks of the Sarmiento line then turned onto Avenida Rivadavia, walking towards Flores. Close to the La Universal pizzeria, inspiration struck. He decided he could afford to take a break and went into the pizzeria. While they served him muscat and he waited for a plate of mozzarella with *fainá* flatbread, he called La Sombra.

"I need you to do some surveillance work and data analysis for me."

"That doesn't come cheap."

"But can you do it?"

"I've got some guys working for me who could help. You already know them: Nick and Bono."

"Not those two again," muttered Federico, remembering the hackers who had sold him some information he needed more than a year ago.

"They're brats, but they know their stuff. Tell me what you need, and I guarantee Nick and Bono will do a good job."

"They have to enter a church in Liniers undetected, find two books of minutes, or records, in an office there, photograph the pages of both books and analyse them."

"What is it you're looking for?"

"The books contain the names of all the people who attend a Catholic help group for alcoholics. One of the guys who went to that group committed suicide a few weeks ago. I need to find someone who used to go to those meetings but doesn't any more, someone who's angry at the Church."

"Send me an email with all the information laid out."

"Change of subject – has Rosenthal come close again to Rinaldi?"

"I wanted to talk to you about that. Verónica Rosenthal called me. She said she didn't want anyone tracking her

246

through her phone, so she threw it away and now I've lost the trail."

"Why didn't you let me know?"

"Because I can't believe that you're mutually stalking each other."

"Stalking? Mutually?"

"You're too old to play at being spies. Send me what I asked for and we'll get Nick and Bono onto this."

The mozzarella was going cold on his plate. Federico cut a piece off and, as he savoured Universal's flatbread, he tried to make sense of what La Sombra had told him about Verónica. And it made no sense.

VI

Verónica felt a little better after her chat with Paula. What would life be without her friend's age-old wisdom? It was like being friends with the Buddha, or Gandhi, or Paulo Coelho.

She picked up her jacket and walked out of the hostel. At the entrance she crossed paths with a blonde couple, German-looking.

Verónica headed for the bar. Few tables were taken and there was no sign of Harrison. She sat down at a table near the back, feeling somewhat deflated. But her spirits lifted when she spotted Harrison emerging from the kitchen. Seeing Verónica, he came towards her with a smile.

"Have you come looking for me?"

"Actually, I was looking for a toasted ham and cheese sandwich and a Coca-Cola."

"I thought you only drank whisky."

"You thought wrong."

Soon afterwards Harrison returned with her order. "Don't tell me this is your supper?"

"I'd be lying if I said it's tomorrow morning's breakfast."

"When was the last time you had proper home cooking?"

Verónica considered this and said: "Home-made things are overrated." As Harrison turned to leave, she quickly added: "What time do you knock off?"

"As soon as the last customers go, we're locking up. Want to wait for me?"

When she had finished, Verónica paid for the sandwich and Coke and went outside to smoke. After a few minutes, Harrison came out, in a change of clothes. They looked each other up and down for a few seconds.

"Do you want to come back to my place? I share it with a friend, but he won't be back until tomorrow."

Verónica pretended to think this over for a few seconds then, smiling, she said: "Sounds good. Let's go."

For a block they walked in silence then, as they reached the junction of Estados Unidos and Pichincha, Harrison lunged at her in a clumsy embrace. Verónica felt the boy's cock hard against her body. She liked the way he made his move so publicly, in the glare of a street lamp.

"Wait, wait! Let's get to your apartment first."

For the next five blocks they kept on kissing, finally arriving at a somewhat antiquated building that looked both under-maintained and under-cleaned. They took the elevator four floors up, Harrison grabbing her ass and pulling her against him.

The apartment, by contrast with the building, was clean and tidy. They went straight to the boy's room and were barely inside it before Harrison had whipped off his pullover and T-shirt and was left only in his jeans.

"You don't hang around, do you?"

He didn't answer, instead starting to take off her clothes. Verónica helped him undo the innumerable buttons on her jacket and shirt, the hooks on her bra. Her trousers quickly came off too, then she pulled off his jeans. Pushing him onto the bed, she contemplated his naked body: his muscles were so defined, he would have made the perfect subject for an anatomy class. She thought of saying that to him, but preferred to use her mouth on his cock. After sucking him for a while, watching him from that horizontal perspective, she stood up and took off her underwear. Harrison moved towards her and pulled her onto him. They kissed while he caressed her, penetrating her with his fingers.

"You've got condoms, right?"

He nodded, then paused. "Wait right there," he said, and left the room. Almost immediately he was back with a packet of condoms. Verónica didn't ask why they weren't in his room and where he had got them from.

She didn't want him to enter her yet, so she pressed the boy's head towards her navel, trusting he would know where to go from there. And she wasn't wrong. His clumsiness during the first kiss was forgotten in his skill at licking and sucking. Perhaps he had done this many times before; all the same, he seemed to have an innate flair for eating pussy. And yes, that was what she wanted. Perhaps she needed nothing else from life: just a guy who knew how to tongue a woman. If Harrison continued like this, she would come any minute. She thought of tugging his hair so that he would come up, penetrate her and they could finish together – but she reckoned she deserved this: to let him finish her with his fingers and tongue.

Eventually she had to ask him to stop, because he could have stayed down there all night. Harrison put on the condom and she observed him with the fascination she always felt watching men handle their dicks. The boy lifted her legs up onto his shoulders and gently entered her, but once he had reached as deep as he could, he moved firmly against her. She reached for her clitoris and rubbed it as he kept roughly pushing into her. He lasted long enough to give her a second orgasm.

"And there was I thinking you were a virgin," she said, teasing him, as they fell exhausted beside one another.

He turned towards her and smiled. "You're the tenth this month."

Verónica decided not to ask if he was being serious, but it would surprise her if the boy lacked for women: he had a spectacular body, incredible eyes, smelled good and fucked like a pro. Plus he was at an age when he could screw teenagers, veterans like herself, older women too.

"You like to work out, right?"

"I take care of myself. I'm an actor, and my body is my instrument."

"Woody Allen's an actor too, and he hasn't got pecs like these."

Harrison laughed. The boy might be a bit slow to think of a witty comeback, but she could take care of the jokes. So long as he kept quiet, kept smiling and kept tonguing her like he had just now, she could only call him perfect. Perhaps it was better to give the repartee a rest for the time being.

"Where did you go to get the condoms?"

"I got them from Tom, the guy I live with. He always has loads."

"Forward planning. Or does he have loads because he never gets to use them?"

"He gets through more than anyone."

During the night, Verónica drifted in a light, dream-filled doze, waking every now and then to Harrison's caresses. He didn't need much recovery time between one screw and the next. Verónica had more orgasms that night than she'd had in a whole year. And it wasn't even morning yet.

Finally Harrison went to sleep, breathing deeply and in an almost foetal position, as naked as she was. He looked like a little boy when sleeping, although his body definitely wasn't a boy's. Verónica was dying of thirst and, not wanting to wake Harrison, decided to get herself some water from the kitchen. She didn't want to leave the room naked, in case she bumped into Harrison's room-mate. So she put on her jeans and the cardigan, with a few buttons done up.

Outside the room, she saw a faint light coming from the kitchen. As she drew closer, Verónica realized Harrison's room-mate was there.

"Sorry – I'm a friend of Harrison's and I wanted to get some water."

The boy greeted her with a peck on the cheek. He must be used to Harrison taking girls to his room. Suppressing an urge to say *We used your condoms*, she opened the fridge and took out a bottle of soda. Tom found her a glass.

"I hope we didn't bother you."

"I've only just got back."

"Harrison said you work nights. And your name's Tom, right?"

"Tomás, Tom. What's your name?"

"Verónica."

Tom was tall and dark. He must have been a few years older than Harrison, perhaps twenty-seven or twenty-eight. He was wearing a tight black shirt and maroon trousers. The shirt was untucked and the light was dim, but she could still distinguish a fine ass and broad shoulders.

"Did he also tell you what I do?"

"Don't think so."

"I'm a rent boy."

"He didn't tell me then – I wouldn't have forgotten that."

The kettle was starting to boil.

"I'm making a tea. Would you like one?"

"I'd feel bad leaving Harrison."

"Tell him to come."

"He's asleep."

"Then have a cup of tea with me."

He made a good case, plus Verónica was intrigued to know what kind of person she was talking to. Was he gay? She never would have known.

Tom made tea for them both and they sat at the table in the kitchen. Verónica realized her cardigan had fewer buttons done up than was decent, but decided to leave it that way.

"Do you enjoy your work?"

"It has its moments. What do you do?"

"I'm a journalist, and that also has its moments."

"Ah, then you can write an article about me. The rent boy who left the suburbs one day to come to the city and sleep with men and women for money."

"Sounds interesting. I thought rent boys only slept with men."

"Men, women, couples. These aren't times for limiting your market."

"So what do you prefer?"

"For work, couples. For life, voluptuous brains."

Verónica took a gulp of tea that burned her insides, although the boy was even hotter than the tea. She was tempted to say: *I'm not wearing any underwear.* Or *Come to Harrison's room and I'll fuck you both.* But she wasn't brave enough. She readjusted her cardigan and washed her cup in the sink, aware of Tom's presence inches from her legs.

"Thanks, Tom. For the tea and the chat."

Back in the bedroom, she took off her clothes and settled into bed, putting an arm around Harrison, who was still asleep.

It was morning when they woke up, not long afterwards, and a hubbub rose from the street. Morning sex turned out not to be as good as the night before, perhaps because Verónica's mind was already on the long day ahead.

Harrison accompanied her down to the front door and she started walking back to the hostel. On the way she stopped for a double espresso and glanced at the morning's front pages. She couldn't stop yawning and considered going back to sleep for a few hours. But she hadn't been back in her room for two minutes when a call came through from María Magdalena.

"I've just arrived at Tonso's printworks. It's closed."

"How strange. Unless they work afternoons and evenings."

"Apparently it's closed due to a bereavement. I spoke to some of the neighbours. They said there was an attempted burglary last night. The people who broke in killed Tonso."

"Are you sure?"

"A hundred per cent. And these people weren't thieves, just as Gómez Brest's death wasn't the result of a road accident. They're trying to stop the investigation into the stolen babies."

Verónica thought about the doctor she was going to meet, about the testimonies María Magdalena was hoping to get from women and from couples who had adopted in this way and were now prepared to speak out about what had happened. All those people were at risk.

"We're going to have to hurry, before they kill other witnesses," Verónica said to María Magdalena.

"We've got to work fast and keep our wits about us if we don't want to be next."

12   *Blind Man's Buff*

I

There are weeks when everything is complicated. Contributors don't hand in their pieces on time, editors go off sick, breaking news necessitates a new layout, two pages on top of what you already had. Patricia Beltrán could grapple with all that and keep her composure. But then these unforeseen problems were rarely connected to a crisis in the magazine's management. At ten o'clock Adela, newsroom secretary and receptionist, called to let her know that there was going to be a meeting of editors at 13.30. Soon afterwards, the new editor of Entertainment confided that the editor-in-chief was leaving and a new one would be coming in. There were lots of names in play and no certainty about the outcome.

At 13.40 the magazine's senior staff were already gathered in the fishbowl, respective coffees in hand. Goicochea, the outgoing editor, wasn't there, and nobody had been able to reach him. A few minutes later the human resources manager, commercial director and representatives of ArgenMedia, the company that owned *Tiempo Nuevo*, made their entrance. They were brief.

"All connection between Goicochea and the company is severed, with immediate effect," said the commercial director. "The new editor-in-chief is Julio Tanatián, a journalist known to all of you. In addition to his new role, Tanatián will head up content management for the ArgenMedia group. There will also be some changes in the newsroom, but those will be announced in due course."

"Can you tell us why Goicochea's leaving?" asked the editor of World and Opinion.

"The company wanted a change of image, a shock to the system to jolt us out of the catatonic state in which the magazine currently finds itself. We need to boost sales, which means improving both content and the synergy of those who provide it."

"When does Tanatián start?" asked Elena Cardozo.

"Next week."

"But we still have to get this week's edition out," said the Entertainment editor anxiously.

"Of course. Atilio Forte will take charge of the news-room, together with the two deputy editors, Vilna and Elena Cardozo."

After the official announcements had been made, the editors remained in the meeting room. Their situation didn't seem much clearer than it had before. Surely management wasn't going to bring in extra staff; it was more likely they would shrink the newsroom. The editors agreed not to convey this grim prognosis to their teams because both writers and designers were capable of going on strike; then, if they wanted the next edition, they'd have to whistle for it. Forte, who hadn't once opened his mouth, left the room and went to the commercial director's office. Ten minutes later he emerged again and returned to the fishbowl.

"Guys, fuck this crap. I'm going to tell you what they don't want to say. They're bringing in a new managing editor, also a coordinating editor to keep an eye on all the section heads. The World section is going and will be merged with Politics in a new section called 'Today'. And they're cutting the staff: at least eight people, including journalists, photographers and designers. I'm out of here. Goodbye and good luck."

Nobody moved, apart from Forte, who stormed out with the energy of someone who has been unhappy for a long time and finally found the perfect pretext to leave. After a few seconds, everyone looked over at the editor of World and Opinion.

"I'll wait until they announce this officially and then see what I do," he said.

"How can they call a section 'Today'? If that's Tanatián's first bright idea, then we're off to a bad start," said the editor of Culture, concerned, as always, with the important things.

"What matters now," said Vilna, perhaps imagining himself managing editor if the company didn't end up bringing in someone new, "is to reassure the journalists. No word about more change being on the way."

"What shall we do with the schedule?" Patricia asked.

"Editorial meeting at three o'clock and let every editor put their section together as they see fit." Vilna seemed happy to take the lead on this.

Patricia walked back to her desk and noticed that the journalists, designers and photographers had gathered on one side of the newsroom. Meanwhile, the intern was still sitting in front of her computer. Patricia asked her what was going on.

"It's a meeting to discuss strike action. Because of the job losses and other changes that have been announced."

"But nothing's been announced."

The intern shrugged. A voice raised at the impromptu meeting carried across the newsroom.

"All those in favour of striking every day between 4 p.m. and 7 p.m., raise your hands."

Every hand went up. It was now 2.30 p.m. She had an hour and a half to work with the writers, certainly not enough time to put a whole issue together. Patricia decided to fill her section with articles that had been on the back burner. If it came to it, she herself could cobble together something off the wire.

Among the articles she had on hold was María Vanini's piece about the allegation against Archbishop Nogués. Patricia had some concerns about it. She didn't doubt the woman's testimony, which was backed up by her official complaint, but she would have liked to have had a statement from the archbishop, even if only to say that he wouldn't be making any statements. María was one of those journalists who only ever amplified one voice, the voice of the people she agreed with. Moreover, the victim had mentioned other cases and María had made no attempt to see if these checked out. Finally, it was Verónica's article that had started this line of investigation. If Patricia wasn't in favour of journalists reserving subjects for themselves, it was also true that María hadn't asked if her colleague had anything new to add to the article. The responsibility for this confused situation lay to a large degree with Verónica, who was staying away from the newsroom. If she had been there, she could have filled in the gaps in María's story, looked for other sources, tried to find more cases.

Now they would have to put the latest edition to bed with no editor-in-chief, no managing editor, two useless deputy editors and with section editors left to their own devices. Not the best conditions for producing a weekly magazine. Patricia decided to open the Society section with María's article. It would, at the very least, enrage an archbishop.

II

Bono and Nick asked Federico to meet them in the Sector Bar at the Spinetto shopping centre. At that time in the afternoon there was hardly anyone there, just a few teenagers nonchalantly playing pool with an air of skipping school. Federico arrived early, ordered a large coffee and sat down, looking towards the youths. He remembered his friends from the Centeno club, and how after school they used to go to the Coto supermarket on Avenida Gaona to play the Daytona arcade game. It was a long way to go, but they didn't care. He wondered where these kids were from.

Nick and Bono appeared, walking towards him from the pool table area. In his tight black shirt and periwinkle trousers, Nick looked like someone who had been at a techno rave. He must have been about six foot five, with red hair and tortoise-shell granny glasses. Bono, on the other hand, looked like someone taking part in a comics convention, with ripped jeans and a long-sleeved T-shirt emblazoned with the image of the Starship *Enterprise*. By no means small, he looked like a midget beside Nick. They noticed Federico and walked straight past him without saying hello. He watched as the pair continued towards the till, ordered two freshly squeezed orange juices and only then came over to his table. They nodded by way of greeting and sat down.

"Generally we don't like people to arrive before us." Nick spoke while Bono glanced around him, as though looking for microphones or paparazzi hiding behind the columns.

"I was running early," said Federico, apologetically, and instantly regretted his tone. Why should he have to give explanations to these two?

"You can give the money to Bono," said Nick, his way of informing Federico that payment would be required before they started talking.

Federico took out the wad of notes he had been carrying in his jacket's inside pocket and passed it to Bono, who put it away without counting it. Nick gulped down some juice, then said:

"We've got what you need. We looked into about two hundred different people over the last ten years. Depending on your requirements, we've got something that could be useful."

Now it was Bono's turn to suck lengthily on his straw, as if orange juice were a prerequisite for speech with these two.

"There was a third book, very old. Inside it, we found the name Sandro Hernández cropped up a lot. A woman's name also appeared frequently: Cristina Reggiardo. She started attending meetings in 2004. The donations are recorded when you arrive and hand over your money. Hernández's and Reggiardo's appear consecutively in the books, so it's logical to deduce that they arrived together. This woman stopped attending meetings two months before the truck driver's suicide."

"Cristina Reggiardo," Nick added, "was the wife of an ultra-nationalist activist murdered in the 1990s. Hernández belonged to the same group. And there's something else: this woman was knocked down by a car the week after Hernández died."

"Did she die?"

"No. She was accidentally saved by a cyclist who was crossing the junction without looking and got between her and the car. The cyclist died, the car drove off and she was left with injuries. She was taken to Penna hospital, which she left without being discharged the day after she was brought in."

"And you lost her at that point."

"No, no. It was tricky, but we located her in Colonia, Uruguay."

Nick took a USB drive out of his trouser pocket. "You'll find everything here: copies of the registers and Cristina Reggiardo's details."

Bono and Nick looked at him with an expression of *That's your lot, mate.* Federico got the message. He put away the USB drive, stood up and said goodbye, already planning to travel to Uruguay the next day.

She decided to wait until the last minute before telling Pablo. The journalist had been in touch to say that the magazine would come out the next day and in a few hours the whole town would know she was the archbishop's lover. Nobody would linger on the fact that the priest had been abusing her since she was too young even to think of seeing a man naked. Nobody would feel compassion for her lost daughter. Everyone's takeaway would be that she was sleeping with a priest. They would look at her with contempt and hatred. Not on account of what had happened for all those years, but because she had dared to speak up. Fabiana knew this, had always known it. If even her mother hadn't protected her when she was a child, what could she expect now from other people? She didn't care about the neighbours, though. What worried her was Pablo's reaction. Would he find a way to understand?

Amanda had shown a lot of solidarity: she had gone with Fabiana to the hospital, then she helped her find a lawyer from the Party who would plead her case against Nogués. Solidarity but not compassion. Perhaps Amanda's coolness was professional – doctors have to be prepared for cases like this, or worse – or perhaps she simply didn't want to appear weak in front of her. Fabiana wished her friend could have held her. Then she would have been able to cry.

She sat in a chair in the kitchen, waiting for Pablo. It felt like an appropriate space to talk about important things. By the time he arrived, it was nearly eight o'clock in the evening. That was the time he usually poured himself a Cinzano and threw himself into an armchair to surf the news and sports channels. Fabiana told him they needed to talk. Pablo made some joke about that phrase and, as though she hadn't heard him, Fabiana said: "When I was ten years old, Archbishop Nogués started abusing me…"

Fabiana told her story as though it had happened to somebody else. She didn't want to go into any unnecessary details, but she tried not to leave out any important episodes. Pablo listened to her in silence, his eyes full of confusion.

"When I went to live with the girls, I didn't go back to the bishop's palace for more than a year. It was like coming out of prison – I felt as though I was breathing fresh air for the first time. Then one day I went back there. I went back with the confidence of a recovered alcoholic who sits in front of a glass full of wine and thinks nothing will happen. I arrived with all this certainty, and it instantly collapsed. And I went back to him. I thought of killing myself, because I realized I was never going to get that man's hands off my body. I was going to die still feeling disgusted by his smell, his touch, his voice in my ear all the time. But I was scared to kill myself, I was a coward, and then I began to lie to myself. The person who spent time at Nogués's house was someone else, not the woman you know. I wasn't leading a double life, I had two distinct, irreconcilable lives, one that I hated and one that I loved, with you, with my friends, with the Party."

Fabiana waited, watching him. She was hoping for a response, but he hung his head and moved his foot, as though making a mark on an earth floor.

He asked her why she had done it. Whatever answers she gave couldn't diminish Pablo's anguish, his pain and anger. The conversation made no sense. Nothing they said could bring them closer now.

They sat in silence. Fabiana couldn't stop looking at him, searching his eyes. Finally Pablo asked her: "And why did you tell a magazine all this before telling me?"

261

"I couldn't talk about it to you. I couldn't, Pablo... I don't want to suffer any more. Help me."

"I don't know how."

"Please don't say that."

Pablo stood up and went towards the door, Fabiana following him with her gaze. He didn't turn around, simply left the house. She stared at his empty chair, then looked at the floor, as though she could read what he had tried to write with his foot. But there was nothing there.

IV

Laura Rivarola's gynaecology clinic was between the Recoleta and Barrio Norte neighbourhoods, a few blocks from where Verónica had grown up. She knew those doctors' offices, so similar to one another, in the old but cared-for buildings that had once been apartment blocks for the middle classes, before they fled to other neighbourhoods with more modern homes.

Verónica felt like a patient as she sat in a Regency chair the doctor must have inherited from a grandparent. There were two women ahead of her waiting to be seen. If Doctor Rivarola carried out abortions, she clearly didn't do it in this clinic. Verónica tried not to think of anything.

The minutes passed. Only one of the two waiting patients had entered the consultation room. Verónica started looking through old entertainment magazines. She imagined herself writing those pieces and thought there must be nothing more hellish than writing up celebrity gossip. Finally, after a fifty-minute wait, the secretary told her to go through.

Doctor Rivarola must have been between fifty-five and sixty years old; she wore bracelets, rings and a necklace of imitation pearls. She seemed neither sympathetic nor friendly, although she visibly softened at the mention of María Magdalena.

"I told the sister that I was prepared to tell you what I know, so long as my name doesn't appear anywhere."

Laura Rivarola told Verónica that she had been married to Salvador Rossi, a successful obstetrician ten years older than her who had three private clinics: in Santiago del Estero, in Posadas, and in Buenos Aires. The son and grandson of doctors, Rossi was also a fervent Catholic with a seat on the Association of Catholic Doctors' board of directors. His first clinic had opened in Posadas, where he and Rivarola lived at the time. Sister Ofelia Dorín, almost from the beginning, had acted as the institution's spiritual advisor. The nun persuaded Rossi that she could help him, through her supposedly pastoral work arranging the adoption of poor children by Christian families. When Ofelia found a poor girl in a risky situation, she had her attend the clinic with all the costs covered by the adoptive family. Laura Rivarola, who also worked there, gradually realized that these poor girls were being deceived: they were led to believe they would be able to keep their child, but after the birth they were told that the baby had died. A provincial judge, Doctor Mores, was responsible for the paperwork that signed the newborn over to its new family.

Not satisfied with that arrangement, the nun and the doctor started touring poor neighbourhoods under the guise of promoting good health, preventative medicine and primary care. In reality they were looking for single mothers or desperate couples with babies they could buy. They promised that the child would have a future if its parents let it go to another family. How could anyone who wanted a better life for their child refuse?

With the help of Sister Ofelia, the Order of the Most Holy Charity and the local archbishop, Arturo Nogués, Rossi opened a second clinic, in Santiago del Estero. In the new place they used the same tricks they had refined in Misiones, and soon they had built an adoption network spanning several provinces, taking in Corrientes, the north of Santa Fe and the south of El Chaco. At the same time, Rossi used his position at the Association of Catholic Doctors to become one of the most strident voices against the decriminalization of abortion. That stance recommended him to the advisory board of the Christian Home Movement, a front for illegal adoptions. In his consulting room Rossi had photos of himself with all the popes from the last forty years.

Rossi and she hadn't divorced, because he wouldn't admit that as an option in their lives. Nor did he want to separate. Laura had to leave him and threaten him with legal action if he pursued her. The Rivarola family was also powerful in Misiones and had political connections in Buenos Aires, so Rossi couldn't act with his usual impunity when it came to his wife. Finally, they thrashed out an agreement: they would share custody of the children, make a fair division of assets, and she would stay out of all of Rossi's medical projects.

"How many children do you have?"

"Three." Laura paused for a moment, then, looking directly at Verónica, added: "They're adopted. We couldn't have children, so I used my husband's services. In all three cases I took particular trouble to meet the families, to be sure my children weren't the fruit of theft or deceit. All three are grown up now, and they know about their origins."

"Doctor, I promise to protect you as a source. But are you aware your testimony would be vital for any prosecution?"

"I'm old enough to have seen things I could never even have imagined. I'm not scared of my children's father. If they send him to prison, I won't do anything to try to save him. And if it's necessary for me to give evidence, I'm prepared to do that."

"You said that there were three clinics, but you've only told me about two."

"I haven't told you anything about the one in Buenos Aires. I want you to understand that what I'm about to reveal isn't motivated by madness or resentment towards Rossi. These aren't inventions but things that really happened and that are still happening today."

"I've never doubted that."

"Nevertheless, what I'm about to tell you will make you doubt my credibility."

Rivarola brought over two glasses of cold water and took a long drink from hers before continuing with her account.

At the time Rossi opened his clinic in Buenos Aires, she said, they hadn't yet separated. Perhaps she would have continued in the marriage, unhappy as it was, if she hadn't discovered what was going on in that clinic. Although "discover" wasn't the most appropriate word here, because much of what she learned came directly from Rossi, a man who found it hard not to share everything with his wife, even the most terrible things.

The clinic was in Floresta, on the same block as the convent, school and church of the Most Holy Charity. In fact, the religious order had been buying up all the properties in that block.

This second clinic took a few years – and a lot of money – to build. It wasn't the same building a clinic in Buenos Aires as it was in Santiago del Estero. The Order of the Most Holy Charity or the bishop of a city in the interior wouldn't have had the means to fund such a project. Sister Ofelia Dorín had family and political contacts who financed the building work and the fitting-out of the clinic. They didn't need the Buenos Aires clinic to handle illegal adoptions. There were already more than enough babies in the provinces, and no compulsion to search the poor neighbourhoods of Buenos Aires. But in a few cases it was necessary to uproot the future mothers during their pregnancies, otherwise they might change their minds under pressure from their families. These girls were brought to Buenos Aires and taken to live in the convent of the Sisters of the Most Holy Charity. The nuns were doing good work, because otherwise these girls would have aborted. They took satisfaction in this worldly mission.

However, arranging adoptions was not the Buenos Aires clinic's chief activity.

Rossi had a partner who was not listed as such but who used the clinic for his own ends. Most likely Rossi wouldn't have asked too many questions when a Misiones businessman said he was going to connect him with a very important person from Buenos Aires. This person had links to the underworld and used the clinic to treat his hitmen, his injured goons or the mules who brought in drugs and arrived, in many cases, on the brink of death.

Many of them did die.

The corpses weren't buried or cremated. They were cut up, like animals in a slaughterhouse. And they were sold. Not in Argentina – the human parts were illegally taken out of the country: legs, arms, bones, skin, perhaps even organs. And if any woman lost her child during the birth or miscarried while pregnant, that little body was sent along too.

This might all sound incredible, but she wasn't mad, or embittered, or imagining things. Even as they spoke, bodies were probably being cut up in the clinic of the Most Holy Charity.

V

Federico contemplated the River Plate with a certain nostalgia as he stretched out in his comfortable seat on the Buquebus ferry. He had thought of asking Rodolfo Corso to go with him to interview Cristina Reggiardo, the woman who had supposedly been close to Sandro Hernández, but in the end he decided to travel alone. Nick and Bono had done a good job: thanks to them, Federico had the address at which this woman was now living.

This was one of the fast Buquebus services. He would have liked to go on the *Eladia Isabel*, which took three hours to cross the river and had that old-world feel he found so attractive. He might not have said anything to Corso, but he would certainly have asked Verónica Rosenthal along if they hadn't been so distant, and if she were helping him with this investigation. They could have spent the day together in Uruguay, enjoying the local food and perhaps checking into some hotel for a quickie, like they had in Tucumán. Enough. Federico couldn't permit himself this nostalgia. He had to remember how unpredictable Verónica was, in both her feelings and her reactions. That was why they had fallen out. And he wasn't someone who enjoyed riding an emotional roller coaster.

A phone call from Rodolfo Corso took him away from these amorous reflections. Evidently the man had something urgent to relay.

"Even the best hunter can miss a hare, which isn't to say I consider myself the best, or that either of us is trying to hunt a poor mammal with the appearance of a large rat. Ever since I found out that both Father Ignacio and Chief Superintendent Barbosa are members of the devout Commission for Action on Addiction, in the worthy archdiocese of Buenos Aires, I've perused the list of members of said commission several times. I didn't find anything suspect, just well-intentioned Catholic folk united in a desire to send potheads to Hell. Among the members there's an elderly woman, I'm tempted to call her a bitch, called Herminia de García. Not a surname that tends to stand out, and it wouldn't have rung alarm bells with me if not for the fact that we're dealing with Juan García, alias the Invisible Man. And yes, my dear Córdova, for thirty-eight years Doña Herminia has been the wife of García. See how the circle is starting to close in on itself?"

Federico called La Sombra from the boat. He asked him to look into possible links between the members of the Catholic commission, especially between Herminia de García, the priest and the chief superintendent. Perhaps there would be another place where all three coincided.

Reggiardo's house was quite close to the Buquebus terminal, a little over a mile, according to Google Maps. Federico decided to go there on foot.

For nearly half an hour he walked through the less touristy part of Colonia. No elegant cobbled streets here, no historic buildings. It was a grim patch of garages, rudimentary housing and stray dogs. The house where his subject lived was modest. On either side of the building was bare earth that aspired to be a garden but looked more like a vacant lot. There was no bell, so Federico clapped his hands to get attention. A woman's voice, from inside the house, asked him what he wanted.

"I'm looking for Cristina Reggiardo. Is that you?"

There was silence on the other side of the door. Federico waited for the sound of a key opening the door, but it never came. Instead, he heard the whine of a creaky back door. Glancing down the side of the house, Federico saw a woman hurrying towards the wire fence that separated her property from the one behind it.

"Señora… Cristina!" Federico shouted.

The woman ignored him. Now she had climbed over the fence and started to run. Without hesitation, Federico went after her. He stepped over a low wall, hoping that would be the biggest obstacle he was going to encounter, then ran the length of the house, came to the back part and crossed the fence between the two adjoining properties. Federico saw the woman emerging into the next street and headed in the same direction, without paying any attention to a dog that had woken from its siesta and started barking in his direction. It was a medium-sized dog, part German shepherd, part stray. Before Federico could reach the sidewalk, the dog had caught up and lunged at his leg. His jeans were no match for the dog's canines, which he felt sinking into his flesh. He swore, kicked the quasi-Alsatian and kept running. This time the dog didn't follow. Federico's leg throbbed and he could feel the wound bleeding. Cristina was about half a block ahead. Worse still, the boat shoes he was wearing weren't made for running. A few locals watched the chase impassively, as though this kind of thing often happened. At the next block the woman turned right and Federico feared he would lose sight of her, but that didn't happen. Instead Cristina carried on running then ducked into a house just before the next corner. Federico followed her to the back of the property. He could hear a woman yelling someone's name: Wilson. From the sound of her voice, she was terrified. Federico reached the back yard and, with his remaining breath, tried to explain to her who he was.

"Cristina, please don't be scared. I'm looking for you because of Sandro Hernández. I'm —"

Federico never finished the sentence, because suddenly he felt a blow to his neck powerful enough to knock him to the ground. He attempted to get up, but rolling onto his side earned him a kick to the kidneys that made him howl. The woman shouted: "Kill him!"

He looked back at the person who had hit him. A tall man, powerfully built and enormous from his perspective on the ground, was pointing a gun at him, eyes full of hatred.

"Please don't," Federico said, but he could hardly speak for the pain, and that effort of begging for mercy was the last thing he was aware of before everything went blank and he felt nothing more.

VI

"Sombra, are you still working for the Rosenthal practice?"

"Yes, when they call me."

"Listen," said Verónica, "I need you to do a job for me. I've got no budget to pay for it, but you could add it to your next invoice for the practice."

"Does your father know about this?"

"No, my father and I aren't speaking. What I'm asking for is a favour. But I do want you to get paid for it."

"You're asking me to overcharge Rosenthal and Associates so that I can do some work for you?"

"Yes."

"Do you want me to investigate Federico Córdova?"

"What? No. Nothing like that."

"OK. I'll bill your father. Tell me what you want."

"I need you to look at a list of names to see if you can find any links with narcos, or any other kind of trafficking: children, sex slaves, weapons, whatever."

"Gotcha. First things first. Is this your new number?"

"Yes, I threw the other one away to get people off my trail."

"You should speak to Federico about that."

"Leave Federico out of this. You're obsessed with him. Write down these names."

Verónica gave him the details she had for Salvador Rossi, Sister Ofelia Dorín, Archbishop Nogués, Father Eduardo, and Tonso, the printer.

The investigation was opening up a lot, and that wasn't always a good thing. She feared losing her way. All the same, the conversation with Doctor Rivarola had been productive. She wasn't surprised to find a man like Rossi in the mix, or even a nun, but it was remarkable to find an archbishop directly involved in the trafficking of children. If she could find some solid evidence and establish a link to Nogués she'd have the makings of a scoop. She should travel to Santiago del Estero and try to interview him.

María Magdalena called her when Verónica was back in her room at the hostel, lying on the bed. Verónica told her about the conversation with the obstetrician and María Magdalena, in turn, said that she had been able to confirm all the stories included by Gómez Brest in the draft of his piece.

"There's something else. One of my best friends in the Order of the Paulines has a younger sister in the Order of the Most Holy Charity, in Buenos Aires. I've known her for ten years. I spoke to my friend, who spoke to her sister, then I spoke to the sister and we agreed to meet in a few days. From what my friend said, and her sister implied, she has information that could be useful to us."

Verónica ended that conversation feeling cheerful. She was in the final stretch of her first important article in a long time. Moreover, she had found a colleague who was as obsessed as she was when it came to hunting down information. María Magdalena was a blessing, if a Jewish girl could allow herself such a Christian turn of phrase.

Her phone rang again. Considering only three people knew this number, it seemed surprisingly busy. It was Harrison.

"I've been thinking about you a lot," said the young waiter.

"That's nice."

"Tom told me you guys met and he made you tea."

"That's right."

"Me and Tom have been talking about you. He really liked you. We want to extend an invitation to you."

Verónica felt a disconcerting tingle travel from her feet to her head. "Both of you want to make this invitation?"

"Both of us. If you accept, you'd need to be in the central hall of the Constitución train station, tomorrow at noon."

"Do we have to meet there? Can't it be somewhere else, your apartment for example? Anyway, aren't you working tomorrow?"

"Tomorrow's a holiday and I'm not working. And yes, it does have to be there, because we've got a little trip planned."

"I'm intrigued! And also alarmed. Where are you taking me?"

"Relax. You're going to have a very good time. We'll see you tomorrow, midday at Constitución."

Verónica ended the call without knowing whether she had done the right thing in accepting Harrison's invitation. There was still time to change her mind. After all, she didn't know Harrison well enough (Tom even less so) to trust him blindly and go somewhere that might be dangerous. It couldn't be a case of sex trafficking, because she was too old for that. She was probably better suited to prolonged torture in a snuff movie. All the same, she would have preferred a more classic encounter, in Harrison's apartment. Why complicate things with a trip out to the suburbs? Her curiosity was stronger than her fears or apprehension, though, so she decided to go and see what the deal was.

She arrived at Constitución to find the boys already waiting for her. They seemed half asleep, and Verónica noticed that all three of them were wearing jeans and leather jackets. She didn't know if hers reflected a certain prejudice, whether it was just a sign of the times, or even a coincidence.

"Let's go – I've got your ticket and there's a train leaving in ten minutes," said Harrison.

"Am I allowed to know where we're going yet?"

"To Wilde. Do you know Wilde?" Tomás asked.

"No, I've never been there."

"What about Avellaneda?"

"I've been to the cemetery there."

"It's a bit further than that, towards La Plata, before Quilmes. Do you know Quilmes?"

"Are you going to ask me about every single station on the Roca line?"

"Ask her if she knew Constitución," said Harrison.

The carriage was fairly empty. Verónica sat down next to the window, opposite Tomás, Harrison next to her. The train began its slow clatter away from the station. Tomás bought some chewing gum from one of the vendors who walked past.

"You can tell me where we're going now."

"Remember the other night in the bar?" Harrison asked.

"What about it in particular?"

"You arrived, you asked for a toasted sandwich. You said it was your dinner. I said it was clearly a long time since you'd had home cooking."

"Harry mentioned it to me. It needed putting right," added Tom.

"I still don't understand," said Verónica, who was beginning to understand but hoped she was misunderstanding.

"We're going to my folks' place in Wilde," said Tomás. "To the home of the inimitable Doña Rosa. My mum's home-made ravioli is something you'll never forget. *Ravioles de seso*. Hardly anyone makes ravioli with brains any more. Followed by the best chicken stew you've ever had in your life."

"You're surprised, right?" said Harrison.

"Extremely."

It took three more train stops for Verónica to accept what was happening. True, she did need to improve her diet and

273

she had never eaten *ravioles de seso* (at first she had heard "de sexo", but her brain quickly autocorrected.) So why not relax and enjoy a trip through Greater Buenos Aires? In any case, when they got back to town she'd take Harrison to his apartment – or to the hostel, or a motel – and have her way with him. A few hours of family life wouldn't kill her.

They got off the train in Wilde and crossed the avenue that ran parallel to the tracks. Verónica had expected to find a quiet neighbourhood of traditional single-storey houses, but there were quite a few buildings and businesses, and a lot of traffic, despite the holiday.

"Shouldn't we arrive with a bottle of wine or something?" she asked.

"No, this is my parents' house."

"Do they know you're coming with two friends?"

"Yeah, it's no big deal anyway because my mum always cooks enough for a whole battalion."

After they had walked a few blocks, the scenery became more suburban: houses of one or two storeys, very little traffic, birdsong, the sound of a radio from a neighbour washing his car.

The house they arrived at was typical of Italian immigrants, with no front garden and the ground floor occupied by a workshop, garage or some other enterprise. The family home was on the first floor.

Tomás rang the intercom and the door opened without anyone asking who was there. Inside, they could hear the ruckus of children, a barking dog and the thwack of a ball being hit against a wall. They went up to the first floor, where they found Tomás's mother, a small woman who wiped her hands on her apron before giving them all a kiss. Also present were Tomás's father, older sister and husband, their three children, his mother's sister and someone else who may have been a neighbour or a widowed friend, Verónica wasn't sure which. There were introductions and kisses all round, and nobody seemed to find it odd that Tomás had arrived with friends. They already knew Harrison, and Tomás's mother asked after his parents. Verónica was offered a Cinzano or a glass of red wine and opted for wine. For lunch they started with aubergines in oil and marinated chicken. Tomás's sister complained about that, because the stew was also made with chicken, and his mother gave her an earful. A loaf of bread was on the table, and each person cut off as much as they wanted to make an impromptu aubergine sandwich. Tomás's father was in charge of grating the cheese and brought it to the table in plastic tubs. Every so often he'd cut off a chunk with a knife and discreetly offer it to a guest. It was an aged provolone, a bit picante, and Verónica got two pieces. In addition to the *ravioles de seso*, Tomás's mother had also made some ravioli with ricotta, for anyone who didn't like brains, which included his two nieces – twins of nine – and his seven-year-old nephew. The stew was a bit oily, but still absolutely delicious. Tomás's mother boasted that everything in it was natural. And they, in turn, praised the ravioli, the sauces and the chicken. Verónica was happy to add her voice to the others'; the food was exquisite. During lunch they talked about politics and television; Verónica's journalistic acumen was called upon to provide the last word in every family dispute. At first she found it awkward to be cast in that role, until she realized that nobody cared that much and, seconds later, they would all be caught up in some other argument which in turn was superseded by a new one soon afterwards. The ravioli, enjoyed by everyone, apart from the children, was followed by home-made crème caramel with dulce de leche and Chantilly cream, whipped up on the spot by Tomás's sister. Two rounds of coffee had to be made to serve them all. When everyone had a cup, Tomás's aunt produced from her handbag some chocolate almonds which she'd had at home, she said, since a birthday celebration some weeks back.

Verónica helped to clear the table and offered to do the dishes, but the family wouldn't hear of it. Tomás's sister washed up while his father, brother-in-law and the neighbour went to the living room and settled down to watch a Champions League soccer game.

Meanwhile, Tomás took Verónica and Harrison to the back part of the house. They crossed a long patio lined with potted plants and home to a hairy dog that was eager to play with the new arrivals. At the back was a garage and an exterior stairway leading to a room above it.

"This was my room when I lived with my parents," said Tomás.

It was a spacious room with a single bed, a desk, a swivel armchair, a small bookcase with a few books and some sporting trophies; in one corner was a hi-fi with ancient speakers and some boxes containing music CDs. There was also a poster of *2 Fast 2 Furious*, the first of the sequels to *The Fast and the Furious*, a photo of Tomás with his classmates at high school in Bariloche, and a few family snaps. The bed was made up as if for a current occupant and there wasn't a speck of dust anywhere in the room. Tom threw himself down on the turquoise quilt, Harrison sprawled in the armchair and Verónica, dropping her backpack onto the floor, perched on a stool beside the window that looked onto the courtyard. From there she could see the front part of the house. All three of them remarked on how much they had eaten and how tired they now felt.

"We could have a siesta in this bed, but I don't think three of us will fit in," said Tom.

Verónica was quite capable of falling asleep even on that uncomfortable chair. She could have asked them to be gentlemen and let her take the armchair or the bed, but she was happy to observe them as they were: Harrison with his legs open, one hand dangling and the other resting on his leg, beside his trouser pocket; Tomás with his T-shirt ridden up, showing his flat stomach, his navel and the fine line of dark hair that disappeared under the silver buckle of his belt.

The patio filled up again with the noise of children who had come out to play with the dog. They shouted, laughed, ran from one side of the courtyard to the other. Verónica watched them and for a few seconds that picture of innocent happiness made her forget the two men in the room with her. Tomás's voice brought her attention back to the room.

"On Sundays, when I was eleven or twelve, I used to come here after lunch with my cousins, Maru and Gonzalo. Maru was the same age as me and Gonza a bit younger."

Tired of sitting on the stool, Verónica moved to perch on the edge of the bed. Tomás shifted his leg over, so that she could sit more comfortably, and carried on speaking.

"Our parents would be arguing or playing cards. We used to play blind man's buff. We blindfolded Mary, took all our clothes off and she had to work out who we were by touching us. But we didn't stay still – we tried not to let her catch us too quickly. To annoy or confuse her we'd grab her ass or climb up on the bed so the first thing she'd touch would be our dicks. Sometimes she'd tell us we were revolting, and other times she'd feel us up for a while before saying our names. She was never wrong about which one was which."

Verónica rested her hand on Tomás's knee, then crept it up his leg. His erection was visible through his jeans. Turning, she looked at Harrison, still sprawled in the chair, smiling beatifically at her. She took that as a sign that everything was fine between them and moved closer to Tomás, undoing his belt and the buttons of his jeans with both hands. She was

277

surprised to see that Tom didn't wear underwear. The fuzz that began at his navel turned darker and more abundant at his pubic area. She took his cock and moved it to her mouth. The silence in the room provided a counterpoint to the hubbub outside in the courtyard. Tom stroked her hair and Harrison moved over to the bed. He squeezed her breasts through her clothes. Verónica kept sucking a bit longer, then removed her mouth to kiss Harrison deeply while still masturbating Tom. Verónica looked into Harrison's eyes. The boy seemed to be awaiting orders. She placed her free hand on Harrison's neck and steered him gently towards Tomás's cock. Harrison took her place and she took the opportunity to move away, watching them, to look for condoms in her backpack and take off her clothes. It was, as Tom had predicted, impossible to fit all three of them on the bed, so they got down on the floor. They all seemed perfectly synchronized with their mouths and hands, as if they had done this before. Only once did Verónica feel obliged to take charge. She made Harrison lie down, lowered herself onto his dick and moved slowly on him then, after a few movements, she stretched along his body and asked Tomás to penetrate her too.

On the train back to the capital, Harrison talked about a new acting course he was starting that week and Tomás described, in detail, a trip he had made to Cuba the previous year. It was still early and the number 53 bus would have suited all of them, but they decided to take a taxi anyway. They dropped Verónica off at the corner by her hostel.

13 *The Bonds of Love*

I

Verónica left the hostel early. She wanted to organize her material over breakfast, before meeting up with María Magdalena. She also needed to call Patricia to update her on the investigation and, while she was at it, to get authorization to travel to Santiago and try to interview Archbishop Nogués. Perhaps she could get some more evidence of children given up for adoption.

It was odd that La Sombra hadn't been in touch with her yet. He usually worked quickly.

The new issue of *Nuestro Tiempo* was already on news stands, and she bought a copy to read over breakfast. She went to her favourite bar for mornings, where the waitress already knew her, and ordered the same as always: a double espresso and a croissant. Sometimes she would order a second croissant, but she never asked for two at the same time. As she listened to the noise of the espresso machine, Verónica started leafing through the magazine. Lionel Messi was on the cover, unshaven and looking a bit tired, above an apocalyptic title: WHAT'S WRONG WITH MESSI? She glanced at the other coverlines and was astonished to read SCANDAL IN SANTIAGO DEL ESTERO: ARCHBISHOP ACCUSED OF SEXUAL ABUSE. The contents page confirmed the name of the archbishop: Arturo Nogués. Her archbishop. Verónica flicked to María Vanini's article and read it, all the while incredulous that the stupid cow had killed her article: a subheading (written by Patricia, presumably) said that the investigation on illegal adoptions had brought forward a new witness. Vanini had interviewed a woman who told how the archbishop had abused her and got her pregnant, then taken away her child and had it adopted. The article also mentioned in passing that there had been other cases of stolen children, but gave no new information about this.

Her coffee was going cold on the table. Verónica read the piece again, incensed. She couldn't believe Patricia had betrayed her by sending Vanini to write that article instead of keeping it for her, given that she was the one investigating illegal adoption. Even more infuriating was the fact that Vanini had struck gold with this new evidence from the young woman and yet the piece she had written was sensationalist and mediocre – a wasted opportunity. She called Patricia, not thinking that it was still very early to be ringing a journalist.

"So you've resurfaced," was the first thing her boss said to her.

"Why did you send that bitch Vanini to cover the story of the woman abused by the archbishop?"

"As I'm sure you know, I don't owe you any explanations about how I run my section. That said, since you no longer come to the office, I will say that María happened to be in Santiago and that it was the victim who approached her, because she had read your article."

"I could kill that woman. I've got proof that the archbishop took part in a network of illegal adoptions involving priests, nuns, a religious order, a Catholic association, a very successful, fascist doctor and other powerful people whose identities I haven't been able to confirm yet."

"Sounds great. In fact, I'm reassured to hear there's more we can pin on the archbishop. I expect I'll get a few calls from the Curia. You know what the Church hierarchy is like."

"But Vanini has ruined my reputation."

"Don't be childish. Get on with finishing your article and perhaps we can put it on the cover."

"One other thing. The woman making the new allegation, did they get her out of Santiago?"

"Not as far as I know."

"Look – these people are dangerous. There are already at least two deaths connected with this investigation. If someone makes an allegation like that they're going to make her be quiet, and they won't ask nicely."

"I'll tell María to warn her."

"She needs to take her somewhere safe."

After the call, Verónica ordered a second croissant without even having started the first. She drank the cold coffee and looked through the rest of the magazine, not finding much else to get angry about, apart from a few pieces by colleagues she didn't like and who couldn't write to save their lives.

When the time came, she set off to meet María Magdalena in a bar in Almagro. It was tempting to carry on to Villa Crespo and her apartment. She missed Chicha, and the little dog must be missing her too. Verónica had left a large bag of dog food, but Chicha must have eaten it all by now. She hoped Marcelo had bought another bag, rather than giving her dog the chopped-up beef, rice with chicken giblets and similar things that he believed essential for a strong, healthy dog, with no need to resort to synthetic food, full of chemicals.

Putting that temptation aside, Verónica got off the bus at Sarmiento and Sánchez Bustamante, then walked to the bar. María Magdalena hadn't arrived yet, so she sat at a table beside the window. Her writing partner arrived five minutes later dressed in the same sober style Verónica remembered from her time at *Vida Cristiana*.

Verónica told her that she had enlisted the help of a hacker. They were unravelling the mystery, but they weren't there yet. They needed something on paper, an incriminating document or something that clearly implicated the Christian Home Movement and the Order of the Most Holy Charity.

"I've visited Mariana, my friend's sister who's also a sister of the Most Holy Order. She's an honest girl, with a genuine religious vocation, and she's absolutely horrified by the things people are saying about the Order inside the convent. Even Sister Ofelia Dorín boasts of helping Catholic couples to adopt children because their mothers are single, or very young, or very poor.

"One of the things she likes to brag about is how she remembers every one of the adoptions that have taken place. According to Mariana, and to a boy who was illegally adopted and went to see Dorín, the nun records all the information pertaining to these cases in a notebook covered in blue paper which she keeps in her office. That room's usually left unlocked."

"Can we ask Mariana to get hold of the book, or at least to photograph it?"

"I've already made both of those suggestions and she wasn't keen on either of them. Passing information and gossip on to an ex-nun is one thing – spying is something else entirely."

"We have to get hold of that notebook, María Magdalena."

"Yes, of course. And I have a plan. In a couple of days there's going to be a Latin American convention of nuns at the Order of the Most Holy Charity's house in Floresta. Many of the nuns will sleep there, and they'll spend much of the day in the cloister. We have to get our hands on that blue book.

So you and I are going to use the religious convention as a way to get into the convent."

"Can anyone attend then?"

"No, it's only for nuns, but they come from many different countries and obviously don't all know each other."

"So you'll get credentials for us?"

"Something better than credentials. Mariana is going to get hold of two habits from the sisters of the Most Holy Charity. One for you and one for me. I hope I got your size right."

"I'm not following you."

"We're going in dressed as nuns. You and I. And may God forgive us."

For once, words failed Verónica. But she had to find them again to answer her phone, which had just begun to ring. It was La Sombra.

"Verónica, we need to meet urgently. Like, tomorrow."

"Have you found something on those names I passed you?"

"This is all getting out of hand. We're going to get together – Federico, you and me."

"What's Federico got to do with my investigation?"

"Everything, Verónica, everything."

II

Federico had never imagined that opening and closing your eyelids could generate so much pain. Every blink was like a knitting needle piercing the nape of his neck. He tried to cry out and it was as though his body were a symphony of pain – a stabbing pain in his stomach exploded out of his mouth. He was lying on the ground, looking at the sky, which was blue and white like the Uruguayan flag. He tried to ask for help and could only moan. A giant shadow covered the sky: it was the man who was going to shoot him or who had already shot

283

him (could one of the pains he was feeling have been caused by a bullet?). Wilson still had the gun in his hand and was still pointing it at Federico.

"We're not murderers," he said, which was somewhat reassuring.

Federico turned his head, looking for Cristina, and saw her standing a few yards away, observing the scene.

"Please, Cristina, I need to speak to you. I don't mean you any harm."

"Who sent you? How did you find her?" said the man, who had at least lowered his weapon.

"I'm an attorney in Buenos Aires. I'm investigating the death of Sandro Hernández. I know Cristina and Sandro spent a lot of time together at a church in Liniers – that's why I'd like to speak to her."

"I'm not going to speak to anyone," said Cristina, without moving from her position.

"Cristina, I promise you that nobody will ask you to make a formal statement. What you tell me won't be published anywhere. At the moment your name is mentioned in the case. If another judge or prosecutor takes up the case, they'll send a warrant to the Uruguayan authorities to make you return and testify in Buenos Aires. I promise you that if you tell me about what happened, no one will know it was you who told me and your name will be erased from the case."

Cristina turned around and walked away, crying. Wilson came over to Federico and helped him get up. If they had peppered him with gunfire, he would have felt less pain than he experienced now, simply trying to stand. Federico leaned against the man, who led him to the kitchen, where Cristina was sitting at a table. She blew her nose and wiped away her tears.

"If you found me, then the others can find me."

"Maybe, but I assure you that those people are going to have bigger problems to worry about than looking for you. What you tell me might even help get them off your back."

"They wanted to kill me. It wasn't an accident."

"I know, and I understand your fear. Was Sandro also threatened?"

"No, not him."

"You knew him well."

"For many years."

"You'd been activists together in the nineties."

"I wasn't the activist – that was my husband."

"Your husband and Sandro were both members of a nationalist group, is that right?"

"They were difficult times."

It was clear Cristina Reggiardo didn't want to talk about what had happened back in the 1990s. Her husband had died in suspicious circumstances, then she had reappeared in the life of Sandro Hernández. But he wasn't in Colonia to investigate a crime committed several decades back. Better to skip that part of the story and concentrate on the church.

"Father Ignacio had a particular soft spot for Sandro."

"Over the years he became a kind of secretary to him. I didn't like that priest."

"Why not?"

"He had a group, almost like crusaders, who followed him everywhere. He encouraged them to feel special, superior to everyone else. Sandro was in that select group."

"May I ask why you were going to the support group?"

"Because I'd had problems with alcohol, like Sandro."

"But you were never in the select group?"

"Never. You had to be very Catholic, a Bible-thumper. They were forever mentioning Jesus, Mary and all the saints. Father Ignacio and the others had brainwashed them."

"You stopped attending a few months before Sandro's death."

"I'd been telling Sandro for a while that these people were crazy. Two years ago, another member of Father Ignacio's crusaders also committed suicide when he got caught with drugs at Ezeiza airport. Everyone acted so surprised, but I'm sure the priest and his friends had something to do with it. Every so often he'd get visits from powerful people."

Federico had taken the precaution of bringing a photo of Chief Superintendent Barbosa with him, and now he showed it to Cristina.

"Yes, that was one of the people who used to have meetings with Father Ignacio. Sandro and the others were made to believe that their mission in the Church was more important than anything else. That they should give their lives for Christ. If Father Ignacio had said you should kill yourself on the next full moon, those poor wretches would have done it. I stopped going to the group when I found out that Sandro was going to have to transport dead bodies. He didn't know where they came from. What if they were people who had been murdered by the priest and his friends? I begged him not to do it, but he didn't take any notice. I was really angry, so I decided not to go to that church any more. What's more, the bodies were all cut up. He told me, because he made several trips."

"Did he know where the order came from?"

"Father Ignacio. His friends. Perhaps this chief superintendent in the photo. He made a couple of trips. Each time when he came back, his whole body was shaking. He said that he'd seen horrible things, mutilated bodies, foetuses. I begged him to leave it, not to go back to the church. The bastards had given him a gun. If anyone stopped him, he had to kill himself. That's what he told me."

"Do you know where they loaded up the bodies?"

"It was a place in Floresta, the back part of a church or something. I don't think even Sandro knew what was going on there."

Federico left Wilson's house a few minutes later with renewed promises that nobody would bother Cristina and that she could probably return to Buenos Aires in a short while. Wilson offered a terse apology for the beating and Federico set off on foot towards the Buquebus terminal. His body hurt a little less, but it was still uncomfortable to walk. Every so often he paused for a rest before continuing.

Fifty minutes later, he reached the Buquebus. It was still two hours before the next boat left. He went to the bar and persuaded the staff to bring him two aspirins along with the tea and the gin he ordered. It was a strange combination, perhaps the right antidote for flu, but Federico was hoping it would also take the edge off his injuries. His phone rang. It was La Sombra.

"We have to speak in person, urgently. Tomorrow."

"Wow, Sombra. You genuinely want to see a human being?"

"This is serious. I don't know what you and Verónica are up to, but you're snapping at each other's heels."

"Has she gone close to the number I gave you?"

"Forget the phones. This is really weird. I'll explain it tomorrow. To you and to Verónica."

"She's coming too? You didn't tell her I've been tracking her, did you?"

"See you tomorrow, Federico."

III

If he believed in anything, it was in the digital life. People who think the virtual world is an illusion, a distraction or a mistake have never experienced the intensity of emotion that can be found in an internet connection. So thought La Sombra, who had built his life on binary codes. They were no less real to him than a person's DNA, the chlorophyll in plants, the cement in buildings. Would he have fallen in love with his wife if he hadn't first known her from the porn films he downloaded with the devotion of a saint at prayer? And it wasn't that he liked her more in the digital world (those videos in which she would always be young and beautiful) than in real life (the woman with whom he hoped to grow old), just that he could make those two universes coexist with the same intensity.

La Sombra interacted with hundreds of people via email, chat rooms, websites, even on the phone, but he rarely saw them in person. Over the years he had felt increasingly phobic of a real world that couldn't be erased by changing screens, nor improved by applying a filter, nor played back as required. For that reason he had surprised himself with his own decision to meet Verónica and Federico in person. Those two were messing with his head more than a gang of Chechen hackers. Either they were both groping in the dark, or they were competing for the same information, or they were spying on each other, as might be inferred from Federico's request that he monitor the phones of Verónica and another person. Better to see them in the flesh, bring them up to speed and let them sort things out between them.

He had asked them to come to an old bar close enough to his house that he could walk there, but far enough that they wouldn't be able to work out exactly where he lived. A hacker must do everything possible to remain untraceable. He arrived half an hour early, to scope out the locale. "Avoid surprises" was his motto.

Federico got there a few minutes later, but he hadn't come alone. He was with a journalist called Rodolfo Corso, who seemed to be enjoying this little drama. Immediately afterwards, Verónica arrived, accompanied by a woman of about fifty, whom she introduced as a journalist who was working on an article with her. Federico and Verónica gave each other a slightly chilly greeting then sat opposite each other at the table, their sidekicks conveniently by their sides.

IV

Before meeting Federico for the first time in seventeen months, Verónica had gone to a lingerie store on Avenida Entre Ríos to buy herself a push-up bra. The terrible memory of the other Verónica's bust had been pursuing her, like that giant breast chasing Woody Allen in one of his 1970s movies. She couldn't go for too much enhancement, though, without looking ridiculous. In the end she bought a padded bra that seemed to fit the bill.

She assumed La Sombra must be summoning her to a meeting with Federico because she had gone into his emails. So was he expecting an apology? Or perhaps Federico had some information that could be useful to her investigation. Federico must have requested this meeting. It was an excuse to see her. Well, she wasn't going to rush to meet him. Verónica still hadn't forgotten how he'd left her in the middle of a crisis, more than six hundred miles from home. He had abandoned her. And now he had a girlfriend. Plus he was flirting with Daniela. Or rather: Daniela was flirting with Federico and he, true to form, was letting her do it. It was exasperating. She put on the new bra: it lifted her boobs a little and her spirit a lot.

Verónica had asked María Magdalena to go with her to the bar. She had started by saying they were meeting a source who might have useful information, then ended up subjecting her friend to the whole Federico story.

"I can't give you any advice about love," said María Magdalena. "But I can tell you how to disguise your feelings and desires. One doesn't spend two hours talking about someone only to finish by saying he isn't important. I think that at some point you should be honest with him. First of all, you should be honest with yourself."

"Honesty in love is overrated."

"Let's suppose it is. What if being honest allows you to get what you want, though? Then we're not talking about an honesty of principles but one of outcomes. Your aim is for him to discover that you're a wonderful human being and that he wants to be with you. Your best card is an honesty imbued with drama. It works in soap operas, after all."

Harrison rang her later to suggest they meet up. Although he was a delight, she said no. He said a couple of things that made her laugh and she nearly changed her mind. But Verónica needed to focus, like a soccer player before a final, on what might happen the following day. That night she fell asleep thinking of Federico.

When she arrived at the bar and saw him there with Rodolfo Corso she felt betrayed. Was he so feeble he needed to bring a chaperone? Did he think she was going to jump on him? Besides, Rodolfo looked at her far too lingeringly. Federico was bound to have talked to him about her. Men never knew how to keep their mouths shut.

"I asked you here because you both require my services," said La Sombra. "I'm not going to get into anything personal, except in relation to the investigations that each of you are carrying out, separately, as far as I understand. Is that right?"

Both Federico and Verónica put on a face intended to convey that there was no question of them working together.

"Federico, you gave me a list of people who are connected to a case of trafficking in cadavers, or rather body parts."

"Body parts?" Verónica queried.

"Yes – please, let me continue. Included on that list was Herminia de García, the wife of Juan García, who's a member of a Catholic commission."

"The Juan García I know?" Verónica asked Federico, who nodded briefly so as not also to be guilty of interrupting La Sombra.

"Meanwhile, Verónica is investigating a case of trafficking babies. Live ones. You gave me a list of people who belong to the Catholic Church, and you believe there are other powerful people behind all this. Among the names are Ofelia Dorín, the Provincial Superior of the Order of the Most Holy Charity. The full name of Juan García's wife is Herminia Dorín de García. The two women are sisters. All this suggests that the powerful people you suspect may be behind the trafficking of children are also the ones under investigation by Federico. As for you, Federico, if you're trying to establish the motivations and connections of these people, Verónica may have the answers you need." La Sombra stood up. "I'll leave you two to catch up."

Moving his shot-putter frame with the agility of a ballerina, La Sombra vanished into the world outside, leaving behind two surprised people and two stupefied ones.

Corso leaned across the table and said to María Magdalena: "Since we're colleagues, what if I invite you to share a table a bit further away from these two? You can tell me everything you both know, and I'll bring you up to speed on our own findings."

And so they were left alone. Verónica, ever the professional, told Federico all about her investigation, from the search for Jazmín to her meeting with Doctor Laura Rivarola. Federico noted down some of what she said. He was particularly interested in Doctor Rossi and his horror clinic in Buenos Aires.

Then he briefed her about Chief Superintendent Barbosa, his connection with the Church and the reappearance of Juan García. Federico studied his notes (to avoid looking her in the eye?) and made a neat copy of all the information they had.

"At the heart of all this is a religious order, the Most Holy Charity, which in its original, medieval emanation rescued Christians from the hands of Muslims and which in the last few decades has concentrated on supplying Catholic families with children. Do we agree?"

"Yes, of course."

"Good. This order has its headquarters in Buenos Aires but is most active in the provinces of north-east Argentina, two in particular: Misiones and Santiago del Estero. There's a nun, currently the order's Provincial Superior, top nun in other words, called Sister Ofelia Dorín, who began her evangelical work in baby theft in the 1960s. As time went on, she gained the support of the inestimable doctor Salvador Rossi, who owned a clinic in Posadas. Then we have the Christian Home Movement, under the directorship of Herminia Dorín de García, sister of Ofelia. Rossi thrives as a medical entrepreneur and opens another clinic in Santiago del Estero. There he is actively supported by Archbishop Arturo Nogués. Since most of the adoptions are channelled through the Christian Home Movement in Buenos Aires, Rossi sets up another clinic here in the capital. We don't know at what point Rossi and García team up, but it seems that when the doctor first arrives in Buenos Aires, he's already able to count on logistical support from the crime lord. And we're not talking about someone innocently lending a hand. García has an associate, Chief Superintendent Barbosa, who needs a clinic in Buenos Aires for businesses related to drug trafficking. I wonder if human trafficking wasn't also organized through that clinic, given that García already has previous in that area.

"Barbosa is another God-lover who rubs shoulders with the leading figures in the Church in Buenos Aires. He creates a support system to help these priests and nuns do their dirty deeds. At a church in Liniers vulnerable people are brainwashed. Not content with his usual trafficking, Barbosa discovers a new revenue stream – selling body parts to other countries."

"Now I understand what Doctor Renzi was trying to tell me when I went to see him. He said that I didn't have enough bodies and you had too many. Renzi realized, before La Sombra, that our investigations were connected. Everything's falling into place."

"Some pieces are still missing, though. If these guys had a whole adoption ring set up, then there's an important element we haven't yet considered: the judges who authorized the adoptions, the registrars who let children be registered as the biological offspring of people who weren't their parents."

"We can fill in those blanks if we can get hold of Sister Ofelia's blue book. Every case of a child surrendered to her organization is there. If we can see their documents, their fake birth certificates or adoption papers, we've got those bastards by the throat."

"What I can't get my head round is why Barbosa's shipment of body parts, and not one of his drugs consignments, was intercepted in the port. Was somebody sending him a message?"

Verónica nodded, and instinctively Federico imitated her. They were like those plastic nodding dogs that some bus or taxi drivers like to put in the window.

"And how are you?" Federico asked, out of the blue.

Verónica wasn't ready for this, having committed every brain cell to the criminal investigation.

"Me? Fine, all good. I got a promotion at the magazine – I'm a deputy editor."

"Congratulations. And the girls told me you have a dog."

"Which girls?"

"Your sisters."

"That's right, Chicha. She was one of Mechi's puppies, remember?"

"You brought a puppy back from Tucumán?"

"It was better than coming back alone."

Verónica had to contain herself. The last thing she wanted was to come across as resentful or angry. And she needed to control the conversation. Ask the questions herself.

"You see my sisters a lot, right?"

"Every now and then. Not much. Work doesn't leave a lot of free time."

"Daniela a bit more so."

"A bit more than…?"

"I mean you and Daniela see each other more often."

"No, far from it. Why do you say that?"

"I always got the impression you and she had a rapport."

"I've known your sisters for so many years that they feel a bit like my sisters now."

"How sweet. I've always wanted a brother."

"I said they felt like sisters. Not you."

"So you're discriminating against me."

"You know what I mean."

"I met your girlfriend a while ago, the one who works in PR."

"Yes, she mentioned it. Are you seeing anyone?"

"Kind of. Nothing serious, not like your thing."

"Well, it's probably just a matter of time."

"And he's very young. Twenty-two."

"Aren't you a bit old for that?"

"Of course, because only older guys can go out with young girls."

"I know, I know, I've read about it in *Cosmopolitan*. Anyway, I have to go. Corso and I have an investigation to get on with. Let's speak. Call me, or I'll call when I have something new."

V

Thirty-three. He was thirty-three and her boyfriend twenty-two. Federico didn't understand why that made him so angry – at the end of the day, the age of Verónica's boyfriend was none of his business. He could be fifty or fifteen, be four feet tall or play basketball for the NBA. It was her life. Dealing with his own girlfriend was tiring enough; he didn't have the energy to indulge in absurd speculation about Verónica's life. But what could she possibly have in common with someone that age, apart from sex? The next time he saw her, he was going to say: keep going out with boys and you'll end up alone at forty. How long would a guy whose target market still included high school girls last with her?

"Do you believe that it's better to go out with a sixteen-year-old than with a woman over thirty? That sooner or later your ex-girlfriend's boyfriend is sure to opt for a schoolgirl? And another question, Federico, are you perhaps watching a lot of pornography?"

"I wouldn't say it's better, but if I were twenty-two I might well have a teenage girlfriend. I don't believe Verónica's relationship with this kid can last. And no, I'm not watching a lot of porn, not even a bit of porn."

"You don't watch porn?"

"I do, but I haven't had much time recently. What with work and Verónica, I've got no time to watch anything."

"Congratulations."

"On not watching porn?"

"Because you've just said 'Verónica' without clarifying that you're talking about your girlfriend. Unless…"

"What?"

"You were referring to Verónica Rosenthal."

"No chance."

"Let's go back to your short monologue earlier. You say that your ex-girlfriend can only be getting sex from this boy, from this *chiquilín*, if you'll pardon the Uruguayism. What do you get from Verónica?"

"From which Verónica?"

"Which one do you think?"

"I think you're referring to my girlfriend. She brings me a lot of peace. And also sex, company, laughs."

"She brings you peace? Is this girl a Blue Helmet in the United Nations? I'm going to tell you something that on its own is worth everything you've paid me this month: when someone, talking about his partner, says she brings him peace, he means she occupies less space in his brain than the weekly shopping list. People don't want a partner for peace, or sex, or company, or the best ever stand-up routine. What people want is someone who gets in their head. Who gets into every neuron. Peace! Listen, psychoanalysis has never promoted physical violence, but I swear that whenever a patient tells me that what their partner brings is peace, I feel like slapping them to see if they wake up."

"You're not a psychoanalyst, though."

"Look, Federico, don't get ontological on me."

Federico was so confused when he left the psychologist that he went to a bar and ordered a Fernet, unusual behaviour for someone who didn't drink bitters, much less at eleven in the morning. Rodolfo Corso rang then and asked if they could meet an hour later at Alameda Sur, a bar on the Costanera promenade. In other circumstances he would have tried to change at least the place of their meeting, but sea air might help clear his mind and refocus it on his case. Of course, now the case was no longer just his and Corso's; it also belonged to Rosenthal and that journalist with the religious name.

He took a taxi to the bar where Rodolfo was waiting for him. Luckily, the venue wasn't one of those typical Costanera food stands where you have to eat a hot dog standing up or sitting at the edge of the sidewalk, but a proper bar, with an indoor room and plenty of tables. Corso was standing at the entrance.

"I'll be so disappointed if you don't order a pork sandwich with all the trimmings and an egg on top."

On Corso's recommendation, then, they ordered two *bondiolas*, a large portion of fries and two cans of Quilmes beer. There weren't many people in the bar and their order came out quickly.

"I've no intention of boring you, so I won't run through the many setbacks I encountered with our collection of ultramontane Catholics. Like you, there's something I'm still puzzled by. How did the Prefecture know that a shipment was coming from Barbosa through the port? If they knew he was trafficking cocaine, why fuck up a shipment that was much less important, economically and legally? I checked up on the pricks in the Prefecture to see if there was any professional link with Barbosa and found someone who seems to have a lot more in common with him than a love of uniforms. They were at school together in a place that specializes in raising young fascists; even its name is a clue to the kind of pupil that comes out: the Doctor Dámaso Centeno Military Social Institute."

"I was at school at the Centeno."

"Seriously? Well, that explains a few things. Anyway, this gentleman, by the name of Patricio Arizmendi, holds the position of prefect responsible for special operations. Guess where Arizmendi was working in the 1990s."

"Hollywood?"

"In the province of Misiones. He almost got booted out for failing to spot a bus carrying two hundred kilos of the finest weed from Pedro Juan Caballero, in Paraguay. Local gossips say that land is registered in the name of a frontman and that the real owner is Arizmendi." Corso paused to take a bite out of his *bondiola*, then wiped his mouth with a paper napkin and continued. "We don't know the reason, and it's not all that important to us, but what's clear is that what happened with the truck full of body parts was some kind of score-settling between two criminals who wear uniforms."

"Between two big mafiosos, in other words."

VI

He had a contempt for melodrama. Nogués couldn't understand people whose reaction to adversity was confusion, shock or suffering. He had always felt closer to the Jesus in the Gospel of Mark, who walks silently towards the Cross, than to the one in Matthew, who talks to everyone at Calvary. Although he was also unconvinced that Jesus would have said, "Father, Father, why have you forsaken me?" It was clear that God had plans for Him and that he must endure them without drama or complaints, much less reproach. That was why Nogués felt such disdain watching his private secretary, Converti, desperately packing their bags and preparing to flee. If Christ had been able to bear His ordeal, then he too could carry the cross of fake news.

Nogués had made mistakes. Unlike the supreme pontiff, an archbishop can't rely on infallibility. His greatest error had been to let Fabiana remain close to him. After the birth he shouldn't have seen her again. Yet there was something he found very attractive in that adolescent growing towards womanhood. Fabiana despised him; she could barely contain her hatred. To bend that hatred and contempt into submission was, for him, hugely enjoyable.

He hadn't expected Fabiana to deliver him such a low blow. Santiago del Estero was alive with gossip and rumours, and soon there would be disdainful looks in his direction. There were bound to be journalists, photographers and TV cameras looking for him. His peace had come to an end, at least for now. He called García, Rossi and Ofelia and noted a certain *froideur*. Although they might not want to say it, they blamed him for letting this affair run for so many years. Everyone agreed that he should leave Santiago for a while. The best plan would be to go and stay with the Brothers of the Most Holy Charity. There he would be protected from the buffeting of the press.

García agreed to take the necessary steps to stop any legal fallout and contain the media reaction. Converti had to work with the crime lord on the wording of a statement of denial that would be published in the press in the next few days.

The car that was going to take him to the airport was already waiting. Converti loaded their suitcases into the back and they drove away.

It was soon after dawn and there were still few people out and about: street cleaners, doormen washing down the sidewalk, the odd store owner opening up. These were his people. He had seen governors, politicians, judges and businesspeople come and go. He wasn't going anywhere. Soon he would be back to occupy his rightful place.

VII

The sky had turned black, and a storm was brewing. Fabiana dressed warmly, put on her bomber jacket and took out her umbrella. She left the house at siesta time. That morning she had appeared on a local radio station and taken a battering. The presenter had called her a mythomaniac, floated the idea that she might be making this allegation for money and had even suggested that she was a dangerous terrorist because she belonged to a left-wing group. She had received an email from the girls at Las Muchas Otras, who planned to travel to Santiago to support her, and a text message from María Vanini, who offered to help and asked her to get in touch if she remembered anything else. As if there were any part of this nightmare she could have forgotten.

Pablo hadn't come home, or been in touch. Nor had any of his friends, apart from Amanda, who was still sticking by her. Fabiana had foreseen this might happen. She wasn't surprised, not even annoyed. Getting all that garbage out from inside her had made her feel so much stronger than anything else could. She did, however, need to speak to her mother.

Everything between them was covered by the greasy patina of Nogués. He was present in all their conversations, in their relationship itself, in every single thing one did for the other. They had been so close. They knew the meaning of pain, of want (although not hunger, because there had always been food on the table), and shared a certainty of being alone in the world. Nobody had helped Fabiana's mother, nor had they helped her, either. But if her mother had made a mistake, there was still a chance to turn things around. To heal wounds. Fabiana would ask her to stop working for the archbishop; she could help her with money and to find a more dignified way of earning a living.

It had suddenly got much darker, and the storm broke with unusual force. The wind turned her umbrella inside out, leaving Fabiana ill-equipped to protect herself against the freezing rain. It was only three blocks to the cathedral, but the sudden deluge made it feel more like ten miles. She arrived soaking wet at the bishop's palace.

The door to the kitchen was locked, which struck her as odd because her mother never locked it. Who would be bold enough to steal from the archbishop's house? She rang the bell and nobody answered. Nogués must be having a siesta, if he was still able to sleep. Fabiana banged hard on the door. She was beginning to worry when her mother appeared, opening the little window above the door.

"Open the door, I'm soaked to the skin." Fabiana was still wrestling with the umbrella, which looked unlikely to withstand another storm.

"I no longer have a daughter," said Luisa, and the door stayed closed.

"Come on, Ma."

"You're an ungrateful person. Have you already forgotten that it was thanks to Father Arturo you got to finish high school? Where do you think we would have ended up, you and I, without his help?" Whenever her mother was angry with Fabiana she addressed her formally, using *usted* instead of *tú*.

"We can talk about this inside. Let me come in."

"No."

"Did Nogués tell you not to let me in?"

"Thanks to you, Father Arturo has had to leave everything and go away. You must feel very pleased with yourself."

"Mamá, I only told the truth."

"The truth? Don't make me laugh. Who cares about the truth?"

"I do, I care."

Before Fabiana could say anything more, Luisa closed the little window and disappeared. Fabiana tried banging on the door again, but to no avail.

Full of anguish, she started walking back home. She hadn't felt this way about Pablo's response or those of the people she had once thought of as friends. She would never be able to communicate with her mother again, unless she could get them both out of the gigantic web into which they had fallen so many years ago. Nogués was the web, and there was only one way to eliminate him from their lives. Fabiana was sure about that now. She had to kill the archbishop. But would she have the spiritual strength to do it? Yes, she knew that she would. She would find him, wherever he was hiding. Finally she would be free.

A flash of lightning lit up the empty street. Something stopped her a few houses before she reached her front door. Perhaps it was instinct, or the habit of caution instilled in her by the Party. Fabiana didn't go any further because she was sure that the car parked by the kerb in front of her property was waiting for her. Instead, she turned and started walking back the way she'd come, hoping they hadn't seen her. But it was already too late. There was a sound of car doors closing. Turning to look, she saw that two men had got out of the car and were walking in her direction. Fabiana threw down the umbrella and started running, even though her legs were trembling. She had always been agile, and it wasn't hard to keep ahead of her pursuers. Heading back to the archbishop's palace, she covered one block, and another. Reaching the back door, she tried to turn the handle, an action she had repeated so many times in the past without giving it a second's thought and which was now impossible: the door was still locked with a key. She rang the bell, insistently, and could hear it ringing inside, the sound muffled by distance and the continuing noise of thunder. Now she had only a few seconds. Her mother had to open up; she would have to throw herself into the house and they would have to get the door closed quickly, before the hitmen caught up. They wouldn't dare come in here. Or at least she would have a few minutes to call the police, or Pablo, or some friends from the Party. Fabiana pounded furiously on the door, begging her mother to open it. She implored her, fists drumming like thunder or bombs: she yelled that she was being chased by people who wanted to kill her. Fabiana didn't see her assailants arrive, because she had decided in those last seconds to trust that her mother was going to appear and let her in, that she would see sense, that she would understand what was at stake. A pain, rising in her back and reaching the pit of her stomach, became more pressing. As she turned slightly, one of the men slashed her across the belly and blood began to gush out, as though from a broken pipe. She pressed her abdomen with both hands to suppress the bleeding and protect herself from more blows, but that meant exposing her face and the next cut caught her cheek, above the cheekbone. The rainwater at her feet was turning dark red. Fabiana collapsed against the door. Her body sounded like another thump on the door, urging her mother to open up. She curled up in an attempt to protect herself. The blows that followed hurt less as her body started yielding to its fate. The storm quietened, the rain subsided and the men became a shapeless shadow. All that remained intact was a longing for her mother to open the door. And that didn't happen. At least not while Fabiana had life left in her body.

14   *The Nuns*

Verónica had tried to resist, but resisting wasn't her forte. After making a Herculean effort to stay away, she went back into Federico's inbox. She needed to know if he had said anything about their meeting. And there it was again, open like a flower offering itself to Verónica's investigative nose.

Although Federico hadn't sent many emails in the last few days, one in particular caught Verónica's attention: an email from "F" to her sister Daniela the night before. Verónica fully expected to find in it proof of a relationship between her sister and Federico, but her confidence soon gave way to a sense of shame. The subject was *Happy…* and Verónica felt her pulse quicken. Federico was sending Daniela birthday greetings. Verónica had completely forgotten it was her middle sister's birthday – a terrible oversight. She closed the laptop and immediately called Daniela.

"Sorrysorrysorrysorrysorrysorry," she said as soon as her sister answered.

Daniela sounded cold and distant, so Verónica had to resort to every possible trick to win her over. She told her sister that she was in the middle of a complicated investigation, that she had moved away from home for a few days, that she often thought of her. That she had thought the eighteenth was tomorrow and not realized it was yesterday. Her sister softened, sounded less dour and urged her not to get into any trouble. Verónica felt like playing with fire, so she asked:

"Do you have any news of Federico?"

"Why – are you interested in him again?"

"No, no, just curious."

"He's going out with some bimbo. They won't last long. He's very busy in the courts and definitely not in a hurry to see Dad again."

"Or me, for that matter."

"He hasn't said anything about you. He's quite reserved when it comes to matters of the heart."

"Sounds like you know a lot about him."

"He comes round every now and then, or he goes to Leticia's. The kids love him."

"And what about you?"

"I adore him."

"That's intense."

"It's a shame you two fell out. Look, I have to go because the guy who drives the bus that brings Santino back from nursery just buzzed my intercom."

"Well, happy birthday a day late."

"Don't be silly, it's fine. And call Federico."

Veronica went back to looking at the new emails but didn't find anything of note. She decided to call Federico; she would tell him about the visit she and María Magdalena were planning to make to the convent of the Most Holy Charity, using that as a pretext to suggest they meet up. Any excuse to see him.

And if there was one thing to be said about Federico, he made it easy for her. He wasn't arrogant or condescending, and certainly not hostile or distant. The idea that they should meet to discuss the case seemed like the most natural thing in the world to him. He didn't even quibble when she asked him to meet her in Dadá at eight that night, hardly the most convenient time or place to be talking about journalistic or legal investigations.

After calling Federico she noticed – and it almost seemed like divine intervention – that there were two missed calls from Harrison. Verónica phoned him back immediately. Better to get the bitter pill out of the way. She told him that they wouldn't be able to see each other tonight, either. That she was very busy and that the next few days were going to be really difficult. Harrison was a kid, but a perspicacious one.

"You're not about to make up with your husband, are you?"

And for a moment she did feel like someone who was about to make up with her husband, except that there was no making up to be done and, come to that, she didn't have a husband.

There was also a more serious problem to resolve: she had no clothes. Apart from two pairs of jeans, a few shirts, T-shirts and jackets, she had nothing to wear. Not that she needed a whole outfit, but a new, pretty item would help her feel more confident. A trip to the Abasto shopping mall shouldn't be too risky. She took the H line on the Metro, changed to the B and walked straight into the mall and into a branch of Portsaid. Verónica lost no time over the shopping expedition, treating it as a commando strike: she bought a sixties-style sweater with a diamond pattern, a white T-shirt to put on underneath and an irresistible jacket with a tartan lining and fur hood, much warmer than her leather one. It was cold enough, she decided, to justify making these credit card purchases. She took the metro back to her hostel, feeling happy. In front of the mirror in her room she tried on the pullover and jacket again, this time with the jeans she was thinking of wearing. Everything was perfect.

Verónica was fifteen minutes late for her meeting with Federico, who was already sitting at one of the tables at the back, an area usually reserved for love cheats and other people who need privacy. It would have been good if his girlfriend had happened to walk past and seen them there. Federico was wearing a smooth grey shirt, black jeans and no tie, which meant that he must have gone back home, changed out of his legal attire and dressed informally for her. He was drinking a Corona.

She asked for a Bloody Mary, some tortilla chips and guacamole. She felt happy, relaxed. Federico represented a continuity in her life, as though all those months in which they hadn't seen each other had never happened. His gestures were all familiar to her, and she liked that.

"I'd pay good money to know what's going through that pretty little head right now," she said, levering guacamole onto a Dorito.

"I'm thinking that we've seen each other twice in less than thirty-six hours. Must be a record."

"Quite dangerous."

"There's always danger when you're around."

"Is that a word you'd use to define me? Dangerous?"

Federico thought. He seemed overly serious, as though ready to reprise the last conversation they'd had in Tucumán, just before he'd left her. But perhaps he didn't want to touch wounds that were still raw; his expression softened and he said simply: "Unpredictable."

"Whereas you're the opposite for me: predictable. I don't mean that as a defect, by the way, quite the contrary."

"Yeah, right. You might as well say I'm a turnip, not as a defect but as a vegetable."

"Being predictable is a positive, if what can be predicted is good. If you support Barcelona, it's predictable that they'll win, and that's cool. On the other hand, it's predictable that Atlanta will lose, and that's not so good."

"So I'm more like Barcelona."

"Let's say you are. In fact, when you weren't predictable with me you tore my heart out. Don't look like that, I'm not getting at you. It was only an example."

"OK. Maybe we should stick to talking about our mutilated corpses and our trafficked children."

Verónica told him about María Magdalena's findings and the plan they had hatched to get hold of Sister Ofelia Dorín's blue book.

"Doctor Rossi's clinic is in the same block, so the two places may be connected. Couldn't María Magdalena also get some priests' clothes, for Corso and me?"

"You could pass for a priest, but Corso's more like the Antichrist."

They ordered another round of drinks and some bruschetta. Verónica didn't want to suggest they go and get dinner somewhere for fear of breaking the spell.

"So it's an early start tomorrow. I'll go to the courts and you to the convent. Mind you, don't end up converting and taking the veil."

"I can't believe it's already eleven o'clock."

Outside, a freezing wind hit their faces. Verónica was glad she had bought herself a jacket.

"If I didn't know you had a girlfriend and a tendency towards loyalty, I'd invite you to a motel. Since you paid in the bar."

Federico laughed nervously. She wanted to kill him when he reacted like that, all innocent and bashful. She'd kill him and then fuck his dead body.

"Vero, Vero. I'll walk you to a taxi. I've missed you a lot all this time."

"I've missed you too."

"I didn't know what would happen when I saw you again."

"And what did happen?"

Again, those shadows across his face, that feeling that part of him was still there, back in Tucumán. Verónica briefly feared that Federico was going to walk out of her life again, that the rendezvous in Dadá, the short walk to Avenida Córdoba was one of those enchanting dreams that turn into a nightmare on waking. She didn't want to wake up, or for him to leave.

"It was lovely to see you," he said.

The relief. To feel relieved – is there any better feeling? Verónica couldn't stop herself. Now that he wasn't abandoning her, the way he had at the hotel in Yacanto del Valle, she wanted to double her stake.

"Nothing more?"

"You should know the answer to that. I'm Mr Predictable, after all."

They arrived at Avenida Córdoba, where the taxis were coming thick and fast. No excuse to keep standing there together, then. Verónica kissed him on the cheek, slowly, smelling him, breathing him in, and Federico touched her hair. She stopped a taxi and got in, grinning through the window at him, and the taxi took off down Avenida Córdoba towards the hostel.

I I

Patricia Beltrán arrived early at the newsroom. The only other person there was the new editor-in-chief, Julio Tanatián, with whom she had got off to a bad start. A few days ago, Tanatián had called her into his office and given her a dressing-down for publishing María Vanini's article. As far as he was concerned, to attack an archbishop was to go against the ecclesiastical hierarchy, and doing that would have repercussions for the magazine's advertising revenue. Or did she not know that the magazine's biggest advertisers were companies that belonged to Catholic families? Patricia had told him that she wasn't aware of that fact, but that the allegation was too important not to be published. Besides, it was an exclusive.

"Did you know that the woman who has made these accusations against the archbishop is a militant Trotskyite?"

"And a Trotskyite can't denounce a priest?"

"This woman has invented a story to attack the Church. And we can't be anyone's stooge. Look, I've just received a statement from the Argentine Episcopal Conference refuting the slander published by us. Make sure you put it out on a double page at the start of the section. And find a good photo of Nogués to illustrate it."

Patricia left the editor's office spitting nails. She disliked Tanatián's style – too much outward negotiating and inward authoritarianism. He behaved more like someone juggling different vested interests than a journalist managing a newsroom. While all the freelancers were trying to protect their own interests, plugging their monthly bulletins or radio shows, Tanatián was toadying to the highest echelons of power. He met with ministers, businesspeople, and church leaders too. If it hadn't been for the chaos that had reigned in the days before his arrival, the allegations against Archbishop Nogués would never have been published.

As the minutes went by, the newsroom began to acquire its usual pulse: the other editors arrived and then the writers and interns; someone put on the television; the receptionist popped in and, visibly annoyed, asked who had ordered a food delivery and nobody owned up until some writer emerged from the bathroom and said it had been him; the assistant editors and the art director were seen going to Tanatián's office; some section head swore because none of the designers had arrived and he needed to get a piece on the page that had been waiting since the day before. A photographer went over to a journalist's desk to arrange a time to go and do an interview, another came over simply to watch the soccer or a gossip show or whatever happened to be on TV. There was a cacophony of ringing phones, of a video playing through someone's computer speakers, of a buzzing printer tossing out pages and more pages, of old-school hacks thumping on their keyboards as though they were typewriters. A normal day, in other words, for Patricia, who had now read the Church's official statement. She wasn't against publishing it – after all, she strongly believed in the right to reply – but the magazine and the author of the article came off so badly that a piece would be needed to put their side and set the Church's accusations in context. She would talk to Tanatián during the editorial meeting.

She looked on the Télam cable and scanned the headlines to check what was happening in the world and see if there was anything useful for her section. And there it was, a statement as cold, indifferent and neutral as any other agency news item: Fabiana Benítez had been stabbed to death. Télam reported that her body had been found at the door of the bishop's palace. According to police sources, Fabiana had been attacked by her partner because of her alleged link to Archbishop Nogués.

It wasn't the first time in her career that Patricia had had to contend with the murder of an article's subject, but she still felt a mixture of shock, indignation and fear. She glanced around for María Vanini, who was arriving in the newsroom wearing her usual scowl. Before she had a chance to put her things down on her desk, Patricia called her over and showed her the wire story. María's hand flew to her mouth. She seemed more surprised than anything else.

"Didn't you get in touch with her when I told you to?"

"Yes, I texted her. I offered her my support, but she didn't get back to me."

"Did you tell her she was in danger?"

"Well, she already knew that. It must have crossed her mind that the guy might attack her."

"You believe it was the boyfriend? The cable says 'police sources'. What if it was Nogués's people?"

"Either way, it was a man. A femicide."

"Yes, but the motives would be different. She shouldn't have stayed in Santiago."

"You can't make an allegation against someone like Nogués and expect a pat on the back, can you?"

"Proximity to evil often makes people lose perspective on the possibility of harm."

María spread her arms in a gesture of resignation. "Pato, we can't be people's guardian angels."

"No, María, you can't be a guardian angel. That much is clear."

"Shall I write a piece about her? I've got up-to-date statistics on femicide, province by province."

Patricia told her to hold off, that she would confirm that later. She called Verónica and read her the whole wire story.

"There are no witnesses yet the police know it was the partner? Did they find the knife at his home? Has he confessed? Sounds far-fetched. It was the priest."

"That's what I thought."

"What are you going to do? I can't cover it because I'm on my way to a convent. I'll tell you about it afterwards."

"I'm going to send someone there. But I'd rather send the office boy than María."

"Have you got a budget for freelancers? Because Corso is working on this case too, and he knows it very well."

"Things here are in such a mess that nobody notices stuff

like that. I'll call Corso. I hope Rodolfo can speak to Fabiana's mother. She's the key to this."

"I was thinking the same."

They ended the call. Patricia knew that there were hard days ahead. If Corso ruled out the partner as a suspect, all suspicion would fall on Nogués, the same archbishop who had denied everything in a communiqué from the Church authorities that Tanatián wanted to splash across a double-page spread. She called Corso, looked up the next flight to Santiago del Estero and asked an admin assistant to book him on it right away. She wasn't going to say anything to Tanatián until she had all the cards in her hand.

I I I

María Magdalena invited Verónica round for lunch before they set off for the convent. She asked her to come to her apartment at midday; they would eat something, get changed, then head for the house of the Sisters of the Most Holy Charity. María Magdalena lived in the Boedo neighbourhood. Her apartment was small but comfortable: a living-dining room separated from the kitchen by a breakfast bar, simple furnishings, no television in sight.

Lunch was a cream of asparagus soup, then a salad of chicken, tomatoes, cheese, egg, carrot and celery, all prepared by María Magdalena.

"Do you ever miss the nun's life?" Verónica asked.

"Sometimes. I miss having my life organized for me, not having to worry about the day-to-day. Not that I don't enjoy this life, but there are times I'd like someone else to point me in the right direction and tell me what to do. I don't even know if it's better to buy celery or leeks, or if in the bakery I should ask for meringues, *felipes* or *miñones*."

"I never know what to ask for in the bakery either."

María Magdalena made coffee while Verónica cleared the table and washed the dishes. Her phone rang: it was Patricia, calling to tell her about Fabiana's murder. After hanging up, she saw María Magdalena looking at her.

"I think it's too risky for us to go ahead with this plan," she said.

"Can they easily find us out?"

"Not easily, but I can't rule it out. And given the direction all this is taking, I think we should have another think about it."

"You mean we shouldn't go?" asked Verónica.

"You shouldn't go. I know my way around a convent like you do a shopping mall, if you'll forgive the typecasting. I mean, I can go shopping in a mall, like you, but it doesn't come naturally, and my awkwardness would immediately be obvious. The same might apply to you in a convent."

"Not a chance. We're both going. I promise that if I took you shopping and you stuck by me nobody would notice that you don't know the difference between prêt-à-porter and haute couture."

When Verónica went into María Magdalena's bedroom, she felt as though she were already inside a convent. The single bed to one side, the tidy desk, a small bookcase, a stack of magazines. On the bed were two folded habits.

"On top of your underwear you wear this cotton skirt and a white turtleneck. Then over that goes the serge tunic, which you can adjust with this three-knotted rope around your waist, but don't make it so tight you look like one of those sexy nuns by Divito. When I see these old uniforms, I'm glad I chose to join the Pauline Order. Next you put on the scapular, which looks so pretty, and you fix it so it doesn't move all over the place. Then the veil goes over your hair. Leave a little hair visible. It's the only touch of coquetry we've achieved after hundreds of years enduring the wimple, which some nuns still wear, by the way. Put on these tights – they're horrible, but very warm. And here are your shoes, plain and comfortable. Everything should be your size, or rather too big, which is the preferred style. Feel free to get changed in my room, and I'll use the bathroom."

Verónica put on the clothes. Before adding the veil, she looked at her reflection in the little mirror in the room. She liked the tunic's greyish-blue colour. She looked odd, but not inordinately so. Dressing as a nun seemed neither particularly strange, nor particularly special.

"Give me a shout when you're ready and I'll help you with the veil. It can be tricky if you're not used to hair clips."

María Magdalena reappeared already dressed. Her face shone. Even if she didn't say so, it was clear that she felt happy in these clothes. Verónica perched on the bed and María Magdalena firmly fixed her veil in place.

"Leave your glasses on – they make you look more pious."

"And where do we carry our phones, money and, I don't know, things we need?"

"There's a little pocket here." She pointed at the habit, below the rope belt. "But I'll also carry a small bag for the two flashlights we're going to need. And to bring back the blue book."

"I thought we would photograph it."

"It'll be quicker to take it."

They went down to the street, and Verónica took her first steps as a nun in the outside world. She expected someone to say something, but almost nobody noticed them. They got into a taxi – she noted that this was much easier to do in a long skirt than in a short or tight one – and María Magdalena gave the driver the address of the convent, which was the same as for the religious school and the church Verónica had visited when she was investigating Jazmín's disappearance.

"Won't Father Anselmo recognize me?"

"You're going to be mixed in with two hundred nuns. The most he'll be doing is celebrating Mass. He won't be in direct contact with us."

They drove past Doctor Rossi's clinic and had the taxi drop them at the corner, right in front of the convent's entrance. Verónica noticed that the nuns milling around outside were wearing a different uniform.

"It's the old version. Some sisters still wear it, especially the ones from Colombia and Ecuador."

They followed these women into the building; some men at the door (who looked more like gardeners or plumbers than bouncers) greeted them with a nod as they passed.

"First we're going to see my friend Mariana."

They walked down corridors bustling with nuns, who didn't particularly notice them and emanated a sense of calm Verónica tried to imitate. She felt she was succeeding. The two women crossed a courtyard with a fountain and walked up some stairs to the first floor, leaving behind them the bustle of the ground floor. A series of identical doors suggested that the bedrooms were here. María Magdalena knocked on one of them and out came a small, young nun wearing thick glasses. The nun took María Magdalena's hands in her own and gave her a kiss on the cheek, then repeated this gesture with Verónica. She didn't ask them into her room, but walked with them down the corridor to a window, from which they could observe the inner courtyard and part of the convent.

"Sister Ofelia is in her office constantly, welcoming the delegations," said Mariana.

"So it's going to be difficult to get in there without being seen," said María Magdalena.

"She definitely won't miss Vespers at seven thirty."

"That could be our moment, then."

"Or after 10 p.m. In any case, you're going to have to be very careful. Since this morning there have been some strange things going on. Here and on the brothers' side. It seems we have visitors."

"In addition to all the nuns from Latin America?" asked Verónica.

Mariana looked at Verónica, then at María Magdalena. She seemed to be hesitating between saying more or keeping quiet. Finally she spoke, lowering her voice a little.

"I shouldn't be telling you this, but Brother Raúl sent me a WhatsApp saying that a surprise guest has arrived in their house. Archbishop Arturo Nogués."

Veronica looked at Mariana, scandalized: monks and nuns use WhatsApp? It was a few seconds before she fully understood the implications of what she had just heard.

IV

If Chief Superintendent Barbosa was running a drug cartel, Federico had no way to prove it. It wasn't clear to him what role the prefect Arizmendi performed, either, except that he opposed Barbosa for some reason. Nor did he have anything solid on Juan García, only suspicions. The scumbag never left a trail, and any accusation of colluding with Barbosa could quickly be dismantled in the first rebuttal by his defence team. However, if he could at least prove the involvement of Barbosa in the corpse trafficking and of Herminia de García in the illegal adoptions, it was likely that Barbosa and García's alibis would collapse and they might give themselves away. The key to both strands of the investigation was Doctor Rossi. He had been involved in the adoptions and in the mutilation and sale of cadavers, never mind that his clinic had also been a hideout for wounded criminals. If he was arrested, perhaps he would supply the evidence that Federico needed on García and Barbosa.

Federico had enough material now, but without a judge's order there wasn't much he could do with it. And the judge presiding over the case of the body trafficking wasn't willing to proceed, raising the suspicion that Barbosa himself, through some intermediary in the courts, had managed to halt the investigation.

These were the conclusions reached by Federico while on his way to meet Verónica, and to break up with her.

They had arranged that he would pick her up at the offices of the PR company where she worked, then go and have a drink and end up at her place. During the eight months of their relationship, he had gone to Verónica's workplace only rarely, perhaps three or four times. They usually met at a bar, at some event or in their respective apartments.

A glass door announced that the offices of D'Alessandro and Associates were on the eighth floor. Federico rang the bell and they let him in. He walked across the soft and springy carpet towards one of the receptionists and asked for Verónica Rinaldi. She appeared almost immediately, in a little tailored suit, grey and form-fitting, worn with a slightly low-cut white blouse and a short, moss-green coat. The outfit gave her the look of a 1950s pin-up.

"Let's go, before they realize I've escaped," said Verónica with a grin, after kissing him in front of the receptionists.

Federico had been awake all night. The meeting with Verónica Rosenthal in Dadá had messed with his head. If his psychologist was right, if love was someone occupying all your neurons, then Verónica Rosenthal was the perfect embodiment of love, because in the last twenty-four hours he had done nothing but think of her.

Verónica Rinaldi didn't deserve that. And he needed to be clear with himself about what he wanted. Verónica Rosenthal reminded him of a giant zip line he had tried in Brazil when he was twelve. From below it had looked like the most amazing experience in the world, a promise of happiness from end to end, the best possible combination of freedom and action, but once he was on it he felt more terrified than he had ever been in his life, as his legs flailed in the void, the harness straps dug into his balls and stomach, and the noise from the cables made him think that at any moment he could plunge into nothingness. He was too old to be flailing about in the air for anyone now.

And yet.

Better to break up with Verónica and see what might happen with Verónica. Everyone was right: he should have picked a girlfriend with a different name.

They got into the elevator and Federico pressed the ground floor button. Verónica slipped her arm around his waist. They were alone. Around the level of the fifth floor it stopped and all the lights went out, apart from a few LEDs that barely illuminated the tiny space.

"Has the power gone off?"

"Maybe," said Federico. "But these buildings have emergency generators. We should be moving again in a few seconds."

They waited for a few minutes, then Federico pressed the emergency call button and the alarm rang out loud and clear. Presently they heard a voice from outside, somewhere beneath them, which said:

"Don't worry. There's been a small failure in the elevator's control system and it's stopped as a security measure, but we'll get it started again soon."

"It's a bit embarrassing that such a modern building has such crappy elevators," Verónica complained.

A young woman's voice came on the line, asking: "Is that you, Verónica? Are you trapped? They'll get you out soon."

"Obviously I'm trapped," Verónica retorted, then under her breath to Federico: "That's one of our juniors. Not the brightest."

Federico nodded. Verónica tugged at his tie. She started speaking in a breathy tone.

"I've always fantasized about making love in an elevator."

Federico gently but decisively moved an inch or two away from his girlfriend.

"Verónica, I've got something to tell you."

She looked suspiciously at him. "What do you mean?"

"We need to take some time. Think about what we want."

"Are you breaking up with me?"

"Not exactly."

"Then what do you mean you need time? That you're going to buy some time in the supermarket or that we're going to stop seeing each other?"

"I think we shouldn't keep seeing each other, at least not for a while."

"What's wrong, Federico?"

"I think our relationship has stalled. You're an incredible, charming, attractive person and I'm an idiot who can't accept all the good things you bring him because he keeps sabotaging his own happiness."

"Are you seeing your ex again?"

"Which one?"

"Don't play the idiot with me."

"One thing has nothing to do with the other."

"You're seeing your ex again."

Verónica started crying and he tried to embrace her, but she pushed him away, beating her fists on his chest.

"Let me go, you bastard. Go off with the other one."

"I'm not going off with anyone, Verónica."

As Federico kept trying to hug her, she stopped hitting him so she could scratch his face instead. Federico put up a feeble defence. His cheek burned and bled. Someone from outside asked if everything was all right. Since Verónica was crying, Federico answered. They were fine, he said. Verónica kept repeating, between hiccups, "Piece of shit."

Suddenly the lights came on and the elevator descended half a floor. The doors opened to reveal all the people who had been waiting for them. Some of Verónica's colleagues from work, the doorman, the electrician, the odd curious bystander. Their initial smiles froze into rictuses of concern. Among the crowd was Agustín. When Verónica saw him she flung herself into his arms, weeping. Federico stepped out of the elevator, hand pressed against his wounded face. Everyone who knew he was Verónica's boyfriend looked at him with contempt, and those who didn't know him thought he was a stranger who must have tried to assault a woman in the elevator. They glared at him with a hatred that seemed about to erupt into violence. Agustín looked like a man prepared to fight a duel there and then. There wasn't much left for Federico to do there. He decided to walk down the last five flights.

V

When Mariana left them in one of the corridors of the convent, Verónica asked María Magdalena why they didn't simply hide in her friend's room until it was time to go looking for the blue book.

"She's frightened. I don't want to expose her too much. At least she let us leave the bag with the flashlights there. Let's take the opportunity to look around a bit."

They returned to the ground floor, crossed a courtyard and arrived at a colonnade. There were only nuns in this area, and the occasional laywoman.

"The second door on the right," said María Magdalena, "is the office of the Provincial Superior. She's going to be at a Mass at the other end of the convent. She doesn't have windows onto the colonnade, so we won't be seen from outside if we use flashlights. If we're careful, we shouldn't have any problems."

The door was slightly open and, as they walked past, out of the corners of their eyes they could see nuns inside. Verónica couldn't make out which one was Ofelia Dorín. They came across a stairway that connected one wing of the building to the other. María Magdalena explained: "That dividing wall separates us from the Order's masculine line."

"And from the clinic?"

"There's no direct link between the convent and the clinic. There is one between the clinic and the house of the Most Holy Charity's brothers."

"But we can't get in there from here."

María Magdalena smiled at her. "Where there's a will, there's a way. You see the chapel over there? Behind the pulpit there's a trapdoor leading to a cellar. That cellar is linked through a series of tunnels with the brothers' house. You come out in a storeroom that leads to their courtyard."

"Wow. Wouldn't it be easier just to have a door in the dividing wall so people can get from one side to the other?"

"But what would Christianity be without its mysteries?"

"Is there also a secret route to the clinic?"

"I have no idea how one would get there from inside the building. That's something Mariana never told her sister, and so I don't know either."

They made a circular tour of the convent and returned to their starting point.

"You know what?" said Verónica as she observed the movement of the nuns with a certain fascination. "When I was a teenager I thought of becoming a rabbi."

"Seriously? You're a believer?"

"No, not really. But back then I thought the best way to rebel against my atheist family was to be religious. Luckily my grandfather Elías talked me out of my delusion."

"I don't think it's delusional."

Verónica needed a piss. María Magdalena went with her to the bathroom, which seemed standard, with a row of cubicles, not dissimilar to what you'd find in a club. The main difference was that there was a crucifix on the wall. Verónica had to wrestle with her tunic and the skirt underneath it before she could relieve herself. She washed her hands and looked in the mirror, feeling ridiculous. She couldn't wait to get out of this garb and back into her usual clothes. She detested uniforms of any kind.

"Is there no bar inside the convent where we can get a coffee?"

"No, but it's time for tea anyway."

They went to a dining room with long tables on which there were already cups and various plates with croissants. In a corner, on a counter, were flasks containing hot drinks. The women poured themselves coffee and went to sit at one of the communal tables. Verónica avoided eye contact with any of the other nuns in case they asked her something. When they prayed aloud she lowered her gaze and tried to follow what they were saying with her lips.

After tea, they were directed to an imposing room, its perimeter lined with stately chairs. The walls had dark wood panelling with religious images in high relief. Above them were images of Jesus carrying the Cross, fallen on the ground and crucified. In the corners were medium-sized statues of

323

nuns similar to the ones Verónica had seen in the Church of the Most Holy Charity (then again, perhaps they were saints). Beside the entrance was a striking organ that looked very old. More nuns were arriving in this room and María Magdalena made a beeline for some seats in the corner, Verónica following her.

"What's going to happen here?" asked Verónica anxiously.

"This is the convent's choir, one of the best places in Buenos Aires to sing. Since a lot of nuns have come from all over the continent to take part, I expect we're about to sing some traditional religious songs."

"'We'?"

"We've got time to fill. And we're going to be safer here than anywhere else in the building. You don't have to sing – just mouth the words."

The next hour and a half was spent singing songs of praise to Jesus and the Virgin Mary. Finally the concert finished with music that sounded familiar to Verónica. She had heard it in a horror movie in which someone gets murdered in a monastery, or something similarly ghoulish.

"Mozart's 'Lacrimosa'," María Magdalena clarified, still emotional as they left the choir.

Most of the nuns now went in one direction, while they took the opposite route.

"It's time for Mass. In a few minutes the coast will be clear."

Verónica felt her phone vibrate. She hoped it wasn't Harrison calling to say he wanted to see her that night. Surreptitiously she took out her phone – she had seen several nuns using them – and saw that it was Rodolfo Corso.

"I got this number from your boss, who's temporarily also my boss," he said. "She told me to call you and tell you about the latest developments. The accusation against Fabiana's partner collapsed immediately. The man was lucky, if he can

324

be said to have been lucky in anything, to have been in a radio interview at the time of the crime. I've also been able to talk to a kid, a teenager, who lives almost opposite Fabiana's house. He saw, from his bedroom, two men waiting for Fabiana in a car and then chasing her when they saw her arriving. She ran off and managed to reach the door of the bishop's palace. The mother doesn't want to talk to anyone. So cross off the partner and put a few more chips on the archbishop."

"I'm less than a hundred yards away from him as we speak."

"Be careful, then. I'll call you with any news."

Verónica updated María Magdalena. Both of them looked towards the brothers' house, as though they might see Nogués through the walls.

It was already dark.

"Come on. Showtime."

Verónica followed her.

15   *Between the Walls*

I

Silence and darkness had fallen over the convent of the Sisters of the Most Holy Charity. The daytime bustle had moved towards the church, leaving the corridors and courtyards deserted. María Magdalena and Verónica walked confidently towards the office of Sister Ofelia Dorín. There was nobody in the colonnade and they could see no sign of movement inside. They waited a few seconds then approached the door, hoping that the nun had not changed her usual practice and locked it. María Magdalena turned the handle and the door opened.

They entered, closed the door and switched on their flashlights. The nun was tidy, ascetic. On her desk was a photograph of Pope John Paul II. On the wall, a crucifix and a photo of the Archbishop of Buenos Aires. A painting reproduced the image of a saint whom Verónica, clueless in these matters, didn't recognize. There were some shelves bearing folders, and an antique cupboard in carved wood. María Magdalena opened it while Verónica shone her flashlight inside. There were some books, more folders and a pile of blue notebooks. They were the Rivadavia type, covered in blue, wipeable paper. Each bore a label with a number on it. The one on the top said *11*.

"This is the one," said María Magdalena, flicking through it.

While Verónica held the flashlight, María Magdalena picked a page at random. In the top corner there was a date: 10 March 2000. On the first line the word *Shade* was underlined. Under that were the words *Liliana, Pozo Hondo, 21, two older children, no husband or family, no work. $800.* Under that entry was the word *Light*, underlined, and then *Family of Hernán and Lorena Gatti, Nuestra Señora de Pompeya, lawyer and teacher*. There followed addresses, telephone numbers and codes or acronyms that were hard to decipher (*3 V, 2 positives, rep. local p. i., I.C.H.P*) and finally, in a hand somewhere between childish and laborious, came a description written in the style of a school composition: *I met Liliana in a room at the Pozo Hondo Society of Development. A dim girl who only knows the Lord's Prayer, never finished elementary school and is ignorant of all that is necessary to save one's Soul. There was no possibility of this girl ever becoming a good Catholic. After several meetings, at last she saw reason and accepted that the fruit of her womb should go to a wholesome and educated family. She accompanied me to Santiago with her two children. We welcomed her to our house and clinic. She gave birth to a son whom the parents have christened Agustín, after our Great Saint Augustine. She returned to Pozo Hondo with her older children and the money we gave her. Blessed be the Name of the Lord who has allowed us to fulfil His mandate.*

"It's despicable," said Verónica, who was reading over María Magdalena's shoulder. "There's something wrong with her."

"An evil woman. A person who believes herself to be pure and therefore above the law."

María Magdalena picked up the book with *10* on it. Inside were more entries, documenting older cases.

"It's not *the* blue book. It's all these blue books. Hundreds of children removed from their mothers by this madwoman."

"If you think of her as mad you take responsibility away from her. She isn't alone. It's the whole order, it's the Christian

Home Movement, it's Rossi's clinic, it's the archbishop. This is a criminal organization."

Verónica motioned her to be quiet; they could hear voices coming from the corridor. They turned off their flashlights and kept silent. Two women came closer, chatting, passed in front of the office door and continued on their way, voices fading.

"Let's go," said María Magdalena, putting all the blue books into her bag and closing the cupboard.

For a few seconds they watched the door then, when they were sure nobody was near, walked out through the colonnade to the other side of the courtyard.

"We've got the books. Nobody will check our bags if we leave the convent now."

"Wait, María Magdalena. Nogués is here and the clinic's right opposite. We can't just leave."

"What else can we do though? We can hardly ask the archbishop for a statement for the magazine."

"But if we could get into the clinic…"

"To see where they cut up the corpses? I don't think it'll be on any signposts."

"We have to try."

"Don't let perfect be the enemy of good, Verónica. We've got eleven books containing hundreds of cases of illegal adoptions. It's enough to sink the nuns and their accomplices."

"And Nogués? He repeatedly abused a teenager, stole her child, had her murdered. That's beyond doubt. And it's also very likely that he's abused other girls, because one is never enough for these guys who think themselves untouchable."

"We haven't got long. As soon as Mass is over, Ofelia Dorín will come back to her office and discover the theft. And then we won't ever get out of here."

"Take the blue books. I'll meet you back at your apartment

in a couple of hours, then I can change out of this ridiculous get-up."

"No, there's no way I'm leaving you here alone. Let's hide the bag in Mariana's room and try to get to the clinic. But at the first sign of trouble or danger we're out of here – OK?"

II

Mariana wasn't in her room, so they left the bag with the blue books behind a cabinet. The women were having to act faster now than was prudent. They kept hold of their flashlights, concealing them in the wide sleeves of their tunics. In the corridor they passed a few nuns, but none paid them any attention.

"We've got less than an hour to go over there and get back. Later on there won't be anyone left in these corridors, and it would look very suspicious if we were found walking around here. And we have to pray Dorín doesn't discover that her books are missing... or at least I have to pray."

Arriving at the little chapel, they went inside and closed the door after them. Moonlight gleamed through the windows of what looked like a compressed, scaled-down version of a church. There was a smell of incense. María Magdalena went towards the altar, crouched down and tapped the floor.

"Here it is. Give me a hand."

Between them the women lifted a trapdoor, hinges creaking as the wood moved. They switched on their flashlights and pointed them into the cellar. A metal ladder led straight down into it. First Verónica descended the ladder, then María Magdalena, carefully closing the trapdoor behind her. They found themselves in a narrow room, with roughly plastered walls. Verónica quickly scanned the space, looking for any insects, spiders' webs, bats hanging from the ceiling or rats around their feet, but she saw none of these. The area must be used regularly, because it was kept tidy and clear enough to allow easy passage.

They advanced along a narrow corridor, ahead of them complete darkness, complete silence. Verónica had a sensation of both blindness and deafness but, while the subterranean passage suppressed some senses, it heightened others: there was a smell of penetrating damp like you find in old, abandoned houses and the feel of the walls on either side was rough and impossible to avoid because of the narrowness of the path.

Although the underground tunnel continued for no more than fifty yards, it felt like miles to Verónica. Finally they arrived at another iron ladder. Verónica shone her flashlight to one side of it and saw that the passage continued.

"Where do you think that goes?" she asked.

"No idea. The clinic?"

"Let's go and see."

María Magdalena didn't seem too sure about this, but once more she followed Verónica's lead. To complicate matters, there were two further bifurcations on the path. They chose one that led to a dead end, retraced their steps and went the other way, which led to another iron stairway. Shining their flashlights at the ceiling, they made out another trapdoor. María Magdalena went up the ladder first and tried without luck to open it; it must need more strength than she had. She passed her flashlight to Verónica and tried again, pushing with all her might and, miraculously, the door opened.

It wasn't a miracle, though. Someone had opened the door from the other side.

"Come on up, Sisters, we've been waiting for you."

A white light shining above them illuminated the face of María Magdalena. Verónica thought of running, but she couldn't abandon her friend.

330

Two young men – stocky and wearing nurses' uniforms – helped them up into the room. The men didn't seem surprised or annoyed, and showed no sign of aggression.

"Doctor Rossi wasn't sure if you were going to come now or later," said one of them.

"You two haven't been before, have you?" the other one asked, suspiciously.

"No, it's the first time," said María Magdalena, without having to lie.

"Follow me, we'll take you to Doctor Rossi's office."

They walked to an elevator then went up to the clinic's top floor, the fifth. Verónica and María Magdalena exchanged glances. They didn't need to speak to acknowledge that they had stumbled into a misunderstanding, one that needed to be maintained if they were going to come through this unscathed.

A strong smell, disagreeable and hard to define, filled the air.

"It's the chemicals they use to treat the skins," explained one of the nurses.

"Don't you want to see how they flay a corpse?" asked the other.

"Leave the poor Sisters alone," said the first one and turned to them. "Did Sister Julia tell you that she fainted?"

"Yes, she did mention it," said María Magdalena.

"I don't think I'd faint," ventured Verónica.

The nurses exchanged glances. One seemed to be seeking the approval of the other, who shrugged. They walked further down the corridor, then opened a door. The visitors didn't enter, but watched from the doorway. María Magdalena raised a hand to her mouth, as though to hold back a scream, or nausea.

On the hospital beds nearest the door were four naked bodies: three adult men and a woman. A male nurse came to get one of the beds and wheeled it to the back of the room. In the middle of the area were glass tables on top of which were what looked like a collection of curved plastic items. In fact they were torsos detached from cadavers. At the back of the room, a power saw was slicing the arms off a body. On one side of it, bones were piled up according to type: tibias in one place, fibulas in another, ribs further on. A man appeared, smoking, the apron and cap he was wearing giving him the appearance of a slaughterer. He was spattered everywhere with blood. This man glanced reprovingly towards the door and the nurses got the message.

"We should go," said one of them.

"And they didn't even faint," added the other.

Neither of the women spoke. Verónica wanted to vomit, to scream. It was impossible to unsee those images or rid herself of that stench of death, impregnated in her nostrils. She tried to concentrate on walking forward.

They were shown into an office where a small, balding man with glasses and a suit greeted them with a handshake. He spoke quietly and softly, as though imitating a priest. Perhaps he imagined that was the way you should talk to nuns.

"I thought Sisters Julia and Mabel were coming."

"They're part of the reception for the nuns attending the convention," said María Magdalena.

Rossi nodded, sat down in a wing chair on the other side of the desk and invited the women to take a seat.

Verónica found it hard to imagine this man married to Doctor Laura Rivarola. He seemed more like a 1940s clerk, fearful for his job.

"Right, have you got the details of the new driver?" he asked.

"Yes," Verónica said quickly, taking a wild gamble. "Didn't you get them?"

Rossi smiled condescendingly. "If I had them, you wouldn't have needed to take the trouble of coming."

"Of course – he's called Ricardo Pérez."

"Is he from the same church as Father Ignacio?"

"He is, and the Father has full confidence in him."

"Have you brought his photograph and the document with all his details?"

Verónica and María Magdalena looked at each other. María Magdalena made as if to check her pocket.

"What an idiot I am. I left it in the choir."

"Never mind. I'll call Sister Ofelia to get someone to look for it and bring the folder over."

Rossi picked up the handset on his desk and dialled a number. Verónica glanced casually behind her. The two nurses were standing at the door.

"It's either switched off or out of coverage. Isn't she in the convent?"

"Yes, but the signal's very bad in some places," said Verónica.

"We should go now," said María Magdalena, standing up.

Rossi dismissed them with another handshake. Verónica noticed disquiet in the doctor's expression but, if he wasn't going to try to keep them there, she saw no reason for trying harder to seem credible. The nurses escorted them to the trapdoor and they went back down the ladder they had come up and then hurried away, breathing in fits and starts.

"It's all there, Verónica. We saw it with our own two eyes," gasped María Magdalena.

"Now we just need to find out what Archbishop Nogués is doing here."

"We need to get back to the convent, grab the books and go."

"Ten minutes."

They had reached the ladder that led to the Brothers' house. Once again, María Magdalena went up first; if they ran into anyone, she would make a more convincing nun than Verónica. This time the door yielded easily, barely creaking as it opened. The room on the other side of it was also dark. María Magdalena peered out, silently: nobody there. They climbed out of the tunnel and found themselves in a storeroom full of tools.

"What now, where do we go?" Verónica asked.

"We can't wander around the whole house looking for Nogués. Apart from anything else, if we meet someone this time we'll have to explain ourselves." She got out her phone and wrote a text. "I'm asking Mariana for advice. She knows this place better."

They stood waiting for the nun's reply, alert to any noises. Two minutes later, the phone buzzed.

"Mariana says that outside here on the right there's a path with a privet hedge leading to a small house. It's usually empty, except for when special guests are staying."

"So Nogués must be there."

Stepping outside the storeroom, they saw a path running alongside a privet hedge high enough to provide some cover. There was no need for flashlights, as the starry night illuminated their way. Twenty yards short of the house, the privet-lined path ended in a garden with shrubs and flower beds through which they cautiously advanced, mindful that lights were on in the house. The women kept low, using the shrubs for cover until they were a few yards from what looked like a living room with an enormous picture window. Inside was a group of people. The archbishop was sitting in a large, throne-like chair. Around him were gathered Sister Ofelia Dorín, Father Anselmo, a woman dressed in everyday clothes, an older man in a suit and a younger man who looked like an assistant: he was serving the others glasses of water and cups of coffee.

Suddenly all the lights went out – not just the ones in the guest house, but some low illumination in the garden and the distant lights of other buildings. The assistant came out into the garden, went to the side of the house and started up an engine. Light returned to the house. The man picked up a can lying nearby and poured its contents into the engine.

"What's he doing?" Verónica asked.

"It's a generator. He's putting in gasoline to keep it going."

The assistant went back inside the house, but nobody paid him any attention. They continued to talk among themselves, with no sign of suspecting the women's presence among the shrubs.

"If only we could get a bit closer to hear what they're talking about."

"No, Verónica, that's far too risky."

"To cap it all, my shitty phone isn't good enough to get a photo from here."

As though hearing this, Ofelia Dorín took her own phone out of her bag. She spoke on it for a few minutes, the others – who had broken off their conversation – listening intently. After ending the call, the nun started telling the rest of the group something that prompted the other woman to grasp her face in the kind of surprised gesture nobody makes any more. The archbishop had got to his feet. He reminded Verónica of Max von Sydow, not when he played a priest in *The Exorcist* but in the movies he made as an old man. He looked like someone who could impose himself in any scenario, one of those people who always get what they want. The most immediate sensation he awoke in Verónica was fear.

Now the other people in the room also stood up. Whatever the nun had told them had alarmed them.

"Let's go. I don't like this at all," said María Magdalena.

"Yes. We should go back."

Then came one of those instants where life stops being what it was and changes for ever. The trigger might be an accident, a piece of news, a decision, something you did or that other people did to you. Verónica and María Magdalena experienced such a pivotal moment when all the patio lights came on. The people they had been observing were now watching them, as in one of those avant-garde pieces of theatre where the actors become the spectators and vice versa.

"Walk," said Doctor Rossi, resisting the temptation to make a speech despite having the attention of the two women, three nurses and an audience behind the window – not to mention the compelling presence of a handgun.

III

Doctor Rossi indicated the entrance to the house, and they walked towards it. It was strange to find themselves inside that living room, a space that seemed too small for so many people. The first person to speak was Father Anselmo, pointing at Verónica.

"She's the journalist who came to interrogate me."

"I told you so," Ofelia Dorín said bitterly, looking at the priest.

Nobody seemed in a hurry to speak, perhaps because there wasn't much to say. Both sides knew what the other wanted. They showed a rare decorum in not overlaying the circumstances – which were already sufficiently dire for everyone – with dramatic rhetoric. The man in civilian dress said, quietly and calmly:

"We need to search them. Weapons, phones, microphones, whatever they have."

There was a brief moment of doubt. The archbishop was an abuser of children, the nun stole babies, the doctor trafficked in bodies and the civilian must have some interesting crimes to his name, but apparently nobody wanted to pat down the women or tell them to strip off. Perhaps their religious uniform protected them. It was the woman in everyday clothes, whose similarity to the nun suggested she was Herminia de García, who took the lead.

"Go through to the bedroom."

Closeted in a room with the Dorín sisters, the women were ordered to take off their tunics and skirts. The sisters took their phones and Verónica's glasses, the only items they had on them. They didn't pat them down or ask them to strip completely.

"You can get dressed. Although you're not worthy to wear the holy habit of our Order."

"You're not worthy of any habit," María Magdalena retorted, seeming ready to hit Ofelia Dorín.

"God has chosen me to do His will."

There was a window in the room and it crossed Verónica's mind that, if she and María Magdalena attacked the women, they might be able to escape – but she doubted they could get as far as the underground tunnel before the guys dressed as nurses caught up with them. She resigned herself to getting dressed again and returning to the main room, where the same people were still waiting.

"We have to put an end to this," said Ofelia Dorín in the same tone of suppressed fury she had used in the bedroom.

"Not here," said the archbishop.

"What are you going to do to us?" asked Verónica. "Are you going to kill us, like you killed Tonso, Gómez Brest and the stolen car dealer?"

"We should take them to the chamber," the man in civilian clothes said to Ofelia Dorín.

"Are you going to stab us to death, like Fabiana Benítez? Did you enjoy that, Nogués, did you enjoy it as much as abusing her?"

The assistant took her arm and hustled her towards the front door. One of the nurses did the same with María Magdalena.

"If you think you won't be punished for this, you're very mistaken," said the ex-nun.

"You assume you know everything, but you know nothing," said the archbishop, directing himself to Verónica.

"You abused her when she was a child and kept on abusing her, you stole her daughter, you wrecked her life and you had her killed. What else do you think I should know?"

The women were taken outside and marched back along the privet-lined path. Sister Ofelia and her assistant went ahead, with Verónica and María Magdalena behind them and the three nurses bringing up the rear. The assistant didn't go with them down into the tunnel; he was charged with closing the trapdoor once the nurses and women had gone through it.

In retrospect, this would seem like the last moment Verónica and María Magdalena were able to exert any control over their lives. As they emerged into the convent's chapel, there was still a hope that other nuns would see them and realize something was wrong. Their captors wouldn't dare shoot them if there were witnesses. But there was no one. At that time in the evening the convent's corridors were empty. So nobody saw the group climb the stairs, pass the nuns' sleeping quarters and go up to the rooftop. There they were confronted with a dismal cement structure, a somewhat violent addition to the convent's harmonious architecture. The women were forced into a windowless room inside it. Ofelia Dorín made them remove their tunics, rope belts and veils. She allowed them to keep on the underskirts and turtlenecks. The nun refused to see them in holy garb any longer.

The room was completely empty: no bed, no blankets, no chairs, no toilet. A bare cell, ten feet by ten, with one door that closed with a thud once the two of them were inside it.

"They call this a retreat chamber, but really it's a punishment cell," said María Magdalena. "At least when they send a nun here they let her bring a blanket and a pillow."

It was so dark in the room that they couldn't see each other, just hear each other's voices.

"Why have they locked us up in here?" asked Verónica. "Why didn't they just kill us?"

"I think what's coming may be worse than death."

IV

The women's plight didn't seem so terrible. If their captors hadn't killed them immediately, that must be because they had another plan. Perhaps they hoped to make some kind of deal: immunity from prosecution in exchange for the women's lives? The fact that they were locked up and not dead allowed Verónica and María Magdalena to believe that the worst possibility wouldn't happen. They weren't going to die. So things couldn't be that bad.

Verónica began a reconnoitre of the room. She walked around it looking for anything – a light switch, a blanket – that might make the cell seem less naked. Her search was fruitless; there was nothing on the floor or on the walls. María Magdalena sat down on one side of the room and Verónica stood at the other side, as though waiting for something to happen. But nothing did. Annoyed, she sat down too, back against the wall. The concrete was uncomfortable and the damp made it feel colder and even more unyielding.

She scratched the floor with her nails, gently rapped her knuckles against it, beating out the rhythm of a song; she held her head in her hands, stretched out her legs and pulled them back up several times. If anyone had asked her how she felt right then, she would have answered: bored. Uncomfortable and bored.

How many hours would they be held there? Their captors must be waiting for the convention of Latin American nuns to end, to cut down the likelihood of witnesses.

It was cold. Verónica curled up and lay down in a corner of the cell. She had taken off her shoes and used them as a pillow.

When would they be given something to eat? She needed a piss. Would they let them out at some point to go to the bathroom?

It must be three or four hours now since they had been flung into this forsaken room. Nobody had looked in even to check that they were still alive, or at least not trying to escape.

She thought she heard a noise in the distance. A door opening and closing. And were those footsteps? The sound grew steadily fainter. Then there was nothing. Might some nun be monitoring them from a distance? She tried hard, but in vain, to hear some movement on the part of this hypothetical guard.

Then she got up, went to the door and banged on it as hard as she could, yelling to get the attention of the nun she imagined might be watching the door of the cell from the other end of the roof terrace.

"Hey, listen! I need to go the bathroom! Are you listening? I need to have a piss! Or do you want us to piss in our clothes?"

She kept banging on the door, but there was no response from the other side. Verónica returned angrily to her corner and sat down against the wall. She really did need to urinate. She would wait a little longer and, if no one came, make such a scene that they would have to come and put her in a straitjacket. Had another hour gone by yet?

"Are you asleep?" she asked María Magdalena.

"No."

"I can't believe no one's coming."

She waited for the other woman to offer some comforting explanation, but her companion said nothing. Verónica heard her lying down. María Magdalena must be stretching out her back, as Verónica had done a while before. She got back to her feet, went to the door and repeated her previous commotion, again with no success.

"Piss at the edge of the room," María Magdalena advised.

"How can I do that?"

"Just do it."

Verónica couldn't hold on any more. She went to the wall furthest from María Magdalena, took down her underpants and squatted as close as possible to the wall. Her need to urinate was such that the flow seemed interminable, and she worried that the stream of piss would reach far into the room. When she had finished, she did something ridiculous: in the dark she tried to work out how far the puddle had extended and, when she found the end of it, she started mopping it up with her underwear, using it like a floor cloth. There was no option but to leave the soaked garment to one side and return to her corner. Verónica felt awful. She lay down again in the foetal position, then dozed sporadically.

Her mouth felt thick; she was hungry and thirsty, her joints hurt and the cold penetrated her bones. It was impossible to sleep deeply. She didn't want to complain, though, or to dishearten María Magdalena or start pleading with the nuns. The darkness around them felt like violence, but the silence outside was worse.

Verónica longed for the hours to pass, for someone to come looking for them and get them out of there. Finally, a white line appeared beneath the door. Dawn must have broken. She still couldn't see María Magdalena.

"Are you awake?"

"Yes."

"Will they come when it's morning?"

"I don't think so."

She heard María Magdalena stand up and go towards the door, saw her as a sketchy shadow. Verónica also stood up and moved towards the line of light.

"I can't hear anything," said María Magdalena, her right ear pressed against the door.

"Perhaps they aren't awake yet."

"They get up at dawn."

Verónica sat down with her back pressed against the door. At least the wood was more comfortable than the concrete walls. María Magdalena also slid down the door, until she was sitting beside her. She took Verónica's hand.

"We're going to have to be strong. I know you're not a believer, but I am, and I know there are tests. You can think of them as life's challenges. We're facing one of those challenges now. You mustn't let yourself be beaten."

"If one of these women would just show up."

"I find it very helpful to pray. My brother once told me that he found serenity in remembering and naming every player on the Argentina soccer teams from the 1978 and 1986 World Cups. However you live out there, find a way to connect with it from in here."

They sat like that for a long time (two or three hours?) until Verónica felt her whole body cramping up. Then she stood up and paced out a straight line. From the door to the back wall: seven steps. She began to feel hungry and needed to piss again. Casting about in the dark, she found her shoes and put them on, then returned to the corner where she had already relieved herself. She kicked the discarded underwear to one side, squatted down and pissed on the floor, which was wet and smelled of urine.

Verónica couldn't bring herself to go back and sit with María Magdalena, but sat instead against the back wall, her elbows resting on her knees, palms against her temples.

The light under the door was growing stronger. It must be nearly midday.

"I'm hungry."

"Think about something else."

But what? She didn't have María Magdalena's faith, nor sufficient strength of mind to convince herself that it was worth trying to focus on something outside this prison. To make things worse, the cold had never completely left her body and the walls' dampness was deep in her bones. Verónica hugged her legs tightly and rested her head on her knees. She tried to remember her first ever friend; it must have been when she was about three and at kindergarten. Then she started making a mental list, chronologically, of all her friends, from her earliest memory until the current day, and entertained herself with the idea of gathering all these girls and women in the same house. It could be a country house with a swimming pool, so everyone could get to know each other and make friends, the ones from kindergarten and the ones who went clubbing at Martataka on Thursdays.

Verónica fell asleep. When she woke up, the light under the door was very faint. Soon it would be dark again.

She got up. Stretched her legs. Her back hurt; her neck was stiff. She thought of talking to María Magdalena, telling her something funny as a way to demonstrate (to each other and to whoever was guarding them) that they still knew how to chat and be cheerful. But she didn't. She didn't know how.

She walked around in a little circle until she felt dizzy, then went back to sit in her corner.

What would all her friends be doing now? Was Harrison phoning with invitations to go out? The poor boy must think

343

she'd gone back to her husband. Neither Paula, nor Patricia, nor her sisters would register her absence. Not Marcelo, either. Verónica thought of Chicha. She wished she could have her little dog jumping all over the bed again while she tried to sleep.

And Federico. Would he realize she had disappeared? Would he think she was deliberately being difficult and not call her for that reason? Or would he look for her? Would he move heaven and earth to find her? Would Prince Charming arrive in time to save Sleeping Beauty? Not that she was beautiful any more. She was less and less herself, becoming something shapeless, disposable, like a mudguard dumped in a scrapyard. She was nothing more than that. And Prince Charmings didn't exist. Or, if they did, they never arrived in time to save anyone.

16   *Aarón Rosenthal*

I

From the moment Verónica had told him she and María Magdalena planned to enter the convent dressed as nuns, Federico suspected this was not a good idea. Their scheme had the makings of a publicity coup: two journalists, one of them an ex-nun, infiltrate enemy lines in search of the evidence that will incriminate a religious order and a Catholic movement. All well and good, as long as they didn't fall into the hands of people who had already killed to avoid capture.

All afternoon he waited for a call from Verónica to confirm that she and María Magdalena were out of danger, with or without the evidence. But Verónica didn't get in touch, and he didn't want to call her for fear of risking her safety.

That night, as he grew increasingly worried, he got a call from Rodolfo Corso in Santiago del Estero. Corso told Federico that he had spoken to Verónica to tell her about the latest events and that she had sounded calm, biding her time until the moment came to get inside the nun's office. Verónica had also told him that Archbishop Nogués was inside the men's living quarters.

"Do you believe that the archbishop ordered the girl's killing?" Corso asked him.

"It's very likely, though with the evidence we already have against him for abuse, plus whatever may emerge from similar

345

cases in the next few days, the son of a bitch is looking at a long spell in prison anyway."

"If he's over seventy, he may slip through the net. They'll send him off to a luxury retirement in some monastery."

"Then we have to pray that God exists and sends him to Hell."

There was no telling how long the two fake nuns might take to get their hands on the books. Federico went anxiously to bed, willing Verónica to get in touch.

But the following morning, she still hadn't made contact. Corso was doubtless still asleep when Federico rang to leave a message asking him to call the minute he had any news.

At midday, he called Verónica's phone. It was either switched off or out of range. He found the telephone number for *Nuestro Tiempo* and spoke to Patricia, who didn't know anything either. He couldn't afford to lose any more time.

Gathering all the evidence he had so far, Federico put his case to Judge Tagliaferro, asking him to issue a search warrant for the convent of the Order of the Most Holy Charity. Despite the urgency of Federico's request to see the judge, and his insistence on the need to act quickly, it was six o'clock in the evening by the time Tagliaferro deigned to see him, hours after the last person had left the court. The judge was clear and blunt: he informed Federico that he was taking him off the case and asked him to hand over his dossier immediately. Citing reasons both formal and far-fetched, Tagliaferro made it clear he wanted Federico nowhere near the case – nor was he prepared to grant a search warrant. Federico couldn't think of any better response than to tell him: "I hope Chief Superintendent Barbosa is paying you well for this, because you're protecting a murderer."

He left the courthouse on Avenida Comodoro Py convinced that his career as a prosecuting attorney was over.

Standing in the street, he realized that it was now more than twenty-four hours since Verónica had made contact with anyone. She could be dead, or trying to avoid death. Because if he was sure of anything, it was that the people working for Barbosa and for the religious order wouldn't hesitate to kill Verónica and María Magdalena. Perhaps the women had had time to hide. If so, the moment to act was now, before they were discovered and it was too late to help them.

He had only one card left, and decided to put everything on it.

He called Aarón Rosenthal.

II

Their building was a smoke-free environment, not something that unduly concerned Aarón Rosenthal every time he lit up a cigarette or, on rare occasions, a cigar. His office was the only place at Rosenthal and Associates where smoking was permitted. Some of his lawyers used the opportunity of a meeting to light up there, avoiding the need to go outside.

Since his secretary had already left for the day and there were few staff still in the office, Aarón had no reason to stay on, but no compelling reason to go back home, either. Nobody was waiting for him there and, between watching television and studying some case in the armchair in his office, he still preferred the second option.

It was a surprise to hear Federico's voice on the telephone. Aarón knew through the grapevine that he was working in the Justice Department; otherwise, there had been no news of the young lawyer since his resignation from the company. If Federico hadn't quit that day, Aarón would have fired him. He had behaved in a clumsy and reckless way in disobeying his orders. Through Federico's error, Rosenthal and Associates had lost important allies, as well as credibility in places where mistakes were costly. The Rosenthal practice, thanks to its most promising lawyer, had shown a lack of gratitude to people who were far too powerful to be crossed. The blame, evidently, lay not with Federico but with Verónica. It was through blindly following her that he had made so many mistakes. It wouldn't be so bad if their liaison had at least culminated in marriage, but no.

Federico sounded nervy, and Aarón was sure that the nerves weren't prompted by speaking to him. Something serious must be happening. He decided to set aside any recriminations and invite him to come to the office. Thirty minutes later, Federico was in front of him.

"Verónica's in danger."

Quickly and clearly, Federico briefed Aarón about the investigation. In desperation, he explained how he had failed to obtain Judge Tagliaferro's support for a raid on the convent.

"Tagliaferro's an idiot. I'm surprised you didn't know that. The raid could be effective if Verónica and her friend are still there. But we run the risk that they've been taken somewhere else and that this action will only serve to have them killed, wherever they are. The raid has to be focussed on exactly the right place, and has to find them within seconds."

"That's almost impossible."

"Not if we have the right intelligence."

III

Aarón stood up, walked around his office with a meditative air and, finally, got out his phone, that gadget that, in his hands, seemed to work like a magic wand: whatever he ordained telephonically came to be. Federico had witnessed this trick on various occasions, always with a mixture of admiration and unease.

"Rogelio, how are you? It's Aarón Rosenthal."

It was that easy for Aarón to reach the private phone of a provincial governor. The person on the other end always picked up. No question of going to voicemail or missed calls, or any other excuse.

"I need you to do me an enormous favour. I have to get in touch urgently with Juan García… Come on, Rogelio, which Juan García do you think? I assure you it's nothing against him. It's just that García has information I need right away."

The governor said he would call him back in a few minutes. Aarón sat in the armchair in his office. Now he too looked worried.

"Why did you let Verónica get into something like this?"

It wasn't a criticism – there was resignation in Aarón's question. Federico didn't recognize in that weary tone the man he had had worked with for so many years.

"Aarón, you know that neither I nor anyone can control her."

The older man nodded, accepting a reality he seemed powerless to change. He was thinking about how to avoid the worst happening.

"You told me that this Barbosa has a dispute with the Prefecture."

"From what we were able to establish."

The telephone rang. It was the governor. Aarón spoke a few words and wrote down something on a piece of paper. He thanked the politician profusely, then ended the call and stood up.

"García's expecting me in half an hour. He's on Avenida Libertador. Can you drive me there?"

They went downstairs to the building's garage and set off in Rosenthal's Audi. Aarón was silent. In addition to the worry about Verónica, Federico had no doubt that his mind was already busy formulating a plan of action.

"Wait for me in the car. I don't think I'll be very long. Are you still an attorney, or have you resigned?"

"No, I'm still an attorney."

"Good. I'm going to need an attorney in a few minutes."

IV

The building preserved the functional, prosaic style of 1970s construction. The nouveaux riches of that era had bequeathed apartments with a view of the Buenos Aires Golf Club, and now their children displayed them like minimalist gems. Yesterday's nouveaux riches were today's tycoons. At least Aarón Rosenthal had had the good taste to buy an apartment in a building that was nearly a hundred years old. He had never felt pressured to secure a foothold in some fashionable area like Avenida Libertador, Barrio Parque or Puerto Madero, either as a home or for his law firm.

A security guard cleared him at the entrance, and Rosenthal took the elevator that went straight to Juan García's floor. A woman who must be García's secretary opened the door to him and showed him into the living room. There seemed not to be anyone else around. García must have his security detail holed up in the kitchen. The lights were dim, perhaps to make the space seem less chilly. There were almost no paintings, photographs or other signs of intimacy. It was clear García didn't spend his days in this apartment.

García made a triumphal entrance in a double-breasted jacket, worn open. He was holding a lit cigarette but quickly abandoned it in an ashtray and didn't touch it again during the course of their conversation. He stretched out his hand to Aarón.

"Doctor Rosenthal, it's an honour to meet you. I'm only sorry that it's in these circumstances."

Each of the men took an armchair.

"Listen, García, I'm not here to do public relations, nor to waste your time. I've come on behalf of my daughter."

"Yes, I realize that. I won't waste your time either. In different circumstances, you and I could sit down to negotiate. You would tell me what you need and I would ask for something in return. We'd come to an understanding."

"I just need my daughter, safe and sound."

"That's the problem, Doctor. Look, you know your daughter Verónica well, don't you?"

Aarón nodded and let García keep talking.

"Imagine if our roles were reversed and I were the one asking you to stop your daughter proceeding with an investigation. There wouldn't be much you could do. I'm sure you wouldn't be able to persuade her. Am I right?"

"Quite possibly."

"We're looking at a similar situation here. A simple phone call can be enough to make governors, ministers, police chiefs dance on the table, if you understand me. But however much I plead, weep or rage, I can't do anything about the decisions my sister-in-law makes. I've known her since she was a novice, and she's always done exactly what she wanted. She's the one who calls the shots. She stands above this venal life, then lets people who are sinful but useful for her purposes, like Barbosa, do her bidding. I assure you that it's my sister-in-law who decides what does and doesn't get done."

"There's your wife, as well."

"You have three daughters, I believe? I don't expect they pay each other much heed. What I'm trying to say is that I'm not going to make a deal here, because there's nothing I can

351

guarantee you. Without wanting to sound cynical, I'd say that your daughter is in God's hands."

"You know, García, that I'm a man who doesn't forget those who have helped him."

"Bear with me for a minute, just a few minutes, while I make some calls."

Juan García went to another room. Aarón looked at his phone. He was hoping to receive a call from Federico to say that everything had been successfully resolved. Then he could put his mind to other matters: how to get Federico back into the company, how to see more of Verónica, at least at family gatherings. They had been estranged for too long. If it was true that Federico had made mistakes, he had made them to protect Verónica. And what did he want to leave as an inheritance to his daughters and grandchildren if not security? The firm had grown thanks to his talent and that of his team. He was proud of the work they had done in the last nearly forty years. But none of that meant anything if he couldn't offer his family the peace of mind that comes with power, prestige and money. If he were to lose his daughter in these circumstances, nothing he had done in his life would make sense. For the first time since his wife had died, he felt stricken; he had to make an effort to hold himself together.

Juan García returned with a printed sheet of paper. Aarón stood up.

"I have some good news for you, Doctor. Your daughter is alive. I swear I feared that it might not be so. Nor can I guarantee her survival in the next few hours. All I know is that she's still in the convent of the Sisters of the Most Holy Charity. You know how this goes: when the cops arrive, the small-time crooks throw their drugs in the toilet and the ones who don't want witnesses liquidate any enemies to hand. You get my drift, don't you? The convent is a big place, but I managed to get them to make a rudimentary plan of where your daughter and her colleague are."

He passed Aarón the sheet and accompanied him to the door. Before Aarón left, García added:

"Two things: the first will be obvious to you, I imagine. Don't send in the Feds, because they won't go or, if they do, your daughter will turn up dead. Second: take this as a plea. In absolutely no circumstances must my sister-in-law find out that I was the one who gave you this information."

V

There were still no calls on Federico's phone, no news of Verónica. He felt useless sitting in the car with nothing to do. Then Aarón came out of the building, talking on the phone. He didn't get into the car but stood at the driver's side while he continued his conversation. Federico got out, and when Aarón had finished the call he said:

"I've just spoken to Lusich. He's signing a search warrant for the convent."

"Are they there?"

"Yes. You're going to attend as an attorney. This plan shows the location of the cell where Verónica and the journalist are being held. It's on the roof terrace."

"But the federal police answer to Barbosa. It would be risky to inform them of the search warrant."

"That's why it's not going to be done by the Feds but by the Prefecture. Who's your contact there?"

"Nobody in particular, but Patricio Arizmendi is there. He's the director of special operations, the one who ordered the detention of Barbosa's truck."

"Here's what we'll do. Go to the Prefecture. I'm going to try to speak to Arizmendi. I want him to oversee the raid personally. We can't leave this to chance. And I want you to be the one who goes in with the Prefecture people to the cell where Verónica is. God forbid anyone should shoot her."

"I understand."

"I'm putting everything in your hands, Federico."

For years the Rosenthal sisters (Verónica included) had ribbed Federico by saying Aarón loved him like a son. Aarón had always kept a certain distance with him, but he had been generous both at the office and at family gatherings. That night, however, Federico realized that Aarón was trusting him as though he were one of the Rosenthals and not just a lawyer friend of the family. Federico wanted to return that gesture of trust with reassurance.

"Don't worry, I'm going to bring Verónica home."

"Take the car. I'll get a taxi. Keep me in the loop."

When Federico arrived at the Prefecture, they were already preparing for the raid. Arizmendi arrived minutes later but walked past without speaking to him and shut himself away in his office. Alarm bells sounded in Federico's head. Who was Arizmendi speaking to on the phone? And what if they were wrong and the guy was an accomplice of Barbosa? He was about to call Aarón to tell him what was happening when Arizmendi came out of his office and grunted at him to come in.

"You're Córdova, the lawyer, is that right?"

"Yes."

"The same Córdova who was present at the operation in the port. But that time the acting judge was Tagliaferro and this time it's Lusich."

"That's right."

"Explain to me why I have to risk my neck taking my men to a raid that has nothing to do with the port or waterfront? Why not the Feds or the metropolitan police or the gendarmerie, who've got nothing to do all day?"

Arizmendi was deliberately being difficult but, if he was there, it must be because Aarón or some friend of Rosenthal's hadn't left him any option.

"Because the judge doesn't trust any of those forces," said Federico, playing along. "We're looking at a religious order and a Christian movement, both linked with the theft of babies and illegal adoptions. They, in turn, are connected with a clinic from which the body parts we found in the port originated. And Chief Superintendent Barbosa took part in all that."

"I know him."

"Yes, you studied together at the Dámaso Centeno."

"You've been investigating me? What the fuck is this?"

"No, Arizmendi, don't get me wrong. I want Barbosa locked up, and you know very well he's a hard nut to crack. I don't know your own reasons for wanting him out of the way, but I assure you we want the same thing."

Arizmendi studied him with a martial air, as though inspecting his prefect's uniform. This guy was probably as big a criminal as Barbosa, thought Federico, but he was past investigating anything now. He just wanted to find Verónica alive.

"None of this can come back to bite me," Arizmendi insisted.

"The judge understands that there's a link between what happened in the port and what's happening in that clinic, which is in turn connected to the convent. He's the one ordering you to proceed, and the Prefecture is simply following orders."

"All right. Grab yourself a bulletproof vest – we'll leave in five minutes."

As they were preparing to go, Federico saw some half-litre bottles of water on the table and put two in his overcoat to take to Verónica and María Magdalena. Hopefully thirst would be the worst of their problems.

The bulletproof waistcoat was uncomfortable, especially with the bottles squeezed into it. Federico was directed to one of the armoured vehicles and they sped through the avenues, sirens wailing. It was a strange sensation to be sitting in that tight spot, surrounded by uniformed men, going to find Verónica. Federico looked out of the narrow window. Buenos Aires seemed to him a phantasmagorical city.

17 *Burnout*

I

She had fallen asleep again and dreamed that she was crying. No. She was awake and crying, hugging her knees. In the darkness she heard María Magdalena coming to sit beside her and she took her hands. They were cold, like her own.

Verónica didn't want to cry. Dropping one of María Magdalena's hands, she wiped away her tears. Though she had lost all notion of time, she calculated that it must be night-time again. She was hungry and thirsty. Despite having done nothing but sit or take a few steps around the cell, she felt exhausted, her body hurt, and she wanted only to sleep. She rested her head in the lap of María Magdalena, who stroked her face as a mother would her daughter's. For the first time since they had been locked up, her body relaxed. And then she did go to sleep.

There was no way of knowing whether five minutes or two hours had passed. First she felt María Magdalena waking her, then she heard steps in the corridor. Someone was coming closer. They sat together, motionless, waiting.

The women heard the scrape of a key and felt that the door was opening; they saw shadows, dressed in habits, against a black background, then a light, exploding full in their faces. Someone was pointing a flashlight at them: it was like sand-paper across the eyes.

Two nuns approached them, another two standing at the door. They grasped Verónica under the arms and lifted her.

"Get off me, bitch, what are you doing?" She tried to free herself and couldn't.

The nuns dragged her outside. In the doorway she saw Ofelia Dorín pointing not a flashlight at her but a small pistol. When the nuns tried to stand her up, Verónica's knees gave way. She felt cramp in every muscle. It was like having the body of a ninety-year-old.

Now they pushed her towards one of the other cells. Were she and María Magdalena going to be separated? One in each room? At least in this new cell there was a small lamp throwing some light into the room. There was a chair, too, in which Verónica was made to sit.

"Where are the books?" asked Sister Ofelia in her hysterical duck voice.

"What books?"

"Where are they?"

"I don't know what you're talking about."

Ofelia Dorín made a sign and one of the nuns slapped Verónica so hard it threw her head back.

"You're deranged!" Verónica shouted. "You and the rest of them."

"Hit her," commanded the nun. One slapped her again and the other grabbed her hair and shook her hard.

Verónica repeated that she had no idea what she was being asked for. Sister Dorín appeared agitated, a state that seemed to be exacerbated by Verónica's deliberate effort to stay calm. She ordered more beatings. One of the nuns twisted Verónica's breast until she cried out with pain. As she tried to stand up, the other nun kneed her hard in the ribs, winding her. She fell down, banging her face against the floor.

"Hit her," Ofelia Dorín said again, her voice a croak.

A nun kicked her in the backside.

"Harder!" shouted the Provincial Sister.

The other nun crouched down and pushed her hand against Verónica's cheek, scraping her face against the floor.

"Harder, hit her harder!" Ofelia Dorín screamed at the top of her voice, as though directing an orchestra of religious goons.

The nun's shouts couldn't drown out the cries of pain. Emboldened by their spiritual leader, the other two rained down blows on Verónica's body. She struggled to protect her head, her face, her chest. Although she tried to stand up, to get away, to move out of the range of their feet, the nuns followed her with more blows. She dragged herself against the wall and the kicking stopped. While Verónica could see through one eye, the other barely opened. Her cheek was bleeding, the result of a kick to the face. Her other cheek was criss-crossed with scratches. A stabbing pain encompassed the area between left thigh and waist. Her breasts burned. Her mouth was full of blood.

Ofelia Dorín was standing beside her.

"Are you going to tell me what you did with the books? Where have you hidden them?"

Verónica tried to say something, but she was winded and her heavy tongue cleaved to her palate.

"There's nothing else for it," said Dorín, turning to look at the nun standing behind her. "If this carries on, we'll have to call Barbosa. He'll know how to make her talk."

Verónica's left ear must have been injured too, because she began to hear a buzzing that intensified her headache. She longed to detach herself from her body.

The other nuns grabbed Verónica under the arms again and dragged her back to the cell. They threw her down like a sack of potatoes and she collapsed without putting up any resistance. Behind her, she heard them taking María

Magdalena out of the cell. Then the door closed and Verónica was on her own.

For a few minutes she sat still, unable to react. She could hear screaming in the distance. *Motherfuckers*, she wanted to shout, but she could scarcely hear her own voice. They were beating María Magdalena. She dragged herself over to the door and banged on it from her position on the floor. Nobody came.

The buzzing in her ear couldn't drown out the screams coming from the torture room. Verónica dragged herself away from the door and towards the back of the cell. She groped around for her shoes, to use as a pillow, but couldn't' find them. Still, she lay down anyway, on the damp floor. She was very, very thirsty. And her stomach hurt. The pain from her beating was compounded by powerful cramps. Since her whole body was in intense pain, there was nothing she could do to lessen the cramps except to sit still, aim for torpor. Her muscles were tensed in response to the suffering in every inch of her body and she couldn't control them. She became aware that she had soiled herself without noticing. Her skirt was dirty and a stench of shit filled the air. She took off the skirt and pushed it away with her feet.

Verónica couldn't even cry. She had lost all control of herself and was nothing now but an amorphous mass, traversed by suffering.

She heard nuns moving in the corridor, the door opening and María Magdalena being thrust onto the floor. Verónica decided to use her last breath to plead.

"Water, please, water."

The nuns didn't even register her presence at the back of the cell.

When they closed the door, María Magdalena pulled herself across the floor until she was able to lean against the wall. "They don't know where the books are. We were too strong for them."

She could picture María Magdalena's smile.

Verónica either went to sleep then, or lost consciousness. She was woken by noises coming from the terrace. Instinctively she moved to a corner of the cell and curled up into a ball. She had found her shoes lying on this side of the room, and clung to them in desperation. Had Barbosa arrived?

No, it wasn't Barbosa.

People were banging on the door – they didn't use a key yet somehow broke the lock. The door opened and flashlights lit up the room as though a bolt of lightning had shone inside. Some women in military uniforms came in. One or two came towards Verónica, who was still sitting in a foetal position, hugging her legs and clutching her shoes. Her face must have been disfigured by fear, because one of the women said:

"Don't worry, everything's all right. We've come to get you out of here." The woman gently wrested the shoes from Verónica's grip and covered her with a blanket.

That was when she saw Federico behind the uniformed women and her relief turned into something nightmarish. She searched for strength where there was none to be found. "Don't let him come in, don't let him —"

But Federico was already there. He crouched beside her while she repeated, "Go away, please, I don't want you to see me like this." Federico took out a bottle of water and brought it to her lips. She took it with shaking hands, choking on the water.

"Slow down, Speedy Gonzales."

Verónica saw María Magdalena. She was leaning against the other wall and had also been given some water. Their eyes met briefly, and María Magdalena smiled: her smile was exactly how Verónica had imagined it in the darkness.

One of the women from the Prefecture got hold of some trousers from a colleague, though it wasn't clear why they would carry spares. Unless perhaps they had foreseen that the women would need clothes, as well as blankets to keep them warm. The trousers were a little big for Verónica, but at least they stayed up. Federico asked one of the people in charge of the operation to call two ambulances. María Magdalena, who was in a better state than Verónica, had managed to walk over to see her. She looked at her with compassion. Verónica tried to seem in better shape than the inflamed face, the cuts and pains all over her body suggested. Walking as best they could, they left that awful cell. Federico wanted them to wait for stretchers, but María Magdalena insisted on going to get the books they had hidden in Sister Mariana's room. Verónica was able to walk down unassisted to the convent's central courtyard.

Everywhere there were people in uniforms, nuns emerging from the cloisters to find out what was going on. She didn't see Ofelia Dorín or either of the nuns who had beaten her, but Verónica knew she could identify them if necessary.

The woman from the Prefecture hung back as Federico led Verónica to a bench to rest.

"I don't want you near me," she told him. "I'm deformed and I smell horrible."

"Don't be silly – sit down and finish the bottle of water."

"They need to arrest Ofelia Dorín and the others."

"Of course. There's already a warrant out for her, the sister, Father Anselmo, Doctor Rossi, and the icing on the cake: an arrest warrant for Chief Superintendent Barbosa."

"And Nogués?"

"We don't have any proof yet of his direct involvement in

the theft of babies or in the trafficking of bodies. There's only Fabiana Benítez's statement."

"But the woman's dead. He can claim that they became lovers after she reached adulthood, and that Fabiana invented the abuse story."

"We'll have to find a way to refute it."

Someone came to tell Federico that he was needed for some paperwork. Federico asked one of the female prefects to make sure that Verónica and María Magdalena were taken to hospital as soon as the ambulances arrived.

The woman came over to Verónica and asked her how she was feeling.

"I've been better. Do you happen to have a cigarette?"

The woman passed over her pack and a Bic lighter. Verónica experienced the first lungful of nicotine as an elixir. Her unsettled stomach had taken away any desire to eat, yet the cigarette made her feel better. Something was clearly awry in her system.

A call came over the walkie-talkie to summon the prefect immediately to the third floor. The prefect asked her charge to wait for her on the bench, and Verónica found herself alone in the convent's courtyard. She could see light and movement, could hear noise. Life. It was what she needed. And with life came fury, frustration, an urge to fight. She couldn't credit that a man like Archbishop Nogués was at liberty and unpunished. Verónica had seen him in the company of all the people who were going to be arrested. He was clearly also responsible for the theft of babies. The man was no less guilty than Ofelia Dorín.

Her pain was undiminished, her face still swollen, but Verónica felt her energy returning. Enough for her to stand up and walk towards the little chapel from where the tunnel towards the house of the Brothers of the Most Holy Charity led.

Her immediate concern was to reach the chapel without being seen by anyone who might try to restrain her. She felt calmer as she crossed the threshold of the chapel and walked towards the area behind the altar. The only problem was that she had no flashlight. Looking around her, she saw a row of candles. She picked one up and lit it with the lighter the prefect had given her. Then she opened the trapdoor and went down into the tunnel.

Each step she took down that straight, iron ladder caused pain to shoot from her head to her feet. On reaching the ground she stood still, waiting to recover her strength and for the pain that was slicing through her to abate.

Verónica perfectly remembered the way to the monks' house. She also knew where to turn off for Rossi's clinic, but this time she kept straight on towards her objective. It was as painful to go up the next ladder as it had been to come down the first. Luckily, this time the trapdoor opened easily. She blew out the candle and threw it onto the floor of the tunnel.

Emerging into the storeroom, Verónica stepped silently out onto the privet-lined path. The silence was absolute, so different to the commotion a hundred yards away.

She reached the shrubbery from which María Magdalena and she had observed the inside of the house. Lights were on in the living room, but there was no sign of Nogués. Boldly she walked towards the bedroom window. Not there, either. Could he have left? Had he been alerted to what was happening next door and fled, as he had from Santiago del Estero? Verónica circled the house, then hid behind the generator that had been started up during the power outage. A few canisters, some containing gasoline, others empty, were piled up on a shelf. From this vantage point, she could see another small chapel, similar to the one on the nuns' side. Some long, narrow stained-glass windows showed a faint light coming from inside. Verónica went towards the door. Carefully, she opened it a crack and glimpsed the central nave. Sitting in the front pew was Arturo Nogués. Praying.

Verónica – an atheist by conviction – found it abhorrent that someone like Nogués should use faith as an alibi for such heinous crimes. The man had no right to pray, to communicate with God (who, although he didn't exist for her, did perhaps have some kind of presence for a believer). The spectacle sickened her. She opened the door wide.

"I don't think God is going to forgive your sins."

The archbishop continued to pray for a few seconds longer before turning to see who was speaking to him. Without even getting up, he said:

"Judge not, and you shall not be judged. Condemn not, and you shall not be condemned. Forgive, and you will be forgiven."

"I imagine that in your Holy Book there are quotes to justify anything."

Nogués stood up, brushed off his knees, as though to remove dust, and crossed himself, looking towards the tiny altar. "Are you a believer?" he asked.

"No."

"For a long time I've thought of atheism as a Jewish sect. In any case, I expect you've read the sacred texts of Judaism. In the book of the prophet Jeremiah it says, 'I will cleanse them from all their iniquity by which they have sinned against Me, and I will pardon all their iniquities by which they have sinned and by which they have transgressed against Me.' Praise be to God."

"Did you also quote from the Bible every time you abused Fabiana Benítez?"

"I never abused anyone."

"She was twelve, thirteen years old."

"Each person leads the life that God has assigned to him – or to her."

"How many other little girls did you abuse?"

The archbishop laughed. "Since you've gone to all the trouble of coming here to display your wounds, I'll tell you something that everyone should know: some minors can consent to a relationship with an adult. They can and indeed they do. There are girls of thirteen years old who are perfectly amenable to this – they want it, in fact."

"You're an evil bastard."

"Fabiana liked being with me. I'm sure she felt closer to God. It was always like that."

"A rapist, a murderer."

"Don't talk nonsense. Fabiana and the others were never as happy with anyone else as they were with me."

"You're going to pay for this."

"The Lord, who sees everything, forgives everything. Now off you go. I don't know how you escaped, but you won't last long like this."

The archbishop turned his back on her and returned to his place in the pew. He continued to pray, on his knees, ignoring her. He seemed even to forget she was present.

Verónica wavered. Fabiana's story kept reverberating in her head, like a fly in a bell jar. In front of her, his back turned, was a murderer, someone who would celebrate Mass the next day, pontificating on good and evil, inviting the trust of his congregation. She took a step towards him, then stopped. Turning around, she walked out of the chapel.

In the garden, someone who seemed to have been a witness to the conversation between herself and the archbishop stepped out of the shadows. Verónica was startled until she saw that the person standing in semi-darkness was María

Magdalena. She was happy, if surprised, to see her friend there.

"What are you doing here?"

"I could ask the same thing."

Could they really be so similar? Seeing María Magdalena was like looking in a broken mirror: she could recognize parts of herself in the other woman's face, in her expression, even in her posture as she walked towards the chapel. Verónica stopped her.

"Wait – where are you going?"

"I need you to go, Verónica."

Verónica grasped María Magdalena's arm, forcing her to stop. "We're going back."

María Magdalena freed herself with a brusque movement and pushed towards the church. Verónica hurriedly caught up with her, made her turn round and took her face in one hand, forcing the ex-nun to look into her eyes.

"Listen to me, María Magdalena. I've already been there. Not there with Nogués, but in your shoes. It's brutal. You think you're doing everything right, that you're obliged to step in where others have failed. Don't do it."

The erstwhile nun shook her head and went towards the generator.

"You'll never find peace, you'll always be thinking about what you did. You'll go to sleep imagining that everything could have been different, then you'll have terrible nightmares. There won't be a minute in the day when you're not thinking about that monster."

María Magdalena continued as though she were alone and Verónica's words were background noise. She picked up two canisters of gasoline and only then spoke to Verónica.

"Hell exists, and I'm not afraid of it," she smiled. "The only thing that frightens me is the thought of that man continuing to hide in God so he can commit his crimes. He has raped and killed and betrayed the Gospel. This is personal, Verónica, please don't get involved. Leave me alone."

Verónica took a few steps away and watched as María Magdalena soaked the walls of the chapel with gasoline. She emptied the two cans then, searching in her pockets, took out a lighter. A flame glowed in the darkness. She threw the lighter towards the wall as though it were a grenade.

Fire spread quickly through the chapel. They heard Nogués scream. A guttural, inhuman cry. The strength in his voice quickly fell away, though. As the flames rose the howls became whimpers, which faded into ever longer silences. María Magdalena watched, fascinated, as the little church burned. Verónica took her arm and yanked her away. This time María Magdalena let herself be pulled. They had to get away fast – but Verónica could hardly walk. Driven on by the fear of discovery, they reached the storeroom. María Magdalena had left the bag with the blue books on a workbench there. Verónica grabbed it and they went back down the ladder, making their way in darkness to the other end, where they climbed up into the nuns' chapel, closed the hatch and went to the convent's main courtyard. Neither Federico nor the prefect was there. The marigolds in the garden area were shivering in the evening breeze. Although Verónica wanted to get as far as the bench, so she could be found exactly where she had been left, she didn't have the strength for it. In vain she tried to hold onto María Magdalena, watching as the bag with the books fell onto the ground. She fainted in the middle of the courtyard.

III

For two days Verónica had been lying in a private room at the Clínica Suizo Argentina, a hospital, her sisters gleefully reminded her, that specialized in maternity. Daniela had already been there, waiting for her, when she arrived in the ambulance and had spoken to a doctor at the Suizo, who assessed Verónica before ordering further tests and treatments. Neither Daniela nor Leticia reproached her for anything, nor did they seem particularly alarmed by her appearance. They must have been briefed by Federico.

"Dad wants to know if he can come and see you," Leticia said.

"Tell him yes."

"Federico wants to know if you'll marry him," added Daniela.

"The idiot said that?"

"No, it's a joke," said Leticia. "If you can call that funny."

Leticia managed to get Verónica a phone with her old number. It didn't make sense to carry on hiding now that the religious gang's leaders were all in prison or awaiting trial. The only people who didn't have her old number were María Magdalena and Harrison.

She texted María Magdalena with her contact details and found the ex-Daughter of Saint Paul in better shape than she was herself. Perhaps the nun-thugs had shown mercy to someone who had once been in the same club. She had been discharged from hospital early that morning. Ever since leaving the convent in their respective ambulances, María Magdalena had refused to let go of the blue books, which she wanted to scan at her brother's office and then get digitized. Then she would hand them over to Federico to be used in the case against Ofelia Dorín.

Verónica didn't give Harrison her new number. She had lost his, anyway, when Rossi and his hoodlums took away her phone.

Early the next morning Paula came to visit her, bringing a packet of churros stuffed with dulce de leche.

"I've taken the day off work and the kid's in school, then a club. So I'm at your disposal."

Her friend went to the hostel, paid the bill for her room up to that day and packed up Verónica's things. She dropped off her laptop at the Suizo then went on to her apartment in Villa Crespo, where Marcelo was waiting. Verónica had already called him, asked to speak to the dog – something that had mildly perturbed the doorman – then explained that her friend would be going round to ready the apartment for her return. Marcelo met her at the door and they went in together. Paula looked at him with a certain distaste, because she was still convinced he was the one who had stolen some underwear she had left in the apartment over a year earlier.

The apartment was in a disastrous state. Marcelo and she tidied up everything together and left it looking respectable, ready for Verónica's return. Marcelo, with more foresight than Paula, checked the fridge and made a note to buy some basic provisions in the supermarket later. Paula returned to the clinic with some pyjamas and the clothes Verónica wanted to wear once she was discharged.

Around lunchtime Patricia dropped by, with news of the latest changes at the magazine. In turn, Verónica told her about everything she and María Magdalena had been through, and about Rodolfo Corso's findings. It certainly had the makings of a cover story. María Magdalena herself arrived shortly afterwards. She seemed tired and more serious than usual. Patricia's eagerness to get the articles written up helped her focus on the job in hand, and the atmosphere lifted when Rodolfo Corso joined the group. The four of them improvised a mini editorial meeting around Verónica's bed, reviewing all the material they had and discussing how to present it. Corso complained because Verónica and María Magdalena had only one article to write between them while he had two: the body trafficking and the role of Archbishop Nogués.

"He hasn't died yet because he has the luck of the devil, but he's in a deep coma. Mind you, given that he's sustained eighty per cent burns all over his body, I don't know if he'll want to wake up."

Patricia returned to the office, while Rodolfo and María Magdalena went to look for a quiet bar in which to work on their article. Every so often they called Verónica, now reunited with her laptop. She found it strange working from a hospital bed, and she missed her cigarettes and whisky. She still didn't know when she might be allowed to leave.

More tests were carried out that afternoon. Verónica had almost recovered from the dehydration, her contusions were progressing as expected and she seemed to have no serious injuries beyond a pair of painful broken ribs. Her eye had been completely saved, and the inflammation around it was starting to come down.

In the evening Verónica's father came to see her, bringing a bunch of flowers. It was the first time in her life he had given her flowers, although he often used to give them to her mother. They greeted one another as though there had never been an estrangement and this was just one of their regular catch-ups.

Aarón's favourite topic of discussion when he was with Verónica was his grandsons, so they talked in detail about all four of them. Not to be outdone, she told him about Chicha. How she had chatted to the dog on the phone. How Marcelo had told her that when she said, "Chichi, Chichi, it's me, Mummy," the little dog had wagged her tail.

"She's so clever," said Verónica, and her father nodded.

As they were saying goodbye, Verónica told him that she knew he was responsible for saving her life: Federico had told her.

"I hope it didn't cost you a lot of money."

"Nothing that can be bought with money is expensive."

"But who helped you find me?"

"As you journalists like to say, 'I have to protect my sources.'"

"Let's have lunch next week."

"Call me. And something else, darling. In reality, the person who did everything to save you, the true hero in all this, is Federico. You do realize that, right?"

Federico. He had been the first person she saw after leaving the emergency room in the clinic. She had been lying on a stretcher, alone, barely conscious, with that white light shining brighter than her eyes could bear. Federico had looked in, assessed the situation, then come back to see her. She had said to him: "I'm a deformed monster."

"Whatever you say."

"I mean that I'm horrible, unpresentable. You shouldn't see me like this."

"Ah. You're forgetting I was the one who took you to hospital that time you had gastroenteritis."

"And you choose to bring that up now?"

"Your eye looks quite pretty, like a purple hillock."

"What a moron. Don't make me laugh, because everything hurts."

"Let's talk about something serious, then."

"You saved me. Prince Charming arrived just in time."

"You're right, you know – there's definitely something princely about me."

There was a silence and Verónica feared that Federico would seize his chance to say goodbye and leave her alone, so she blurted the first thing that came into her mind:

"To think that by now I could have been chopped up into little pieces, ready for export to Korea or some other strange place."

"True. They might have been selling you in little bottles of formaldehyde."

Verónica tried to make herself more comfortable on the bed. Federico helped her, then kept hold of her hand.

"Perhaps I would have been worth something in little pieces," she said quietly, too weak to squeeze Federico's hand.

"I'm sure you would. I for one would have liked a piece of you."

"Seriously? Which bit?"

"I'm not telling."

"Go on…"

"Nope."

"All men are the same. I can imagine which bit you would have taken."

Gently Federico withdrew his hand and moved away the hair that had fallen over her injured eyelid. He looked into her eyes and smiled.

"Your heart. It's always been your heart I wanted."

18 *On Loneliness*

I

Verónica had learned to ignore dreams. She tried to leave that oneiric universe quickly and enter the real world, the only one that, with all its dangers, evil and injustice, could guarantee her a measure of peace. Dreams were too beautiful and serene. Beauty and serenity could conceal monsters.

Anyway, she had discovered a mantra that worked as a spell to scare away the tranquillity of dreams. Her first thought in the morning was: Federico, this won't last. She said it to herself when she was alone, when Chicha woke her up or when she found Federico's hand on her breast and him still sleeping beside her.

Despite the love they felt, or perhaps because of it, they regarded each other with a certain suspicion. He had abandoned her when her morale was at its lowest; she had ignored him for years. They watched each other, as though waiting for one to betray the other.

And here was a paradox: that mutual mistrust, which nobody close to them knew about, was something else they had in common, and so it brought them closer, it made them love each other more.

They loved each other because they knew they could walk away, that one day that might happen and their lives would spin off in different directions.

Her sisters were delighted that Verónica was going out with Federico. She couldn't understand their devotion. After all, her life wasn't so extreme that they should act as if a junkie, strung out on heroin, had been restored to normal life.

One afternoon when Daniela came round to drop off Santino, she took the opportunity to talk to her.

"Have you got a thing for Federico?"

"Are you mad?"

"Answer me."

"No, madwoman. Why would I have a thing for him? Obviously I think he's a genius and the best brother-in-law in the world, especially compared with Leti's husband."

"You talk to him a lot."

"You're not jealous, are you?"

"No, I just wanted to know."

"Did he tell you that we often talk?"

"No, I just noticed."

"You wouldn't be reading his emails, by any chance?"

"No – but once he left his inbox open and I happened to notice that there were a few emails from you."

"You're reading his emails. God help you, woman."

"Fuck off."

Aarón Rosenthal was the only person in her circle who hadn't passed judgement on the relationship between them. Perhaps he knew them better than the others and for that reason kept his counsel. He didn't say anything to her, not even when father and daughter met for lunch alone. If he made any reference to Federico, it was always to do with his work. Federico had returned to Rosenthal and Associates, a decision that hadn't been hard to make when things got complicated in the Justice Department. Judge Tagliaferro had been spreading the rumour that Federico's every action had only one objective: to cover the drug deals of the chief of special operations in the Prefecture. Verónica knew that her father would give Federico an opportunity to get his revenge.

Her friends, meanwhile, put her to the test. They wanted to know if, now she was more or less Federico's girlfriend (you could never be sure with Verónica), she would still meet up with them, or if – as so often happens when two people hook up – she would paint them out of the picture. Verónica didn't disappoint. She kept going to Martataka, to launch parties, to every kind of bar. She never brought Federico along. Nor was she interested in going out to dinner with him and his friends from high school. She preferred to hear an embellished version of the event when they were alone together.

Verónica no longer saw much of Paula, much to the regret of both parties. It wasn't that they loved each other less or didn't want to meet up, just that those long conversations analysing their travails in a male world no longer made much sense. Happiness doesn't lend itself to an extended narrative; you can't wax lyrical without falling into cliché or boring your listener. What could she have told her friend? Who would be interested in knowing how happy Verónica had felt when she found out that, like her, Federico hadn't seen the last season of *Lost*, how she had taken this as a sign that they should be together and how they had spent a weekend ensconced in his apartment watching all eighteen episodes of the sixth season, slightly drunk, pausing only for pizza or sex or to look up ridiculous trivia about the series on the internet. Nobody. And yet that had been one of the happiest and most important weekends of her life.

Perhaps we should expect no more of love than this.

And it wasn't that she was seeking transcendence, or to protect her freedom, or was eager to have new experiences, or longed for extreme emotions. She loved Federico, deeply. She had known that for more than a year and a half. They had spent so many months apart and if there was one thing she wanted, it was not to lose him again.

It was at the end of October that something unexpected happened.

Nuria, Leticia's younger daughter, was turning seven. They were going to celebrate at an indoor ball park at six o'clock that evening; afterwards the three sisters and their partners would have dinner at Leticia's house. Verónica and Federico arranged to meet at seven o'clock in Notorious to eat something before going on to the ball park towards the end of the party, in time for the cake-cutting and to sing "Happy Birthday". Verónica went to buy a present for Nuria. She wanted to get her a really nice book, but she had to be quick about it because it was already time to meet Federico. She got out of a taxi at the door of the Ateneo Grand Splendid and went down to the basement. As she scanned the bookshelves for her niece's reading age, she alighted on Darío Valrossa's *Witches in Sandals*.

Verónica couldn't say she had never thought about Darío in all those months, but she hadn't let those thoughts develop; she cut them off as soon as they came to mind. And yet coming face to face with one of his books was like encountering something material from his life. She glanced at the date of the edition: the book had been published two years ago. Darío's daughter would have been about one then, and perhaps he and his wife hadn't yet begun to hate each other.

She started reading the illustrated story. All around her, children were grabbing books under the unworried gaze of their mothers.

She read to the end of *Witches in Sandals*, then looked for other books by Darío. There were several others and she took them off the shelf, ran her hand over them like a caress, as she had once caressed Darío. And Lucio.

Her phone rang. It was Federico, but she didn't pick up. She sat down on one side of the room, like an exhausted mother, or like a child discovering fiction, and set about reading each one of those books. She tried to picture him writing them, inventing those stories, with Jazmín, a baby, and then a little girl, playing beside him, growing under his watchful eye. Verónica's phone rang a second and third time. She turned it off.

Had Darío ever been happy with Cecilia? How had they journeyed from love to such a searing hatred? And what was Verónica herself looking for? What did she fear? What did she need? Verónica had no answers to any of these questions, just confused feelings about what was happening to her.

She had Federico. He didn't need answers, or grand gestures, or theatrics to be at her side.

Was it enough? Was it too much?

Neither her sisters nor her friends nor anyone else seemed to appreciate that being with someone didn't mean not being alone.

Verónica left the bookstore at about half past eight, without having bought anything. When she came outside, the world seemed strange, alien.

She walked up Avenida Santa Fe towards Avenida Pueyrredón, then switched her phone back on. There were more missed calls from Federico and from Daniela. She wrote one short text to Federico. Two words: *Forgive me.* The awful thing was that when he saw that message he would ascribe a much more banal meaning to it; she would never be able to put into words what was going on inside her head.

A new message pinged on her phone. It must be Federico, replying. He was probably annoyed, or fed up, or disconcerted. But his message simply said *You're still in time.* In time for what? To sing "Happy Birthday" to her niece? To save what they had been building from love yet also from fear and mistrust? Not to take a wrong turn?

"You're still in time," she repeated to herself, and it seemed the most pathetic form of self-deceit ever. A platitude, to mask her loneliness. But she hadn't said it – Federico had. Verónica sent him another text: *Pueyrredón and Santa Fe*. A few seconds later the phone pinged in her hands again: *There in 10.*

She took her cigarettes out of her bag, lit one and prepared to wait.

II

Every morning Darío walked along the beach from Santa Teresita to the far side of Mar del Tuyú. He liked feeling the cold winter wind in his face. On those walks he thought up stories that featured Jazmín as a protagonist. In his imagination, his daughter turned into a magical being who could speak to spiders, travel on a magic carpet, turn into a butterfly and travel to China; she could bake the biggest cake in the universe and even find time to befriend some extraterrestrial bears. Darío was often surprised to find himself smiling as he imagined his daughter on these adventures. When he got back to Lucía's house, where they lived together now, in rooms above the bar, he would have a shower then write until midday.

Then Lucía and he would spend the rest of the day together. Darío had to learn many things about running a bar, including how to manage suppliers, inspectors, staff, food and drink. It was Lucía, though, who took charge of the most complicated jobs. Then, on Friday nights, she sang her own songs and played the guitar alongside a pianist and drummer. Darío was always there to hear her.

After their first day together, Darío and Lucía didn't speak again about Jazmín, or Cecilia, or Lucio. She stopped buying

Nuestro Tiempo. He kept in touch only with Emilse, his editor, and every so often he called his parents to let them know he was well.

Darío approached Lucía's body with the same sense of surprise and expectation he had felt as a teenager staying in an apartment yards away from the home they now shared. Her body was different from the one he and Lucio had seen and touched for the first time. And yet it was that adolescent body he remembered every time he touched her.

What had Lucía been doing all those years? How had they remained connected for more than twenty-five years? Lucía had never married or had children, nor did she dream of starting a family. She was happy with her bar, her music, the sea nearby and Darío's company, which came with no conditions attached.

They never took precautions when they fucked. Darío thought she might get pregnant at any time, but that didn't happen.

He finished *Jazmín's Stories* one Friday in October. He read it through, revising it countless times and, when he finally felt he could make no more corrections, sent it to Emilse. The book had turned out to be very long. His editor read it quickly and said she loved the stories but thought it better to divide the book into two volumes, and Darío agreed. She sent him the contract, which he signed without reading and posted back. The first volume was dedicated *To Jazmín, who lived through all these adventures and many more.* The second carried the same inscription, this time with an addition: *And to Lucía, who taught me that the sea of my childhood and the one I know now are one and the same.*

"We're in for a hot summer," Lucía said, returning from the market. She had bought avocados, green apples and shrimp. Her skin shone with sweat. She took the coffee Darío served her and started softly singing one of her songs as she cut the avocados, peeled the apples and washed the shrimp. Darío came up behind her and caressed her bare shoulders, revealed by her black vest. She kept singing to herself as he ran his fingertips over the body he had never forgotten. He ran them down the ridges of her back, put his lips to her neck and kissed her slowly, softly, making her smile and stop singing. Lucía turned round, kissed him back and said: "Hey, you."

"I'm going to the beach."

"OK."

They didn't kiss again or say anything more.

The wind that had accompanied him through the winter as he invented Jazmín's stories had gone now, leaving only a soft breeze, a premonition of summer that could make you forget spring would soon bring more windy days. Walkers were arriving on the beach; people were standing, staring at the sea, taking in the sun. Darío walked to the beginning of the beach at Mar del Tuyú. He was sweating; he remembered Lucía's sweat, the salty taste of her neck. Lucía smelled like the sea.

Darío took off his shoes, socks and T-shirt, not caring that the scars from his accident would be exposed. He left his shorts on and walked towards the sea. The water was less cold than he had expected. Looking right and left, he saw nobody swimming. He went further in and now he noticed the water was much colder, something that wasn't unusual here, even on the hottest summer days. As always, the best way not to feel cold was to get in quickly. He waded a few steps further, then threw himself onto a wave. Now his body was covered by the salty, effervescent water. Darío started to swim and noticed how his muscles warmed him up. He felt really good. Lucio and he used to pretend they were swimming to South Africa. Beyond the horizon lay a world of adventures, of wild animals and unexplored lands. It was the world of children's books.

Sandokan, Captain Nemo and Jim Hawkins were there. Lucio and he would jump the waves, defying the wind and the currents to swim to the horizon, then return to the beach to find the end of their adventures in books. They wanted to swim to South Africa. They were happy swimming. Death didn't exist then. Lucio hadn't hit anyone with his train; he hadn't been shot, in the dark, on the tracks. Darío didn't know then that happiness would be watching Jazmín grow up. The sea. The waves lashed his scars like whips. Darío was swimming towards the horizon. A wave pushed him over, spinning him around to face the deserted beach. Darío turned back again, looking for the line of the horizon. He swallowed some water. Salty sea, like Lucía's adolescent skin. Salty sea, like Lucía's neck as she sang. Lucía's smile. *To South Africa!* he would have shouted had Lucio been there, and they would have laughed until they spluttered and choked on swallowed water. He could hear Lucio's laughter, Jazmín's contagious guffaw, Lucía's gentle laughter. But he couldn't keep swimming any more. He rested his arms and looked at the horizon for the last time.

October 2014–May 2015